FROM OUT OF THE BLUE . . .

The dead and dying were everywhere in the City of Dreams.

Citizens clinging to life, having no hope of rescue, looked in shock at the fate of their city: collapsed buildings, cratered streets, piles of broken humanity cluttering entrances to over-filled shelters. It was more than shock and pain that gripped them in the last moments of their lives. It was the *unfairness* of this death.

Until the Great Battle of eight years ago every world in the seven galaxies had lived in fear of an attack like this one. But since that time the Fleets were said to be virtually paralyzed. On thousands of worlds, the silver ships and the gold ships arrived *in peace*. They came to trade technology for supplies, and it was said that this was the future for the worlds, and for the Fleets. There were reports of a few—*a few!*—raids. Nothing like the way it was before. The odds of being attacked now were said to be too great to merit consideration. In the City of Dreams, stricken citizens wondered . . . why *my* world? Why *my* city? Why *me*?

But this time the victims claimed one privilege never known by their antecedents: revenge.

Ace Books by Rutledge Etheridge

LEGEND OF THE DUELIST
THE FIRST DUELIST
AGENT OF DESTRUCTION
AGENT OF CHAOS

AGENT OF CHAOS

CHAOS

RUTLEDGE ETHERIDGE

ACE BOOKS, NEW YORK

This book is an Ace original edition,
and has never been previously published.

AGENT OF CHAOS

An Ace Book / published by arrangement with
the author

PRINTING HISTORY
Ace edition / August 1997

The Putnam Berkley World Wide Web site address is
http://www.berkley.com

Make sure to check out *PB Plug*,
the science fiction/fantasy newsletter, at
http://www.pbplug.com

ISBN: 0-441-00464-4

ACE®
Ace Books are published by The Berkley Publishing Group,
200 Madison Avenue, New York, NY 10016.
ACE and the "A" design are trademarks
belonging to Charter Communications, Inc.

PRINTED IN THE UNITED STATES OF AMERICA

10 9 8 7 6 5 4 3 2 1

AGENT OF
CHAOS

PROLOGUE

Surprising only the ever-present dreamers among us, the human species carried its faults, as well as its hopes, to the stars. Scarcely a hundred years after the first great migration into the galaxy, the new worlds were making war upon one another; for trade, for glory, for vanity, for power. Warships traveled for months to attack any of countless enemies—and often were met by ships equally distant from their own homes. When one engagement ended, survivors set a new course. Not for home, but for yet another attack, or another battle, moving deeper and deeper into the cold emptiness of space.

Success for these tiny fleets meant generations away from the worlds that sent them out. Their crews lived by plunder. They died by the thousands. When they did find a way home, they learned that far from being honored as noble defenders, they were strangers, ridiculed and feared. And sent out again, against newly designated enemies.

After humankind had reached to seven galaxies, a revelation burst upon the hundreds of fledgling war fleets and

1

spread like a nova among them: They all lived the same lives; none of them had homes, other than their ships; all they knew of life was battle, and preparation for battle. They were alike. Who then, was the real enemy? The worlds were the real enemy. And so they began to bond with the only brothers and sisters the universe provided for them— each other. Ten ships linked with twelve, forming a new entity that went on to link with fifty more ships, to fight against another new grouping. Survivors were absorbed by the victor. The formula repeated itself over centuries until two massive Fleets emerged—the Silver Fleet and the Gold Fleet, each commanding warships numbering in the hundreds of thousands. The settled worlds were divided between them, to be subjugated and raided at will for supplies. The Fleets were harsh masters; they would never forget how their ancestors had been sent to die in petty, never-ending disputes. And they saw themselves as benefactors; never again would any world have the power to attack its neighbor.

And then the Fleets went to war.

After six centuries of unceasing conflict, the Silver and the Gold Fleets met in the most destructive single confrontation in human history. Three hundred sixty thousand ships, carrying six hundred nineteen million human beings, were destroyed in a matter of hours. The Great Battle, as it came to be called, ended in stalemate. Neither side could claim victory.

But there was a secretive transgalactic organization that could.

From their inception, both Fleets had practiced slavery. Unknown to them, for the past two centuries a very few of the men, women, and often children they took captive from the worlds were agents of this organization, known to its members as The Stem. As their leader had often observed, "The Fleets can be envisioned as the two halves of a single brain. We will become the brain stem. Once we have placed ourselves properly, neither half will be able to survive without us. Then we will vanish, and direct the fall of a dead colossus.''

The Stem agents were adepts in an advanced science of behavior control. With these skills they beguiled the leaders of the two Fleets into waging the battle, then subtly directed its course to assure the desired outcome: maximum casualties, with no winner. For with the Fleets temporarily crippled, the worlds might have a chance to develop defensive alliances and weaponry to protect themselves and one another from the predators.

This would be enough, until The Stem could destroy them utterly.

Eight years after the Battle came a span of one hundred days in which two agents of The Stem would profoundly affect the course of history.

Day 1

Galaxy M-14,
Sentaura System,
Canopal,
City of Dreams

In the public square was a statue, millennia old, cast from an antiquated metal too ancient to be of modern use. The edifice had been part of a first colonization package on three previous worlds, before it arrived with the hopeful settlers who named their new home Canopal. For twenty-two generations it had graced the little manicured area set aside for it, reminding visitors that while as individuals they were new to life, and while their planet was a recent addition to the domain of humankind, they were all part of a great history and a noble march into the future. The metal tended to turn green every few years and was lovingly restored to its deep auburn tincture by artisans who admired its simplicity of form and message: a young man, a young woman, cradling an infant between them, eyes fixed steadily on the sky above. By tradition the statue was called City of Dreams; and its name was given to the first settlement on each of the four worlds it had seen come to life.

Though their "eyes" were pointed in the right direction, the young man and the young woman could not see the objects that had appeared out of a perfect morning sky and now circled overhead. But thousands of others had seen. The dead and the dying were everywhere in the City of Dreams.

Citizens clinging to life, having no hope of rescue, now saw the fate of their city: collapsed buildings, cratered streets, piles of broken humanity cluttering entrances to overfilled shelters. It was more than shock and pain that gripped them in the last moments of their lives. It was the *unfairness* of this death.

Until the Great Battle of eight years ago, every world in the seven galaxies had lived in fear of an attack like this one. But since that time the Fleets were said to be virtually paralyzed. On thousands of worlds, the silver ships and the gold ships arrived *in peace*. They came to trade technology for supplies, and it was said that this was the future for the worlds, and for the Fleets. There were reports of a few—*a few!* raids. Nothing like the way it was before. The odds of being attacked now were said to be too great to merit consideration. In the City of Dreams, stricken citizens wondered . . . why *my* world? Why *my* city? Why *me*?

But this time the victims claimed one privilege never known by their antecedents: revenge.

Those still able to think coherently could look up at the late morning sky, a sky that only hours earlier had held nothing more ominous than a passing flock of birds and a few feathered white clouds. Their view was direct, real; not the screen images monitored within installations half a mile beneath the surface. There was value in that.

They saw forty ships, half-spheres reflecting silver light,

hovering above the city and receiving into themselves shuttles laden with precious metals, food stocks, gems, newly taken slaves . . . They saw two of the ships rock suddenly, as pits of blackness appeared like sunspots on their hulls. Seconds later the two predators evaporated in bursts of orange and silver.

Death was a high price to pay for the privilege of witnessing firsthand that Canopal's new weapons systems worked. But before the remaining silver ships intensified their fire and reduced the City of Dreams to flowing slag, some of the condemned knew a last moment of satisfaction.

Silver Fleet vessel `Dalkag`
Deep space

Dane Steppart found it helpful to use stylus and paper when organizing her thoughts. It was a habit she'd developed as a three-year-old on her native Walden. And even though it wasn't necessary, and could be extremely dangerous, twenty-one years later she still found comfort in the archaic formality of watching each word form from her hand, of giving each one a physical reality. It was Dane's location that made the practice dangerous, and her memory that made it unnecessary. Nothing her senses encountered was ever lost. Words read or heard, a taste, a sensation, a thought, an impression, anything seen, all were indelibly recorded in her memory and subject to instant recall.

She bent over the sheet of paper and allowed her mind to wander for a moment. What came was *They're monsters. They're my new family. I worry about them. But I want to destroy everything they stand for. They're killers. But sometimes I love them. Why?*

She wrote:

"Forgive me, Mother, when I think of Jenny Marsham and Buto Shimas as my parents. And Alfred, I know you will understand about my 'brothers,' Jarred and little Sato. Jenny Marsham and Buto Shimas took me aboard their ships as a slave, and I should hate them for that. (But of course my capture wasn't their idea; it was mine.) Given the work I am engaged in, it would be better, or at least simpler, if I could hate them. But I don't. The one time you met Jenny, Mother, she told you that I kept them alive during the Battle. There is some truth to that. Now they have adopted me as their own, and I have developed affection for them. All the while, I work to unravel their way of life. I have never been able to resolve this conflict within myself. I mention it here only to tell you that however confused my feelings may be toward them, they are clear where you are concerned, and growing daily. It would be so good to see Walden and Vermilion City again. I said good-bye to you eight years ago. I said that no matter what the cost, it was important that I continue my work for The Stem. I was sixteen. I didn't understand, then, how very much I would—''

Dane set the stylus down and brushed a number of droplets from the paper. *This isn't what I set out to write*, she thought, drying her eyes with the back of a hand. But Jenny, and Buto, and Jarred . . . They'd gone out to negotiate with Karnas Kay-Raike. A rogue, and a dangerous traitor. Would they come back alive? She gave herself a few seconds and began writing again.

''The Fleets are behaving as we had planned, after the Battle. Trade is a new art to these people. They're learning and adapting quickly, despite the expected (inevitable) internal opposition. Jenny and Buto are quite senior in the Silver Fleet command structure now. They have appointed me as a trade negotiator and assigned me to devise a standardized set of regulations and practices. That work has taken more than two years to complete, but I am happy to say that it is nearly done. Next, the war is not the all-consuming passion it once was. The Fleets do meet and fight, but the encounters are fewer and smaller than before. All of this means (as it was intended to mean) that the worlds are safer now than they have been in centuries.

There are incidents; but again, they are fewer and smaller than before.

"There are three possibilities which concern me now. One is that either, or both, of the Fleets will revert to its former way of life. The second is that they will fall apart too quickly, before the worlds have armed sufficiently and before there are enough Stem agents in place to (as Brian Whitlock was fond of saying) 'direct the fall of a dead colossus.' The third possibility is the one which frightens me most. That is that the Fleets will abandon their mutual hostility and combine. I see no signs of this at present. But then, I have had no contact with The Stem for eight years. I know what Jenny and Buto know, but they are not privy to the inner workings of Sovereign Command Council. Until I have direct access to the council (there are rumors that Jenny may become a member) or until I am contacted by a Stem agent who does have such access, I will continue in a state of worried ignorance. A merger of the Fleets would mean one single power, more than a million ships strong, with no energy focused in the war, but all energy focused against the worlds. Life under such conditions is beyond imagining. It is on my mind now, because I have had recent dreams in which this has occurred.

"Jenny and Buto believe that my dreams are prophetic. (I used the idea of 'dreams' to give them information I should not have had, before and during the Battle. This is how Momed Pwanda and I were able to set the Fleet formations, ensuring a stalemate. I wish I could tell you that story, Mother and Alfred.) But if by some cruel chance my dreams *do* have prophetic meaning" . . .

Dane set the stylus down again and concentrated for several minutes, rereading what she'd etched onto the paper. It all seemed so simple in concept: We've had some success; now there are three things to worry about. In fact there were ten thousand or more things that could go wrong. But it was easier to think in three categories than to list the ten thousand details, any and all of which could affect any and all of the others. That, Dane thought, was the value of sitting with stylus in hand and pouring one's mind out onto paper. She looked again at her final sentence fragment, "But if by some cruel chance my dreams do have prophetic meaning" and wrote,

... "then it would have been better for me to have stayed on Walden, living out what life was possible with you and others I love, and waiting with you to die when gold or silver ships arrived. Because if the Fleets combine, then everything The Stem has done in the past eight years will have been for nothing. No, not for nothing. Much worse. By causing the Battle and therefore the events that will continue to flow from it, I and others like me will have brought an end to any hope the worlds have had. We will be guilty of murder on a scale the individual Fleets never visited upon us."

There was no need for Dane to read the pages again before she atomized them in a garbage chute. She would always remember what she'd written. Especially that last sentence.

Above Canopal
Aleç flagship of the outlaw Kay-Raike clan

"They have no range," Karnas Kay-Raike said with contempt. A mere three hundred miles above the shattered city below, the renegade Silver Fleet ships could detect nothing from the weapons that had destroyed two of their number and severely damaged eight others. "The solution is obvious," he continued. "Point one is that next time we will do our preliminary work from this distance and send in the supply shuttles afterward." Kay-Raike was seated with twelve officers around the ship's War Table. Centered above the table was a sphere of blackness in which was displayed the local sun, its eight planets and their eleven moons, and, in exaggerated scale, his thirty still-functional ships. "But," Kay-Raike said, "there is point two. For the first time in more than four centuries a world has fired upon one of us. They need to be reminded how serious a crime that is.''

"I agree, sir," said Kay-Raike's brother, Mendel. Although nine years his brother's senior, Mendel was three grades junior to him in rank. "But the time involved?" Mendel was a large man, long-limbed with a wide face that was florid both from anger and from the prodigious amounts of alcohol he regularly consumed. He was terrified of his brother, who massed less than seventy percent of his own weight. Karnas had succeeded their grandfather Olton as head of the clan. And like the late Senior General, Karnas made a specialty of meting out discipline; against Grounders, ships' personnel, or clan members, it made no difference to him. Mendel's question was carefully phrased. It would not be wise at this time to remind his brother directly of their other obligations; not when Karnas was thinking of diversions that he considered to be more pleasant.

"Time?" Karnas repeated distractedly, gazing at the display. He turned to face Mendel. "What is the condition of our three guests?"

"They're still unconscious, sir, as you ordered."

Nodding, the smaller man said, "It would be interesting to wake them now and explain where they are, and what they've been a part of. The boy's response would be meaningless, of course. General Marsham would carry on about Fleet this, Fleet that, new agreements, delicate considerations, and other verbal debris. Equally meaningless. But General Shimas . . . would . . . what would he do, Mendel?"

"I don't know, sir. Half of what he says supports us. The other half is debris, as you said."

"That isn't much of an answer, Brother."

"Waking him now could be dangerous, sir."

"Exactly right. That's why it would be interesting." Returning his attention to the War Table display, Karnas pointed at the world they were orbiting and asked, "How long would it take?"

Mendel looked around the table at the others, hoping to be freed from what he had to say. The eleven remained silent. "Sir, with a planet that size, and as you know we have only thirty ships fully functional, and normally we would have a squadron of one hundred—"

"A number, Mendel. How long?"

"To guarantee no survivors, sir, I'd estimate twenty days. At least twenty."

Karnas sighed, wiping a hand across his forehead and focusing sharp brown eyes on the overhead. His brother was an idiot. Mendel had forgotten already that an unknown number of the Grounders had been detected as much as half a mile beneath the surface—another violation of Fleet rules governing the worlds. The time involved to be sure, which he had already roughly calculated, would be at least twice what Mendel had suggested. "Very well," he said. "We have a delivery to make, and I intend to arrive early enough to have a little fun. We'll return here . . . what is the name of this rock?"

"Canopal, sir."

An idea struck Kay-Raike, and as it grew in his mind it displaced the rage he'd felt. Brilliant, he thought. Dazzling . . . simple. Worthy of the clan name. Suddenly he was grateful to the citizens of this world; used correctly, what they had given him was the key to his every dream. "Very well. We'll return when the time is right to deal with Canopal. For now, a symbolic gesture will have to do. How many Grounders did we take from Canopal?"

"Roughly eighteen hundred women, fifteen hundred men, and two hundred children, sir. I can get an exact count if you like."

"No, it's not important. Execute them all, in groups of ten. Record the executions and send the tapes to my quarters. Have my wife deliver them personally. Begin now, Mendel."

"Yes, sir."

Six hours passed before there was a knock at Kay-Raike's stateroom door. He opened it to see his young wife, the latest of a succession of five, holding a package in her hands.

"It's the holo tapes you wanted," she said dully, looking at the floor.

"Come in," Karnas said. "Set them up in the projector. Then take off your uniform."

=2=

Day 4

```
Dalkag
```
Deep space

As he'd taken a seat across from her, Dane had made the mistake of asking, politely, for his name. That was ten minutes ago.

"I have nothing against Grounders, you understand," the young man was saying. "Aboard my own ship, some of my best friends—"

"Of course," Dane said, having lost interest in her untouched breakfast, and her uninvited companion. In ten minutes he'd used the phrase "my own ship" eight times, and the word "Grounder" six. Grandiose and condescending. She'd hoped for better. The dining room aboard the vessel *Dalkag* was nearly empty at this early hour. The compartment was sixty feet by sixty, beneath twelve-foot ceilings from which hung models of historically important

Silver Fleet ships. There were hundreds of them; any ten-year-old child aboard could identify each and give a stirring account of its accomplishments. The compartment lighting was uniform throughout; just subdued enough to be restful. Attendants, still referred to informally as Grounders, bustled with practiced efficiency as they set up tables to accommodate the officers who would soon be arriving for a meal before they reported for watch. Another section of the room, more casual in decor, was being readied to serve dinner to those coming off duty.

"But," the man continued, "now that I'm assigned here, I feel it's important to establish myself with everyone, to avoid future problems. You would be interested to know that this habit of mine is one of the reasons I've advanced so far, all before the age of thirty, which I will reach in a few days. And so given your, ah, previous status . . ." He paused to look pointedly at her unadorned maroon uniform. The moment stretched beyond his original intent.

"Yes?" Dane said.

His eyes met hers again. "In answer to your question, it's only proper that you address me as Colonel. Perhaps as we become better friends, you may call me William. That's my name, William Saddhurst. But for now . . ." He put a section of apple in his mouth and said around it, "I hope you're not offended."

"I'm curious, more than anything," Dane replied. "There are twenty-two tables in this section, and nineteen of them are unused at the moment. Why did you choose this one?"

Saddhurst said, "You look like pleasant company. What better way to begin a new day, and a new assignment?" As she'd expected. He'd interpreted her question not as an invitation to sit elsewhere, but as a sign that she was impressed with him, and hoped for a compliment. He was stocky, with blond shaggy hair, and a youthful face that seemed always on the verge of a smile—but hadn't yet made the transition. He plunged ahead, unmindful of the slight roll she'd done with her eyes. "And you listen well."

Dane nearly laughed. Listening was something she did exceptionally well. From early childhood she'd been trained by the best minds available to do just that, and then to use what she'd heard. Or more accurately, absorbed. "Your eyes are an unusual blue," Saddhurst went on. "I'd almost call them phosphorescent. And you're . . . in a word, I'd describe you as willowy."

" 'Willowy'?" Dane lifted a fork and dropped it abruptly on her plate. She pushed back her chair, which glided along grooves in the flooring and locked into position with an emphatic *click*.

Saddhurst asked, "Did I say something wrong? That's a Grounder word, isn't it? Like 'phosphorescent'? Someone told me that 'willowy' is a compliment. It means—"

"A tree," Dane said, keeping her face composed. The man was behaving like a boor, and had ruined her breakfast. The least he could do now was provide a little entertainment. "Have you ever *seen* a tree?"

"Well, no, not personally. But . . . did I tell you that I'm considered to be one of the brightest minds in the field of propulsion? On my own ship—"

"You're a bright mind, eh? And yet you're telling me that I'm wooden, have *no* mind, and that I bend with every passing breeze. Again, I'm curious, Colonel. Were the female officers on *your own* ship so impressed with you that they accepted such insults? Or were your clumsy attempts at charm limited to Grounders? *Your own*, of course."

"Now see here!" Saddhurst's face was flushed. "In deference to my position, you will kindly—"

Dane laughed, subtly mimicking the sound she'd projected that his own laugh would make. She raised her eyebrows and tilted her head to the same angle he obviously associated with charm, and waited. The young man was confused as he saw something intimately familiar in her expression, but was unable to identify it. Dane could see the disorienting effect her subtle manipulation was having. Finally she laughed to break the moment of strangeness. Saddhurst shook his head, clearing his mind. "A joke," he said. "You were joking with me, weren't you?"

"Welcome aboard *Dalkag*, Colonel," she said, standing and extending her hand. He took it and smiled up at her.

"Grounders don't usually make me nervous," he said. "But you have clan status, which means that you're exceptional. And . . . And I've spent so much time talking, I never asked; what is your name?"

"Dane."

The flush returned to Saddhurst's face. He groaned low in his throat. "Wonderful. Just wonderful. Look, I'm not going to ask if you're *that* Dane. But do you suppose you could refrain from mentioning to your parents that I made a fool of myself, or at least give me time to kill myself before you do?"

"Buto Shimas has a favorite expression," Dane said. "It is, 'Now we are even in the matter of jokes.' Please excuse me, Colonel, I—"

"William?"

"William. I have a class to teach."

Saddhurst watched her leave the compartment. When she'd gone he muttered, "Physics, William. Stick to physics."

"Sir?"

Startled, he turned to see a young male attendant behind him. "Nothing," he said. "I'm finished here. You may clear the table." To be safe, he added, "Please."

"Yes, sir."

The man was tall and slim, ebony-skinned, and suffering painful leg cramps. Breather-pellets in his nose provided adequate oxygen, but after an hour they were becoming hot and uncomfortable. And he had serious doubts about his legs ever working again. He ached to stretch them. Or to shift his weight, somehow, within the small metal box he'd chosen for concealment. But the least movement would betray his presence; small children have big ears. He waited, submerging his discomfort in the steady, sometimes thundering, tide of their voices. The child speaking now took on a new tone. No longer a part of the ebb and flow, he reminded the man of a fledgling sea eagle, circling aloft to see what the tide offered. The man listened, fascinated.

"There are only thirty of them," eight-year-old Sato Shimas Marsham continued, lowering his voice and leaving his seat to tap the screen. His bearing and voice announced that he was out of his engaging-little-boy mode and into another that he managed with equal, sometimes frightening, skill. His eyes were dark and direct, like his father's. At this moment they held Dane Steppart in a way that was almost physical. "Why do you think we should talk with them?" he demanded after a moment of waiting for her to respond. "We know they're Kay-Raike ships." In his budding warrior mind, identifying and killing an enemy was one act, not two. "Let's do it, and get on to our destination."

Sato's statement brought mixed murmurs of assent and disagreement from the class of fifteen similarly aged students. Dane allowed the debate to progress, mentally recording comments for later discussion. It wasn't time yet to tell the children that they were watching a replay of events that had begun nine hours before, while they slept. Very few aboard *Dalkag* knew yet what had happened.

"Why haven't they attacked us?" Dane asked, prodding.

"Sato already explained that," a girl answered. "There are only thirty of them. And there are ninety-seven of us." She smiled toward the boy, received a curt nod in return, and blushed from the unexpected acknowledgment. Sato was often the most friendly of her companions. But not when he was acting this way.

"Have you forgotten?" Dane went on gently. "He also said that they're from the Kay-Raike clan." Those who hadn't given this factor the weight it deserved understood at once. A number of things could be said about the Kay-Raikes: They were an ancient clan, never far from power. They were fanatics. Their reputation for cruelty and unnecessary killing was not embellished by legend; it was fact. They were now in a state of open rebellion against Fleet authority; the Supreme Generals were again threatening to exterminate the clan, along with all of its followers. Many things could be said. But despite a poor showing in the Battle, no one could reasonably question their courage, skill, or zest for battle. The Kay-Raikes would consider ninety-seven ships against thirty of their own to be favorable odds.

"They haven't attacked," Sato replied impatiently, "because we have something they want. They expect us to behave like cowards and surrender it."

"And what would that be?"

"You, Dane. They believe you poisoned Senior General Olton Kay-Raike just before the Battle."

"That's not true!" a boy replied. "If it weren't for Dane, no one would have lived through the Battle. None of us would have been born! And she didn't poison—"

Sato glared at the boy until he was silent, and went on. "The Kay-Raikes say that if the Senior General had lived, we'd have won against the Gold Fleet. They say that because of you, we were hurt badly. That's why we live in disgrace."

"Disgrace? Would you explain that, Sato?"

"Yes. We have to be 'nice' to the worlds now. We used to take what we wanted from them whenever we wanted. In return we made sure they never got strong enough to make war on each other again. That was fair. That's the way things were supposed to be. And *are* supposed to be."

Incredible, thought the man, fighting cramps in his legs and hearing every word clearly. She murdered a Senior General, along with everything else she's done to cripple the Silver Fleet. He pictured himself moving up on her from behind, getting close . . . Would she hear him, remember the sound of his footsteps, his breathing? Say his name even before she turned around and saw him? Eight years was a long time. But then, she never forgot anything, did she? He smiled, and for a moment forgot about the pain in his legs.

Dane accepted Sato's explanation without comment and waited for the others to express themselves. Everything the

boy had said about the Kay-Raikes' beliefs, he clearly believed also. And with one exception—at the last moment
she had changed her plan to poison Olton Kay-Raike—it
was all true. But it was only part of the truth. She had
arranged for the Silver Fleet to suffer maximum casualties.
Just as her counterpart in the Gold Fleet, Momed Pwanda,
had manipulated events to ensure parallel results. But later
analysis of the Battle demonstrated that had the Kay-Raikes
fought to their accustomed, exceptional standards, the outcome might have been victory for their own Silver Fleet.
Still costly, but a victory. As a result of the analysis, former
Fleet Leader Arlana Mestoeffer had been allowed to live
and to retire. But in disgrace. Major Generals Jenny Marsham and Buto Shimas, Sato's parents, retained their ranks
and were credited with avoiding a rout.

The Kay-Raikes believed themselves to be held in wide-
spread contempt. Their pride was an open wound that fes-
tered for five years. And then . . .

"But," Sato continued, "I'd rather die than give you to
them. We've accepted you as a member of the Marsham
clan, even though you were born a Grounder. Also, we
don't negotiate with pirates, we kill them. That's what we
should be doing right now."

Dane asked, "If you were squadron leader, you would
order an attack?"

"Immediate and total," Sato replied confidently.

"And how many would die as a result? Might that in-
clude your friends on this ship, and the children here in this
room?"

"The point is that the Kay-Raikes would—"

"Learn a lesson?"

"That's right, older sister," he said defiantly.

"Good." This was the point she'd been building toward.
"I agree that there is something to be learned here." She
looked at the determined boy and decided that for his sake,
this should be a lesson learned privately. She dismissed the
class, all but Sato. "Watch the screen," she said, gesturing
him back to his seat.

The thirty ships were in tight formation, seemingly at rest, perfectly matching the course and speed of the squadron. But as Dane manipulated the controls, the sense of real time was lost. The ships appeared to jerk from side to side as subtle positioning maneuvers were viewed in fractions of seconds.

Sato pounded his desk. "That's a recording!"

"Keep watching." Moments later a shaft of light streaked from one of the Kay-Raike vessels toward the ship they were on. Sato jumped in his chair as if they'd been fired upon. Dane slowed the action. The streak revealed itself as a shuttlecraft and disappeared from view. Another view, this one inside one of *Dalkag*'s airlock/hangars.

"The Kay-Raike ships departed at this time," Dane explained. "They never communicated their intentions until seconds before the shuttle arrived. They were daring us to launch the attack you'd have ordered, younger brother."

On the screen a wide door was seen to open in the shuttle's port side. Six crew members rushed into the small vehicle. Moments later they returned, bearing three stretchers between them. On them, in full dress uniform, unconscious but clearly breathing, were Jenny Marsham, Buto Shimas, and Jenny's son, Jarred.

"They're all right," Dane said. "They were drugged, but show no ill effects. The doctors are sure of a full recovery."

Sato turned his face from the screen, and away from Dane. "They weren't due back for two days," he said. "I'd have killed them." His young voice quavered, then hardened. "But that doesn't prove I'm wrong. It only proves that they should never have tried to negotiate with the Kay-Raikes. That was a mistake. Foolish." He turned to her then, with dry, dark and commanding eyes. "I'll thank you for one thing, Dane. For sending my friends out before you humiliated me. You can be sure I won't forget that. Or any of this." He stood, snapped expertly to attention, and left the classroom.

Dane Steppart switched off the screen and sat tiredly in

one of the students' seats. She'd been awake for more than thirty hours, most of that time devoted to completing the new trade guidelines the council had assigned to Jenny Marsham and Buto Shimas. Idly, she looked up at the compartment monitors. By special permission they were deactivated whenever she conducted class. It was her argument, successfully pursued, that students should be encouraged to ask whatever questions formed within their young minds; to bring their ideas out where they could be discussed without fear of future recrimination. Without such freedom, Sato would never have ventured an opinion about the situation he saw developing. He would, as would any of them, have said only that the squadron leader was in command, and that whatever she chose to do would be the correct course of action.

Sato had ended the class session by stating that his parents, both major generals, had been foolish to attempt a peaceable discussion with the Kay-Raikes. It was encouraging to know that he and the others trusted her enough to speak words that, only a few years before, would have been acted upon as treason—even from an eight-year-old. That was progress, she thought. But the ideas that Sato expressed were disheartening. His solution to any problem involving the Kay-Raikes, or the Gold Fleet, or any world that demanded more in trade than he thought reasonable, was to attack. Obliterate. As if six centuries of unbroken war between the Fleets had entered into his genetic code, nullifying all other possibilities. Perhaps she was hoping for too much, too soon. But time was precious . . .

Everything that she and Momed Pwanda, and other agents of The Stem, had accomplished was ephemeral. For eight years following the cataclysmic Battle the Fleets had virtually withdrawn from the galaxies, mending losses, with a few notable exceptions approaching the worlds only to trade, bartering technology for the materials and supplies they required. As a result the worlds were growing stronger. Associations were forming between them. The great lie—that they possessed weapons capable of defending themselves against Fleet attack—was becoming true. But as former Stem leader Brian Whitlock had foreseen, the effects of the Battle could not last. Rebellions such as the one perpetrated by the Kay-Raikes were fracturing both Fleets. Strong leaders were rising up through the chaos. There were not enough of them to duplicate the galaxies-wide damage done by the Fleets, but the breakaways were growing desperate. Cut off from the new technologies developing among their former comrades, they found themselves unable to compete for trade. More and more, they were relying upon brute strength to obtain what they needed from the worlds. And to the extent that they were successful, many officers remaining loyal to either Fleet began to question the new ways: Why trade? The worlds were not as powerful as they had feared. Why not return to the old ways—the natural order of things?

All of this had been anticipated. On the day of their last meeting Brian Whitlock had given Dane his vision of the post-Battle universe. His predictions, and the reality Dane was living, were identical. He'd said, *"We will face three primary problems. One is that the Fleets may fracture prematurely, before we are in position to safely direct their demise. The second is that they may revert to their parasitic natures, before the worlds can develop the capability to defend themselves adequately. The third is the greatest danger of all, and here we must perform a most difficult feat of balance: We must see that the Fleets find selected areas of agreement in order to prevent a full-scale regeneration of the war between them. At the same time we cannot allow them to become overly cooperative or trusting of one another. I don't need to tell you, Dane, that if they end their differences and combine forces against the worlds, there is no hope."*

Dane was the first Grounder in Silver Fleet history to be accepted into a clan. Her ascension set a pattern that was becoming more common. Grounders, formally called attendants, who rendered exceptional service could be rewarded with freedom and the opportunity to advance—though never as Fleet officers. The precedent she'd set allowed Dane and, she hoped, other Stem operatives a measure of optimism in approaching the next phase of Whitlock's plan. Agents were to make themselves indispensable to the Fleets in every way possible: Become trade negotiators; doctors; ambassadors to the worlds; personnel and communications specialists. They were to dominate a few crucial professions, until it became standard for Fleet officers to look upon these vocations as beneath them, as career paths that only Grounders—former slaves—followed.

And of course, teachers.

Agents of The Stem were to change what they could for the present, waiting for the time when they were so indispensable that by ceasing work, by creating harmonized acts of sabotage, they would plunge the Fleets into carefully controlled chaos—breaking them, rendering them incapable of ever again threatening entire galaxies. The fractured pieces would, Whitlock had planned, be commanded by leaders who had become accustomed over time to dealing peaceably with newly powerful alliances of worlds. And, to the extent possible, with each other. But the Fleets would never form again. New generations of Stem agents would be trained to prevent that from occurring.

For this reason it was vital to reach the young minds and help prepare them for life in a universe they would not dominate.

Dane was both a trade negotiator and a teacher. She'd expected extreme difficulties in the former role, and time had proved her correct. Building trust between former predators and victims was a long and arduous process. But to her great surprise, the biggest challenge she faced was Sato . . . He was not typical, for which she was grateful. Clan influence and tradition aside, most of the children who shared his views did so because of the force of his personality. At eight years of age, he was a leader; in many respects her classes were verbal duels between herself and her younger brother.

She closed her eyes, recalling another precocious child

who at that age had demonstrated a talent for bending the
will and shaping the minds of others. That child was Dane
Steppart, and it was that ability that had attracted the attention of The Stem. She allowed her body to relax into the
chair and recalled her initial day of formal instruction.
"The first thing you will learn is how little you know." To
which Dane had responded, "Sir, I'm three years old. Of
course I don't know much!" And the reply: "My remark
was directed toward the adults here, Dane. But since you
don't know much, will you help me explain to them what
that means?" "I'd say I don't know *how* to explain that,
but if you're right, then I don't know that, either." Crinkles
over his brow, surprised laughter. Martingale was his name,
smart eyes, bony face, voice like Alfred's flute, soft, hard,
make you mad, cry, laugh, with just a little change; the
next hour he could sound and even look like any of them
there, scare you, or make you want to jump up into his
arms. When he wasn't teaching he turned out to be a funny
old . . .

   "Ouch!"

Dane slapped at a sudden sting in her neck and leapt
from the chair. At the same moment she heard excited
shouts from the corridor outside the classroom. Disoriented,
she realized that she'd been asleep.

"I wasn't here," a voice whispered from behind her.
Dane turned and nearly collapsed. "Momed!" she began
to call out, but strong fingers covered her mouth and what
emerged was a muffled grunt.

"I'm sorry, I thought we'd have time to talk privately,"
Momed Pwanda whispered. "Don't worry about your neck,
Dane. You'll understand after we meet formally, tonight."

She stared, uncomprehending. Her former partner in The
Stem opened his left hand. In it was a thin, inch-long metallic tube, with a smear of redness at one sharp end. She
looked at the hand she'd held against her neck. There, too,
was a spot of blood.

"Trust me," he said quietly but urgently. "And hide me.
I wasn't here."

All but one of the voices in the corridor moved away. "Dane, are you in there?" The door began to open. She turned to see Momed Pwanda folding himself into a small portable locker. She rushed to the box and pushed the lid down securely, turning and stepping away just as the door opened fully.

"Dane—"

"Oh, hello, Colonel Hormat." Stretching and yawning, she said to the larger woman, "I confess. I fell asleep after the class. You'd be doing me a favor if you'd order me to my quarters for a day or two." Giel Hormat was only four years older than Dane. During the final five hours of the Battle she'd been raised from Lieutenant to Captain to Major. She was one of the very few who remembered that day with fondness.

"You do look as though you need rest," Hormat said. "But not for long, today. Your parents will need your assistance this evening."

"How are they?"

"Sluggish, but not harmed. The officers and crew have been informed of what's happened to them. They're not to be disturbed for now." Her eyes narrowed. "*Kay-Raikes*," she said disgustedly. "You want to hear a *real* confession, Dane? Eleven years ago that filthy clan approached my mother. Do you know why? They wanted me transferred to one of their ships. If I proved 'acceptable' after a year, they would assign one of their junior clan members to be my husband." The woman's strong features were changing to a bright red.

"Obviously, your mother didn't accept."

"Yes, she did. I informed her that if the orders were not rescinded immediately, I would kill her, and then myself. I meant it."

"That was difficult, Giel," Dane said gently. "And it was a long time ago."

"She betrayed me. In return I threatened murder and treason. Two good officers were dishonored that day. That is what association with the Kay-Raikes brings." Realizing that she'd gone too far, Hormat said, "I mean no implied criticism of Major Generals Marsham and Shimas."

"Giel, the monitors are off."

"I know that. You'd have warned me otherwise." She laughed. "You're too easy to talk to, Dane. Sometimes I say things to you I'd never dream of saying to anyone else. I don't know if that's your weakness, or mine. The reason I came here . . . have you seen . . . er, anyone . . . well, unusual, in the last few hours?"

"Other than my little brother?"

Hormat looked at her curiously, smiled vaguely. "Never mind."

"There seems to be a problem, Colonel."

"It's nothing, really. A trade delegation came aboard last night. One of their representatives seems to have lost his way."

"Trade delegation?"

"Yes, that's right."

The dreams Dane had had in the past weeks took on a sudden hard reality. In the months prior to the Battle, Momed Pwanda had been her counterpart—a slave who rose to become an unofficial advisor—within the opposing Gold Fleet. On a number of worlds she'd visited in the past years, she'd met people who'd encountered him. She'd learned that, like herself, he now held a formal position. His presence here as a trade delegate implied a level of peace and formal cooperation between the Fleets that was beyond anything Dane had heard of up until now. Events were moving too fast, and in the wrong order. The Stem's plan called for the Fleets to be far more fractured than they were now, before cooperative meetings took place at high levels. There was a personal paradox for Dane here: While Momed's presence could mean the worst, it was also true that if the worst were coming, there was no one she wanted to see more. The news he would have for her, and his counsel, would be valuable. But in their brief encounter he'd seemed doubtful that they would have private time together . . . she thought again of the injection he had given her. Dane's expertise, an art refined and practiced in secret by The Stem over centuries, was the study and manipulation of human behavior. Not for the first time, her partner had baffled her.

But Giel Hormat's demeanor in asking about him was transparent. Dane and Momed Pwanda had been taken captive within three days of one another, from her home world of Walden. In order to remain with her as they carried on their work for The Stem, he'd made a request of Buto Shimas in return for a valuable service he'd performed. Buto agreed. The two of them could remain together, under one circumstance. And so Momed Pwanda became, and according to Fleet law he remained, Dane's husband. No doubt her adoptive parents had spent many hours laughing together, imagining the reaction Dane would have upon seeing her "husband" again. The husband, in name only, whom she had denounced to Marsham as a traitor, in order to have him sent as a "gift," meant as an insult, to the Gold Fleet.

"When does my work with this delegation begin?" Dane asked.

"There will be a reception at the end of the evening watch. You'll be there, of course. And then we'll see how, ah, negotiations, proceed."

"In that case, and since my parents aren't ready for company, I'm going to my quarters and sleep for now." There was a gentle throbbing in her neck, a new pulse point, and an odd tickling sensation as if something were moving upward from the injection site. Her impulse was to see a doctor, or to rip open the locker and demand an explanation from Pwanda.

She nodded to Hormat and left the room.

A few steps into the corridor she was overtaken by a feeling of warm serenity, like the secure softness of a favorite blanket. Yes, she thought. It had to be imagination. There was nothing moving in her neck. But if there were . . . ? Momed Pwanda was a good man. Unpredictable, as always. But still worthy of her trust, as he had been in the past.

⇒3⇐

Day 4

Whatever it was, she knew two hours later that it was real. Corresponding to mild contractions in her larynx was definite movement that had gone from her neck to her head. She couldn't pinpoint the precise location. It was something she sensed more than felt, a shadow passing over a nerve, and then gone again. It caused her no concern whatever.

She'd put on her night clothes in anticipation of a restful sleep, then decided to review her final work on the proposed trade manual. The words began to float before her eyes in interesting patterns that continued even as she looked away from the work and toward the bare walls of her quarters. It was a pleasant phenomenon, but not productive. After a few minutes she stretched out and fell asleep easily.

"Sato," she murmured sometime later. "What do you want?" He'd wakened her as he had since he was a toddler, by putting his hand lightly on her left foot and waiting for her to respond.

"He was told to knock first." Jenny Marsham's voice came from the other side of the door. "I would appreciate it if you'd tell him that yourself." With her eyes still closed, Dane agreed. In the past few hours she'd had enough of people touching her unexpectedly.

"I'm sorry about before," Sato said. "It was the sight of those Kay-Raikes. I was worried about Mom and Dad and Jarred, and seeing those ships reminded me of it. I didn't mean anything bad. You're my sister, Dane. No matter what."

"No matter what," Dane repeated. She sat up in bed and pulled him to her. No longer the fierce warrior he'd been that morning, he was now a little boy again, hugging his big sister and relieved that she wasn't angry. "You know, Jenny is right," Dane said. "You're becoming a man so quickly that from now on you'll have to announce yourself before you go into a young woman's quarters."

"Really? Why?"

"Those are the rules."

"Oh? Very well, then." He said with a proud smile, "I'll bet some boys have to wait until they're ten before they become a man so quickly."

"Why don't you go outside and wait with Mom—"

"And Dad."

"And Dad, while I—"

"And Jarred."

"Sato—"

"All right, I'll go! Before you get mad again. But hurry and get dressed. We have some surprises for you."

Not as many as you believe, Dane thought as she was left alone. Changing out of her nightclothes and into the unadorned maroon uniform that signified a former Grounder, she thought again of the odd dichotomy within people of the Fleet. It was the cause of the ambivalence she'd tried to describe on paper, three days before. Like Sato, the people she now lived with were warm and human at times. But often they were cold automatons that no amount of destruction could satisfy. It was as if their minds could forge no connection between destroying ships and killing the people aboard them. Most—the Kay-Raikes notably not among them—could not bear to watch another person suffer and die. But none would hesitate to fire weapons designed to tear an opposing ship into spaceborne shrapnel, snuffing out all life aboard. Anonymous life, she'd come to think of it. Unseen, and therefore not real. It was the way they'd felt for centuries about Grounders.

She finished dressing and entered the corridor.

There could be no mistake, seeing them together, that Lieutenant Jarred Marsham was Jenny's son. He was twenty-six, while she had just celebrated her fifty-first birthday. The two were of identical height, with the same auburn shade of hair, and matching patterns of freckles along the cheeks and bridge of the nose. Buto Shimas Marsham was dark of eye and hair, short and broad, reminding Dane of a great oak, with the same strength and sense of permanence. Sato favored his father, except in body shape. He seemed destined to be thin and, judging from his present size, taller than any of them. Already he was a mere six inches shorter than his sister.

Dane was of median height and slender, blue-eyed, with black hair that she wore cut just below her earlobes. She knew that men found her attractive. But they did not pursue her. This was beneficial to her overall plans; she did not need the complication of a suitor or a lover from among these people. There were moments, however, when she wished it were otherwise. Colonel William Saddhurst had been the first in a long while to approach her with such clear intentions. She admitted to herself that despite a boorish beginning, he was not unpleasant. Under better circumstances she might find him appealing. But now he knew who she was; his ardor would translate into distant, careful pleasantries. She would understand, as she did with the others. How could she expect otherwise? She was, though only by Fleet law, married. And the daughter—again, only by Fleet law—of two very senior officers.

Just how senior, she was soon to learn. It was the first of the surprises that Sato had mentioned.

No one was ready to answer Dane's questions. Jenny, Buto, and Jarred appeared unharmed. Well rested, she thought, and in surprisingly good humor after six days with the Kay-Raikes, the last three of which had been spent in drug-induced unconsciousness. Officers and crew walked past them as they made their way forward through two compartments and up three levels. All nodded respectfully to the two major generals, but none spoke. Only in matters of duty were junior officers permitted to initiate conversation.

Sato was squirming in his seat within five minutes of entering the small private dining room. He continued to fidget as attendants served the meal. Dane nodded her thanks to a middle-aged man as he placed a large plate of salad and breadsticks in front of her. The fresh-baked aroma reminded her that she'd had virtually nothing for breakfast, and had last eaten more than eighteen hours before that. As his own plate was set before him, Sato burst out, "Dad's going to be a council member!"

"Sato!" Jarred slapped the table in frustration.

Dane looked up, the food suddenly forgotten. "Is that true, Buto? There have been rumors for months now . . . but they were about Jenny."

"That's irrelevant," Jenny said, beaming a wide smile at her husband. "And yes, it appears to be true. There will be a formal interview aboard *Sovereign* when we arrive there."

Jarred had hoped to break the news himself. He said dejectedly, "Do you want to know how we learned of this?"

"The Kay-Raikes," Sato announced. "They have spies everywhere. Karnas Kay-Raike told them about it. He had a copy of the official orders."

Glaring at his brother, Jarred continued the story. "As you know, the council has to replace Hivad Sepal."

"He's sick. He'll probably be dead soon."

Ignoring him, Jarred went on. "Because of the Battle and her seniority, Jenny seemed to be the most likely candidate. But there are a number of factors to consider. Buto is immensely popular with just about every faction. His loyalty to the Fleet is beyond question, but he's never denied that he has some sympathy with those who want to go back to the way things were." Jarred pronounced his next words with obvious distaste. "Even the Kay-Raikes support his promotion."

"That's why they drugged them," Sato said, snapping open a breadstick and pulling out the soft center. He discarded it and crunched down on the crusty shell.

"Someone will have to explain that," Dane said. There was an air of unreality about this meeting. As if she were watching, but not actually connected to the conversation. Could it be the—whatever it was—moving again within her head? It was not an alarming feeling. Just . . . very odd.

Buto spoke for the first time. "Jenny and I didn't understand until a few hours ago," he said. "I was waiting to regain my full faculties, before adding to the criminal charges against Karnas Kay-Raike and his clan. Then it came to me. Or Jenny; I'm not sure who thought of it first. They—"

With a sudden insight, Dane understood. "They're calling off their vendetta against me. They believe I poisoned the leader of their clan. Symbolically, they've just taken revenge. The message is that the matter is settled."

"For now," Jenny cautioned. "While they believe Buto can help them."

"While they believe I *will* help them," Buto corrected.

"And will you?" Dane asked.

"That's a matter of perception, isn't it? The Kay-Raikes want a return to . . . well, you know what they want." Dane did know, and it was not a comfortable subject for discussion between them. "For now," he continued, "I'm content to trade with the worlds. The danger is in allowing them to become too powerful again. We can't forget that when they were . . . **aaayne caanooo eermee** . . ."

Dane stared at him and at the others. Buto was still speaking, and no one had changed expression. It was apparent that only she was hearing the strange "sound."

It died away as he continued. "... war with each other constantly, and sent our ancestors out to die for them, giving them nothing in return except disrespect and ... **aaayne caanooo eermee** ..." There it was again, exactly as before. Again, only Dane was affected. "... never like that again," Shimas was saying. "My position is that the only way to prevent that, and it could happen within fifty or sixty years it we don't ... **aaayne caanooo eermee** ..."

She brought her hands to her face and rubbed her eyes.

"Dane," Jarred asked, "what is it?"

Buto barked a short laugh. "I know you disagree, Dane. But don't drift away, argue with me! I need you to sharpen my mind for the council interview."

Dane looked up at him. "Something ..."

"She's ill," Jenny said, reaching across the table to take Dane's hand. "Can you walk, or shall we have a doctor brought here?"

"No, it's ..." *What* was it? A tickling sensation; a mild current, as if in a wire reaching from ear to ear. Larynx contracting again, as if she were trying to speak. It was gone now, along with the ... sounds? Not sounds. It was more the absence of them, specific ones, that the mind anticipated. A glass shatters on the floor in utter silence. Still, the mind creates an image of the sound it expected to process. That was as close as she could come to describing it. What had Momed Pwanda done to her? "I'm sorry," she said. "You were speaking about trade, Buto. Will that be the topic at tonight's meeting?"

"You know about that?"

"I know that we have a delegation of some sort aboard." She was careful not to mention the Gold Fleet. Only by seeing Pwanda could she have known the origin of the delegation. "Colonel Hormat told me that one of its members was missing."

"Oh, they found him," Jarred said, warning Sato to silence with a glare. "He was curious, and wandered. No harm done."

"About the manual?" Buto asked, pointedly changing the subject.

"Finished," Dane replied.

"Good! After the meal, have it brought it to Jenny and me. Once we've gone over it, we'll have it transposed into formal language so that no one else can even hope to know what it says. When the new regulations take effect, there will be three legitimate experts, all of them in the Marsham clan."

Jenny looked around at her children. "Does anyone doubt," she asked with a grin, "that your father is ready for the council?"

Two hours later Dane was dressing for the evening's activities. Her uniform was plain as before, but for two small insignia. Over her right breast was the shaded silver swirl that made up the Marsham crest. Opposite it was a patch of checkered design, green and white, which she thought unbearably ugly, identifying her as a senior trade negotiator. She noted as she pulled on the monolithic, form-shaped garment that its fit was looser than it had been only two weeks before. Jenny would notice, as she always did. Another lecture would follow on the importance of eating regularly.

Her throat contracted. . . . **itch petter, gnow, esss? ool oonersnan zoon, tayne** . . .

"Yes, it's better now," she said aloud.

. . . **kood, kood. hile zeee ooo zoon** . . .

How does this work? she thought. There was no reply. She nodded, beginning to understand.

Above the bare minimum necessary, Karnas Kay-Raike hated light. Light was something Grounders craved, the better to view their loathsome planets: from the scars of disintegration they called mountains, to the uncontrolled and dangerous waste that was their oceans. He'd touched a

planet, once. A boy at the time, he'd taken a single step
from his shuttle and made the fool's error of looking up.
No overhead . . . nothing there. He'd felt himself falling
into that lighted nothingness and fainted. His father cursed
him as a coward. The doctors called it vertigo. A Grounder
disease. One second, and he'd been contaminated for life.

At the far side of his stateroom was a holostat of his
father, perched on the desk like a malevolent animal frozen
in its own bile. Only its outline was visible, but Karnas
could feel the eyes of it peering outward. "Coward?" he
said in a monotone whisper. "I've killed more ships than
you ever thought of running away from." He kept the holostat for reasons of clan solidarity. Tirus Kay-Raike was
revered as a hero. Karnas knew better. He'd been with his
esteemed father, watched their formation of ships on the
War Table display, and witnessed the hesitation . . . An attack against the Gold Fleet at that moment would have
ended in the destruction of their own squadron. But the
Enemy would have been distracted, unable to mass as it
did, prior to that last killing offensive . . . the Battle could
have been won. They were right when they blamed the
Kay-Raikes for the disgrace that followed. Olton Kay-
Raike's leadership was missing, but that was no excuse for
his father's cowardice. His clan had failed. It was a stain
on his honor that he would never escape. Like the Grounder
disease.

Beside the holostat of his father was one of his mother.
This had its own illumination, and shone brightly to any
point in the dim stateroom. Mother and son had been together only once; the moment of his birth was the last of
her life. She'd known, and had made the choice. It was the
Kay-Raike way: Death is a small thing to offer the clan. A
touch at the base of the holostat would bring her voice
again, her final words, meant only for him. He no longer
activated the recording. There was no need, because her
words never left his mind. She'd wished him a long career,
marked with distinction. And said that he was *the* one; he
would be the first of the clan to take a seat on the council.

Karnas marveled again at her face. Wise, without fear, vi-
sionary, dedicated . . . captured on holo when she was his
present age, it was a feminine mirror of his own.

A voice blared from the wall. "Squadron Leader?"

He sat up in bed, startled at the voice and at the sight of
the woman beside him. He'd forgotten she was there. "Get
out," he said, shoving his wife to her feet. "You can dress
in the corridor." When she'd gone he reached up and behind him, toggling the speaker. "Yes."

"Sir," a man's voice said, "the delegation is aboard.
There are five of them, without security, as negotiated.
Shall we keep them confined to their shuttle until you ar-
rive?"

"Have they been searched?"

"Thoroughly, sir."

Karnas chuckled. "Then they'll be angry. Good. Yes,
keep them isolated there. Have attendants bring them food,
but Grounder rations only. Call me again an hour after
they've eaten."

"You'll arrive with the doctors?"

"Yes."

"Understood, sir."

"I protest this inexcusable treatment," the woman said
weakly. Unlike the others in her party, she had refused the
sleeping medication that would take them through the stomach sickness.

"You have my apologies, of course," Karnas Kay-Raike
said solicitously. "Your quarantine aboard the shuttle was
for your own protection, as much as ours. But this"—he
indicated the half-empty bowls of pink gel being removed
from the table between them—"*is* inexcusable. You are our
honored guests. This is intended only for Grounders."

"Grounders?"

"I believe you refer to them as Dirts," he said. "This
food is formulated to their needs. It is not meant for people.
Along with my apology, please accept my assurance that
those responsible will be punished." As if the idea had just

occurred to him, he asked, "Would you care to be a witness?"

The woman glanced up at two men, one old and one middle-aged, who stood mutely across the small compartment. They wore identical gray tunics and kept their eyes lowered. What strength she had, she summoned as anger. "No, I would not. But in my Fleet they would be hanged by the heels until they were unconscious."

"We're not so cruel," Karnas said lightly. "Once all pressure is bled from the airlock, the door opens and they're expelled into space. It's quick, and relatively painless." He waved a hand dismissively, and the two attendants were led away. He did not add that, conveniently, the two attendants had reached the age of mandatory retirement. They were scheduled for the airlock anyway, but now their deaths served a purpose other than the disposal of Grounders who'd outlived their usefulness. With this ruse he had learned a great deal about the Gold Fleet representatives by watching them through the shuttle's monitors. Of the five, only this woman had demonstrated any real strength. And yet she was not senior among them. That honor belonged to a much younger woman, Supervisor Handley, who had been the first to accept an escape from discomfort through sleep. From this he inferred that leadership was not a function of merit within the Gold Fleet. The alternatives were favoritism, or heredity. A valuable bit of knowledge, which they certainly would not have volunteered. The other three, all men, had been the most shameless in their complaints. Handley had made no attempt to silence or discipline them. Incredible.

The woman pulled herself up to an erect sitting position. "I am Coordinator Jamel. Under the circumstances I will speak for Supervisor Handley and these three crew. We wish to be taken to more appropriate quarters and allowed time to recuperate from this, ah, incident."

"I've already given that order," Karnas said. He had not, but his officers responded immediately. Attendants were brought in to carry the four. Jamel insisted on walking, unassisted.

"I want one thing," Kay-Raike said to Jamel as he escorted her to the doorway. "And that is change. Must we accept Grounders *telling* us what they are willing to *trade* for? This must stop. I believe that many in your Fleet are of the same mind."

"You can discuss that with Supervisor Handley," Jamel said with immense dignity, "when she has recovered from your gesture of good will and cooperation."

When they were gone, Karnas paced the small shuttle compartment and said aloud, to no one in particular, "This is not an auspicious beginning. Look what the Gold Fleet has sent us. With the exception of that one woman, these representatives are beneath contempt. It is not possible that they have the authority to hear my ideas and react to them. Sending them here was a deliberate insult."

Dismissing the other officers, Mendel Kay-Raike came to stand beside his younger brother and nodded thoughtfully. "The Gold Fleet doesn't know your power, sir, or the quiet support you have throughout our own Fleet."

"Your point, Brother?"

"They chose these people to meet with you because they believe that you're merely a renegade. I would advise saying very little to this group, beyond convincing them that their superiors should show you the proper respect. That will strengthen our position and ensure that next time, the people we deal with will have the authority to agree to your proposals."

"Yes, that's wise."

Emboldened, Mendel continued. "On the other hand . . . I wonder, sir. Perhaps this *is* the best they have left, after . . ." He could not bring himself to mention by name the catastrophe of eight years before.

"Then we're lost," Karnas snapped. "If this is their best, they're useless as allies. And without allies we have no hope against the council."

"Shimas, sir?"

"What about him? To gain power over us, he'll present arguments in our behalf. And we will pretend to trust him. That's useful in gaining time, and it is the only reason he left this ship alive. But he won't stand against them. Eventually he'll vote for our destruction."

"Without the Kay-Raike clan, this present madness will continue, and our Fleet will die."

"You've heard me say it often enough, Brother."

"So Shimas is a traitor."

"He's worse. He knows we're right, but he hasn't the courage to stand with us. And as for his 'daughter,' that . . . that . . ." Immediate rage led to a fit of coughing, which left Karnas unable to speak.

Mendel Kay-Raike held his brother by the shoulders to steady him. "I understand what you need, sir. It will be done as soon as we can arrange it. Sir, can you hear me?" With a sigh, Mendel lowered his brother gently to the deck and sat with him until the shaking stopped.

Momed Pwanda, as senior delegate, was the last to enter the meeting room.

Standing at relaxed attention along with thirty of *Dalkag*'s officers, Dane had mentally rehearsed her reaction to the sight of him. Buto and Jenny expected shock, followed by a flash of anger, and then speechless embarrassment. She'd planned to accommodate them. But watching Pwanda's slow, regal walk, the blank look of piety on his face, the golden knee-length robe he wore, the oversized gold boots, the crimson, ball-shaped hat on his head . . . she burst out laughing.

Very unprofessional, Dane. And don't get me started.

The almost-sound was clear this time as her larynx moved, framing the words he'd sent. She gained control of her expression and looked at Jenny and Buto. Both maintained outward calm, but she recognized the anger in their stiff bearing. Jenny began to speak, was interrupted in Dane's mind by **I didn't make the costume, you know** and Dane laughed again.

"It is so pleasant to see you after so long," Pwanda said, saving the moment by breaking protocol and coming forward to embrace Dane. He stood back and offered a hand in turn to Jenny, and then Buto. "I am pleased that your side is prepared to honor this first meeting with a gesture of informality and personal warmth. My patrons might not have been so bold, in your place."

"We thought it only appropriate," Buto said.

"And we hope that this is a harbinger of our future dealings," Jenny added.

Smooth, Pwanda sent.

Escorted to their seats and presented with the carafes of chilled water they'd specified, the Gold Fleet representatives waited for Jenny Marsham to deliver the opening remarks. To Momed's left were a man and a woman, Supervisors Hecht and Sensen. Hecht was thin-faced, ebony-skinned like Pwanda, with a receding hairline that was close-shaven and resembled a thin cap. Sensen appeared to be roughly the same age as Dane, but in contrast was a large woman with eyes that seemed permanently locked in an expression of concentration. To Pwanda's immediate right was his understudy, also a former slave, dressed in an abbreviated version of Pwanda's uniform. Colin Vestry was a young, brown-haired man whose every feature suggested "average." Dane understood immediately that to have been chosen by Momed Pwanda, he was anything but average. To Vestry's right was another supervisor. She was a woman whose age Dane would estimate at mid-thirties, and whose appearance Dane would describe as startling. She was extraordinarily beautiful. Her hair was golden and cut short, framing wide green eyes that seemed to take in everything at once. The credentials Pwanda had earlier delivered to Jenny gave her name as Nass.

You're right, she's not what she appears to be. Dane looked at Pwanda and saw him watching her. **I'll explain later. But find a way to tell your patrons that she's very important. They should pay close attention to her as we proceed tonight. Also, here's the trick to this. Purse**

your lips very slightly. Pretend you're making words in your throat, and imagine them being sent to me.

yike yiss?

Almost 'like this.' Relax your throat. You're holding it like you're gargling poison, afraid to swallow. It'll become natural very soon. By now everything's in place, mechanically. You can think the transmitter on, or off. More later. Let's enjoy the show. Be sure to tell your patrons about Nass.

Ayre gny karents gnow.

Parents? Wow.

As Jenny began her remarks, the remainder of the Silver Fleet officers sat down. Dane wrote and passed a note to Buto, offering her opinion that Supervisor Nass appeared to be a woman of more authority that her credentials indicated. Shimas took the suggestion seriously. Dane's "impressions" about people were usually—thinking about it, he couldn't recall an exception—correct.

As the meeting progressed, Dane was relieved to see that this encounter was more symbolic than substantive. After completing his own brief remarks, praising the concepts of cooperation and friendship, Pwanda deferred to Supervisor Hecht. For half an hour the elderly man recited a litany of historical wrongs perpetrated by the Silver Fleet that required compensation prior to any further agreement. Buto Shimas rose angrily and began to respond in kind.

Boring, isn't it?

Momed, how serious is your side about . . . can anyone else . . . for want of a better word, 'hear' us?

Excellent! You've got it just right. The answer is no. For now, only you and I have the transmitters in place. I can communicate with our leadership on two worlds, but those units are in mechanical devices and require a separate frequency. You have that capability also, Dane. But it will be a number of weeks before you develop the fine control to access it. Or perhaps less, judging by how quickly you've mastered sending.

Then The Stem knows what's taking place.

Of course.

Momed, we can't allow this to go forward. We do need the Fleets to cooperate in small matters, to prevent a return to large-scale warfare. But an official delegation . . . this is too much, too soon.

Whitlock gave me the same lecture he gave you, Dane, and I am in total agreement. My counsel is this: You take care of yours, and I'll see to mine. As to this present farce, don't worry. It will comfort you to know that this meeting is the first of its kind. And it will be the last for quite some time. The woman you thought of as startling and beautiful . . . you formed those words as you thought them, so be careful you don't reveal how devastatingly handsome you consider me to be . . . is No'ln Beviney. In the Gold Fleet hierarchy there is the Nomarch, and then her. But that's misleading. The Nomarch is . . . let me just say that No'ln Beviney is the highest-ranking *competent* person among us. And she hates you, all of you, with an intensity that is difficult to describe.

Yes, that's very comforting. Why are you here, then?

The transmitter, of course. To accomplish that, I convinced Beviney that there are advantages to deceiving you about our intentions.

You knew where I was?

A "sound," which she took to be a laugh. You're not unknown, Dane. Whenever you've been seen, it was in the company of Jenny or Buto, usually both. When No'ln Beviney contacted your council through another supervisor, she specified that she wanted to meet with those two.

How did you arrange that?

Easily. They led the battle against her, and she was curious. She wanted to see the faces of the people she intends to have revenge against.

But, Momed, they weren't scheduled to be back here for two more days.

Yes, that was a surprise. I thought we were two days

early, which would give me the opportunity to speak with you about the transmitter.

Before stabbing me in the neck.

It didn't really hurt, did it? If you'd known it was coming, you'd scarcely have felt it.

I suppose that's true.

Besides, now there will be . . . oops, I'm called to center stage again.

Buto Shimas had resumed his seat. Into the thick silence that followed his oration, Momed Pwanda stepped smoothly. "I am delighted," he said with a voice of quiet authority, "that despite our histories, or perhaps because of them, we have been able to meet and to speak with such encouraging candor. As senior delegate representing the Nomarch of the Great Command, I express his gratitude to our hosts. And I am authorized to say that the unpleasantries of the past six hundred years notwithstanding, it is the Nomarch's intention that the two Fleets will find common space in which to pursue our individual and collective interests. The Nomarch realizes that the step we have taken here today is a small one. Hostilities between our Fleets will not cease because of it." There followed a subtle change in Pwanda's tone and vocal cadence, a clear signal to Dane that he was reciting the next words. " 'But there will be a time, a place, a circumstance, in which our ships will meet in agreement to a common purpose. I believe that that purpose will be the peaceful pursuit of trade among the thousands of worlds throughout the seven galaxies. And I say with confidence that when our hosts share that belief, which is the vision of our Nomarch, that chance encounters between our ships will begin with communication, and not weapons fire. It is a beginning.' " Pwanda paused, pretending to drink from his carafe.

Don't believe a word of it, Dane. Beviney wrote that last bit. She has something in mind. I'll contact you when I know what it is.

"We had hoped to be with you longer," Pwanda continued. "But due to the fortuitous early return of Major Generals Buto Shimas and Jenny Marsham, we find that our business is concluded. My instructions were to depart when that moment arrived. May I assume that a full presentation of our meeting will be transmitted to your council?''

''It will be done,'' Jenny said, standing. ''We regret your departure so soon, however. There are so many . . . other things that could be discussed, informally.'' She glanced at Dane questioningly, and seemed bewildered by the disinterested shrug she received in response. ''But we do understand. A shuttle is ready to return you to your ship immediately. May I add, I'm pleased to see that you've done so well.''

Pwanda smiled. ''Your decision to send me to the Gold Fleet came as a shock, General. I'm grateful for the opportunity to thank you for that. Good-bye.'' The five of them stood and walked toward the door with that same regal pace they'd affected while entering before.

Don't look, Dane. You'll burst into tears.

Or die laughing.

That night Dane slept very well. While Momed was traveling back to his ship *Noldron* they'd had a long conversation, mostly personal. At first candor had been difficult, more strange to her than accepting the reality of the implanted transmitter. But gradually she'd accepted the astounding fact that she was no longer alone. The journals she had written and then destroyed had helped ease her sense of isolation. They had never been enough, however. Now she could tell another human being what she hoped for, what she feared, what she felt. For the first time in more than eight years she could discuss her work. As sleep overtook her, Dane found herself giving a silent chuckle; minutes after their last conversation, he'd accidentally sent, **"She thinks Beviney is beautiful? My God, isn't there a mirror aboard that ship?"** Professor of Engineering Momed Kwasii Pwanda-Pwanda wasn't as expert in their new communication as he believed. Or, she wondered, was he?

≈4≈

Day 5

"I meant to give you this yesterday," Jarred said at breakfast. Except for a few attendants, the two of them were alone in the mammoth dining room, the first to arrive. Dane ate with an appetite she hadn't had in recent memory. The peaches seemed especially good this morning. Like all of the fruits and vegetables grown deep within *Dalkag*, they were produced according to the innovations introduced by Paul Hardaway. Paul was her cousin, a farmer on her home world of Walden who'd been taken captive shortly after she and Pwanda had been. Now he was free again. The succulent array of fruits on the table brought Dane a smile. Paul would examine each one minutely. And then, grudgingly, approve.

"Dane?"

"What?"

"Don't you want this? You mentioned it at least ten times before we left, and getting it for you wasn't exactly easy. Or safe."

"Thank you," she said, accepting the thumb-sized cylinder. "How many of them were you able to record?"

"Only Karnas, I'm afraid. We were searched whenever we left our quarters. I kept this on a table, and you were right. They had no interest in anything that was out for them to see. On the second day there, Karnas came to speak with Buto. Jenny took the opportunity to begin an argument with him, and I recorded his responses. Or *response*, I should say. Once he began, no one else had the chance to speak. Nearly forty minutes, Dane. That officer is obsessed." He added reflectively, "But I don't understand why you wanted it."

"If he had pledged to kill you, wouldn't you want to know something about him? At least what he looks and sounds like?"

Jarred popped an olive into his mouth and nodded. "I understand what you mean. Until yesterday, none of us had seen a living member of the Gold Fleet, and they've wanted to kill us for centuries. Yes, I was curious." Dane saw the sudden inspiration in his eyes, and knew what was coming. "While we're on that subject, curiosity and the Gold Fleet, I've been wondering what it was like for you. The meeting last night."

"I was disappointed," she said. Jarred nodded, ready to offer sympathy. "We all hoped for more than an exchange of accusations, didn't we?"

"Dane, I risked my life for you, and you know that's not what I'm referring to!" His freckles stood out, a sign of quick anger. "I meant you and . . . you know what I'm asking about."

"Colonel Saddhurst!" Dane called over Jarred's shoulder.

The stocky man approached, surprised and pleased at the greeting. "Good morning, Dane. Good morning, Lieutenant."

"William, have you met my brother?"

"No, I haven't."

Jarred leapt to his feet to acknowledge the senior officer.

Dane made the introductions and added, "William, my brother is fascinated by your field, propulsion physics. I'm sure he has many ideas he'd like to discuss with you."

Saddhurst accepted the implied invitation and sat down, gesturing for Jarred to join them and continue his meal. "That would be my pleasure, Lieutenant. Perhaps we'll find the time at a later date."

"Why not now?" Dane asked. "I need to prepare for a class, so I won't be here to annoy you with uneducated questions." Before either man could voice a polite objection, she picked up the cylinder and stood, wishing them both a pleasant morning as she left.

After completing outlines for the day's classes, Dane arranged for a substitute to replace her and played the holo in her quarters. More than a year had passed since she'd last tracked a human being; for this and other reasons she knew from the outset that Karnas Kay-Raike was going to be a challenge. He had an odd way of moving. Pacing as he spoke, he took steps of irregular and seemingly random length. She knew that there was a pattern, but found it elusive at first. In most people, long strides indicated boldness, emotion, confidence, or the expression of a large and important concept. By contrast, short paces denoted careful thought, indecisiveness, or falsehood. These principles, taken together with gestures, head and eye movement, changes in inflection or tone, stiffening or relaxing body posture, could be correlated with the words spoken, silences, pauses, the rhythm of speech, as well as facial expression, to create a composite impression of the target. Karnas Kay-Raike employed all of these modalities of expression: to some extent consciously, which meant that deliberate deception was possible. To some extent unconsciously, and these were the key signifiers. It was Dane's art to discern which was which.

But Kay-Raike was a jumble of contradiction. Within a single sentence, moving and gesturing, he would combine telltales of sincerity, deceit, anger, happiness, surety, and bewilderment. At times he would stop and hunch his shoul-

ders, clenching his fists at his stomach and closing his eyes
. . . all with no break in the context or rhythm of his speech.

Dane played the tape twice and then shut off the holo.
It was time to enter the physical phase of her work, the
segment that went beyond traditional methods of observation. This procedure was the invention of Brian Whitlock.
When successful, it led to a depth of empathy that allowed
the tracker not only to understand and anticipate, but often
to control, the target.

Again checking that her compartment monitors were disabled, she began. During the first tracking run she mouthed
each word Karnas had spoken, imitating perfectly his inflection. She paced her quarters while matching every
movement and gesture the target had made. Next she halved
Kay-Raike's speed, and went through his entire performance once again. By the end of this second run she was
no longer consciously aware of Dane Steppart. She was a
blank entity, building and coming to understand a new *self*.
Each minute movement and word had offered clues to explain the new self more completely. Her mind sifted
through them, singly and together, while her body rested,
unmoving. She was an entity seeking to define itself. *Who
am I who shouts like this, breathes like this?* She looked
everywhere, and saw nothing. She was aware only of what
she had just said and done. Her entire world must be built
from only that. Or she would go mad. She was lost, alone,
and terribly frightened.

She soon had help. In response to her conditioning for
this procedure, the fear triggered a return of Dane's self-
awareness. The relief she felt was overwhelming. Perspiring heavily, she took a few moments to calm herself. When
she was ready, she plunged ahead. Her mind probed deeper
and deeper into her task as she went through everything
Kay-Raike had done a final time, at actual speed. At a specific moment—she was never able to recall when this
occurred—she again lost all conscious perception of Dane
Steppart. Suddenly everything she was doing made sense.
She *was* Karnas Kay-Raike: angrily denouncing, subtly ly-

ing, boldly proclaiming, promising, threatening, reviewing history, defining the future. Feeling pain when he clenched his fists, but ignoring it with perfect control; hating Buto Shimas, inspired by and attracted to the defiant Jenny Marsham, *afraid*, ignoring the fool who was her son.

When it was over, Dane remained in the final pose of the holo, expecting a reply from the strangely silent and progressively immaterial guests. *Why aren't they responding? Are they overwhelmed? Convinced? Afraid? Did I make a mistake, reveal too much? Are they laughing at me? Damn them! Do they, too, believe that I am a coward? Is it safe to let them return to . . .*

Dane, it's over. You've finished.

When she again knew who and where she was, Dane collapsed on her bed facedown. She could not remember being so drained and exhausted. Tracking had never hurt this much. It was an effort even to respond to Momed.

My transmitter was . . . ?

For the past nineteen minutes. I'd say that's when you became Kay-Raike. Rest, Dane. Let everything pull itself together. I'll go now.

Thank you.

But I should point out . . .

Not now, Momed. I'll . . . She was asleep before the thought could be completed. There were the words **you know he's insane, don't you?** but she didn't know whose they were.

She had never tracked anyone like Karnas Kay-Raike. And there were limitations implicit in using a holo tape as the tracking medium. Not until she saw him in the flesh would she know if she'd been successful—only then would she know whether or not, in the parlance of her Stem training, she *owned* him. Somehow she didn't think so.

⇒5⇐

Day 16

Intergalactic space

Sovereign appeared on the War Room screen as half of a dim silvered sun, still and majestic, orbited by seven miniatures of itself. Its base circumference was four times that of the average Silver Fleet vessel of war, with proportional interior space. *Dalkag*'s officers, crew, and attendants numbered 2,320. Aboard *Sovereign* the number was twenty times that, with thousands of visitors aboard at any given moment.

As *Dalkag*'s senior staff watched the War Room display, one of the seven ships guarding *Sovereign* broke from its orbital pattern and approached. Jenny and Buto nodded to one another in mild surprise at the honor being extended.

"General Marsham, General Shimas." The image of a young, dark-haired woman appeared at the top of a screen on the wall across from them. There were gasps from every officer present. Buto blinked deliberately to clear his eyes. Were it not for the uniform the woman wore, and had he not passed his daughter in the corridor only minutes before, he would have bet his life that Dane had taken a shuttle to the outrider ship and was now speaking to them from there. The resemblance . . . no, not resemblance, *duplication* . . . appeared to be perfect. He knew that given uncounted billions of people alive, the probability of every person having one or more doubles approached, perhaps reached, certainty. But what were the odds of *meeting* two such people?

"Is there something wrong?" the woman asked, seeing the consternation throughout *Dalkag*'s War Room. Then she smiled. "Ah, you know who I am. But nevertheless, I must observe protocol. I am Captain Naomi Kay-Raike. A reverse renegade, you might say."

Jenny and Buto exchanged bewildered glances; two shocks, not one.

Naomi continued, "I've been given the privilege of welcoming you on behalf of the Generals and Sovereign Command Council. I'm coming aboard to pilot your shuttle to *Sovereign*. After that, *Dalkag* will take up station at the standard distance for visitors."

"Understood, Captain. Thank you," Jenny said.

"As you see by my uniform, 'Captain' is my rank, not my position aboard this vessel. I am to make myself available to you during your stay. Then if you . . ." Naomi turned toward someone near her and listened for a few seconds to something the monitor did not relay. She stiffened her expression and faced the screen again. "We'll discuss that at an appropriate time, with your permission."

"Of course," Buto replied as the image left the screen.

"I don't believe what I just saw," Jenny said.

"What choice do we have?" Buto answered. "At least her voice is different."

Dane was prepared for the meeting; Naomi was not. When she saw Dane standing between Jenny and Buto as she exited her small craft, Naomi went visibly weak at the knees. She greeted the major generals perfunctorily and said to Dane, ''I've never seen a likeness of you. Now I understand why . . .'' The shock and loathing in her expression was gradually overcome by one of anguish. She tried to speak again, and fainted.

Shimas caught her before she fell and lowered her gently to the floor. ''It was a surprise to all of us,'' he said to Jenny. ''But to react like that . . . an officer of the Fleet, and a Kay-Raike. It's shameful.''

''There's obviously more to this that we know, Buto,'' Jenny said with some anger.

''Ah, yes, of course there is,'' he answered, looking away from his wife. ''Exactly my point.''

''Help me with her.''

Half an hour later Naomi Kay-Raike was sitting up in a dispensary bed and assuring Jenny that she was well, and capable of performing her duty. ''General Marsham, I ask only for a few minutes alone here. We have sufficient time for your scheduled arrival aboard *Sovereign*. With your permission, I'll meet all of you in the shuttle.''

''Very well,'' Jenny said. She was unable to dismiss the feeling that she was speaking to her daughter. She agreed to Kay-Raike's request on the basis of professionalism. An officer needed to carry out her assignment and would be shamed by a refusal based on the perception of personal weakness.

When Naomi entered the small craft, she said nothing before taking the pilot's seat and strapping in. ''We're ready,'' she announced a minute later, after the preflight inspection. No one commented on the fact that she had trimmed her hair to one inch in length and thus reduced her resemblance to Dane.

The shuttle touched down in a hangar that was similar to one aboard *Dalkag*, except three times the size. Prior to the Battle, Dalkag had been refitted to resemble *Sovereign* by order of Arlana Mestoeffer, a council member who'd been selected against her will to serve as Fleet Leader in the confrontation.

Other than *Dalkag*, no ship in the Silver Fleet came close to the opulence that characterized *Sovereign*. Emerging from the shuttle with Buto, Naomi Kay-Raike, and Dane, Jenny recalled her first impressions of *Dalkag*, which now seemed a poor imitation of this original. The hangar was fabulous; as she'd thought of its smaller counterpart, it was something from a storyteller with too vivid an imagination. Floor and walls appeared to be fashioned of genuine silver, a lustrous sheen interrupted by inlaid murals of precious stones. The murals depicted ships in combat, along with facial likenesses of officers who'd distinguished themselves in battle over the centuries. As aboard *Dalkag*, there was one work of art that dominated all the others. Set above the exit door was a mosaic of multicolored gems, thirty feet or more in height. The mosaic depicted two faces, one male, one female, touching one another at the cheek and facing out toward the viewer. These were the Generals, Mosh Trikal and Tabba Depluss, who reigned over the council and thus over all of the Fleet. Jenny recalled her reaction to viewing the visages of the preceding Generals, Menta Carole and Tobok Ishmahan. She'd seen them as projecting confidence, strength, and wisdom; looking ahead and reflecting back on a future more glorious than the common mind could comprehend. Depluss and Trikal were not lesser leaders. But the future they represented was far less certain than that embodied by their predecessors.

"This ship is the soul of the Silver Fleet," Shimas said quietly.

Dane agreed silently. To her, the hangar was an obscenity. Everything displayed here, the metals, the gems, even the artistic minds and arduous labor that had combined to create this splendor, had been stolen from worlds brutally invaded and left in destitution—left in broken poverty that future generations would inherit and make it their life's work to repair. That thought fed her determination that the Fleets would never merge, nor would they return to their

old patterns. It was her duty to see that they were irrevocably changed. And then, dissolved.

Dane was genuinely fond of Jenny and Buto. They accepted her as their own child and, to the extent possible
concerning a Grounder, they loved her. But they were prod-
ucts of their own history. Each had led numerous "supply
runs," leaving behind devastated worlds and unknowable
misery. They'd come to power by skillfully and enthusiastically killing anyone their Fleet designated as enemy, or
victim. Under orders they would do so again, without hesitation. Jarred was different. Despite everything he'd been
taught as a child, he hated war more than he hated the Gold
Fleet. Of all of the spaceborn people she knew, he was the
most dedicated to the idea that human beings who lived all
of their lives aboard ships, and those whose homes were
planets, could and must find mutual accommodation and
exist as complements to one another. And Sato . . . After
Jenny and Buto, Dane had been next to hold the squalling
infant and feel the strength of his fingers touching her face,
and the warmth of his small body in her arms. She adored
Sato, even though at times she was distressed and repulsed
by the thought of what he could, and seemed to want to,
become. She had told these people that they were her family now. They trusted and depended on her. And yet she
knew that if their deaths, or hers, were required to further
the goals of The Stem, she would help to make it so.

"I left my clan eleven days ago," Naomi said to Buto
as they exited the hangar and proceeded into a jeweled
corridor. The walk-space was twenty feet in width, twice
that of other ships. "I believed I'd be taken directly to the
council. But I was held for interrogation. It seemed it would
never end. After a while I thought . . . I didn't expect to be
here."

"Neither did I, until recently," Buto said, scarcely no-
ticing the young officer's breach of courtesy in speaking
first. He was as awed as Jenny or Naomi. The ceiling above
them was gently arched, peaking at fifteen or more feet.
Long silvered bars lined walls and ceiling, running parallel

to the floor. These were braces to be used by personnel when the ship pitched or rolled in battle, or when sudden acceleration was enough to overcome balance. Here the bars were ceremonial; *Sovereign* had never participated directly in combat. If it ever did, it would be to the shame of the entire Fleet, whose every officer—every *loyal* officer, Buto thought, glancing curiously again at Naomi Kay-Raike—owed this singular vessel absolute fealty and protection. It was every ship captain's dream to command one of the seven outriders that orbited *Sovereign*. To be so appointed was an honor second only to council membership. Those seven men and women were acknowledged to be the finest warriors the Fleet could produce; there was nothing ceremonial about *them*.

The three officers had been provided a partial schematic of *Sovereign*, and knew the route they were to take. By long-ingrained habit they were measuring distance by counting paces as they walked. They were in unfamiliar territory, but in case of emergency would be expected to be able to move quickly through any spaces they had traversed, in total darkness. The corridor stretched for one hundred nineteen feet before they passed the first intersection. They had still seen no one, but all knew that their every step was monitored. The emptiness only added to the sense of grandeur, and the officers understood that the ungreeted simplicity of their arrival was a rare privilege. No traditional honor guard had met them for the same reason an officer as junior as Naomi Kay-Raike had been dispatched to bring them aboard: They were to be welcomed first by the council itself. At the third intersection they turned to the right. Another thirty feet, another intersection, this one leading toward the center of *Sovereign*. Four hundred feet, three levels upward, and another short walk. They came to a compartment door that opened at their approach.

The four spaced themselves carefully and lined up outside the door in order of rank: Jenny, Buto, Naomi, and, three paces behind, Dane. They entered the room in that order, keeping their eyes straight ahead.

As soon as Dane was across the threshold, the door slid shut again. The four came to a simultaneous halt.

The room was another surprise in a day that seemed destined to bring a lot of them. In extreme contrast to what they'd seen thus far, this compartment was starkly bare. The walls were soft brown and without decoration of any kind. The ceiling was of similar color, marked only by lights that were spaced at three-foot intervals and emitted a glare-free luminescence. Neither bright nor subdued, it reminded Dane of a slightly overcast autumn afternoon. Were it not for the large table and the silent officers who sat in the eleven ornately carved chairs around it, this area could be a detention cell.

At the head of the table were the Generals. Rarely viewed except in mosaic representations, their appearance was discomfiting at first. Tabba Depluss and Mosh Trikal were two persons surgically joined so that they shared a common arm and hand. The hand had been rebuilt; it bore two opposing thumbs and could close in either direction. Their common arm was wrapped in lengths of thick silver cord. The Generals were of approximately the same age, mid-nineties. Both were graying, and both had sharp eyes that were attentive and piercing. Depluss was smiling. Trikal appeared incapable of ever doing so.

"I welcome you and invite you to stand at ease," Trikal said, referring both to himself and Depluss. As the "attack" half of the Generals, he was considered senior. It was his duty and prerogative to speak first at all council functions. He appeared to be taken from the same mold as his predecessor, Menta Carole. Or perhaps, Jenny thought, he was emulating her. His gray hair was pulled tightly back and tied at the base of the neck with a thinner version of the cord that bound their shared arm—his left, Depluss's right.

The "defend" half of the Generals had a softer appearance—not unlike that of her own predecessor, Tobok Ishmahan.

From their positions at the table, the nine council members eyed the four visitors with a range of expressions. The only member recognizable to Jenny or Buto was Hivad Sepal. Known to be dying, it was rumored that he no longer sat in on council meetings. He was tall and extremely thin. His emaciation might otherwise be credited to his wasting disease, but it was in fact a common clan trait. His grandson Tam had been company leader to Jenny and Buto when they were both squadron leaders. Jenny and Dane had been forced to watch Tam slowly and painfully put to death on the orders of Arlana Mestoeffer. His execution was the result of Mestoeffer's vendetta against the Sepals; it was Hivad who had engineered her leaving the council to take command of the debacle that came to be known simply as the Battle. Mestoeffer was now, again by rumor, said to be in hiding from Hivad Sepal. As a retirement gift, he had publicly promised her a year's forbearance before he conferred on her the same ignominious death she had given his grandson.

Seeing Sepal here reminded Dane of the environment her new family was soon to be a part of. No council member had ever caused physical harm to another while in active service. Immediate family was also safe. But vendettas against more distant clan members, though rare, were firmly established in Fleet tradition. Mestoeffer had been an exception to the concept of rarity. In her years on the council she had instituted no less than four, some said ten or more, such vendettas. The Marsham clan had been the target of one of the known four.

Yes, Dane thought, recalling Buto's earlier words. This was the soul of the Silver Fleet. And depending on today's events, it could be her future home.

"Captain Kay-Raike," Depluss said, "your testimony has been reviewed and found to be satisfactory. Your request is under consideration. You are now free to leave us." When Naomi had gone, she continued. "Major General Marsham, Major General Shimas, Senior Negotiator Steppart, welcome. It has long been my intention to meet with you personally." Trikal scowled, but by tradition the words were accepted as coming from both of them.

"Thank you for the privilege, Generals," Jenny answered.

"Hivad Sepal will soon be dead," Trikal said with characteristic bluntness. "Shimas, come to attention. Are you prepared for membership in the council?"

Shimas snapped to. The interview was under way, with a sharp opening salvo. Trikal's question was a model of simplicity and cunning. The inquiry was not into whether Buto Shimas wanted the position; it was into whether he believed that a major general with only eight years in rank, who was half of the council's average age, could be qualified to fill it. Shimas avoided the trap of feigning surprise at his candidacy. If Karnas Kay-Raike had spies aboard *Sovereign*, only a fool would believe that the Generals did not have them aboard *Dalkag*. "Yes, Generals," he answered without hesitation. "I am."

"Tell me why," Trikal challenged.

"They're fiends," Shimas said eleven hours later in the shuttle, as it made its way back to *Dalkag*. He was only half joking. "Every detail of my life . . . yes, I cried when I broke my thumb. I was three years old! *'Are you still disabled by minor pain?' 'If that were a child of yours, wouldn't you be ashamed?' 'Our Fleet has been injured. Is it your advice that we all collapse and weep?' 'Shimas, stand at attention!'* " He accepted a fresh towel from Dane and wiped the budding perspiration from his face. " *'How shall we deal with traitors?' 'Who* are *the traitors, those who counsel trade, or those who counsel war?' 'How long were you and Arlana Mestoeffer lovers before she promoted you to major general?' 'How did you coerce a fine officer like Jenny Marsham into marrying a blatant opportunist like you?' 'Is it true that she despises you, that Sato is not your son?' 'Why didn't you kill Karnas Kay-Raike when you had the opportunity?' 'What secret agreements do you have with him?' 'Shimas, stand at attention!'* All shouting at once. It's a miracle I heard any of them individually."

"I've never seen anything so . . . vicious," Jenny said,

still shaken. "When I've thought of the council and the Generals, I've pictured sedate, experienced, carefully spoken officers. Honor and tradition, brilliant insights. The wisdom of age."

"Ten hours," Buto said, breaking a smile. "I, an exemplar of physical perfection, was exhausted. Those old warriors never slowed down! After they finished with my mind, I thought they were going to leap from their chairs and tear the rest of me to shreds."

"You did very well," Dane said.

"We'll know tomorrow," Shimas replied.

Dane was relieved to be returning to *Dalkag*. Shimas *had* done well. So well that she feared his acceptance would be announced immediately, and that the three of them would remain aboard *Sovereign*. That frightening moment was the first time she'd thought of *Dalkag* as home. She wanted to go home, and leave the soul of the Silver Fleet as a bad memory never to be revisited. It was a profound relief to hear that they were to return to *Dalkag* while the council made its determination.

"If I'm accepted," Buto continued, "this is my first official decision. The next time we rehearse for a council function, I want you both screaming and throwing knives at me while I dance and juggle waist-deep in excrement. That will put me in the appropriate frame of mind. For Trikal, especially. *'How long until you realize, fool, that you're here for our amusement? A* matter of jokes, *as you would say? Can't you see that we're all laughing at you?'* What is that Grounder expression . . . *mad dog*?"

"I'm surprised you would say that," Dane said.

"There is no danger of being monitored here," Buto answered.

"It was Trikal who sponsored you," Dane said seriously.

"What?"

"The council is shrouded in legend and misinformation. Only members really understand how it works. But Arlana Mestoeffer used to speak about it frequently."

"Yes," Jenny said. "She was bitter about leaving and

wanted to go back. She'd go on for hours about her importance there."

"Exactly," Dane said to Buto. "And judging from what Mestoeffer said, the Generals preside over debates and then make final decisions. That's a very old tradition. So doesn't it seem unlikely that one of them would take part directly in an exchange of that nature? And to use Jenny's word, be the most vicious among them all? Depluss didn't say a word, you'll remember."

Buto thought for a moment before realization lit his eyes. "Yes, that's true!"

"My guess is that he wanted to prove to the others that he'd chosen correctly." Which, she did not add, meant that there was unusually hostile opposition to Buto's nomination. Given Trikal's unprecedented intervention, she judged that it was not enough to keep him from membership. But everything she'd observed and concluded indicated that there were some on the council who regarded Shimas as a deadly enemy. Dane was certain that she'd identified two of them; Merrill Rhodes and Yvonne Tillic, who appeared to be the most influential members. Dane suspected that there might be more. The question was, why? Along with Jenny, Buto was revered throughout the Fleet for his performance in the Battle. In political terms he was popular because he represented a bridge between the old and the new, with sincere convictions representing both sides. So, then, was this extreme opposition based on his sympathies with those who called for a return to the old ways? Or was he perceived as not sympathetic *enough*? It was clear now just how powerful an issue that was. Karnas Kay-Raike apparently had more support in the Fleet than she had suspected. Buto's interview convinced Dane that despite centuries of stability and absolute control, the council itself was in danger of crumbling beneath the weight of the problem. And that in turn threatened the work of The Stem; as she'd told Momed, the Fleet must not be permitted to grow. But just as important, it must not fall apart before enough agents were in place to safely direct its demise.

Putting these thoughts together for the first time since the disturbing council meeting, Dane was ashamed of her reluctance to live aboard *Sovereign*. For eight years she'd quietly and patiently gone about her work, lulled by the hope that events were proceeding as planned, and by the knowledge that without contact from The Stem, there was nothing more she could do. But now she recognized momentous changes, fractures, coming from within and without. Buto's new position and the influence she had gained over him throughout the years were too vital to be complicated by personal considerations. She needed, as she'd written not long ago, direct access to the council.

The small compartment's overhead speakers carried the calm voice of Naomi Kay-Raike. *"Brace for collision."*

Shimas was on his feet and through the door before the sound died out. Three paces carried him through a narrow corridor and into the pilot's chamber. "What is it?" He strapped himself into the seat to her right.

"Nothing on visual or instruments, sir," Naomi said. "Just the alarm so far." She gestured toward a rapidly blinking red light on the console ahead of her.

"Malfunction?"

Naomi shrugged. "We have to respond to the alarm, but it's obvious that it isn't working properly."

"Agreed. There is no corresponding audio signal."

"If you'll take the controls, sir, I'll trace the system and see what the problem is. You can see our course and speed. We're forty minutes from *Dalkag*."

"Go ahead, Captain. I relieve you."

Naomi transferred power to Buto's station and slipped out of her seat. Shimas spoke into the intercom. "It appears to be nothing, but remain strapped in until we're sure," he reported to Jenny and Dane. "Captain Kay-Raike is . . ." The shuttle bucked and rolled at that instant, throwing Shimas hard against the seat restraints. The stars visible through the port took on a sudden whirling pattern as he began to manipulate the craft to stop the roll. After a few seconds the controls brought no response. Reaching forward and between the seats, Shimas gripped a thin shaft with his left hand and yanked it back and upright, snapping it into position. He pulled it lightly toward him and was gratified to feel the resistance; the hydraulics were engaged and operating, rotating the maneuvering jets. But the correction he applied to the stick had no effect. The shuttle continued rolling.

A quick glance at the console ahead of him confirmed that the jets were without power. He sensed, as he reached ahead to activate the auxiliary power supply, that it would not help. He was right. A frustrated pull on the stick told him that the hydraulics had now failed. As he watched the console, the primary engine also shut down.

The shuttle was drifting, with no means to control it.

Automatically his hand went to the distress switch, keyed to *Dalkag*'s emergency frequency. The indicator light pulsed once, but so dimly that Shimas could not be certain it had functioned at all. A moment later he verified that all outside communication was out of commission.

"Captain Kay-Raike," he said into the intercom, "what have you found?"

If there was a reply, Buto Shimas did not hear it, for at that moment another alarm sounded. Gravity was gone, and air pressure was dropping steeply. A gauge told the story. The compartment's oxygen reading was dropping toward critical. He should be hearing the hiss of backup tanks releasing air into the compartment. There was nothing; life support was out. As crucial seconds passed he unstrapped and moved carefully from the seat, losing his equilibrium, finally orienting himself and reaching a transverse bulkhead three feet behind the pilot's station. He tore open the emergency locker. There were no breather masks, no oxygen pellets. The locker was empty.

Air pressure continued to bleed away. Shimas felt his eyes and inner ears bulging. He was desperate for a full breath.

He glanced at the airtight door leading into the larger compartment that held Jenny and Dane. He tried to picture what might lay beyond that door, but could not consider opening it. If pressure and oxygen were trapped in there, they would be lost the moment he broke the seal.

As unconsciousness began to overtake him, he moved clumsily back to the pilot seat. He looked at the intercom, willing it to speak and tell him that his wife and daughter were safe and would live. It gave no sound.

"We didn't know," the man said miserably. Spread-eagled, he was held securely by tie-downs running from both wrists and both ankles to four eyebolts in the floor of the cargo hold. A crew member stood next to his head, looking into a nonexistent distance and saying nothing.

"It was your assignment," Karnas Kay-Raike said calmly. "Your people." In a cheerful voice he asked, "What did you expect would happen to you?"

"Sir, I expected success, nothing else. We had all the information we needed, from the highest source. Shimas and his family were to stay aboard *Sovereign*. Their quarters were already prepared! Naomi was to take the shuttle to *Dalkag* and pick up Jarred and Sato, along with their belongings. That was decided days ago . . . you saw the four separate confirmations I received. Sir, I didn't fail. We were betrayed."

"By whom?"

"Who else could it be? Only a council member could arrange for Shimas and his family to be on that shuttle."

"Give me a name."

"Sir, I don't know. The four sympathizers we've recruited aboard *Sovereign* have never told me. They refuse to trust us with that information."

"So we have a member of the council who agrees with us, who is kept informed of what we intend, but who won't argue in our behalf, won't reveal him or herself, and feels perfectly free to ruin me."

"Yes, sir. The plan was deliberately sabotaged. I'm not responsible for what happened."

A dark smile appeared on Karnas's face. "Now you're

being ridiculous. When a crew fails, the commander is at fault. That is the Kay-Raike way.''

''Sir, I'll find out who the council member is. I'll—''

''I have been very clear that Shimas was valuable to me, at least for a while. Now he and his wife are dead. And that . . . that . . . *she* . . . had an easy death. You *know* what I had planned for her! The only good to come of this is that the only Kay-Raike ever to desert her clan is also dead. And that in a few minutes I'll be free of you.'' Karnas walked out of the man's sight for a moment and returned with a long, heavy tool. ''Grounders call this a sledge,'' he said pleasantly. ''The head weighs a mere nine pounds. But you will be amazed at the force it can generate as it is lifted high, and brought smashing down in an arch. And the sound it makes, and the . . . well, you'll see! The secret is in the handle, which is three feet long.''

''Sir, please . . . I've been a loyal officer, a friend . . .''

Karnas gestured to the crew member and passed him the sledgehammer. ''Do your duty, young man.''

''Yes, sir.''

''Sir, please don't do this to me! We're brothers!''

''Mendel, a little decorum, if you please.''

''Karnas!''

The younger Kay-Raike stepped backward and sat in a cushioned chair that was mounted in the hold permanently for rituals such as this. Pulling protective sheeting over himself, he placed his hands in his lap and set his shoulders erect. ''Proceed, young man. Begin with the legs and take your time. There's no hurry.''

Mendel shrieked. The hammer came down in a powerful arch and crushed the prosthetic shin below his right knee.

Karnas was on his feet, shaking with laughter. Mendel had fainted. ''Good, good. That's enough. Return the instrument to its clamps and go about your duty.''

''Yes, sir.''

Karnas knelt down beside his unconscious brother and broke a capsule beneath Mendel's nose. When he was awake, Karnas said, ''You lost your leg honorably, in battle. By destroying the prosthetic, I am telling you that I no longer credit you with any honor at all. And yet I have been gentle with you this time, compared to what I will do if you make another stupid blunder. Do you understand?''

Mendel's eyes widened.

"Good. Soon you'll be returning to *Sovereign*. I want to know who our council member is. I want access to high-level information which I can pass along to our new friends in the Gold Fleet. That will impress their superiors, don't you agree?''

Mendel nodded.

''I think you understand now how important this is. But to be certain, you will remain as you are for a few days. Rest well, Brother.''

Day 17

''Heat-exchange rods? I would never have thought to try something like that.''

''Fortunately, sir, we had enough spares,'' Naomi Kay-Raike said. ''Once they're pushed through the seals, they become unbearably cold and brittle within seconds.''

''And there I was,'' Jenny said, ''believing that my husband knew everything.''

''Thank you, Captain. For all of us.''

''I did it for selfish reasons, sir. I have an aversion to losing passengers. It looks bad on my record.''

Shimas offered her his hand and grimaced at the thoughtlessness of the gesture. New bone mass would grow in her hands within a few weeks, and then permanent skin could be overlaid. But there was doubt concerning muscle and nerve regeneration.

Naomi Kay-Raike had found the shuttle's one remaining pressure suit, sealed the compartment, and brought the shuttle's primary engine back on line by using the rods to activate an external control panel that was used by maintenance workers for testing purposes. The work was too delicate for the suit's external gloves; she'd had to remove them. In the process of opening the panel and starting the engine, the rods had become cold enough to destroy her hands. After leaving the compartment she'd diverted the engine's power into the life-support systems, using her elbows, feet, and mouth to manipulate the necessary controls. The shuttle was still losing air through a series of minute holes drilled through the inner hull and then plugged with material that had frozen and cracked after a short time. But once activated, the emergency tanks had been enough to sustain them until help from *Dalkag* arrived.

"You mentioned once that there was something you wanted to discuss with us," Jenny said. "I can't think of a more appropriate time."

Dane opened the stateroom door and leaned inside. "The call is ready."

Buto and Jenny stood, each checking the uniform of the other for the perfection demanded by the moment about to arrive.

"Very simply," Naomi said. "I'd requested assignment to your personal staff. Either of you. The Generals have given conditional approval. Under the circumstances," she said, looking quickly toward Dane and then away, "I may withdraw the request. But while I decide, would you consider it?"

"Yes," Jenny said. "But we'll need to know more about you, before making a decision."

"Thank you. I'll take my leave now."

Dane and Naomi passed in the doorway. "I haven't had the chance to thank—" Dane began. Naomi brushed by without acknowledgment.

After Dane, Jarred and Sato entered their parents' stateroom. All wore full dress uniforms: Sato's was unadorned, while Jarred's shoulders bore the insignia of his rank. Dane was dressed as she had been during the meeting with Momed and the Gold Fleet officers. Jenny and Buto each wore a wide blue sash that extended from left shoulder to right waist, upon which were the medals and award markers they'd earned in battle. Both had ceremonial swords slung at the left hip.

The five drew to attention as a large screen came on across the stateroom. Tabba Depluss and Mosh Trikal appeared in equally formal dress, of necessity standing together, flanked by the council.

"This is our first induction since Mestoeffer retired," Trikal began. "It is the first induction in more than two centuries which will not take place aboard *Sovereign*." His scowl was firmly in place.

"But I thought it prudent," Depluss said, "in light of the assassination attempt. You are presently believed to be dead. But once we are finished here you will be one of us, Major General Shimas. In all of our history, no council member has been the target of assassins. We celebrate your survival and look forward to informing the Fleet that you and your companions remain in our service. Soon we will welcome you all aboard your new home."

To a man and to a woman, the eight officers standing behind the Generals were smiling in agreement. Buto knew that until the next induction ceremony this would be the last time he would see them at this level of outward harmony. The eight stood at measured distances apart, which highlighted a vacancy among them. Hivad Sepal was gone. Although he was still clinging to life, his career was now a matter of Fleet history.

"Your sword, Shimas," Trikal said.

Buto removed the treasured blade from its scabbard and held it chest high, parallel to the floor, with both hands open and palms up. Depluss and Trikal extended their free arms toward the screen. In their place Jenny moved solemnly in front of her husband and took the weapon.

"This is my pledge," Buto said as Jenny about-faced, held out the sword, and stepped away.

"It is accepted," the Generals replied together.

"The announcement is now broadcast to the seven galaxies," Trikal recited, "to every vessel within Sovereign Command. I order a moment of respect from our friends and invite our enemies to note what we have done here. Buto Patrick Shimas Marsham has pledged to strike against you while there is breath in his body. He is of the Sovereign Command Council.''

The Generals relaxed visibly while the eight officers behind them began milling away, already engaged in discussion and argument. ''There is a meeting of the council three days from now at the beginning of first watch,'' Trikal said. ''Your time belongs to you and your clan until then. Welcome, Buto.'' To the consternation of the Marshams, Mosh Trikal showed that he could smile.

The screen darkened.

''That's *all*?'' Jarred asked incredulously.

Jenny stared at her husband from beneath raised eyebrows. *''Patrick?''*

''I told you,'' Buto said as he slid the sash up and over his broad shoulders. ''Those fiends know everything about me.''

Sato ran giggling from the stateroom. ''Patrick! Patrick!''

''Don't you dare!'' Buto called after him. As the door slammed shut, he turned around. ''Jarred, hunt down your brother and lock him where I can't find him for about ten years.''

Day 22

The shuttle carried only two officers. Jenny piloted while Naomi repeated the interior inspection she'd given the vessel prior to their departure from *Sovereign*. When she was finished, she returned to the cabin. "All systems are satisfactory, General," she reported. "I'm ready to relieve you at the controls."

"That won't be necessary," Jenny replied. "Sit down, Naomi."

The younger woman took the seat and glanced first at the instrument console, and then out the viewport. "General?" she asked. She had timed her inspection to avoid being interviewed by General Marsham. They should now be preparing to enter the outrider *Nabal*. Instead they were circling, controls on automatic, nowhere near the approach route she expected.

"Until I say differently," Jenny began, "rank is suspended. I told you that I needed to understand you better. Now is the time, Naomi."

"That isn't an order, then?"

"No, it isn't."

"In that case . . . all right, I *do* want to speak with you. Why have you had those four attendants watching me? Is it because I'm a Kay-Raike, and all Kay-Raikes are traitors?"

"No. And you know the answer to your question, Naomi."

"The Generals found my testimony to be satisfactory. Do you question their judgment?"

Jenny nodded. "Very well, then. We'll end this now and move on to *Nabal*. Please let me know what you would prefer as your next assignment. We owe you that."

"No, wait. General Marsham—"

"Jenny."

"That won't be easy. But all right. Jenny. You think I'm a threat to Dane, don't you?"

"If you are, you have an odd way of concealing your intentions. Your hostility toward her has been blatant. But yes, I do have to think along those lines. If you had a child, you'd understand."

Naomi blushed. "I *do* have a child! A son. He's one year old. At least, he . . ." Naomi slumped in the seat and wept, bringing bandaged hands to her face. The anger and stiff self-control she'd carried like twin shields dissolved in an instant. She blurted out, *"I am Karnas Kay-Raike's wife!"*

In that instant Jenny Marsham knew as much about Naomi as if she'd spoken for hours. Her own tears came, flowing up hot and stinging.

"Oh, no," she said softly, again and again. Jenny shifted her position and cradled the younger woman in her arms. She didn't know, or care, how much time passed as they sat together. She thought of the unimaginable horror and degradation this woman had been subjected to; and of the danger to Dane, which was far greater than she'd suspected. After a long while Naomi stopped shaking. Exhausted, held by arms that did not hurt her, she had fallen asleep.

• • •

The room Shimas entered was round and high-ceilinged, thirty feet in diameter, sumptuously furnished, with a small War Table at its center. Above the War Table was a three-dimensional blackness containing eight silver motes: *Sovereign* and its seven guardians, in real time. Buto and Jenny, Dane, Jarred, and Sato had been assigned individual sleeping quarters that surrounded the common room. Only Dane was present to greet him. "Buto, how are you?"

"Where is Jenny?" he demanded.

We'll talk later, Dane.

Yes. "She's touring the seven outriders," Dane said. "Naomi is with her."

"Yes, yes, I remember now. She's not due back until tomorrow."

"Yes, sir. We can contact her, though."

"No, she has her own responsibilities. You and I will go out alone."

"Sir?"

"We're going as soon as I change my uniform. Choose a hangar at random. Call and have a shuttle ready in fifteen minutes. No, call three at random. I'll decide which one to take while we're walking." He strode to his and Jenny's private quarters and slammed the door behind him.

Nothing was said until forty minutes later, after they had passed beyond the most distant of the outriders. Buto cut thrust and programmed the maneuvering jets to keep the vessel in a wide circular pattern. Dane assumed, wrongly, that the precautions were to guard against another sabotaged excursion.

"Monitors," he said at last, unstrapping from the pilot's seat. Dane watched as he carefully inspected the small compartment. Satisfied, he returned to the seat beside her. "Tell me your impressions," he said, "of Tillic and Rhodes."

Dane looked at him thoughtfully. During Shimas's interview she had identified Yvonne Tillic and Merrill Rhodes as wielding enormous power within the council. Before she could reply, Buto continued. "Two days ago at my first council meeting they were the most polite of all the members, and the most solicitous of my opinions. Today they behaved as though I were a beloved son. I don't trust them.''

"They hate you," Dane said.

Shimas nodded. "As I thought. I know when I'm being courted, but those two . . . Good, I'm glad we agree on that. Next. Have you had any significant dreams recently?"

Dane knew what he was asking. She had twice saved Shimas's life. The first time it was due to her training, the ability to discern the motives of others and project their behavior. The second time, it was a deception she'd arranged with her cousin Paul Hardaway. She'd represented both incidents to Shimas as the results of "dreams." After the second time, he'd believed her. She'd become his advisor to "watch his back," and from that position had been able to influence the outcome of the Battle. Again, by means of a "dream."

"Nothing specific," she answered carefully. "Buto, what's wrong?" By now she understood what this was about, and was relieved that he'd brought it up. She didn't need his answer. But she needed to ask for it. The alternative was to tell him that an hour before, she'd "spoken" with Momed Pwanda.

"I'll start from the beginning. You recall our meeting with the Gold Fleet delegation. Momed Pwanda told us that his Nomarch looked forward to the time when encounters between our ships would begin with communication, not weapons fire.''

"Yes. But I think he said *chance* encounters." Those words, she recalled, had been scripted by Supervisor Nass, the woman Pwanda called No'ln Beviney.

"Exactly so. It was not a proposal, merely a thought. But half of the council wants to proceed as if a formal offer had been made. The Gold Fleet has been contacted and informed that we are considering sending a number of our ships to meet an equal number of theirs. With weapons *deactivated*. Tillic says yes, Rhodes says no. Each of them

represents three other members on the question. My vote
will create a majority decision.''

''But it's the Generals who decide,'' Dane offered after
a few seconds of thought.

''I did not accept council membership to avoid responsibility,'' Shimas said angrily. ''A full squadron of one
hundred ships could be at risk. I've sent hundreds of
thousands of ships to meet the Gold Fleet, Dane. I've ordered hundreds into certain death. And I'll do so again, if
it's in our best interests. But how can I ask even one ship's
captain to go out with weapons *deactivated*? And yet to
vote no, after the Gold Fleet has been notified . . . they'll
believe we're afraid of them.''

''My point is that a decision may already have been
reached,'' Dane said. As in fact it had. An hour ago Pwanda
had given her this information, which he'd learned directly
from No'ln Beviney. ''I wonder, would we have contacted
their Nomarch if we weren't prepared to go forward?''

''Yes. That was discussed and argued at length. It was
to test their reaction.''

''And if they were to agree?''

''Then we'd have no choice. That would settle the matter, regardless of any vote. We're unanimous on that.''

''But if they decline, Buto?''

''I'm sure that's what the council is hoping for. Then
we'll have proved their insincerity and won the confrontation.''

Dane looked at Shimas, waiting for him to see the flaw
in the argument.

''But only,'' he said slowly, ''if *we* were committed to
taking the chance. Only if we've told the Gold Fleet that
we're ready. Not 'considering,' but agreed and ready.'' Shimas jumped to his feet and glared out the viewport, where
Sovereign hung suspended in emptiness. ''You're right,
Dane,'' he said finally. ''The decision has already been
made. The Gold Fleet has been told that we're sending out
an unarmed squadron. We've challenged them to make the
same gesture.'' He continued, speaking in disjointed bursts.

"We argued this for an hour today. It was a farce, nothing but another test for me. Last time I was ready to be tested. This time I wasn't expecting it. I was so caught up in the idea of being *one* of them . . . like my first assignment as a sublieutenant, among experienced officers . . . I was lucky to get my uniform on correctly that morning." Turning to Dane and sighing, he said, "They got me."

"I doubt if you're the first, Buto."

"I suppose not," he said, nodding. Much of the anger had drained from his face. "When we return to *Sovereign* I'll send the Generals my yes vote, along with the reasoning we've just discussed." A smile crossed his face. "This was the idea of Tillic and Rhodes. Now I owe them one, in the matter of jokes."

Dane could not reveal to Shimas what Pwanda had told her; she could only suggest. "This weaponless confrontation," she began, "could be dangerous."

"I believe I made that point a few minutes ago. What do you have in mind?"

"How long would it take to reactivate the weapons?"

"One minute, no more. But that's an eternity if you're being fired on. At close range the entire squadron could be lost in fifteen seconds. Are you . . . what, dreaming? That this is a trap?"

"Before you returned to our quarters today," Dane said, and let the words hang in the air, inviting him to draw his own conclusion. "Maybe there's a correlation, I don't know. It's about pebble-hand."

"Well, that's clear enough," he said impatiently.

"It was a children's game we played on Walden. Go behind a tree and put a large pebble in one hand and nothing in the other, and close them. Your opponent does the same. When you meet, you've got one try to touch your pebble-hand to hers. Naturally, she'll form both hands as if each contained a pebble, hoping to lure you into a mistake. But you have the option of starting with your empty hand. If she's trying to fool you and is successful, then in that case she loses because you're both holding out empty hands. Touch her other hand with yours, and you can't miss. Pebble-hand to pebble-hand.''

"But then you'd always start with your empty hand, because . . . no, you wouldn't. Not if your opponent had a history of tricking you successfully. You'd make your best possible guess about the pebble, and assume you were going to be wrong again. In which case you'd win.''

"That's right.''

"I understand. Or at least I'll pretend to. I assume you dreamed of a particular time you played the game, or you wouldn't have mentioned it. So, what happened? What was the winning combination? And please, put it in terms of us and the Gold Fleet.''

"If you wanted to entice an enemy to fire at you, how would you do it?''

"Without firing first?''

"That's right.''

"Easy enough, if there's tension between you. Make a sudden, concerted maneuver. Run up your power for no apparent reason. There are dozens of ways. Why?''

"If there's a correlation, it involves two separate 'games.' First they're going to hold out nothing, pretending it's something. When our ships meet theirs—''

"They're going to try to provoke us into . . . all right, into leading with our 'pebble-hand.' Into firing at one of them. If we do, there will be an incident. And we, not they, will have broken the agreement.''

"We would probably kill one or two of theirs before we realized the mistake. They'll accept their casualties and withdraw without firing back. Later they'll offer us a chance to redeem ourselves. The experiment will be tried again, with more ships. This time our weapons will be more severely disabled. And *that* will be the trap. Whatever number of ships we send will be slaughtered. And the Gold Fleet will claim that its action was justified by the first encounter. We'll be angry, but—''

"But they'll be right. Our own people will believe that just as they did, we've got to accept our losses without retaliation. Otherwise we admit that we're less honorable and courageous than they are. No council member will do that.''

"First the empty hand, and we guess wrong. Next the pebble-hand, and we're wrong again. We lose a squadron or more, and there is nothing we can do about it. I believe that's what they have in mind." It was exactly what No'ln Beviney had in mind. The incidents would bring to a halt any thoughts of combining the Fleets in the foreseeable future, a goal that was apparently shared by No'ln Beviney. But Dane could not remain silent when the possibility existed that the same end could be achieved without unnecessary loss of life.

"I see your point," Buto said. "During that first encounter we can't fire, under any circumstances. That's assuming that your dream was correct. But you've always been right, haven't you?" Without waiting for an answer, Shimas asked, "So tell me. Who was it you were dreaming about, who beat you so badly at that game?"

"Buto," Dane replied honestly, "I always won."

I am Karnas Kay-Raike's wife. The words still hung in the warm air, as if too laden with weight simply to drift away. Or were cruel enough to stab deeply into Naomi's emotional center and linger, a voyeur entranced by the flood of pain that followed. Naomi woke again and, like the disciplined officer she was, waited until she was again in command of herself before speaking.

"Karnas saw me aboard one of his ships a week after my husband and I arrived," she said, speaking in a subdued monotone. "I remember that he stared. Nothing was said; he just stared as I walked past him. My husband Benton was junior to me, a lieutenant. He took my clan name, Jeffers, when we were married. His father was a Kay-Raike, but he had also married a senior officer. So Benton never took the name. But Karnas was finding *all* clan members, no matter how distant, and having them transferred aboard his ships."

"Who authorized that?" Jenny asked.

Naomi shrugged. "Our orders were signed by my ship's captain. That's all I knew."

"Please, go on."

"Benton was killed in a training accident two days later. But of course it wasn't an accident. At least I don't believe it was. I filed requests for an investigation. They accused me of treason. Our son Terrance was taken from me and given to more 'loyal' parents aboard another ship. While I was in detention waiting for forced retirement, Mendel Kay-Raike . . . do you know who he is?"

"I've met him," Jenny said.

"He told me that I could live, and that Terrance would be returned to me. If I married Karnas and proved to be a 'suitable' wife. I would have preferred to die, Jenny. But I wanted my son. So I agreed. I didn't know why Karnas wanted me."

"Now you do."

"Yes. But my resemblance to Dane wasn't as strong then. We could have been mistaken for sisters, maybe even twins. But not identical."

"Surgery."

"That's right. Until I saw Dane, I didn't understand why *this* face was what he wanted. Then I understood. When he . . . *used* me . . . it hurt. He hurt me badly, Jenny. While he was watching holos I won't describe to you. I thought at first that it was because he hated me and regretted our marriage, wanted to force me into suicide so he could re-marry."

"Terrance."

"Yes. I'd never leave my son, no matter what the price. I said that to Karnas. It was the only time he looked at me with anything but loathing. He said a mother's loyalty to her son was important and commendable. But nothing changed. And now I know—"

"It wasn't you, Naomi. It never was. You know that now, but you've got to *accept* it. He used you in the most cruel way imaginable. But it wasn't you. He's insane. It was Dane he wanted to humiliate, and hurt.''

"You're saying that it wasn't her fault either. I know that, Jenny. But every time I see her I'm reminded of why I lost my husband, why my son was taken from me, why I was surgically altered, why Karnas did the things he did.''

"How long did this go on?"

"Seven weeks, three days."

"Then you escaped." It was difficult to proceed, but Jenny needed to know. Naomi saved her from asking the question.

"Terrance died," she said. "I was shown a holo of his body before he was sent into space. He'd always been sickly. That was one reason I needed to stay alive. The people he was sent to didn't know how to take care of my little baby." That was all she could bear to say.

"Naomi, do you want to continue our tour of the outriders?"

The younger woman nodded.

"Then please take the controls."

"Thank you, Jenny."

Jenny understood perfectly why the young woman had asked to join her personal staff, or that of Buto. Naomi knew the mind of Karnas Kay-Raike. The Marsham clan knew what it was to be targeted and abused by higher authority.

Naomi wanted revenge.

"Buto will go before the council and petition to give you back your clan name, Captain Jeffers. Welcome to my staff."

"Thank you, General Marsham."

⇛ 7 ⇚

Day 24

The preparations were complete. To his chagrin, Shimas had been informed that a council member could not be spared to lead such an inconsequential expedition. He stressed to them the innovative trap he anticipated; that the Silver Fleet must not fire, regardless of provocation. This argument was met with a mixture of silence, agreement, and counterargument. Yvonne Tillic abandoned her charade and was openly hostile toward Shimas, pointing out his age and relative inexperience. How, Tillic wanted to know, could he expect the council to believe that he and he alone had perceived such a complex threat? What *exactly* had been the nature of his contact with representatives of the Gold Fleet? What secret information had they given him, information that he could use to advance his career? What had he promised in return? Why had he not reported this to the council?

In the end, the Generals made the decision. They agreed

that under the circumstances, only one officer in the squadron was to have authority to order weapons fire at the Gold Fleet. Shimas was successful in having the most able officer he knew appointed to lead the squadron. His choice was based partly on the fact that Major General Jenny Marsham had equal faith in Dane's dreams, believing as he did that they were alive today because of them. To the council he pointed out that Jenny's high rank sent the clear message that the Silver Fleet was approaching this historic experiment with formal sincerity. And that her reputation was such that no matter what they were to encounter, the one hundred ship's captains would trust her judgment and would not act without direct authorization. On this, the council agreed unanimously.

Lastly, Shimas knew that Jenny was growing bored with duties that were largely ceremonial. She would welcome the assignment.

As the meeting drew to a close, Yvonne Tillic said, "Shimas. If we lose one ship, I will personally lead the effort to have you impeached and forcibly retired."

"And you would be perfectly correct to do so," Shimas replied evenly.

Depluss waited until Shimas was gone before she said, "Yvonne, I made the decision to proceed as we are. What he suggested is easily within the scope of Gold Fleet deceit and treachery. If he's right, our best defense is to do nothing. But if he's wrong, tell me this. Were you impeached after your first mistake?"

"No, Generals," Tillic said, delight adding color to her worn face. "All of us here recognize that my statement was out of order and absurd. But it's noteworthy that he concurred with it. I think you'll agree, first, that he's overconfident. Second, that he has a lot to learn about protecting himself. And by extension, the Fleet."

"Yes," Depluss said. "That is abundantly clear."

Trikal scowled, saying nothing.

•   •   •

Watching Jenny's shuttle depart to meet with her designated squadron, Dane sent, **Momed, you'd better be right about this.**

She received, **I don't know what you're referring to specifically, but as a general principle 'right' is the only way I function. Now if you'll excuse me, I'm busy spreading confusion and discontent among the troops.**

=8=

Day 27

Deep space

They were two days' travel from any Fleet concentration. The display above *Halley*'s War Table reflected a situation that had not taken place in more than six centuries. One hundred Silver Fleet ships faced an equal number of smaller vessels, all identical in appearance, flattened ovals, elongated and golden. The unprecedented encounter was marked by four distinctive circumstances. None of the ships was on battle alert. There was no maneuvering for position. Relative speed was cut to allow each group to approach the other slowly. And there was communication between them.

They'd been in instrument range for two hours, and had passed within weapons range thirty minutes before. Now they were closing to a distance that allowed clear visual contact. And here, as Jenny Marsham thought it might, the game began.

Seated at the War Table, Jenny watched as a large screen to her left came to life and was filled with a familiar image. "Supervisor Nass," she said in recognition. "I wasn't aware that you were here. I'm pleased to see you again."

"I had intended to say something equally meaningless," Nass/Beviney said, frowning. "But my superiors direct me to tell you that they are shocked and disappointed at this deliberate insult."

"Please explain, Supervisor Nass."

"We hoped for an honest encounter, General Marsham. The ships you see are our finest. You, however, have arrived with one hundred broken-down derelicts. Would you please explain your reason for this?"

"Supervisor Nass, I have the pleasure of leading the foremost squadron of XG212 Company, which has a long history of distinction in battle."

"You're lying, Marsham," Beviney snapped. She was good, Jenny thought. Nass's face was reddening as she spoke, and her voice carried a convincing note of indignation. Had it not been for Dane's warning, the attempt to anger her might have succeeded. Beviney continued, "I've personally sent thousands of your ships to their death. None of them was competent in battle, which is true of all of you. But they were fighting ships, Marsham. I take it as a personal affront when you suggest that I don't know the difference between them, and the garbage you've brought with you. Are you so terrified of us that you don't have the courage to risk losing *real* ships?"

"It saddens me," Jenny replied, "that you feel personally affronted, Supervisor. But is that your prerogative?"

"What do you mean by that?"

"I'm sure you'll agree that your Fleet should be represented by a more mature and stable officer. Kindly step aside and allow me to speak directly with one of your superiors."

Beviney's face seemed to turn to stone. Her voice, likewise, gave up the heat of feigned passion. "I am no longer affronted, General Marsham," she said. "I am mortally insulted. Defend yourself." The hint of a smile appeared on her lips. Her eyes glowed with victory. The screen went blank.

Seated next to Jenny at the War Table, Naomi said, "This should be interesting. But I'm convinced they won't fire."

"I hope you're right, Dane," Jenny whispered.

Naomi turned to her, mouth agape. "General Marsham, it's *me*, not Dane. Are you all right?"

"Of course. I was thinking of something Dane said before we left." It was about the seniority of "Supervisor Nass," which the woman had just been duped into revealing. How long would it be, Jenny wondered, before "Nass" realized that she'd lost in this game of deceit, that the Silver Fleet knew her to be a liar, and had recorded her actions to prove it? And what would she do then?

"Adjutant Armstead," Jenny called to the third officer in *Halley*'s War Room. He was a thick-chested man who stood by the Operations comm unit. "Relay to all ships, 'The Gold Fleet intends to rush aggressively toward us and close to collision range. Do not respond. I say again, do not respond.' "

"Understood, General."

When it was done Jenny ordered, "Now repeat the first sentence of the message on a channel that isn't secure. Let's allow our friends to wonder whether we've made a mistake, or if we just don't care what they hear."

"Or whether we're harassing them by announcing that we've anticipated their next move?" Naomi asked, warming to the game. "And making them wonder how, knowing that they won't surprise us, we intend to react?"

"There is that," Jenny admitted with a laugh. *Pebblehand*, she thought. Simple probability, easily diagrammed with box algebra, but easily manipulated by deception. Expose the opponent's attempt to deceive, and you've disarmed her. *But you don't win*, she thought. *There will be a second game.*

Movement within the War Table display caught her attention. The Gold Fleet ships were retreating. All, she saw, but one. That single vessel moved slowly toward the Silver Fleet position.

"It's raised its shields," Armstead reported.

The screen came to life with the image of Nass. Her face was pale. "General Marsham, please listen. My name is No'ln Beviney. I am second in command of our Fleet. As you surmised, we had planned to provoke you. What you see on your displays is not a part of that plan. I say, on record and formally, that under my authority the agreement between your council and my Nomarch is suspended."

"Why?" Jenny asked.

"I have ordered a retreat. The ship approaching you has refused to comply with the order."

"A mutineer, No'ln Beviney?"

"Yes, General. That ship is no longer a part of my Fleet. I request that you withdraw, as we are. But if you are attacked, you are free to defend yourselves to the extent you deem appropriate. No action will be taken, or claim made against you."

"With respect, No'ln Beviney, you do not have the authority to rescind an agreement reached by my council. Second, I will not act as executioner on your behalf. That vessel is your responsibility. You can kill your own renegade."

"No, we cannot," Beviney responded. "My ships are incapable of firing. We need more than an hour to reactivate."

"Why then, should we be concerned about one ship with no weapons capacity?"

"Because it is a *mutineer*," Beviney said impatiently. "Do you understand the word? The vessel *D72B* is beyond my control. Its systems *were never deactivated*!"

"Closing," Armstead reported. "General, that ship is one minute away from point-blank range." Meaning that very soon, maneuvering or escape would not be possible. And a reminder that one minute was the time required to empower the Silver Fleet's armament. "Orders?"

Jenny left Beviney's screen activated as she responded. "All weapons are to be left in deactivation, Adjutant."

Beviney stared hotly as the seconds passed. "I have given you every assurance I could," she said. "Any damage you incur—"

Armstead interrupted. "General, the ship is firing!"

"Acknowledged," Jenny said quietly. "Your orders remain unchanged."

"Understood," Armstead replied.

"Damage?" She kept her eyes on No'ln Beviney's.

"Nothing reported," Armstead announced. "The ship is still firing. But what, I don't know."

Beviney continued to stare, and then offered a reluctant smile. "All right, General Marsham. We've tested you. To my surprise, you are capable of keeping your word."

"I agree that that is the best face you can put on it," Jenny said, nodding.

Armstead announced, unnecessarily, "The ship is withdrawing." Its movement was faithfully reproduced above the War Table.

"No'ln Beviney," Jenny said. "During what we refer to as the Battle, I witnessed numbers of your ships forming and breaking intricate formations much too quickly to allow for individual control by ships' captains. We have run analyses which confirmed my observations, and that of others. For eight years it has been common knowledge among us that you employ centralized control for that type of maneuvering."

Nonplussed, Beviney said, "And if that ship had overridden this imaginary control you say we have?"

"That is not possible. When you told me who you are, a number of things became clear. You don't trust your officers, No'ln Beviney. If you did, you would not personally have attended that first meeting between our Fleets. Nor would you be present now. It is therefore inconceivable that you would allow any ship the capability of overriding your direct command."

"I repeat," Beviney said. "We tested you. We were

never a threat to you. As you say, the ship we sent to you is harmless. And as you see it is now withdrawing, peaceably, under my order.'' And then she narrowed her eyes and grinned.

Jenny leapt to her feet, feeling as if a stone had formed in her stomach. ''All ships reverse course!'' she ordered. ''Withdraw, I say again, withdraw. Battle stations, all ships at maximum speed!''

It was too late. Throughout the squadron, those watching through electronic viewports and those watching War Table displays saw it simultaneously. The Gold Fleet ship rocked as if hit from astern while moving away from Jenny's ships. Twice more the vessel shook before they heard on all channels, ''This is Supervisor Nogales, commanding *D72B*. Silver Fleet vessels, why are you killing us? We are *unarmed*! We are *retreating*!'' The man's voice continued, ''I formally protest this . . .'' And that was all. The ship spun completely around once, and disappeared in a half-second of brilliance.

''The core,'' Jenny called out. ''All ships, dispersal patterns, evade.''

Jenny disregarded Beviney's voiced outrage and gestured for the screen to be turned off. The damage was less than might have occurred. One Silver Fleet vessel, *Tarpas*, received through its shield a solid blow from the radiation loosed by the Gold Fleet ship's disintegrating weapons core. Its captain reported extensive loss of life. Structural integrity had held for sixty percent of the ship, but was not expected to hold for long. Propulsion was reduced to minimum. Jenny ordered the squadron slowed to shuttle speed and rescue procedures to begin immediately.

''She's trying to reach you,'' Naomi said from the secondary communications console that was her battle station.

''Ignore her,'' Jenny replied angrily. The anger she felt was self-directed. Dane had been right, she thought. Beviney had led first with an ''empty hand.'' And in the next game, as predicted, the pebble was there. But Jenny had not fully comprehended her own thought of just minutes

before. . . . *But you don't win. There will be a second game.*
She had failed to anticipate that the second game might
begin immediately.

"The Gold Fleet ships have departed into hyperspace,"
Armstead reported.

"Very well, Adjutant. Evacuate the survivors aboard
Tarpas and detonate the vessel. Then take us back with all
speed. If there are inquiries from *Sovereign*, route them to
my stateroom."

"Understood. I relieve you, General."

"I stand relieved," Jenny said. Leaving the War Room,
she thought, *Very possibly for the rest of my life.*

Day 31

Sovereign

The austere council room was empty but for three informally dressed officers. Buto Shimas sat tight-lipped, hands firmly linked together on the table, face impassive. To his right, Jenny Marsham sat at apparent ease, her expression mildly curious.

"To begin," Yvonne Tillic said, "thank you both for agreeing to meet with me. I know that this is a difficult time for you and that you would prefer to use these next days to prepare your case. I promise not to keep you long."

"There is nothing to prepare," Jenny said. "What happened has nothing to do with Buto, and I plan to answer the Generals' questions. That is all."

"Our exchange will not be recorded," Tillic pointed out.

"That is irrelevant," Buto said. "What I have to say will be added to the record. If not now, then later. Your threat was that if we lost a ship in the encounter, you would

press for my impeachment and forcible retirement. I'm prepared to meet you on that basis, formally, with the council.
But taking Jenny before a court-martial can only be seen
as a personal and vindictive strike against me. Her decisions
as commander at the scene were based on good military
reasoning and were in accord with the instructions she was
given.''

Jenny said to Tillic, ''I am not a council member and
shouldn't be a part of this discussion. With your permission, I will excuse myself.''

''You were not ordered here, Jenny. You are free to go.
I thought you might like to hear what I have to say, directly.''

''My husband can tell me what I need to know,'' Jenny
said, bristling at the implied insult. ''Without distortion.''

Tillic sat back with a sigh, running a hand through her
gray hair. ''I am not your enemy,'' she said. ''What will
occur here in three days is not personal or vindictive. And
it was not I who requested the court-martial.''

''Who, then?'' Buto asked.

''That is known by whoever initiated the action, and the
Generals,'' Tillic said. ''Buto, what I said to you at the end
of that council meeting was not a threat. It was a jibe, a
. . . for want of a better word, it was a way we have of
teasing new members.''

''Testing?''

''If you prefer, yes. Everyone there understood that, except you. Let me speak frankly. We were all disappointed
by your reaction.''

''I've heard enough,'' Jenny said. With a momentary
touch to Buto's shoulder, she stood and left the room.

Tillic watched her go, then lowered her eyes. ''I'm not
handling this well.'' Buto noticed for the first time a slight
trembling in her hands. Looking at him again, Tillic said,
''Buto, you are an able young man. You're held in higher
regard than you may think. You became . . . *earned* your
rank as major general during the most complex and difficult
confrontation our Fleet has ever faced. Your performance,

and Jenny's, are acknowledged as the reason that twenty thousand of our ships survived that day."

"That's gratifying to hear," Buto said noncommittally.

"Your problem . . . again, I'm speaking frankly and off the record . . . is that you are perceived as lacking direction."

"Direction? Not experience?"

"All of us arrived here with inadequate experience," Tillic responded. "Although admittedly, you are exceptional in that regard. What I am referring to is—"

"I know what you're referring to," Buto said. "I've spoken for both sides of an issue that has divided the council. Do we continue as we have for the past eight years, or do we resume our previous course? You've chosen to pursue trade."

"That's right, Buto, and that is my point. I've *chosen*. You need to do the same."

"Yvonne," he began, "I'll be as 'frank' as you've been. Despite what you've said here, you do consider me to be a fool." He raised his left hand, waving away her protest. "You want my support. Jenny was invited here as a visible offering. You'll help her at the court-martial if I agree. That's about it, isn't it?" His words came out clipped and short. "So let me say, 'frankly': For whatever time I'm here, my performance on the council will be based on my best judgment. Never, ever, on intimidation." He stood, pushing back the chair.

"General Shimas," Tillic said, "sit down. Please," she added.

Buto complied and glared at her, stone-faced.

"You have accused me . . . any act of coercion against a council member is treason."

"As you say, this is off the record."

"I do not intend either to help or to harm your wife. She will be facing the Generals and the council member who accused her. I will not be there."

"What is it you want, Yvonne?"

"Precisely what I said before. I want you to help yourself, and all of us, by taking a stand. The sooner you do, the sooner we can move past interminable debate and make the strong and clear recommendations we are obliged to present to the Generals. The Fleet is in danger of fragmenting, Buto. It is our responsibility to see that it doesn't. To that end I would prefer to lose the debate than to go on as we are. I am not concerned with which side you take. Only that you take a solid position and defend it to the best of your ability. *Direction*, Buto. All of us have doubts. As council members we cannot afford the luxury of being absolutely sure, before we commit ourselves. You've trained ship's captains?''

''Of course.''

''And you impressed upon each of them that when action is imminent, any decision is better than no decision. That was never so true as now.''

Buto sat quietly. He felt like a child who'd expected bribes and threats, only to find a patient elder offering judicious advice. He understood that Tillic was not offering a truce; she and the others would continue to test the new addition to their group. Nor would he trust her. But it was difficult to find a flaw in what she'd said to him. ''Why was Jenny asked to be present?'' he asked.

''I was married for fifty-six years,'' Tillic said. ''That included my first eleven years on the council. I was invariably better able to deal with problems when Ross was fully involved.'' She pushed herself to a straight sitting position and began to stand, slowly and with difficulty.

''Indulge me for a second,'' Buto said. ''Why did you choose to meet with us now? I think you'll agree that the timing invites speculation about your motives.''

''No,'' Tillic said, sitting again. ''I don't agree. But I'll forgive you the youthful indiscretion. The answer to your question is that I won't see you before the next full council meeting. I'm leaving *Sovereign* for five days. Will you consider what I've said to you?''

''Yes. May I ask—''

''Officially, I've requested time to be alone and think.

Your status entitles you to know the truth, however. But this is not to be discussed with anyone beyond the council. That includes Jenny.''

"I understand.''

"I've been diagnosed with Gerrun Syndrome. Are you familiar with it?''

"No.''

"Neither was I, until two days ago. Gerrun Syndrome is a rapid, body-wide degeneration of nerve tissue. There is no need to provide you with details, which are not pleasant. I've arranged privately for a shuttle to be specially equipped. It will carry me, a team of physicians, and the equipment they'll need. The work will be done away from the officers and crew of *Sovereign* to avoid any speculation that my condition is terminal.''

"Is it, Yvonne?''

"Probably. But I refuse to succumb before the Fleet is committed. One way or the other.''

"Then you *are* offering a truce.''

Tillic smiled and pointed a thin finger at him, unable to hold it steady. "You'd have become a fine enemy,'' she said wistfully, returning her hand to the table. She made an unsuccessful attempt to stand.

"Do you need assistance?''

"No, thank you,'' Tillic said, pushing slowly to her feet. "I'll make my own way.''

"Good-bye, then. And good luck.'' Shimas nodded to her and left.

When Tillic was alone she sat down again and waited fifteen minutes before leaving the room and making her way forward. On the way to her suite of staterooms, she passed a male attendant who nodded, neither looking at Tillic nor breaking his stride. She continued walking and entered a lavatory. A bearded man waited inside. His visitor's badge identified him as an aide to a visiting Senior General. He was tall, but stood with shoulders hunched forward, bent at the waist. Their eyes were nearly at the same level.

"I was told to wait for you here," he said politely.

"By whom?"

"By four friends of mutual acquaintance."

Tillic moved closer to examine the visitor's badge. It bore the pseudonym she'd specified, and was correctly encoded.

"You're Mendel Kay-Raike?"

"Yes."

"I have a holostat of you that is five weeks old. You've mastered a new posture," she said approvingly. "And aged ten years. Cosmetics, or surgery?"

Mendel shrugged. Neither had been necessary. "I was told that you have information and a question for me. May we begin?"

"You know who I am now. I'm sure you understand that the risk is yours."

"I do."

"Naomi has been restored to the Jeffers clan and assigned to General Marsham's personal staff. Any attempt to harm her will be perceived as a direct attack on Buto Shimas and his family. Is it necessary to explain what that would mean to your brother's plans? And therefore, mine?"

"Shimas is a council member, untouchable. Karnas would lose all of his support. We would be hunted like criminals. I understand." *But it won't be me who tells him about Naomi,* Mendel thought, feeling sick again with fear. It struck him then that the suicide he contemplated so often these days would be more meaningful if he withheld this information entirely. *Let him kill her, and destroy himself.* He could think of no finer way to repay Karnas. But then, his wife would be condemned also.

"Good," Tillic said. "Tell me about the 'astonishing' achievement Karnas claims."

"I'll tell you where he is. I think that will answer your question."

•   •   •

Departing soon afterward on the renovated shuttle, Yvonne Tillic fell back against her seat beneath a surge of weakness that crushed down on her like a collapsing bulkhead. *The weight . . . is it the Syndrome, or duty? Or is it treason?* She refused to move toward the quiet, restful place her mind showed her. *I won't go. Not until my Fleet is safe.*

Deep space
Gold Fleet vessel Noldron

"He is from the *Silver* Fleet?" the Nomarch asked. His name was Noldron, the name all Nomarchs had taken for eight centuries. And like his Gold Fleet predecessors, he was the product of one family that had never accepted another into its lineage. He was thirty years old, small and frail, dark-haired, with blue eyes separated by a stylus-thin ridge that ended in flat nostrils. "Why did you bring him here? Is this Nomarch supposed to kill him all by this Nomarch's self?"

Karnas Kay-Raike focused his eyes on a point two feet above the Nomarch's head, face expressionless, as he'd been ordered. *Everything about them is deception,* he thought with a mixture of admiration and anger. He'd been warned that morning to show no fear in the presence of the Nomarch; warned many times, always with an air of dread suggesting that he was about to be dragged before a great and terrible god. It had been enough to shake his confidence. But now . . . *fear?* To the Nomarch's left stood another deception. He was an old man, bald, solid, with deep-socketed eyes and shaggy brows. Kay-Raike had scarcely noticed him the first time they'd met. He'd been one of the three crew to whom he'd fed Grounder food, who'd whined over the resulting stomach sickness like a shameless child. He was now revealed to be No'ln Bishop, second among the No'ln Supervisors.

"Well?" the Nomarch said, scratching at an ear and frowning.

"Before smashing this man to his knees," No'ln Bishop said, "the Nomarch may wish to hear him speak."

"This Nomarch does not think that would be an amusing trick. Everyone in this Nomarch's Fleet can speak."

"And the Nomarch best of all," came a chorus of voices from behind a curtain to the Nomarch's rear.

The meeting room was massive, displaying every conceivable shade of the goldlike metal that formed the exterior hulls of the Nomarch's ships and gave his Fleet its name. The Nomarch's chair was plated with the color, as was the forty-foot-wide curtain that hung behind him and stretched twenty-five feet from gold-marbled floor to a ceiling of the same material. Throughout the room were thick pedestals permeated with gritty bits of gemstone: purples, reds, and greens. Atop each was a bust, cast in the inevitable color, of a past Nomarch. To Kay-Raike, most of them looked to be identical.

Fifty feet across the room from the Nomarch were the spectators. This silent group was made up of all ranks aboard the ship *Noldron*. Individuals departed at will and were replaced so that their number remained a constant thirty.

Kay Raike stood alone, fifteen feet from No'ln Bishop and the leader—titular, he now understood—of the Gold Fleet. "The Nomarch is always making us smile with his jokes," Bishop said smoothly. "But the Nomarch will want to hear what this man has to say because he is the first enemy officer to come aboard *Noldron*."

"Was he invited?"

"Yes, Nomarch."

"Then that is what this Nomarch wants to hear. Go ahead, first enemy officer."

Bishop nodded to Kay-Raike. "Exactly as you told me," he said, warning him not to condescend.

"Nomarch," he began, "we have fought against one another for a very long time. This has been beneficial, because in this way we have destroyed the unfit and strengthened the fit within both our Fleets. And we have prevented the worlds from advancing, knowing that if left to themselves they would regain and use the power they once held over us. It was a good way to live, honorable and important to humankind as a whole. But now we can no longer be enemies.''

''We can't?'' the Nomarch asked, eyes wide. ''Not ever?''

''Not now,'' Kay-Raike said. ''There are worlds in rebellion. We need to work together to stop them. Less than a month ago my ships were attacked, illegally and without provocation, by a world called Canopal. I have information that—''

''Caponal is there?''

''I don't understand, Nomarch.''

''Calopon is in Rebellion?''

''Yes, Nomarch, in rebellion.''

''No'ln Bishop, does this Nomarch have any ships in Rebellion?''

''No, Nomarch. Never.''

To Kay-Raike he said, ''Then you will have to go back to Rebellion yourself and tell them to stop attacking you.''

Kay-Raike coughed nervously. ''We will, Nomarch. But I have information that . . . there are places like this Rebellion . . . in all seven galaxies. Our ships, and your ships, have tried a new arrangement with them. But it has not worked. They want to control us again. We need our combined strength to stop them now, before they become a greater threat than they are.''

Bishop interjected, ''The Nomarch will wish to hear how many others in the Silver Fleet agree with this officer.''

''He will? How did you know that?''

''You have trained me well, Nomarch.''

''None better than the Nomarch,'' came the hidden voices.

''Go ahead, enemy first officer.''

Kay-Raike chose his next words with extreme care. ''Nomarch, nearly everyone in my Fleet understands what I have told you. But there are . . .'' He was going to say "superior," but caught himself in time. ". . . *other* officers who don't understand. If I can tell my friends that the Nomarch agrees with us, those other officers will be . . . they will understand that the Nomarch is right." He gave Bishop a helpless glance. How *else* could he explain outright mutiny to this man?

Bishop nodded his approval and said, "The Nomarch would then be required to lead twice as many ships as he now does. He will want to discuss this with No'ln Beviney, and consider whether he is willing to work so hard."

"Yes he will, No'ln Bishop. This Nomarch is already bored with so much work. Can the first enemy officer to come aboard *Noldron* do anything not boring?"

Bishop thought for a second and smiled. He placed a hand over his stomach, a reminder of their first meeting. Looking directly at Kay-Raike, he said, "Yes, he can, Nomarch. He can dance."

"Oh, good!"

"Momed, you're not leaving *now*, are you? This will be the best part!"

"Work, Coordinator Fields. Always, work."

"Us, cooperating with those Silver Fleet butchers. Can you imagine anything so crazy?"

"Yes."

"Well, take my word for it. When No'ln Beviney returns, the Nomarch is going to hang that idiot and send him back in a Dirt uniform. Ah, no offense intended. I'll record the whole thing for you."

Please, God, Momed thought. *Let that be exactly what the Nomarch does.* "Thank you," he said. He left the room, easing past the other grinning spectators and allowing a grateful woman to hurry in and take his place. **That's all of it for now, Dane.**

Momed, I need Beviney's reaction. You can't remain where you are?

You know why I have to go. But don't worry. No'ln Beviney won't make a decision without her most trusted advisor. And if all goes according to schedule, I'll be back here before anything happens.

⇉1◉⇇

Day 34

```
Sovereign
```
"The captain of *Tarpas* has died of sustained injuries,"
Merrill Rhodes said, leaning forward in his chair and bringing both hands down on the table. He was a thin man,
bearded, with a prominent nose and ears. "And the weapons records did not survive damage to the ship's archives.
I do not know if these facts help, or hinder, Major General
Marsham. What I do know is that an apparently disarmed
and verifiably retreating Gold Fleet vessel appears to have
been fired upon. I know that General Marsham denies giving the order. I know that her denial is irrelevant, in that
she was responsible for the actions of all ship's captains
assigned to her. I know that this incident could have been
avoided if she had withdrawn her ships, as requested. No,
that is not the right word. The opposing commander had
identified herself as second in command of the Gold Fleet.

She admitted planning a trap. She was withdrawing her ships. And she was *pleading* with General Marsham to withdraw as well, without dishonor and without threat. Lastly''—he looked directly toward Jenny, who met his eyes calmly—''I know that we lost eight hundred thirteen people. Needlessly. I ask respectfully that this officer be reprimanded and lowered in grade as a result of her performance.''

The common hand shared by the Generals reached forward and pulled a lever on the table between them. An opaque field formed around them while they deliberated, unseen and unheard. Five minutes passed while Rhodes refused to meet Jenny's eyes.

When the field dissolved, Trikal spoke. ''General Marsham, I am disturbed that you have not given a statement. Do you wish to reconsider?''

''No, Generals. Everything I said and did was recorded. I've answered your questions regarding the thoughts that governed my decisions. I have nothing to add, and will accept your judgment without appeal.''

''I have another question,'' Depluss said. ''General Marsham, do you feel responsible for the loss of eight hundred thirteen of our people?''

''Yes, Generals. As Council Member Rhodes has pointed out, I could have withdrawn.''

''Why didn't you?''

''I saw no military reason to do so. And I believed at the time that No'ln Beviney was acting solely to avoid embarrassment. Given her behavior up to that point, I had no wish to accommodate that attempt.''

''You were not authorized to engage in a personal contest,'' Rhodes said.

''With respect, sir,'' Jenny said, ''that statement is incomprehensible.''

''I agree,'' Trikal said. ''And you, Merrill, are not authorized to interrupt.''

''I apologize, Generals.''

''Unlike the Gold Fleet,'' Depluss said, ''we do not exert

direct control over individual ships. We send officers who are trained to exercise individual judgment. That is, both professional and *personal* judgment. The question before me is whether or not General Marsham did so correctly."

Rhodes nodded, accepting both rebukes.

"I do not believe," Trikal said to Jenny, "that our ships fired on that Gold Fleet vessel. The message purporting to originate from it could have been relayed through its communications arrays from anywhere within the enemy detachment. And I have no doubt that this No'ln Beviney had the capability for remote detonation, as well as the motivation and the will to use it. I conclude that she intentionally sacrificed one of her crews. Assuming that the ship was crewed at all."

"But," Depluss said, "she could not have done so with effect if you had withdrawn, General Marsham. None of your ships would have been damaged."

"I acknowledge that," Jenny said. "It is the reason I have offered no statement or defense."

The opaque field formed again and held for eleven minutes. When it dissipated, both Generals were uncharacteristically flushed. Trikal said, "Very well, I have deliberated. Our decision is this." The word "our" startled both Jenny and Rhodes. "Half of me," Trikal continued, "would have moved the squadron away. The other half would *never* have *retreated*. Under the circumstances—"

"Either decision is supportable under the circumstances," Depluss said in a conciliatory voice. "It is possible that Council Member Shimas was correct in his belief that the Gold Fleet intended to suffer casualties in this encounter. But the data are inconclusive."

"Therefore," Trikal finished tersely, "we find that there is *no* finding. That is all." Once again the field enveloped the Generals.

Neither officer spoke. Jenny stood and entered the corridor, followed by Rhodes. When they'd gone a few steps, Rhodes overtook her. "I would rather," he said quietly, "have been ruled against and reprimanded, or ordered into retirement, than to see the Generals divided. And . . . *bickering,* in our presence. Jenny, I've fought more battles than I can remember, and survived the destruction of two ships. But I have never been as frightened as I am now."

At the first corridor Jenny turned to her right while the council member proceeded on. She had not acknowledged his statement, although she agreed with it wholeheartedly.

Noldron

"This is your holo, and it's your projector. How am I to know this will be accurate?"

"No'ln Beviney, I came here alone on a hyperspace-capable shuttle. Only my brother and by now one other individual know where I am. You could take me prisoner or have me killed, and my own ships would never know about it."

"You're telling me nothing I don't know. What is your point?"

"I'm trusting you with my life. Can't you trust me with a simple picture?"

"No. But proceed."

The scene took form in the center of *Noldron*'s ward-room. There was a long downward pan of city streets, of commerce moving among tall and bulbous buildings, of square brown patches of ground, which tighter focus revealed to be covered with people: walking in small groups, children running, athletic games, families cooking over black pots and eating at tables spread over the open areas in no discernible pattern. "Chaos," Beviney muttered. "It's as though no one has command over those Dirts."

"I agree," Karnas Kay-Raike said. "But it is not as it appears. There is a structure there, and a hostile one."

"Go on," Beviney said.

"Watch," Kay-Raike instructed, pointing. Many of the people below looked skyward for a few moments before returning to their activities. "You can see that our presence didn't alarm them at all," he said, recalling that the people had been watching a group of birds. His ships had not yet entered the atmosphere. "This next was taken from a shuttle." The vehicle circled the city before setting down on one of the brown patches. The view shifted to inside the craft, and showed the door opening outward. A few people were watching from a distance. They were in green uniforms, gesturing broadly at the shuttle.

"They're angry," Beviney said.

As they should be, Kay-Raike thought. *We'd just taken twenty-one of them aboard.* "We assumed we'd inadvertently violated a Grounder ordinance by landing there," he said.

"Why *were* you there?"

Kay-Raike shrugged. "Curiosity," he answered. "I had contacted their city leadership and was told that they would meet with me here"—he back-sequenced the holo and pointed to a prominent gray bulb-shaped building toward the city's center—"after an hour. Some of my people wanted to see what Grounders do when they're not working."

"What is the significance of this area?" Beviney asked in a tone that conveyed boredom and mistrust.

Kay-Raike moved the holo ahead in fast sequence and slowed it again. "This," he said. The brown patch shrunk in size as the shuttle lifted off. A tiny black dot formed in a vacant area of the brown patch. Changing the focus, Kay-Raike centered the view on the enlarging dot, which was revealed to be a widening hole. Something gleamed dully within. The scene shifted smoothly to a Silver Fleet ship that grew in perspective as the shuttle approached. "It wasn't until afterward that anyone looked at the recordings we'd made and saw that pit," Kay-Raike said.

"Afterward?"

"Yes." The holo next showed a ship under attack. Dark spots appeared on its surface, followed by a brilliant ball of white that engulfed the vessel. Seconds later it exploded in an outward rush of flame and debris.

"That was one of two," Kay-Raike said as the holo dissipated to nothing. "I have a tape of our retaliation against the city. It's quite interesting, and often amusing. Would you care to see it?"

"No. I have seen your weapons in action, and am not impressed. What interests me is the death of your ship. I've never seen anything that works in that way. Nothing of ours, and nothing of yours." Beviney stood and began pacing the wardroom. "Eight years ago we began losing ships on what you call supply runs," she said, clasping her hands together at the small of her back. "We suspected that it may have been mass sabotage, but we couldn't disregard the possibility that the worlds had armed. Since we began trading with them, there have been no incidents. That has left the question open to speculation."

"This is proof," Kay-Raike said. "They're well armed, which is a breach of law and a mistake they will regret. Both of our Fleets have been tolerant, No'ln Beviney. Now they've grown bold enough to attack us without cause."

"A holo is not sufficient evidence, Kay-Raike."

"I agree. Eight more of my ships were hit, badly enough that the repairs have not yet been completed. We've analyzed the damage. I am prepared to offer you the results, as well as hull samples you can examine for yourself."

"In return for what?"

"Call it a gesture of good faith if you like. I want you to see the threat as clearly as I do."

"And then what do you want?" She took a seat again, facing him from across the table.

"My Fleet is paralyzed with indecision. If you begin an offensive against the worlds—"

"And take casualties while you do nothing?"

"Yes," Kay-Raike said. "It shames me to say so, but yes."

"That's an honest answer. Go ahead."

"If you take the lead in this, my Fleet will follow. There are tens of thousands of officers who believe that we should take the initiative now, before the worlds grow even stronger and bolder. But others are hesitant. For five years I've tried to convince them that the more technology we trade away, the more we allow their interplanetary trade vessels to go unmolested, the more we endanger ourselves and our posterity. We can't wait any longer. When you act, they will understand that you've reached the same conclusion.''

''Your officers would trust my appraisal?'' Beviney asked, amused.

''Why wouldn't they? You've earned their respect, along with their hatred. I will point out to them that we have the same interests you do because we're all facing the same threat. And that your Fleet was formed for the same reason ours was, in response to hundreds of years of domination by the worlds.''

''You're somewhat convincing, Kay-Raike. But if you fail? If your council allies itself with the worlds against us?''

''They won't. They'll act.''

''How can you be certain?''

He leaned back, spreading his hands. ''I understand my Fleet, No'ln Beviney. Once you begin, an overwhelming majority will see that I was right all along. They will not allow you to surpass us in doing what must be done. Those who stand in the way will be brushed aside.''

''Including your Generals and members of your council?''

Kay-Raike shrugged. ''That's inevitable, I suppose.''

''That is the point of all of this, isn't it?'' Beviney asked. ''I'm to help overturn your leadership and ensure that you take their place.''

''All by acting in your own interest,'' Kay-Raike persisted. ''Once we've restored order to the worlds, we can settle our differences in whatever way you—and *I*—decide.''

Beviney leaned back in her chair and considered all that had been said so far. ''For now,'' she asked, ''will your council allow you to answer that specific attack on you? Or are you satisfied with the retaliation you mentioned?''

Kay-Raike looked at her, surprised at the question. ''Of course we'll return. There will be no survivors anywhere on that world. That is the justice demanded by all who bear my name. And as head of the clan I don't need permission. But before I act, I plan to show the council my proof, both as a sign of obedience and to strengthen my case. They won't dare to refuse me. It is likely that they'll send witnesses.''

''When?''

''Soon. Do you wish to be there?''

Beviney thought for a moment and said, ''No.'' For the first time, she regretted the joke she'd played on General Marsham. Perhaps she'd destroyed the woman's career as she'd intended. But in the process she'd cut short the possibility of intra-Fleet cooperation, which would have allowed her to participate directly in Kay-Raike's plan. She had decided that his ideas had merit, but she did not trust his ability to accomplish them without her guidance. And so she took the first step in bringing him gradually under her control. With a smile Beviney said, ''Given recent events, our ships won't be working together any time soon. That is, not until you've taken command of your Fleet.''

Kay-Raike breathed a long sigh as the tension of weeks drained from him. ''Then you agree?''

''I'll accept your weapons analyses and ship fragments. If they are what you say they are, we have reason to proceed. But before I make a final decision, I want something from you.''

He was consciously aware for the first time of how desirable a woman Beviney was. He assumed that her loathing toward him matched his own toward her; a coupling would be an interesting test of power. ''You have it, No'ln Beviney. Anything.''

''When that world . . . what was it?''

''Canopal.''

''Canopal . . . We have a tradition. The greatest dishonor one of us can suffer is to be abandoned on a planet. It's a punishment we've used only twice in my lifetime."

Kay-Raike shuddered, unable to imagine an end more demeaning or horrifying. "Yes?"

"When Canopal burns, there will be two extra Dirts on it. Buto Shimas and Jenny Marsham."

"But—" He swallowed hard. How . . . ? To kill a council member . . . Never mind. Success would bring him everything. He'd find a way. "Very well, No'ln Beviney. Both of them will be there."

"They have children, I believe? I've met one of them."

"There are three."

"Five, then. Five extra Dirts."

"So it will be." His impulse was to say nothing more, but he decided that his relationship with Beviney should harbor no surprises she might later hold against him. And there was a second, personal reason. "No'ln Beviney, when we first met today I recognized you as Supervisor Nass."

"You saw the meeting with Shimas and Marsham?"

"A record of it. This is none of my concern, but the man who appeared to lead your delegation—"

"Momed Pwanda."

"Yes. Are you aware that he is the husband of Shimas's daughter?"

"Of course I am. My staff has no secrets from me. That was eight years ago, and he was ordered into the marriage. It is meaningless now. But just the same, I do not intend to tell him about it."

Kay-Raike nodded, disappointed. "Pardon me for mentioning it." He had still hoped to have *that Grounder* for himself. Impossible now, if Beviney wanted her to die on Canopal. But his disappointment passed as he found a solution that would satisfy Beviney and avoid liability to himself.

"Why are you smiling, Kay-Raike? It doesn't suit you."

He was smiling because Martin, his only son, a danger to him, would finally be of use to the clan. He would die along with Shimas and the rest. A father would grieve;

Kay-Raike was very good at grieving. Even those who hated him would believe that their deaths were a tragic accident. "Success," he said. "What else in life is there to smile about?"

Day 38

Sovereign

Dane knew, within five minutes of seeing his image appear on the screen, that she'd been at least partially successful in tracking Karnas Kay-Raike. A part of her mind mimicked his every word and movement, as if it were she who was speaking. And the signs she recognized in him—his posture, inflection, movement, eye contact—pointed to one conclusion. He was lying. But, she admitted to herself, he lied very convincingly. Jenny and Buto made little effort to hide their disdain for the officer as their own images and voices were transmitted back to him. But they seemed to believe what he was telling them. Thirty minutes had passed, with neither asking a substantive question. Dane sat apart from Buto and Jenny, watching on a separate repeating screen, out of two-way range.

The three of them were alone in the family quarters. Sato

was in class, while Jarred was busy with his new mentor, Colonel William Saddhurst, who had lived up to his boast; his grasp of propulsion physics was phenomenal. He was now permanently assigned to *Sovereign* and placed with others like himself in a special unit devoted to theory and research. Jarred's talent was lesser, but sufficient to give Saddhurst a reasonable excuse to request his assistance. Jarred had leapt at the opportunity to learn from a genius, understanding as they all did that he was Saddhurst's link to Dane.

"After losing those two ships, we withdrew as you see here," Kay-Raike said, "to an altitude of three hundred miles."

"And still they fired?" Shimas asked.

"Yes, sir. We remained long enough to punish the city, but eight more of us were damaged in the process. I don't have an accurate estimate of their range. That was a mistake, and makes it imperative that the council send me back there."

"Continue," Jenny said.

"I have a ship only two days from you," Kay-Raike said. "It can deliver a copy of the holo you've seen along with several fragments of damaged hull from our surviving casualties. I apologize again for troubling you, sir. Naturally I would prefer to present this to the council personally. But—"

"It's the evidence that will be judged," Shimas said, interrupting. "Not you."

"Sir, it will take me six days to reach *Sovereign*. But if the council could be prepared in the meantime, and the exhibits verified, we can settle this expeditiously."

"Why is time a factor?" Jenny asked.

Kay-Raike looked back at her, attempting a smile. "I'm aware of your feelings on this matter, General Marsham. But I ask you to consider this: Canopal and its allies will mistake our waiting for a lack of resolve. This would encourage other incidents, endangering all involved. I refer to our ships *and* the worlds."

"Who have you contacted about this?" Shimas asked.

Kay-Raike hesitated, surprise on his face, lips and jaw tightening, the signs gone in a fraction of a second. To Dane it was illuminated tracks in a forest. *Another lie ahead, a big one.* "You're the first, General Shimas," he said, "and the logical choice. Both factions trust you."

He's confident that Buto doesn't know. But terrified that he might know . . . what? She glanced to her side. *Jenny caught something, too. How can I tell them that he's met with the Nomarch? I can't. What about No'ln Beviney? Has he seen her, as well? Did she refuse him, and is that why he's coming to Buto for help? Momed, you should have stayed!*

Shimas thought for a moment. To Jenny's visible relief he said, "I decline, Kay-Raike."

"Sir, please reconsider. I am willing to submit to drugged interrogation, if you doubt what I've told and shown you."

"Kay-Raike, this is a secure channel, so I'll speak freely. First, you know that there can be no such interrogation. That is reserved for Grounders, and rarely, Fleet personnel suspected of a crime. In this instance no one on the council would agree to it, and so your offer is empty. Next. When this incident occurred, General Marsham and I were aboard your flagship. You would not need to make any presentation at all if you'd brought us back to consciousness and allowed us to see what was going on."

"Sir, I was wrong in what I did to you. And my impulse *was* to awaken you. But my physicians advised against it at that time, for your safety."

"Next," Buto said, waving away Kay-Raike's reply. "When your case is presented, I will listen and vote on its merits. Next. I support your claim that we must remain firm with the worlds. However, I consider you a disgrace to the Fleet. I mean no offense to your clan. But I want nothing to do with you personally."

"You're not alone in that sentiment," Kay-Raike said, flushed but keeping his voice level. *He expected that an-*

swer. "I came to you because you are among the most outspoken of those who feel that way. General Shimas, you know that as head of my clan I don't need permission to respond to an attack against our ships. But I'm tired of being an outcast."

"That's by your own choice," Buto said.

"I agree, sir. And so I am asking you for an opportunity to submit to the will of the council. That will be most clearly understood if it is you who presents my evidence."

He was responding to a statement he'd anticipated. He's had time to prepare a clever lie. But every word of his answer was the truth. Dane felt the forest closing in on her, the tracks no longer lighted. There was something grotesque hiding in the darkness, but Kay-Raike gave no indication of what that might be. Looking toward Buto, she knew that he felt trapped. And he was; he could not turn away a clear attempt by Kay-Raike to comply with the council. She also knew that when Kay-Raike arrived aboard *Sovereign*, her adoptive father would need all of his self-control to restrain himself from killing the man with his bare hands. He still could not look at Naomi Jeffers without trembling, knowing why her face had been made identical with Dane's. Naomi had refused the surgery that would restore her original appearance. First she wanted to confront Kay-Raike directly, ridicule him publicly, in the same physical condition he'd left her. Naomi's hands were functional now, but she was far from being healed. Jenny and Buto were ready to defend her.

"Very well," Buto said quietly. "I agree. When your evidence arrives in two days, I'll review it and present it to the council. Along with what you've just said."

"Thank you, General Shimas. And sir, I understand your reluctance, and respect it. But I hope you meant what you said, that your appraisal of me does not extend to all members of my clan."

"You're implying that I am a liar, Kay-Raike?"

"No, sir. I wanted you to know that my son is aboard that ship. It is he who will give you my package. Martin is

. . . let me say that he is very close philosophically to your son Jarred. They're of the same age and rank. I thought they might enjoy meeting one another. With your permission,'' he added, addressing both Jenny and Buto. *More truth.*

"You tolerate dissent?'' Buto asked.

Kay-Raike smiled, with no hint of effort. "He's my son, sir. His views make him no less important to me.'' *And something hideous behind that truth, hiding.*

"Yes,'' Jenny said. "We'll be pleased to receive him.''

Shimas grunted and reached forward, severing the connection. He glared at Jenny. "We're going to 'receive' that monster's son? Don't you see that Kay-Raike is offering him as a hostage to his good intentions? His own son! I'm going to bathe.'' He stood and strode toward his and Jenny's sleeping quarters.

"Buto,'' Jenny called after him. "He's talking about a boy. No matter what he intends, Martin is not a hostage. As for the rest of it . . . wait, I'll join you.''

Shimas stopped and turned, holding out his hand for her. "Three seconds,'' he said, grinning. "I've never been angry at you for this long.''

"We'll work on your attitude,'' Jenny said, taking his hand. She looked at Dane and flushed, as if she'd forgotten she was there. "Please excuse us,'' she said.

Dane laughed and waved them away, concealing her distress. Kay-Raike's holo was a fraud; either it had been presented out of sequence, or the land scenes had come from a world other than Canopal. But he *had* lost two entire crews, with eight more ships damaged beyond repair, to ground fire there; he'd told the truth about that, and lied convincingly when he claimed that the attacks had been unprovoked. The council would approve his petition, both as a return gesture of conciliation and to fulfill a law of retribution that was older than either Fleet. There was also confusion in Dane's mind. Jenny and Buto regarded the population of an entire world as a mere political point, which, settled for now, had less meaning than the anticipation of physical intimacy. Karnas Kay-Raike was complex but easily defined, and in broad terms made predictable by the purity of his character: He was cruel, ambitious, unrestrained by personal conscience or moral principles. But Jenny, Buto, even Sato . . . adept, empathetic, whatever The Stem assured her that she was, Dane knew that she would never understand these people.

On one point there was no confusion. The citizens of Canopal, a world that could not be much different from her native Walden, were condemned to a brutish death for the crime of defending themselves against predators. Every family, every child, every hope would be killed. And there was no one to speak for them. Or the others who would follow. Kay-Raike would not stop at one. His words "Canopal and its allies" had been deliberate. If Gold Fleet co-operation was a part of his plan, the worst she had feared would soon be reality.

She entered her private quarters and stood in the middle of the room, stunned by the realization that Kay-Raike had framed his lies perfectly, beyond her ability to expose them. He was going to win. Unless . . .

Never reveal yourself. The words came like a shouted warning. Not from Pwanda. A sentinel, the sum total of her training, standing guard to watch for reckless thoughts. *No single planet is greater than the work of The Stem.* Dane replied angrily, "There *is* no *single* world. This is *every* world!" and stopped her voice when she realized she'd spoken aloud. There was a way, a procedure . . . and a candidate whose political power and physical weakness could be used. *It's permanent, unpredictable.* She felt herself at the edge of a precipice, toes already committed to the empty air, leaning outward, arms wide. *They won't break your fall; come back.* She took the step, on one level merely falling into bed and feeling its softness catch her. But part of her continued to tumble. *I am more than The Stem. I am also a human being.* It was her own voice. The sentinel was far behind, above, crouched at the edge, looking down helplessly, small in its silence.

Day 40

"What did General Shimas tell you about me?"

"Nothing, Council Member," Dane replied. She was not confident that what she was about to attempt would be successful. If she failed, it was possible that she, and her work, would be exposed. But she had come up with no better ideas; this was the best chance she had to save the people of Canopal, and the other worlds whose citizens would be sacrificed to the ambitions of Karnas Kay-Raike. "Nothing," she repeated, "until after you returned and the doctors had confirmed that your treatment was successful."

"I suppose it was, for now," Yvonne Tillic said. "Did he tell you that I'm blind?"

"No, he didn't."

"Good. Perhaps no one knows but you, now that you've seen me. The condition is not systemic, I'm told. It is the result of trauma and should pass within a day or so." Tillic lay beneath a white blanket, most of her face covered in bandages. She was unable to move her head. "Seven hundred sixteen incisions, miles of new nerve tissue. Normally the work would be done over several months, but I did not have the luxury of time. The medical staff was both brutal and brilliant. When the pain stops, I may promote them all."

"Should I call for medication?" Dane asked.

"I won't accept it. My mind needs to be clear for tomorrow's meeting." She couldn't see Dane, and so missed the younger woman's expression of relief. "Why did you ask to see me?"

Dane's voice conveyed the smile Tillic could not see. "When I was young, I was confined to a hospital bed for eleven days. It helped to see my friends from school. But what I remember most were the visits of my mother and brother. My family was . . . I'm sorry, Council Member. That was indelicate of me."

"Dane, my husband was the last of my clan. He died more than ten years ago. I've adjusted. 'Friends from school'? That would be analogous to my associates, whom I will not allow to see me in this state of weakness. If the doctors are correct, I'll be stronger tomorrow. I'll meet with them then. You seem to imply that your father didn't send you here. Is that true?''

"Yes, Council Member. It was my own idea.''

Dane watched as Tillic's unseeing eyes widened in surprise. "Was it, now? All of the council asked to visit me. I assumed that because I'd refused, your father had asked you to bring a private message.''

"I'm sorry, he didn't. I hope you're not disappointed. Do you want me to go?''

Tillic took a deep breath and winced from the pain. "No,'' she said in a hoarse voice. "It never occurred to me that anyone would . . . for purely personal reasons. There should be a towel here somewhere. Can you find it? I seem to be perspiring.'' Only her eyes were moist. "Thank you for coming, then,'' she said a moment later when Dane had dabbed her face with the towel. "Speaking is uncomfortable,'' she said, "but I would be grateful if you'd stay for a while and talk to me.''

"Of course I will,'' Dane replied. She had performed an abbreviated tracking on Tillic shortly after arriving aboard *Sovereign*, and garnered only vague impressions. Buto seemed to understand his colleague well enough that Dane's help wasn't necessary, beyond those vague impressions. But during the previous day she'd gathered several holos of Tillic speaking and suspended most other activities to concentrate. She'd found surprisingly little personal ambition, but deceit when Tillic declared her position on the issue that had divided the council. Outwardly she was the leading proponent of the faction that favored the new trade policies. Recalling lessons she'd learned from her mother, a leading politician on Walden, Dane intuited that Tillic planned to lose the debate in such a crushing manner that those who followed her would cast their votes with Merrill Rhodes—who led the opposition and demanded a return to the old ways. Dane also found, as she had before, the one attribute that was now most valuable to her. Tillic was lonely. "What would you like me to talk about, Council Member?"

"It doesn't matter. Although I'd like to think of something besides the Fleet, if only for a few minutes. And while you're here, please call me Yvonne."

"I could tell you a story," Dane said. "But the only ones I know are Grounder stories."

"That will do," Tillic said. "But don't be offended when I fall asleep."

Dane began by explaining what wolves and rabbits were, and that in Grounder stories they were intelligent beings who thought and spoke, and could feel as human beings felt. "Let me tell you about where they lived, Yvonne," she continued. Tillic was near sleep, but she smiled. Dane told her about the softness of new grass, the living aromas of wood and countryside, the freshness and joy of cool air after hot summers, the startling white of a field of new snow . . . and again the new grass, ephemeral as air and persistent as time. She made her voice to be all of those things she described, using rhythms that flowed along with Tillic's breathing, after a while leading, keeping Tillic poised between consciousness and sleep. The moment arrived when Dane lost perception of herself. She and Tillic were united, a family in the wood and countryside, living her story, part of the air and part of time. First they were wolves who ate rabbits and became rabbits, and then rabbits who were eaten and became wolves. The killing, the hatred, the coldness, and Dane gently wiped their eyes. The hot red agony of being torn apart, and they shuddered, not far from their own postsurgical torment. They were family who grew above and outside it all, who knew all of it at once, all the seasons and all the changes, the hatred and the agony that curled together into a rolling ball that would not stop, would never stop.

Dane was asleep in her chair, breathing in tandem with

Tillic, when a team of doctors arrived and asked her to leave while the bandages were removed. "I won't be far, Yvonne," she said.

"Thank you, Dane."

=12=

Day 41

Sovereign

Tall, light-haired, hazel-eyed, thick in the waist, nervous, quiet and withdrawn, Martin Kay-Raike was a study in contrast to his father. He towered over Jarred. Neither young man was prone to establish power over others, but it was easily seen from the way they walked together, Martin a half-pace behind and attentive to every word spoken by a strangely talkative Jarred, that they had found a balance comfortable to both.

Buto could only shake his head in wonder as he saw them in the corridor leading to the council room. "Good morning, Lieutenant Kay-Raike, Lieutenant Marsham," he said.

"Good morning, General Shimas, Captain Jeffers," they said together as they passed by.

Naomi answered Buto's question without being asked.

"Martin is his natural son," she said, "as difficult as that is to believe. I'd never met him before yesterday, but I knew of him. Not from Karnas, by the way. I don't think they've spoken since Martin's mother died." And answering another unspoken question, she added, "That was in the Battle. They say that Karnas isolated himself and grieved for three days." She hefted a bundle of papers and offered them to Shimas. "You'll find General Marsham's comments in the last three pages."

"Good. I have just enough time to review them. Thank you, Naomi."

"If I may ask, sir, is there any doubt what the decision will be?"

"I don't believe so," Shimas replied. "By the time Karnas arrives, he'll have the council behind him on this. That will give him what he's looking for."

"I see."

"Tell Jenny I anticipate a short meeting. I should be free to join her for lunch, if she isn't occupied."

"Yes, sir."

Shimas was wrong. The meeting stretched past morning and was the most animated session he had yet attended. Opposition to Kay-Raike's petition was led by Yvonne Tillic, with a level of energy that would be impressive in an officer half her age. Her first words of the meeting had been "I can see now. Better than before." She lay on a cot behind her chair, attended by a physician named Heintz who bore the hopeless task of keeping her relatively calm. Her skin was pocked with pink welts that stood out like ship beacons when she became emotional. This she did often, in a radical departure from the cold logic she customarily employed. Across from her empty chair Merrill Rhodes gaped, found difficulty in speaking, and gave Shimas the impression of a man who felt personally betrayed. Their exchanges went well beyond the normal level of disagreement he had learned to expect. On four occasions Rhodes stood and ran from the room, coughing, fists clenched ahead of him as though he were planning to burst through the closed door.

The opaque curtain formed and dissolved numerous times, but the Generals offered nothing to the debate.

Shimas had displayed the holo and passed to everyone present a copy of the analyses performed on the samples sent from Kay-Raike's damaged ships. Tillic began by calling the holo into question, pointing out that Karnas Kay-Raike was a known liar and could not be trusted to provide an honest record of events. No one, including Rhodes, argued the point. She pressed on and for more than an hour verbally dismembered Karnas Kay-Raike. She characterized him as a creature of mindless hatred, a diseased rogue—she used the term "mad wolf" a number of times but did not pause to define the term—who'd deserted the Fleet and gone mad with killing frenzy.

After an in-room lunch during which council members read through the documentation Shimas had provided, Yvonne Tillic struck directly at the physical evidence.

"I have obtained a separate analysis, from another point of view," she announced.

"By what right did you usurp—" Rhodes began.

"By the authority and *obligation* of a responsible member of this council, Merrill. Last night Shimas offered all of us an advance look at the holo and the analysis, along with Kay-Raike's testimony. You declined. I did not." The words were spoken so forcefully that Rhodes flinched and did not reply. Shimas began to suspect that Tillic was closer to death than her physicians had reported; he had seen dying comrades perform extraordinary feats in a final discharge of energy.

Tillic nodded to the hovering, frowning physician. He withdrew a sheaf of papers from beneath her cover and distributed them. "I expected," she began, "to find that Kay-Raike had created these samples himself using retrograde technology, simulating weapons a developing world might have produced. I was wrong about that. The damage was inflicted by something new to us, in the sense that it is based on principles we would never apply to weaponry. And that is because the power-in to power-out ratio is inefficient. An adequate defense should not be long in coming."

"Then what is your *objection*?" Rhodes shouted. "The ships were attacked, as he said they were."

Tillic continued, ignoring the question. "The officer who did this work," she said, "is a Colonel William Saddhurst. He's new to us, and quite brilliant. Colonel Saddhurst highlighted a fact that appears in Shimas's report in addendum, but only as raw chemical data not directly associated with the weapon's operation." She cleared her throat, took several rasping breaths, and continued. "Kay-Raike claims that this damage was received at an altitude of three hundred miles. *But there are abundant planetary gases fused into the hull samples.* If anything, there should be only the occasional traces, consistent with that altitude. The concentration of gases on the samples is indisputable. This damage occurred less than six miles from the surface of that world."

"Is *that* all you have, Yvonne?" Rhodes cried out, his voice breaking. "Is *this* the reason you've wasted our time? This is irrelevant!"

"Is it irrelevant that Kay-Raike has presented false testimony to the council? That is grounds for instant retirement, Merrill."

"These particular hits could have occurred while the ships were retreating."

"All *five* of them? And Kay-Raike wouldn't know that? He lied, Rhodes, and you're making a fool of yourself trying to explain it away."

The hands of the elderly man trembled as he narrowed his eyes and glared at her empty chair. "He may not have misrepresented himself," he said through clenched teeth. "An innocent mistake, or . . . Who is to say? Planetary gases may *be* a part of the weapon's operation."

"That is not physically possible," Shimas said. He was looking over the chemical table included with the original report. The researchers had not been told where the attack had occurred, only that a planet had been involved. Atmospheric traces would not have seemed out of place to them. And neither he, nor apparently Jenny, had read past the heading that declared it to be unrelated data.

Tillic said hotly, "Merrill, read what I gave you. When you find a way to bind oxygen, nitrogen, free carbon, and *airborne water vapor* and send them undisturbed, in naturally occurring proportions, through miles of relative vacuum, I'll listen to you. Until that time, save your ranting for the fools who listen to people like you and Karnas Kay-Raike."

For the fifth time, Rhodes clenched his fists and fled the room. This time Yvonne Tillic did not taunt him, calling after him as she had before. Shimas turned to look at her and saw that the color had drained from her face.

"Generals," Heintz said, bending over his patient, "Council Member Tillic is near exhaustion. I ask respectfully that you allow me to take her back to the dispensary."

"Yes," Depluss said at once. As the doctor entered the corridor and motioned for two attendants to assist him, Depluss said, "Karnas Kay-Raike will arrive here in four days. Under no circumstances is any of this to be relayed to him. He can explain for himself the apparent inconsistency Yvonne has pointed out. The council will make its recommendation at that time." For the second time, Shimas saw Mosh Trikal smile.

Day 45

She was much stronger now. Yvonne Tillic scarcely noticed the team of physicians around her, and felt only minor discomfort as the tubes delivering medication and nutrient were withdrawn. Her friend stood by, the one she could see new things and dream with, holding her hand. She'd been there for four days. Tillic knew about Dane's mother Linda and her brother Alfred, and about the lifelong study she'd made of the human mind and behavior. Dane told her about her teachers, who belonged to an organization that for centuries had developed the psychological sciences to levels not otherwise known. It was by a new technique of theirs— not mysticism, but an understanding of the many levels of human communication—that a marvelous illusion was created. It was as if the two of them could think together, she seeing through Dane's mind, and Dane through hers. She knew, because Dane had warned her, that the more they did this, the more dependent they would become on one another. It wasn't a difficult decision to make. Dane gave her new thoughts, but never attacked the ones that were her own. Tillic responded in the same manner.

Most of the new thoughts were about Dane's home. Tillic understood what it was to live for years beneath the same stars; to have no control over climate; to stand beneath an open daylit sky and feel not terror, but awe; to travel in ships that rolled with strong ocean currents and to feel white spray that stung the eyes and brought laughter to the lips; to live and work for something other than the destruction of enemies; to lose everything at the hand of strangers who knew nothing about you, but hated you. It was more than understanding. Tillic felt as though she had lived all of these things, and was profoundly affected. As she discussed with Dane the changes she felt within herself, the young woman had taken her hands and wept openly.

She looked up at Dane and felt an overwhelming dread. Today's council meeting was fast approaching. She knew it would be her last. And that her long career was to end in disgrace. But of all the events that would flow from the meeting, the only one that terrified her was that she would not see Dane again. After she denounced Kay-Raike to his face and revealed that she had worked with him secretly, that with her knowledge he had visited and conspired with the Gold Fleet to depose the Generals and dissolve the council . . . she would admit that these were goals she had once shared with Kay-Raike because the Generals were weak and the council was chasing itself in circles with endless rounds of empty debate. She'd known that Karnas Kay-Raike was a poor choice for power. But as she'd told Shimas, a poor decision was better than no decision at all. Kay-Raike was in a position to *take* power, to give the Fleet *direction*. She had placed no value on the countless millions of Grounders, human beings who would die as a result. Just as she had placed no value on Dane and her family when she'd arranged to have them transported on the shuttle she'd allowed Mendel Kay-Raike's henchmen to sabotage.

Her confession would be complete. Days of interrogation would follow, and then death. Today, Dane would hear the crimes she had committed but did not have the courage to confess privately to her friend. No planet dweller could forgive her for what she had conspired to do. She would be alone again.

"You're as fit as can be expected," Heintz said. Dane smiled and squeezed her hand.

Karnas Kay-Raike entered the room without escort and stood at attention until he was formally recognized by Trikal. When given permission to stand at ease, he looked around himself with an air of casual confidence, nodding by turns to the Generals and to the individual members of the council. His eyes lingered for a moment on the seated Yvonne Tillic, who smiled. Then, glancing back to just inside the doorway, he went stiff with shock.

"To avoid confusion," the young woman said, "I am Dane Steppart Marsham."

"I don't understand," Kay-Raike said.

"My daughter is attending Council Member Tillic, at her request," Shimas said. He turned away and addressed the Generals. "May we begin?"

Trikal said, "This portion of the meeting is for the discussion of your petition, Kay-Raike. That is all this is about."

Reassured, Kay-Raike answered, "Thank you, Generals."

"I have a statement," Tillic said.

"No!" Rhodes's fists were clenched. "Yvonne, you disrupted and dominated the last meeting with irrelevant nonsense. I ask the Generals to forbid you to do so again." The elderly man was shaking. Shimas looked at him curiously. Rhodes still behaved as if Tillic's performance of four days before had been a personal betrayal. That was odd, in that the two had been political enemies since the Battle, and regularly assailed one another.

"The council owes this officer the courtesy of speaking first, Yvonne," Depluss said to Tillic. "You will have an opportunity to respond."

"I will be brief, Generals," Tillic said. "On my honor as an officer of this Fleet, you will want to hear what I have to say."

Kay-Raike looked to be confused, but was again reassured by the smile she offered him. "Generals," he said, "I have heard that the health of the esteemed council member is delicate. So as not to tire her, I ask that you allow her to speak before I address you."

"Very well," Trikal said. "Go ahead, Yvonne."

"No!" Rhodes shouted, pounding on the table. "Yvonne, you've misled . . . your promises . . ." Unable to continue, he stood and ran for the door. But instead of leaving the room, he turned and strode toward Tillic, shaking a trembling finger at her. "Deceiver!" he shouted, his voice thin and rasping. "Deceiver!"

Shimas rose from the opposite end of the table to catch Rhodes before he collapsed. Dane saw something else. "Buto, help her! Help *her*!" Her outcry came too late. Rhodes fell across Tillic, his hands at her face. She lifted her arms to protect herself as Rhodes braced his feet under him and pushed with all his strength. The chair wavered and tipped backward. Tillic screamed an instant before a sharp crack echoed through the room, sounding to Dane like a dry log snapping apart in fire. Buto arrived in time to catch the chair's back and lower it quickly but gently to the floor before he reached for Rhodes.

Dane opened the door and shouted for Doctor Heintz, who was waiting only steps away.

By now the Generals and members of the council were on their feet. "Stay back," Buto warned. "Her neck is twisted." He stood with an unconscious Merrill Rhodes in his arms. Heintz arrived and bent over Tillic. A medical attendant took Rhodes from Shimas and held him while two more brought in a stretcher.

"We'll have to carry her as she is, in the chair," Heintz announced. "But first I need a brace." He ordered the attendant who'd held Rhodes back to the dispensary, calling out to the young woman the type and size he needed. She was gone as quickly as he spoke.

"What is her condition?" Shimas asked.

"Sir," Heintz replied after a few seconds, "these are called extraordinary measures."

"Please explain," Depluss said.

"It is a custom when dealing with officers of this rank, Generals. I am carrying on my duty without a patient. Council Member Tillic is dead."

So in part was Dane, who had fallen unnoticed behind the opened door. Her last impression before the universe ceased to exist was of a wide-eyed young girl asking about the fragrance of new grass.

Day 46

It's permanent. Unpredictable.

Dane watched numbly as an unadorned gray metal box was carried by four council members and placed gently at the center of the airlock floor. She felt as though a blindness had been lifted, only to come again, leaving her aware of darkness for the first time. Toward everything around her— the cold bulkheads and sinewy conduits, inlaid emblems of *Sovereign* and the Fleet, the officers who stood in silent respect, uniforms perfect—she felt pride. Affection. Belonging. The emotions were not hers, but Yvonne's. They did not compete against her own feelings, her own history. They were complementary; an added dimension of understanding. But it was terribly, terribly incomplete. And empty. A new place to explore, but suddenly without warmth or light. The link she had established with Yvonne was stronger than she could have foreseen. She had shared her friend's moment of death. She knew that her mind would not survive that experience again. *You were warned.*

⇒13⇐

Day 48

William Saddhurst had been invited to the meal in the hope
that his presence would make a difference. He'd been solicitous and amusing, but his laughter was clearly forced.
After a while he looked helplessly at Jenny. She nodded,
giving him permission to excuse himself. Dane watched
him as he left but did not speak. At a glance from Buto,
Jarred and Sato also excused themselves.

Shimas had made only polite conversation with Saddhurst present. Now he resumed a discussion he and Jenny
had begun before the arrival of their children and their
guest. He spoke more loudly than normal, hoping that Dane
would listen and that her presence of mind would return
and anticipate what he was leading up to. The doctors could
not explain Dane's reaction to Tillic's death. He hoped to
spare his daughter the method they recommended for
breaking through the barrier that surrounded her. "There
are few things," he said, "more valuable to an officer than

130

the trust of superiors and subordinates. But if I hear it once more . . . *'you are trusted by both factions'* . . . I'm going to go as mad as Merrill Rhodes.''

Dane glanced at him, mouth agape, and turned away. Shimas regretted his choice of words. Rhodes had not spoken a coherent word since killing Tillic. Left alone for only a few minutes in the ship's dispensary, he had swallowed enough cleaning fluids to give himself a slow death that the doctors could not prevent.

''I still don't understand the council's decision,'' Jenny said, ignoring the exchange and pressing on. ''Kay-Raike was caught in a flagrant lie.''

''A majority of them wanted to believe him,'' Buto said. ''They were willing to overlook a 'mistake.' But it's worse than that, Jenny. You told me that at your court-martial the Generals were divided.''

''Yes.''

''They were again.''

Dane reached for a breadstick and brought it to her plate. Jenny watched her, silently encouraging, but she merely looked at it. Dane had rarely spoken during the past days. She'd eaten small amounts, but only under the direct orders and supervision of Jenny or Buto. Momed Pwanda was still away from *Noldron* and had nothing new to report. She did not want to discuss with him the breach of Stem protocol she'd committed, or its consequences, and so she declined to ''speak'' with him at all. He'd expressed concern, but did not press.

Shimas caught Jenny's eye and shook his head sadly. He mouthed the word ''now.''

Jenny hesitated. He shrugged, a helpless gesture, and nodded. She said, ''And so Kay-Raike has authorization to proceed?''

''Yes.'' They watched Dane as tears formed in her eyes. Her small form seemed to diminish as she closed her hands over her face and wept for the first time in their presence. The doctors had said that this would be a positive reaction. Jenny stood and took the chair next to Dane's, wrapping her arms around the smaller woman. After a while she said, "Dane, I want you to listen to what your father has to say." Dane nodded.

"Yvonne was right in everything she said, Dane," Buto told her. "We'll miss her too. At the meeting I took on her role. I pressed for Kay-Raike's conviction and forced retirement."

"Thank you," Dane said, keeping her eyes averted. "But it didn't help, did it?"

"I don't know," Buto replied. "It may have. Kay-Raike has received permission to return to Canopal. But before he can act . . . Dane, are you listening?"

"Yes, sir."

"The Generals—I should say, General Depluss—wants testimony from residents of that world." Dane looked at him, surprised and confused. Shimas continued, "If Kay-Raike's visit there was recorded by diverse enough sources to eliminate any chance of deceit, she wants that information transmitted to *Sovereign*."

Dane sat up straight. "Testimony from *Grounders*?"

Buto smiled. "That pretty well describes the reaction of everyone at the meeting, including me. Kay-Raike was livid."

"Buto, I want you to send me there. Please."

"Think what is at stake, Dane," Jenny said. "If Kay-Raike is telling the truth—"

"He isn't. He attacked first, and Canopal merely tried to defend itself."

"I believe that also, but if he can't be refuted it won't matter. Dane, you would be there while . . . you couldn't bear it. It would kill you."

Dane laughed, a bitter sound. "Jenny, do you think *that's* important to me?" She was out in the open now, committed to another long fall. "If Canopal dies, so will the fictitious 'allies' Kay-Raike spoke about. The Fleet will be as it was before, but this time with vengeance added to mindless tradition and callousness."

Buto's eyes narrowed in anger. He ignored the emotion,

having been advised to expect irrational outbursts. "That is not an accurate characterization, Dane."

"You agree with me, though, that what Kay-Raike is doing is wrong."

"Yes, but for different reasons. Mine is that he's using Canopal to force a change in Fleet policy. No single officer can be allowed to do that."

"Buto, I'm a Grounder. I can find who I need to find. They'll talk to me. *Please.* I've got to go there."

"He's unstable," Shimas said to her. "You wouldn't be safe. Particularly if it's you who finds the proof against him."

"Buto!"

"I said something before about trust being a curse," he said.

"I heard you."

"I wanted you to reason it out for yourself."

"What?"

"Kay-Raike nearly lost control of himself when the Generals gave him their decision. But then he accepted it. He actually smiled. He went on to make the point—until I was sick of hearing it—that both sides of the argument *trust* me. At his insistence and with the consent of the council, the Generals have assigned me to gather the information Depluss wants. Or, failing that, to be a witness."

"You'll take me with you?"

"Dane, you didn't see him at the meeting. One moment he was calm, and the next ready to kill on impulse. We've ordered Naomi to stay away from him. Can we do less for our daughter?"

"I want an answer," Dane insisted.

Jenny said, "We're not convinced that you're needed on Canopal. But we are convinced that you need to go there. Is that enough of an answer?"

Perhaps it was Tillic's influence, but for the first time Dane fully understood that she was loved by these two officers of the Fleet. And that she loved them in return.

⇒14⇐

Day 51

Deep space
Kay-Raike vessel Alee

"Why is it so dark?" Sato wanted to know.

"This is the way it was last time," Jarred answered. "Karnas Kay-Raike says his eyes are overly sensitive to light. You'll adjust soon, don't worry."

"I'm quickly becoming a man, Jarred. I wasn't worried, just curious."

"Sato," Martin said, "the first time I went aboard a vessel with normal lighting, I was older than you are now. I thought it was some kind of plan to make my father uncomfortable."

"Why did you think that, sir?"

"Because he told me it was. And you don't need to call me 'sir.' I don't have any duties aboard my ship. All I have is the uniform. And the name."

The stooped-over man leading them through a dim corridor said, "Martin, the boy has never been aboard one of our ships. There's so much for him to see and learn, I'm sure he finds your personal concerns to be distracting."

"No, I—" Sato began, but was stopped by a warning hand on his shoulder.

Jenny said, "Mendel, you might explain to him why none of your family has official rank."

Though his features were indistinct from five paces ahead, the man's stiffened bearing and hesitant voice made clear his reaction to the suggestion as he turned to answer. "You're correct, General Marsham. While the misunderstandings and false claims concerning my brother persist, our clan does not enjoy full acceptance within the Fleet. I might add that as a result of this, we are under no obligation to observe traditional protocols."

"What do you mean by that?" Shimas asked, as Mendel turned to lead the way again.

"It means, sir," Mendel called back to him, "that aboard *Alee* your rank has the same weight ours does aboard *Sovereign*. You are here as guests and observers. Not as superior officers."

"I assume you were ordered to make that remark," Shimas said. "And so I'll take it up with your brother, not you."

"Thank you, sir," Mendel said, with relief in his voice. "Your quarters are just ahead. Please let me know if they are inadequate in any way."

Dane could not recall a person as terrified of another as Mendel Kay-Raike was of Karnas. He'd been assigned as their escort, and she believed that he viewed the assignment in two ways: as a welcome chance to be away from his younger brother, but also dangerous in that his performance was under close scrutiny.

They were assigned three adjoining staterooms. Dane inspected hers at once and found that Karnas Kay-Raike had begun his psychological assault on her. The standard two monitors were in place and functioning, but she found a third and a fourth hidden in the overhead, one pointed at her dressing table, the other at her bed. She knew she'd been meant to find them. Just as she'd been meant to find a holostat that lay facedown on the dressing table. It was of Karnas Kay-Raike and the surgically altered Naomi, arms linked as they left the scene of their wedding. Kay-Raike's eyes showed a mixture of triumph and anticipation. Naomi bore Dane's own face, eyes wide with the horror that had just begun for her.

Dane returned the holostat to its original position and spent five minutes disabling all of the monitors. She assumed that more of them would be hidden in her stateroom while she was elsewhere, but she was confident that for now her reaction to Kay-Raike's predictability would go unrecorded. She was smiling, eager to begin the contest.

"Another 'mistake,' Kay-Raike?" Shimas asked mildly after dinner. The others had finished and gone, leaving the two alone in a darkened dining room. Dane had cautioned him that Kay-Raike might hope for a sharp confrontation early in their journey, to use as a counterweight to any damaging evidence they might uncover concerning Kay-Raike's previous visit to Canopal. As a result, he kept his words and tone temperate. During the meal Shimas had seen Kay-Raike glancing furtively toward Dane. She was a fine performer, he thought. The feigned nervousness she displayed had seemed to please Kay-Raike enormously.

"Of course it was a mistake, sir. That was my wife's stateroom. The holostat should have been removed along with the rest of her personal effects."

"And the extra monitors?"

"The relationship between a husband and a wife is none of your concern," Kay-Raike said. "For the record, I'd ordered the equipment taken out after she deserted me. It was not. There is nothing more to be said on the subject."

"And the monitors in the other two staterooms?"

"They're customary, Council Member Shimas. I have not objected to their deactivation. Now if you'll pardon me, it is my habit to be in the War Room when my ships leave hyperspace. You're welcome to join me there, of course.''

"I'm here to observe," Shimas said, standing and preceding his host to the door. "Given your relationship with
the concept of truth, I want to be sure you've taken us to
the right galaxy."

"That is an insult, Council Member."

"Why yes, I believe it is, Kay-Raike," Shimas replied
with a laugh. He was rather proud of his restraint. After
hearing what had been done to his daughter, his inclination
had been to smash Kay-Raike's skull against the nearest
bulkhead. But there would be time enough later for amusement, he thought.

Alee's War Room was empty but for Kay-Raike, Shimas,
and Jenny. Above the War Table hung a cloud of blackness
in which two lighted forms hovered. Both were saucer-
shaped, thick in the middle and dwindling out gradually to
the star-flecked emptiness surrounding them.

"This was recorded at our last normal-space observation
two days ago," a red-faced Karnas Kay-Raike said as he
used a pointer to jab at the leftmost form. "This," he continued, moving the pointer to the other form, "is a generated simulation of the galaxy as it would have appeared at
precisely that time and from precisely that distance and
viewpoint."

Jenny manipulated the display controls and brought the
two images together. They matched perfectly. "Very
well," she said, smiling toward Shimas. "I confirm that
this is Galaxy M-14."

As the display changed scale twice, the double-image
procedure was repeated to verify the identity of the Sentaura System they had entered, and the world they were
approaching.

The display changed again to represent the twenty-nine
Kay-Raike ships in formation around *Alee*.

"Call your Control Center," Shimas said to Kay-Raike.
"All ships to dead slow for now. We'll make our nearest
approach tomorrow, after my family and I have rested. In

the meantime, prepare five shuttles. We'll decide which one to use when we're ready to debark.''

"And of course we'll inspect it thoroughly before we leave,'' Jenny added.

Kay-Raike's face remained flushed as he spoke through gritted teeth. "Yes, Generals,'' he said with angry sarcasm. He opened a comm link to the hangar crews and issued the required orders.

"That's all for now,'' Shimas said. "On your way out, lower the lights to minimum and leave the display as it is so we can monitor your ships' movements.'' Two minutes later, alone with Jenny in the darkness broken only by the War Table display, he said, "This is pleasant, isn't it?'' He moved closer to his wife and reciprocated when she slid her arm around his shoulder. "There's something to be said for Dane's idea.''

"Which one?''

"Let Kay-Raike be the first to lose his temper. His reaction should be of interest to the council.''

"He's dangerous, Buto, but he's not a fool. Unless we find something on Canopal that goes against him . . . actually, even then the most he'll do is raise his voice to you.''

"Yes, I know. But I can hope. Say, when was the last time we were alone in a dark War Room?''

"You talk too much,'' she said, sidling closer.

And so how was the meeting, Momed?

The Stem leadership has become boring, I'm afraid. Endless squabbles about electing new officers. And a full day's debate on the reasons recruitment of new agents is down. Naturally, I attempted to enlighten them. Recruitment has fallen off because the worlds see themselves basically at peace with the Fleets. But of course that's too simple for the leadership to grasp. So I excused myself and gorged in the dining room until I was ordered back in to sit through more inane discussions.

You sound discouraged.

I am. It was a waste of time. I'm just an agent, with

no power to influence their decisions. I should have stayed with Beviney and worked on the information you need. But never mind that now. You're going down to Canopal tomorrow?

Yes. I need to know whether or not Kay-Raike made an arrangement with No'ln Beviney. If he didn't, then he's totally dependent on Shimas's report.

But if he did, it may not matter what you find. He could be using this time to finalize plans with her. I understand. But, Dane, I won't be arriving on *Noldron* until tomorrow. And it's not certain that I'll see No'ln Beviney right away. Can't you postpone your trip down to the planet?

No. Jenny and Buto are still worried about me. If I ask for a delay, they might change their minds about allowing me to go.

They believe that Kay-Raike will strike at you while you're down there? It seems to me that you'd be in greater danger left aboard his ship, while Jenny and Buto are away.

That's not it, Momed. Kay-Raike wouldn't dare harm me directly. Buto would kill him, and he knows it. They're concerned that if I can't find evidence against Kay-Raike on Canopal, I'll run away and hide somewhere.

Would that stop them from killing that world, if it's found guilty?

They don't want to face that question. But no, I don't believe it would stop them.

We agree on that, so I don't need to worry about your doing something foolish. I'm glad you're speaking with me again, Dane. Will you tell me why you wouldn't, for so long?

'Something foolish' is the right choice of words, Momed. I'll tell you someday. But for now it still hurts too much.

We'll leave it at that, then. I'll contact you as soon as I've spoken with No'ln Beviney. Good luck in the meantime.

Thank you.

Day 52

Alee

An angry voice blared from the speaker. "You really don't trust me, General Shimas."

"I believe I've made that clear, Kay-Raike," Shimas said into the shuttle's intercom. Beside him sat Jenny, while in the passenger compartment were Dane, Sato, and Jarred, along with Mendel and Martin Kay-Raike. "Now, what do you want? I'm waiting for clearance to depart."

"It appears, sir, that your guard has become careless. I don't question your right to bring them along, but by not informing me about this, you risked having them intercepted and fired upon by my trailing ships."

"What are you talking about?"

"Your ships, Council Member. One of them has just entered the system."

"Once more, Kay-Raike. What are you talking about?"

"It's well outside of normal detection range," Kay-Raike said, "but it has now created subtle distortions in the readings from two first-magnitude stars. I'm patching a comm link through to your shuttle. I respectfully ask that you contact that ship, sir, and order it to identify itself properly before coming any closer."

Buto and Jenny exchanged a glance, each shrugging. "I know of no one following us here," Shimas said.

"Very well, then," Kay-Raike replied. "Your answer is on record."

"Have you made any attempt to communicate?"

"Yes, sir, also on record. There has been no response."

"Then you don't know whose ship it is."

"Correct, sir. I will deal with it as I would any unidentified presence in hostile space."

"I expect you to follow *established* procedure, Kay-Raike. Not your own."

"Of course, sir. Your orders were that I am not to initiate contact with you for three days. Do you wish to be informed of any developments that might occur during that time?"

"Only if a threat is involved."

"Very well. Take good care of my son, General."

Shimas considered accepting the comm link patch and trying to reach the intruder. Due to the lack of space necessary to house sufficient amplifiers and antennae to boost a voice signal into hyperspace, no shuttle was equipped for communication beyond standard radio limitations. But he had no way to be certain that his attempt would be relayed from *Alee*. Nor, he realized, could he be confident that the intruder in fact existed. He decided it would be best to find out before severing contact for three days. "Kay-Raike, where are you?"

"In the Control Center, sir."

"I'll be there in ten minutes."

Forty minutes later, Shimas returned to the shuttle. "Someone is out there," he told Jenny as he strapped into the pilot's seat. "One ship that we can find. I'll have to admit that Kay-Raike's people deserve their reputation. I wouldn't have noticed the traces if they weren't pointed out to me."

"It isn't answering?"

"No response at all."

"It could be the Generals."

"What?"

"I wouldn't be surprised if they sent a ship to keep an eye on things here."

"But how? Nothing is going to get close to Kay-Raike without his knowing about it."

"There's a way," Jenny said. "It's something my father devised a few years before his death. I don't know all the details, but I know that it's been done successfully."

"I see. Then we may have a guardian out there somewhere."

"It's possible."

"I think you know more than you're telling me."

"The fact that the capability is not widely known tells

me the Generals would prefer to keep it to themselves.''
Her facial expression said that the discussion would proceed no further.

Shimas knew it was useless to pursue the matter. ''Has
anything changed here?''

''No. The airlock is set to local control. It will open as
soon as you throw the toggle.''

''Let's go, then.''

15

Canopal

"What is that dark area there?" Sato asked. His eyes had not left the repeater screen since it became filled with the image of the planet below. "And those white things?"

"The dark area is a continent," Dane explained. "It's land. The green and blue around it is water. The white things are clouds. Do you see that white swirl to the west of the continent?"

"Yes."

"That's a large storm."

"Radiation? Meteors?"

"No, it's wind and rain. It must be hundreds of miles across. Does eighty miles in one hour sound like fast travel to you?"

"Of course not. That's dead stop."

"But think of wind moving at that speed, Sato. It's strong enough to knock you down and carry you away as if you weighed nothing."

"*Air?* It's barely pressurized at all on planets! I don't believe that."

"It's strong enough to make billions of tons of seawater stand up like mountains."

"Dane!" Sato laughed, a child's delighted laughter. "You're making this up!"

"It's all true," Jarred said. "And on the land there are animals. I don't mean the meat we grow, but actual living animals with minds and families of their own. They're in the oceans, too. On some worlds they're as big as this shuttle."

"No!"

Dane was pleased that Sato had been given permission to accompany them. Jenny and Buto had reasoned that there was no special threat to him, as there might be to her. The boy's reaction to visiting a world was exactly what she'd hoped it would be: interest, rather than hostility.

Martin Kay-Raike listened to their conversation, fascinated. Beside him, Mendel was turning a sickly shade of gray. His orders were to wait for at least a day, and under no circumstances was he to act before they had made personal contact with Grounders. If only he could do it now, he thought miserably, and send the retrieval signal before they touched down on the nightmare below.

"Now," Shimas said as he moved the controls to check the shuttle's steep descent. "We're below commerce level. Is there any indication that we've been detected?"

"None," Jenny replied.

"I'm not surprised. This continent seemed to be uninhabited. I wonder why that is."

"Surface temperature," Jenny said, reading from the gauges. "Ice is everywhere. The inhabited areas are all nearer the equator."

"You sound like a Grounder already."

"It's lovely in a strange way, isn't it? For as far as you can see, there are nothing but broad expanses of brown, white, and gray. It's like a mural that goes on forever."

"I don't think 'lovely' is the word to describe so much chaos and waste, Jenny. What value can there be—"

"Look! Buto, something is moving down there!"

Instantly Shimas pressed a recessed console button, which brought the shuttle's light weaponry to readiness. "Where? Is it a ship?"

"No, it's . . . I don't know what it is!" She pointed. "There. Can you see it?"

"Where . . . oh, yes, there it is. It's flying, Jenny."

"Get us closer."

The shuttle made a quick turn and eased downward in a slow spiral.

"Dad, Mom!" Sato's voice came through the intercom. "Dane says that's a bird, but we shouldn't get too close."

"It's huge," Jenny said, reading from a statimeter. "Twenty feet or more across from tip to tip. Sato, ask her if it's dangerous."

"She says not to us, but if it's a mother with young ones around, it might fly into the shuttle to protect them. If it does, it will kill itself."

Jenny had an odd feeling, watching the brown-and-white bird as it began to circle beneath them, ascending the spiral they were descending. Yes, it was protecting something below it. This was a lesser species on Canopal, lower on the rungs of life than humans. And it was doing exactly as she would have done in its place.

Shimas changed course and sped northward toward the equator, leaving the bird to resume its undisturbed life.

"This close," he said, "the curvature of the planet limits us to just a few miles of radio range. But I want them to hear us before they see us coming." He dialed the transmitter to all-frequency and recorded, "This is Major General Buto Shimas from vessel *Alee*, Silver Fleet. We want to speak with someone of planetary authority. We are not a threat to you, but will respond if attacked." He set the message to repeat indefinitely.

A reply came forty-one minutes later as the shuttle streaked across a calm ocean. "General Shimas, this is

Boothe TillBatus Ten aboard my ship *Suram*. Are you in distress?''

"No," Shimas answered. "I want . . . how are you addressed, sir?''

"I told you, my name is Boothe TillBatus. Since we're using titles, mine is Ten. But it's also a name. So call me that.''

"That must be him," Jenny whispered. The screen showed a tiny dot sixty miles north of their position.

"Ten, we'll be passing over you in about two minutes. Don't fire.''

"You mean shoot at you?" There was laughter from Ten, and others in the background. "General, if one of my people gets too excited you might get a hard-shell tossed in your direction, but that's about all we can do. Besides, we're at peace now, aren't we?''

"Ten," Jenny said, "I'm Major General Marsham. How long has it been since you've been home?''

"Sounds like you've got lots of generals there," Ten replied. "You must be a pretty important ship. Listen, if you want to trade something for a share of the best catch you ever saw, stop in before you pass by. But about your question, I *am* home. We're due ashore in another year or so to empty and fill.''

"You don't communicate with . . . ashore?''

"Don't like to get that close, thank you. Listen, I hear you people have some exciting stuff. Can we deal?''

Dane came through the compartment door and whispered to Shimas. A moment later he said, "We're not carrying cargo. But if you could help us, we might be able to find something you'd be interested in.''

"Fifty tons of haul!''

"What was that, Ten?''

"It means good and maybe better, General. I see you now up there. Can you put down in water and get up again?''

"We can hover beside *Suram*," Shimas said. "I assume you have procedures for moving from one ship to another.''

There was more laughter. "We'll do our best, General. But let's get it done quick. I smell a blow coming this way."

"I don't understand."

"It's all the same to me and my people," Ten explained. "But you might not want to cross over with the ocean clawing at your legs."

Shimas went pale. "Ah, Ten, my idea was for you to come aboard here."

"Hundred tons of haul! Come on down here, General. Just open the door and I'll be there."

Shimas eased down beside the two-hundred-foot vessel and pulled to a position directly opposite a group of men, women, and children who stood in a flat area at the rear of the ship. He cracked the shuttle's seals gradually to equalize pressure and nearly vomited as cool, salt-laden air rushed in. "Are you *sure* this is breathable?" he asked Jenny. She had the same reaction, but nodded in the affirmative. Dane took a deep breath. The initial strangeness passed quickly, and she thought she had never smelled anything so sweet. Instantly she was on Walden again, setting off with her mother Linda on one of their frequent fishing expeditions together. Her brother Alfred, and while he was alive her father Daniel, had always reacted to the sea as Jenny and Buto were. Despite herself, Dane laughed at the retching sounds emanating from the passenger compartment behind her.

The shuttle's door began to open. Before it had reached full aperture, a man leapt through, landing nimbly three feet inside the opening, just behind the pilot's seat. He was tall and lean, balding, with bare arms that were corded with muscle. His hands were large and crusted with calluses and scar tissue. "I'm Boothe TillBatus Ten," he said, turning to face them. "Your ship here stinks, General. Were you about out of air?"

"We are now," Shimas replied. "Welcome aboard, Ten."

Ten grunted and waved absently as he turned away,

seeming to look in every direction at once. "Two, two fifty hundred tons," he muttered in amazement. "How much net can this thing haul?" he asked. And then, "Never mind. No room for catch. But it goes right up there," he said, pointing skyward, "out to the moons and farther on? This little thing?" He looked at Jenny for an answer.

"Yes," she said.

Ten whistled and shook his head. "I always thought your Fleet ships were bigger than mine." He said to Dane, "I know these two by their voice. I'm Boothe TillBatus Ten, and I'm luckier than I knew before today. Who are you?"

"Dane Steppart Marsham," she said.

"You're not a spacer, are you?"

"How did you know?"

"These two are turning green. You look like you're enjoying yourself."

"I am, Ten."

Ten cocked an ear toward the passenger compartment. "Sounds like there's more spacers back there turning green. How many people you carry aboard one of these things?"

"This is just a shuttle," Dane said. "It's what you'd call a dinghy. There are seven of us aboard. Most ships carry about two thousand."

"Are you a general too?"

"No. I'm their daughter."

"I see. You're from a planet but they second-familied you. I have two daughters and five sons that way. Their first families drowned." To Jenny he said, "I've never seen one of your big ships, and you haven't seen my catch. But I'll give you half of mine if you'll take me and Mill to one of yours. I just want to see one before I die. Can we deal?"

Shimas, still not in control of his stomach, nodded for Dane to continue. "We can talk," Dane said. "Can we offer you something to eat?"

Ten frowned, his knowing dark eyes piercing hers. "You had bad air, you probably have bad food. Can you open the door again?"

As the shuttle door opened, Ten went to the edge and

leaned outboard, his feet planted as firmly as iron pillars. He shouted, "Boothe Mar! Toss over that sack!" A white canvas bundle flew through the opening and landed next to Ten. "Prime," he said proudly as he bent down to lift it. "Not dead an hour yet. Where's your cooker?"

He untied the bundle. A slender, purplish tentacle fell out and dangled toward the floor. Jenny and Buto pushed past Dane, hands over their mouths.

"We don't have a cooker aboard," Dane said.

"Just as well," Ten said, looking disapprovingly toward the door Jenny and Buto had slammed behind them. "Listen, they may be a while from the looks of them. Why don't you come with me and have something decent to eat? It's probably been a long time."

"It has," Dane admitted.

"Come on, then, I'll help you across."

"Go ahead, Ten. I've got to tell someone where I'm going. You said there was a strong wind coming. How long will it last?"

Ten shrugged. "Maybe through dinner. Not much longer. They seldom do, this time of the year."

Dane found her family and the two Kay-Raikes seated together between the two lavatories in the passenger compartment. Sato appeared to be more ill from the misery around him than he was from any internal distress.

"I've been invited to dinner," she said to Jenny. "Why don't I take Sato with me?"

"Please!" Sato answered, looking thankfully at her.

"Go ahead, if you think it's safe," Jenny said. "But don't be long. Ten apparently doesn't know what's happened, so I doubt that he'll be able to tell you anything that's valuable to us."

"He'll give me an idea of their society and government," Dane replied. "That will help us know where to look. Before we go, I'll set the controls to wait for five minutes and then take you to a thousand feet. That should keep you out of the turbulence."

"Bless you," Jarred said. "As soon as I can move from

here, I'll evacuate the air and cycle in a new supply from the tanks.''

"No," Shimas said to him. "We'll adjust to the air. We'll need that later on, and it can't be any more difficult than Dane's becoming accustomed to our food eight years ago.''

Dane grinned at him. "That took three days, Buto."

"Can we go now?" Sato asked. "Sick people make me sick.''

At the doorway Sato startled Dane by jumping without hesitation across six feet of openness and down onto the fishing vessel. She followed and was steadied by a woman who caught her shoulders and held them until Dane's footing was secure. "I'm Boothe MillAnses Ten," the woman said by way of introduction. "Welcome to my ship." She'd pronounced "Ten" with a vowel sound slightly more elongated than that used by the man who Dane supposed must be her husband and co-master of the ship. She was the physical opposite of Ten. Short, rounded, with straw-colored hair and blue-white eyes that suggested clouds beneath a daylit sky, she appeared to be in her mid-fifties. "Please call me Mill," she said pleasantly. "You're Dane, the one who's not a spacer?"

"Yes, I am. That is my brother, Sato." She pointed toward the boy, who was on hands and knees examining the deck. "I thought I might slip," he said when he looked up and saw that he had Dane's attention. "But I didn't, and this metal is why. It's got little pits in it." Sato sprung to his feet. He approached the woman and asked, "Are all Grounder floating ships like this one?"

"The best ones are," Mill said with a smile. "But I thought now that there's no more war, we weren't 'Grounders' and 'Dirts' anymore."

"But you call us spacers."

"I suppose we do."

"I didn't mean it as an insult," Sato said, holding her eyes. "I just don't know a better word."

"Canopalese," Mill suggested. "Or Metians, from the

port of Metia we use. Or simply people. In my case, it's Mill.''

"And I'm Sato," he said. "But you have permission to call me a spacer if you want. I like it.''

Mill glanced at Dane, who merely shrugged. She had as little knowledge of how Canopalese children were expected to behave as Mill knew of Fleet customs. But the shrug said it all, and Mill seemed to understand. Sato was Sato.

The children in the group were mostly small and stood behind the adults, peeking out at times toward either Dane or Sato. They seemed more curious than afraid of the strangers. The adults wore neutral expressions, neither hostile nor friendly. They ranged in age and size, all wearing tunics of coarse brown cloth belted at the waist and high boots that rose to mid-thigh. All were bare-armed, as were Ten and Mill. All of their hands bore the marks of the rough manual work they performed.

Ten climbed up through an open hatchway behind Mill and came to stand with her, placing an arm affectionately around her shoulders. "Dinner is cooking," he said to Dane. "Why don't you and your brother take the time to explore a little? Go anywhere you like, but don't cross over any open live-catch tanks. Someone will find you when the food is ready.''

Something was wrong, Dane knew. Ten's voice had lost its exuberance, and he looked at her with guarded eyes. She turned as the shuttle pulled away from the fishing ship and quickly gained altitude. Dane nodded to Ten and reached for Sato's hand. Avoiding her, the boy ran to the hatchway and began climbing down. "Come on, Dane!" he called as his head disappeared from sight.

When Dane was gone, Ten looked around himself and said, "Go back to work, all of you. You'll see our guests again." The group dispersed immediately. Ten and Mill began walking forward, his arm still around her shoulder. "I reached Powter Bin Ten," he said. "She just left Metia a few weeks ago.''

''And?'' The first gust of high wind pushed from behind them.

''There's trouble, MillAnses. Bad trouble with the spacers again.''

≕16≔

Day 52

Noldron

No'ln Beviney had kept Pwanda waiting numerous times in the eight years they'd worked together, but this was the first time she had refused to meet his eyes when they spoke. Instead she looked from one area of her stateroom to another, feigning interest in battle mementos and furniture as if she were seeing them for the first time. She had read the trade-scout reports he'd compiled on the four worlds he'd visited during his trip. But her disinterested questioning told him that she'd paid no attention to detail in her perusal of the reports. Normally she demanded hours of his time for each document, reveling in the hunt for greater return in exchange for lesser offerings to each world. Now she asked about the trip itself, his health, the performance of the ship assigned to him and its crew. And she waited with uncharacteristic patience while he completed each answer.

She was giving him nothing he could use to learn what he needed to know from her, leaving him no space for subtlety. Pwanda waited until she seemed totally absorbed in her own thoughts before he asked bluntly, "What was the result of your meeting with Karnas Kay-Raike?"

Now she looked directly at him, her wide eyes flashing at the impertinence of a brusque question from a former Dirt. But there was more than anger there. Pwanda had known for many years that she cared for him personally, and that she did not pursue a liaison because it was unseemly for a No'ln Supervisor to approach a junior in such matters. That was a part of what he saw. Such emotion manifesting itself in this context told the Stem agent that she was withholding information based on a concern for his protection. But protection from what? What could she have arranged, or not arranged, with Kay-Raike that she thought would have an impact on him? No'ln Beviney believed that his loyalty was to her, who had raised him from a slave to become a respected member of the Gold Fleet. She believed that he carried out his duties as trade representative based on that loyalty; that he had no regard for the worlds he visited in her name. Certainly, he had been as ruthless and sometimes deceptive a negotiator as she wanted him to be. And she believed that he cared nothing for or about the Silver Fleet, which had first made him a slave. Why, then, would she think that an agreement between her and Karnas Kay-Raike was something to be hidden from Momed Pwanda? The answer was, only if it threatened something he did care about. Or something that she thought—or was afraid—he might care about. *After eight years of close proximity with her.*

His wife. Dane.

It could only be Dane. On an isolated world, with Kay-Raike ships the closest to her. Right now. But No'ln Beviney wasn't answering. She sat back and crossed her hands over her stomach, indicating that their meeting was over.

As Pwanda stood he sent, **Dane, there's something go-**

ing on between No'ln Beviney and Kay-Raike that involves you.

That's why I asked for your help, Momed, remember? We assumed that they met together.

I just confirmed that they did. But that is all I know, except that you're in danger.

I would appreciate any details you can provide.

You're getting good at this, Dane. Your sarcasm comes through quite nicely.

And so does your concern, Momed. Don't worry about me, just perform your usual magic. I'll be waiting for more information.

You'll have it. *Soon*, he thought, breaking the connection.

"You've been dismissed," Beviney said. "Or is there something else?"

Pwanda looked down at her, pondering a step he knew would complicate his life in unpredictable ways. But he could not stand idly by and allow his partner to die and her mission to fail. The vestige of training that Dane thought of as a sentinel had a counterpart in every Stem agent. Pwanda's began to shriek.

"Yes," he said. "There is."

Suram rocked gently from side to side in the building sea, then settled into a rhythmic pitching as its bow was swung around to face the new direction of oncoming swells. Dane found the motion restful, even sleep-inducing, after the fullest meal she'd eaten in many years. She'd forgotten how satisfying an ocean and its bounty could be. At the far end of the table, Sato was engaged in a game with two children who sat across from him. The object was to time the motion of *Suram* correctly so that a small sphere carved of bone could be rolled from one side of the table to the other, arriving for points in an overturned cup. Sato was losing, badly.

Ten and Mill returned to the table after a long absence. As seemed customary with them, Ten's arm was around

Mill's shoulder. Her own arm encircled his waist. They took seats opposite Dane and waited for a few seconds while conversation all along the table ceased.

Mill began, "You and your family wouldn't be down here by yourselves if you wanted a war with us."

"Generals never go first," Ten offered.

"But Powter Bin Ten thinks otherwise," Mill continued. "She believes you may not be what you claim to be. She says maybe you're one of a number of small ships sent here to find out about the weapons Canopal has now. And that maybe when you find out, you'll think they aren't enough to worry you. So those larger ships might go ahead and start the 'revenge' you told us about."

"That's Bin's idea, not ours," Ten told Dane. "She's my older sister, and I'd never say she was a trusting person. But then, she's got the biggest and newest ship out of Metia because she's not wrong very often."

"But you believe me?" Dane asked. She noted that the motion of *Suram* was slowly easing.

"We do," Mill said. "That's why we're telling you it's dangerous to go near what's left of the City of Dreams. Bin says even the supply and rebuild people don't like to fly near there now. The citizens are afraid and likely to shoot at anything coming in from above ground level. Bin says the damage was so bad that there are still areas where the bodies haven't been recovered. Once the survivors hear about you, I can't say what they'll do."

"How is help getting in?"

"By ground, of course," Ten replied. "That's why it's taking so long."

"Then that's how we'll go," Dane said. "I need to speak with people who saw the attack and recorded it. And Generals Marsham and Shimas need to see the damage at close range for themselves."

"Why?" Ten asked. "They could be a thousand miles away and get good pictures."

"I want them to *know* what's been done," Dane said.

"I want them to walk those streets and smell, and touch, and hear. And talk to the survivors."

"You're getting angry, aren't you?" Mill asked.

"Not *getting* angry," Sato called from down the table. "She's just showing it, for once."

Dane looked at him, amazed. He winked at her.

"You've finished with your meal?" Ten asked.

"Yes, and thank you."

"We do better when we know company is coming," he said. "It's all settled, then. I'll go now and call your ship. The blow'll be over in a few minutes. Then I'll tell my sister what we're going to do. She's closer to Metia and can send word ahead of us."

"Us?"

"I come from a big family," Ten told her. "My brother's mayor of Metia and smarter than I ever hope to be. He'll know what to do next. But he's a lot like Powter Bin Ten, so you'll need me and Mill there. Otherwise he won't listen to you."

"I don't understand," Dane said, "why your sister didn't tell you about what's happened, before today."

"Because there's no reason to worry over what we can't do anything about. She told me now because, as she put it, you and your ship are my catch. Of course, I'm not going to do what she recommended."

"What was that?"

Ten grinned at her. "Are you sure you won't have more shredded eel?"

Dane shuddered. "I see. And once we've all been processed, the shuttle would sink in a matter of minutes. There would be no trace left of us."

Ten looked worried. "That little ship doesn't float? I wish you hadn't told me that."

"Then we're even in the matter of jokes," Dane said.

Metia was a city stretched out over four hills overlooking a natural harbor. From a thousand feet Dane could see palatial estates atop the hills, and smaller homes nestled along winding roads leading down to the wharf areas. To the west the sun was still above the horizon, but at ground level long shadows were beginning to form across the city and harbor. The lights of lorries and groundcars seemed to chase one another in serpentine patterns that ran from dozens of moored ships to enormous flat warehouses. There was no other air traffic.

"My brother lives at the top of that easternmost hill," Ten announced from behind Shimas. "He likes to be the first to check the sun in the morning. That tells him if he'll go to work that day."

"I don't understand," Jenny said.

"Foul weather," Ten explained. "He was at sea more than fifty years. Now he's mayor. It was a habit then, and now it's a privilege."

Jenny and Buto exchanged questioning glances, but did not inquire further. As the shuttle lost altitude, Shimas saw the four people he'd been told to expect. They formed a large square south of the residence and waved lights to indicate his landing spot. He was grateful that darkness would fall in a matter of minutes. Walking out beneath a distant, daylit sky was something he'd done often enough on supply runs, but he had never been comfortable with it. He was accustomed to a solid overhead just a few feet above him. On planets there was always the urge to crouch low to the ground and to grasp whatever was available to guard against the irrational but real sensation of falling into that sky. He'd seen others surrender to that urge, immediately losing the professional demeanor an officer must maintain. Along with his respect.

"That's him," Ten said, pointing. Boothe KetSonal Mayor was taller, leaner, and hardier-looking than his younger brother. He wore a dark blouse and trousers belted around with a wide green sash. Four darker green clusters decorated the sash, in a pattern that Shimas took to be representative of the four hills of Metia. Shimas raised his hand in a greeting that was not returned. As he stepped down from the shuttle steps and approached the four, a woman and two men took positions to either side of and behind him.

"Sir," he said, "I am Major General Shimas, representing the Council of the Silver Fleet. Your brother tells me that you are properly addressed as Mayor."

"My brother is always welcome here," Mayor responded. "By tradition, that welcome includes his guests. You and your party may enter my residence if you wish."

"Thank you, but no," Shimas replied. He received a thinly disguised smile of relief in return. "We have work to do at the City of Dreams. Your assistance would be appreciated, but is not necessary."

"And your presence here is neither," Mayor said. "You may inform your masters that—"

"KetSonal!" Ten's voice came from the shuttle. Shimas turned to see the man jump lightly down and stride toward them. The brothers embraced warmly. "Three years!" Ten cried out. "You've aged at least ten!"

"And you stink of bilge," Mayor said, grinning and pounding his brother on the back. "Soft, TillBatus. You've grown soft!"

"And I'll grow fat too," Ten replied, "as soon as you have the decency to die and pass your job along to me."

"This work is only for adequate minds, TillBatus. Powter Bin Ten inherits if she'll change her name. Maybe your wife next. But you, never."

"I'd never take the job, Mayor," Ten answered in a sudden change of tone. "Not if it means you lose your manners."

Mayor answered in kind. "I've been to the City of Dreams since the attack, Ten. You haven't."

"Then you know what could happen to all of Canopal," the younger brother said. "This officer and his wife are both generals. He is a member of what they call their council. What they find here will decide what happens next."

"I agree," Mayor said. "If they find that we can defend ourselves, their Fleet may leave us forever. If they decide that we're relatively defenseless, we have no hope."

"Which of those propositions is true?" Shimas asked.

Mayor looked at him coldly. "I don't think your Fleet will take a chance, General, if you can't report anything at all. That might save both sides from a lot of death."

"If you believe that, then your best course of action is to kill us all."

"Yes, I agree. And our sister recommends that we do just that. But there may be more of you here. And sadly, General, that is not our way."

"You don't attack first?"

"That is what you came here to learn, according to the young woman accompanying you."

"But you don't believe that."

"I don't believe that either of the Fleets is concerned about niceties such as guilt or innocence. Not where a planetary world is involved."

"You face a difficult decision, sir."

"No. The decision is made."

"I see," Shimas said. He would not harm Ten unless it was necessary, but he was confident that he could kill this man and his three companions within seconds. The shuttle might be able to escape. But whether it did or not, Karnas Kay-Raike would have won. And instead of facing mandatory retirement, the renegade would gain new prominence within the Fleet. "For your sake," Shimas said sincerely, "I hope you've considered—"

"We have a saying, General, and I've seen it proved so often that I believe it. 'Twice in every fool's life he is wiser than the wise.' My brother here invited MillAnses into marriage on the day before I had planned to ask her. That was thirty-eight years ago. He is due to be correct again."

Shimas was tempted to smile, but saw that Mayor was completely serious.

"And so," Mayor continued, reaching into his blouse and retrieving a document, "I've made arrangements. Boothe LawNis Regent could not be reached after I spoke with Powter Bin Ten and my brother today. I'll continue to try. But if I can't, this will introduce you to her. That is, if you're allowed to enter the City of Dreams alive. Regent may not have my faith in the luck of fools.''

Ten took the document and passed it to Shimas. ''This will only be necessary if we're separated,'' he said. ''Otherwise I'll make the introduction personally.''

Mayor shook his head. ''I might have known you'd go. But you should leave MillAnses here.''

Ten smiled. ''You never did understand her, KetSonal. I've always been grateful for that.''

''You still smell of bilge,'' Mayor said, clapping Ten on the shoulder. ''Be careful, TillBatus.'' Without a glance at Shimas, he turned and began walking toward the steps leading to his residence, followed by his companions.

As the shuttle door closed behind them, Shimas asked, ''Boothe LawNis Regent. She's another of your relatives?''

Ten nodded and said, ''She's second-family to Mayor and me, and third-family to Powter Bin Ten. Nearly all leaders on Canopal are Boothe. It's hereditary, but not always. In most places anyone can become an area leader if he or she is willing to take the name. As I told Dane, I come from a big family.''

''Will we need to speak with anyone except Regent to enter the city?''

''No. One person rules at a time. We don't have anything like your council that Dane told me about. Now, if you don't have any more questions, I want to see Mill.''

As Ten departed, Shimas had a thought. Taking the pilot's seat, he dialed in *Alee*'s frequency. Five minutes later came Karnas Kay-Raike's voice. ''Yes, Council Member Shimas?''

''Kay-Raike, what is the status of that contact?''

''It appears to have left the system, sir. We've had nothing since the sighting you witnessed.''

''Very well,'' he said, thinking that Jenny may have been right about the identity of the intruder. ''Oh, there's something else. You testified that before you were attacked, you had contacted the officials of that city for permission to trade.''

"Yes, that's right."

"Do you remember any names?"

"No, sir. There were so many of them."

"I was hoping you could tell us whom to ask for."

"I'm sorry, sir, I can't. Since you've initiated contact, may I ask if my son is well?"

"Yes, Martin is well."

"I have something important for Mendel. May I relay a message to him?"

"Wait."

Jenny went to the passenger compartment and brought Mendel forward.

"Yes, sir?" he asked when Shimas told him who it was he'd be speaking to.

"Mendel, you are due to be a father!"

"What?" The stooped man slumped and sat heavily next to the pilot's seat.

"Dorothy took a fall last night. She wasn't hurt badly, but while examining her the doctors discovered that she's three weeks pregnant. She's all right, Mendel. And so is your daughter."

"Thank you for taking care of them, sir."

Kay-Raike replied, "I was planning to wait until the two of you were together, but I'll tell you this now. I've approved your new command, effective immediately upon your return here. Congratulations, Captain."

"Thank you, sir."

"No thanks are necessary, Brother. Concentrate for now on helping General Shimas with his work. There will be time for your new family and duties later."

"I understand, sir."

"That's all I have for now, unless General Shimas wants to speak with me." Shimas waved a hand, and Mendel broke the connection.

"We're pleased for you," Jenny said as Mendel rose slowly from the seat. "This is your first child?"

"Yes," Mendel said. "Yes, of course it is." Hands shaking, he bent and massaged his right leg below the knee.

When he straightened he said, "If you'll excuse me, I need to lie down for a while."

"Of course," Jenny said. "You've had a shock."

"It's the air," Mendel said. "Everything else is fine, General Marsham. Just fine." He made his way unsteadily back to the passenger compartment and closed the door after him.

"So," Jenny said. "Kay-Raike needed only one contact for permission to trade in that city. He says there were many. We have another verification that he was lying to the council."

"Or as his defenders would say, another 'mistake,'" Shimas answered.

"Why did Mendel react that way?"

"What do you mean?"

"Buto, when you learned that I was carrying our son, we were under fire from the Gold Fleet. Most ship's systems were out, and we were less than a minute from being rammed. But you still had the presence of mind to make a fool of yourself when I told you."

"I don't remember it quite that way, but I see your point. Mendel is about to become a father and take command of a ship. Both for the first time. He behaved as though . . . I don't know, it made no sense."

"As though he were a junior officer learning that his stateroom failed inspection."

Shimas nodded. "Yes, that's it exactly. And that his performance had better improve immediately."

"What do you suppose his instructions really are?"

"To watch us, of course. To report everything to his brother when we return to *Alee*. To testify that whatever we find contrary to Kay-Raike's testimony, we distorted."

"But so far he's showed no interest at all in what we're doing or what we may have learned from Ten and Mill."

"Yes, I've noted that. Your conclusions?"

"None, except that we can't trust him."

"We never did, Jenny."

"You're right. But I'm going to ask Dane to watch him carefully. That is, if she isn't already."

"I agree. Would you ask everyone to strap in back there? I want to be near the city before darkness lifts."

⇛17⇚

Day 53

"Mayor must have gotten through," Ten said nine hours later. "We're a hundred miles out and no one's shot at us." He stood behind Jenny as she piloted the shuttle through dark grayness that was beginning to hint at morning. Cloud cover above and the lack of any artificial illumination below had made their journey seem as if it were through hyperspace, devoid of visible stars. Next to Jenny, Shimas snored in tearing rasps. "Loud horn on that one," Ten observed.

"I don't want to approach much closer than this for now," Jenny said.

"That's good sense. I'd go ahead slow until they start tracking you. Then make some circles up here until I can talk to them."

Jenny cut speed and altitude until the shuttle crept along a hundred feet above the treeline. Fourteen minutes later she watched as a console light indicated electronic range-finding from below. "There they are," she said. The radio came on moments later.

"Is Boothe TillBatus Ten aboard?" a woman's voice demanded. "Answer quickly; we are trained on you."

"He is aboard," Jenny replied. Shimas came awake next to her and read their speed and altitude. He stood and motioned for Ten to take his place. "Key it here," he whispered, pointing to a switch on the console.

"LawNis!" Ten transmitted enthusiastically. "It's fifty tons at least to hear that bottom-scraping voice again."

"You're inland now, TillBatus. You can speak like a human being, if you remember how."

Ten winked at Shimas, finding it funny that the spacer still showed surprise at a common custom such as using insults as greetings.

"Can we come on in?" Ten asked.

"Not with a guarantee of safety," Regent answered.

"All right, wait." Ten switched off communication. He said, "That's a foul sign, my friends. It means that Regent isn't in full control down there. If we go farther, we could be attacked by people who don't answer to her anymore."

"What do you suggest?" Jenny asked.

Ten shrugged. "Remember, I'm the fool in the family. She'll have something in mind." He keyed the transmitter again. "Tell me what you've arranged, LawNis."

"Put down just south of the River Complex and stay in that ship until I rattle the door."

"You're there?"

"Of course I'm here. I've got groundcars and enough Patrol to get us through."

"One thing. The prevailing wind is from the north this time of year, isn't it?"

"That's right."

"Then meet us north of the complex. These are guests, Regent. I won't have you landing them downwind of that place."

"All right, TillBatus. North it is."

Ten laughed after the connection was severed. "You

spacers were in more danger than I thought. The smell of that place would . . . well, never mind. But it would.''

"How far will we be from the city?" Shimas asked.

"Seventy miles or so. There's a good road that follows the power lines, but I'm sure Regent will stay off that. So I don't know how long it will take to get there." He gave Jenny the location of the complex and held on while she gained altitude and went to high speed. Two minutes later they circled north of a vast array of buildings, many of them releasing smoke that drifted south. They landed in the only available field.

"We'll just wait now," Ten announced. "It won't take them long to get here."

Twelve minutes later Jenny said, "What *is* that?"

Shimas and Ten seemed to smell it at the same time. "The complex," Ten answered. "Believe me, it's much worse to the—"

"Ventilation should be entirely self-contained right now," Shimas said, jumping for the passenger compartment door. He flung it open and was nearly overcome by the wall of stench that met him. The door leading outside was still shut. His children, Mill, and the two Kay-Raikes were all asleep on the mats and seats they normally used, and he wondered how they could possibly have avoided coming awake. Then for the first time he became aware of a faint metallic whirring sound to his left. As he watched, a small hole appeared in the bulkhead a foot from the deck. A metal bit protruded and withdrew, to be followed by a capsule that dropped through the hole and rolled a few inches before it stopped. The capsule began to dissolve, releasing a brown mist that dissipated in the air.

He turned to shout a warning to Jenny and Ten to find a mask thrust into his hands. Jenny's was already in place. The moment Shimas began putting his on, she returned to Ten and helped him with the unfamiliar procedure. Ten had dropped to his knees.

Mask in place, Shimas began checking and masking the others, beginning with Sato. The boy's breathing was deep and regular. He was moving toward Dane and saw Jenny about to reach Jarred when the gas he'd already inhaled struck. His legs felt insubstantial as air as he collapsed.

Dane's first contact with the waking world was a gibberish of sounds that soon became recognizable as words. She identified Ten's voice as the louder of two voices, the other one female. Understanding them was nearly impossible because of the distracting and frantic twitching in her larynx. Pwanda was trying to reach her. That sensation eased and then stopped as he apparently decided to wait and try again. It was just as well, she thought. She needed time to understand her own situation before she could give proper attention to whatever Momed had to report.

The passenger compartment door was open to the outside, from where the voices emanated. Dane estimated from the truncated shadow cast by the shuttle that local noon was either approaching or had just passed. The odor that she'd awakened to in the near darkness was gone. She was still on the bench seat she used for a bed, and saw that the others, all but Sato, remained asleep where she'd seen them last. None seemed to be harmed in any way. Jarred had rolled onto his back and was snoring lightly. Mendel Kay-Raike was curled into a tight ball, gripping his right leg just below the knee.

Dane knew she'd been gassed, but felt no dizziness as she slowly stood. She went forward to the pilot compartment and found Jenny asleep between the seats and the rear bulkhead. Sato was sitting next to her. When he saw Dane he whispered, "She's all right. I took her mask off." Dane nodded and looked toward the pilot console. Sections of it were missing.

A search of the vessel determined that Shimas was not aboard.

She returned to the open door and peered out. The steps had not been extended. To her left, at the stern of the shuttle, Ten was standing face to face with a woman who dwarfed him in size. Only slightly taller than he was, she appeared to be more than twice his weight. Her thick arms were bent so that her hands rested on her hips. Both leaned forward toward the other, nose to nose, but neither was speaking now. There seemed to be a silent contest of wills taking place.

"Move back inside," Dane heard from the other direction. She turned to see two men approaching, dressed in identical green uniforms. One of them pointed what was evidently a weapon in her direction. "Go on, spacer, move," the one with the weapon said. She stepped back from the doorway. "Where is General Shimas?" she called out. There was no answer.

She returned to her seat and waited as the others in the compartment stirred to wakefulness. Mendel Kay-Raike was the first to stand. He looked around himself with an expression of confusion. And then, to Dane's surprise, he smiled. He saw her watching him and reddened. Without a word he entered one of the lavatories and pushed the door shut behind him.

"What happened?" Jarred asked, sitting up.

"I don't know yet," Dane answered.

"Well, I do," Mill said. She stood and went to the door to look outside.

"Move back," said the same voice as before.

"Go beach yourself," Mill called out, and jumped the seven feet to the ground below. A second later Dane heard her voice again. "Touch me, young man, and I'll kick you so hard you'll be pissing out your nose!" And then, "That's it, Ten, don't you back away. Or you and that harridan can both deal with me!"

Dane moved to the door again, but this time was not challenged. The two men were facing away from her, as interested as she was in the confrontation taking place.

The large woman stared resolutely into the eyes of Ten as Mill walked around them both, whispering in a voice too soft for Dane to understand. Finally the woman threw up her hands in exasperation. "Cheat!" she shouted. "You called in the sharks!"

"And you lost, LawNis."

Boothe LawNis Regent spun to face Mill and lunged at her. The two women met with an audible crush of bodies. A second passed before Dane realized that they were embracing, and not attempting to crush the life out of each other. Apparently violence and hostility were more ritual than reality here, she thought. Could the council be persuaded that people like this were not likely to strike unexpectedly after the friendly overtures Kay-Raike claimed he had made? Possibly, she reasoned, if enough additional evidence were presented. But the action Boothe LawNis Regent had taken against the shuttle would be strong testimony in support of Kay-Raike's accusations.

Jenny was awake when Dane returned to check on her. She was seated at the pilot's station, comparing a checklist with the equipment remaining in the console. "They meant to cripple us," she said, "and they did. All communication and flight control are gone. The only things they missed are life support and access to the weapons bank. But those may have been disabled locally; I haven't checked yet."

"Where is Sato?"

"He's taking inventory of the spare parts lockers. Is everyone all right? Is Buto awake yet?"

"The rest of us are awake and well. Buto is gone."

Anger flashed across Jenny's face. "They'll regret that."

"I don't think they intend any of us harm, Jenny. Regent did what she believed was necessary."

To Dane's surprise, Jenny nodded in agreement. "Disabling a potential enemy is usually not a bad tactic. But in this case it will work against her."

"They're afraid. You can understand that, can't you?"

"Yes, but that's irrelevant. They've taken away our mobility and made us hostages. Under these circumstances, the council will never accept our report as comprehensive. Kay-Raike will win by default."

"Then we've got to make that point to Regent."

"Not us, Dane. *You.* Buto and I had a long conversation last night. The condensed version is that we don't know what the outcome of this trip will be. But whatever happens, you've got to know that you did everything possible to prove what happened here seven weeks ago. You're an able negotiator. In fact you're the best I've seen. And as you pointed out, you share a common heritage with the citizens of this world. So as of now, with your father's agreement, I'm offering you command. If you accept, the first thing you'll need to do is to convince these people not to commit themselves to certain death."

"You're referring to the shuttle?"

"I'm referring to Buto. He will allow them some time to come to their senses. But if they don't release him, and quickly, he'll lose himself in worry over you children and me. Then he will kill his captors. Or force them to kill him. And if that happens, I will personally lead the reprisal against this world."

"Jenny—"

"Command is not easy, Dane. And it always involves life-or-death responsibility. Do you want it, or not?"

"Yes," she answered after a moment's thought. "Yes, I do."

"Then, with your permission, Sato and I will continue the assessment of our capabilities. Please let me know what else I can do. But, Dane, I hope for everyone's sake you understand the most important duty you face right now. I want my husband back."

It was a different stench, more powerful but less constant than the other. Shimas determined to remain still with his eyes closed until the snippets of conversation he occasionally heard revealed where he was and what they intended to do with him. He knew that he was alone in a small enclosure. He assumed the presence of an internal monitor. His wide shoulders touched against opposite walls, while his breath bounced back from a ceiling he estimated to be a foot or less from his face. Other than the horrific smell, it was not unlike the sleeping quarters he'd been assigned as a young lieutenant while serving on a small scouting ship. As minutes passed he noted another difference; the scouting ship had not featured small animals that squeaked and scampered across his legs.

When the air blew in from his left side, the stench dissipated. "North," he recalled Ten as saying. "Prevailing winds." Those were totally useless concepts in his natural environment. Stellar wind had not been an important factor in space travel for millennia, and what Dane had explained as "compass direction" referred only to ground-based calculations. But here, he realized, they meant something. The "prevailing winds" brought reasonably breathable air and told him that he was somewhat to the "north" of that which stunk so badly. And that would likely be what Ten called the River Complex. Possibly, then, he was not far from where he'd been abducted. He recalled that Boothe LawNis Regent had first ordered them to the other, "south" side. So the gassing and abduction had been planned well before their arrival, but they'd intended to hide him a greater distance from the others.

It came to him that the conversations had stopped minutes ago.

By concentrating he could hear people moving around to his right, "south," at first in a group and then separating. There were rasping noises, unlubricated hinges opening or closing slowly. And then all movement and sound stopped. He had the impression that his captors had taken up defensive positions and were waiting for something. The small animals in his enclosure paused in their random skittering and then ran away as a unit.

He heard a grunt, followed by more dry surfaces grating together. The action came from his right and above him, and ended with the unmistakable sound of a human body falling from a height and thudding dully against a hard surface at deck—or ground—level.

Two things were clear: A battle was being waged, with Buto Shimas as the prize. And Buto Shimas had no intention of waiting to be claimed by the victor.

He opened his eyes into the close darkness and saw that

he was confined in some sort of slatted crate. No monitor was visible. He'd also been wrong about the construction of the enclosure; the slats were not of metal. They were constructed from a fibrous material, certainly organic. He placed his arms to push against the ceiling and discovered that the building material was somewhat flexible. It bent outward with every exertion but returned again to its original position when he relaxed his arms. Frustrated, Shimas doubled his effort and heard a gratifying tearing sound as the top lifted away from the remainder of the crate and was soon loose in his hands. As he tossed it to one side, his uniform sleeve was caught on one of the sharp spikes that had held the top in place. It took a piece of material with it and left a shallow scratch on his arm, which he ignored. He sat up and climbed out to the floor.

The muffled sounds of battle were still coming from ''south'' of him. He headed in the opposite direction, across a floor made of the same fibrous material as the crate. He came to a door and passed through, entering a nearly identical empty room. Time after time he repeated the procedure until his sense of direction was lost. There were no more sounds to guide him away from the fighting. Eventually— he guessed ten minutes had passed since his escape—he came to a door that led him outside. He kept his eyes to the ground to avoid looking at the sky and ran into the wind, certain that this was ''north'' and would lead him back to Jenny and the others. But Ten had not explained to him that a northerly wind can shift in a heartbeat.

Shimas ran between large structures similar to the one he had left, encountering no one. Finally he left the complex and entered the deep woods that, unknown to him, stretched hundreds of miles to the east.

Shimas had never walked a distance greater than the breadth of *Sovereign*. Most Fleet officers maintained a daily regimen of stationary physical activity designed to sustain strength and endurance. Shimas went further than most, always striving for improvement. And like all members of the Shimas clan, and as he had insisted upon with Sato, he had trained from early childhood in traditional modes of physical combat: unarmed, and with sword or dagger. But since leaving *Dalkag* he had not found an adequate training partner. And he had allowed his new activities as a council member to dominate his waking hours. As a result his arms and legs maintained the extraordinary power suggested by their size, but his stamina had fallen to a level he would not have guessed. This became clear to him after an hour of running and walking through dense vegetation. Nearly exhausted, he sat down and rested with his back against a sturdy stalk—a "tree," as he recalled the word. And it occurred to him then for the first time that he had no idea of what he could safely eat or drink in this completely alien environment. Within his sight were a hundred varieties of plants. Were they all safe, or none of them? Did they all provide nutrition, or none of them? People ate meat, of course. But how could he do so here, where the animals bearing that meat possessed minds, and would likely run away from him if he approached? And even if they did not, he had no knife, and no idea of just where in an animal the meat was located. And there was no cooker available. How did Grounders *survive?*

It didn't matter, he decided; he could live for days without food or water if necessary. The important thing was to find Jenny and their children, to satisfy himself that they were alive and unharmed. And if they weren't . . . Canopal was an enormous place from the ground. But from space it was not nearly large enough to absorb the anger growing within him.

⇛18⇚

Noldron

No'ln Supervisor Beviney understood desire. She also understood duty, tradition, and loyalty. Until now she had believed that these were the factors that kept a woman and a man together for a lifetime. It was proper to love a ship. One naturally, being human, loved command, combat, victory, promotion, the destruction of enemies, and the anticipation of all these things that made life the glory that it was. But a *man?* Could one *love* a man? Yes, she knew for the first time. One could.

They had confessed secrets. Momed Kwasii Pwanda Pwanda was not native to the world called Walden, from which he had been taken by the Silver Fleet. He had been born on Pan'Omo, in another galaxy. (He had lied to her about that. But what mattered was that he had not originated on the same planet as the woman he later married. He was therefore as close in heritage to herself as he was to Dane Steppart.) Momed was a professor of engineering

175

and mathematics, and a student of the mind. Another lie confessed. And another: His marriage to Dane had not been forced—*or consummated*—but was based on his wish to work with her in opposition to the system of Fleet dominance that had been in place for so many centuries. There were others, like-minded. (That too was forgivable; what could so few do to upset the natural order?)

No, the lies were not important. What mattered was the way he had looked at her, asking to speak to her as one person to another, for the first time in eight years. She didn't recall everything that had been said. But she remembered how the hours drew to a close, him sitting with her head cradled in his lap, stroking her temples, speaking so softly, creating pictures in her mind with that magnificent voice that soared and whispered, comforted, excited, brought her to tears, laughter, and made it so easy to find stories and hopes that she had not known were still in her mind. When she told him about them, he heard what she told him. He understood everything, because he was so close he was part of everything. Momed Pwanda knew her, as no one ever had. And he approved.

It could have gone on for hours more, with no awareness of time. But then the Nomarch had summoned her, and when she said she had to leave, he wore a face so open and needful that she—Marana Beviney—had laughed and cried in the same breath. Because she knew that the face he wore was not his alone. "Alone" no longer existed.

Remembering now, thinking of Momed Kwasii Pwanda Pwanda, she knew she'd decided on the perfect gift for him. After the naively trusting Kay-Raike delivered it to her, she would give Momed the Silver Fleet; she'd first take from it what she wanted and then let him destroy the rest in any way that pleased him. The result? A Gold Fleet stronger than ever before, unchallenged throughout the seven galaxies. Marana Beviney in solid command. And at her side, forever, a content and grateful Momed Pwanda. Yes, it was perfect.

She was glad now that there hadn't been time to tell him

everything. Nor would she; the surprise on his handsome
face would make a tiny deception worthwhile.

Canopal

Dane jumped down from the shuttle and approached Regent
and Ten. The two uniformed men glared uncertainly at her,
finally looking to Regent for instructions.

"Never mind her," the large woman said. "Continue
your patrol." The two nodded and walked away in opposite
directions.

"I need to speak with General Marsham," Ten said. "Is
she awake?"

"She is," Dane replied. "But it's me you need to speak
with." To Regent she said, "My name is Dane Steppart.
I'm not a spacer, but I am now leading this group. Ten has
told you why we're here. Abducting General Shimas was a
mistake, Regent. We can't help you while he's a prisoner."

"I know that," Regent said.

"And we need control of the shuttle," Dane continued.

"TillBatus has won the point that we have no option but
to trust you. I'll begin by explaining what's happened here.
To begin with, it was not me who gassed you or took General Shimas. That was done by a Patrol element I no longer
control."

A shout came from one of the Patrol, out of sight on the
far side of the vehicle. "Regent! Our people are coming
back."

"Follow me," Regent said. The four of them walked
around the shuttle to see three women and two men emerging from the woods to the south of the landing field. One
of the women was supported by two of her companions,
her legs bound together by a bloody wraparound bandage.
One of the men ran forward to report.

"We found the renegade Patrol, Regent," he said. "But
after we had them beaten, they stole clothes from the people

who operate the complex and mixed in with them. The workers were afraid to identify them. There wasn't time to sort it out.''

"And General Shimas?''

"We didn't see anyone wearing a spacer uniform. But we found a scrap of cloth that could have been a part of one. We think the general escaped while we were trying to get to him.''

"Where are the others, Poda Nem?'' Regent asked.

"Five are looking for the general,'' Nem answered. "Three are dead.''

"Dead?"

"Warna Tal, Samuels Reste, and Hochsman Burr. Regent, I've never seen anything so brutal. We followed drag-marks after the fight. They were pulled into a building and killed. With a knife.''

"Is that how Warna Mas was hurt?''

"No, Regent. She fell from a building. She has a compound leg fracture.''

"So she wasn't with her brother and the other two.''

"No.''

Turning to Dane, Regent said angrily, "We were set up to the south of the complex, where we could have protected you. By the time we got around to this field, your party was unconscious and your general was gone. I sent out my Patrol to look for him. And three of them were *killed.*''

"I'm very sorry,'' Dane said.

"You still don't understand, do you? You were assaulted by people who are no longer loyal to me. Since the destruction at the City of Dreams, they've broken away and formed units to protect themselves and their families from you spacers. They're illegal, but they're still *Patrol.*''

"You're correct, Regent. I don't understand.''

"Patrol does *not* kill, except under the most extreme circumstances. But spacers kill as readily as they breathe. TillBatus says that your general looks as though he could bend iron.''

"They kept him in a nailed-shut crate,'' Nem offered.

"He tore it apart from inside. I don't know anyone who could have done that."

Regent nodded. "What happened is obvious. He found those three unconscious and dragged them out of sight. And he butchered them."

"Regent, Buto Shimas would never—"

"Your lives and his were never in danger. The ones who did this probably thought that taking a hostage and crippling your ship would give them something to bargain with. They were wrong in what they did, but no one had to die."

"Regent, Buto Shimas would not kill helpless people."

The large woman's eyes went wide. "Oh? Then why are you here? You're looking for evidence that your Fleet attacked us first. If you can't find it, this entire world is to be judged guilty and every woman, man, and child is to be executed. Would your general refuse, or even hesitate, to give that order?"

"No," Dane admitted.

"There are more than a hundred fifty million of us. So please, don't tell me he wouldn't kill three."

There was a difference, Dane began to tell her. But the difference was only a matter of personal involvement and cultural background. Killing three unconscious people was an act of cowardice that Shimas would never perform. But the annihilation of a world's people . . . yes, he would do that. And call it duty.

Regent said to Poda Nem, "What instructions did you give for finding him?"

"If it's not possible to bring him here alive, they'll let him go. You were very clear that we were not to harm him."

Regent turned to Dane and said, "You see the difference between us, little woman. And maybe you weren't born a spacer. But you should think very carefully before saying you're not one now." Before Dane could answer she said, "My people are tired, and one of them needs my assistance. Undoubtedly the components taken from your ship are hidden or buried somewhere nearby. So if *your* people aren't too busy, you might have them start a search.''

Poda Nem ran to help his companions. Mill and Ten looked sadly at Dane and followed Regent as she walked away.

Twilight had begun when Jarred, Martin, and Sato located a pile of loose dirt in a stand of trees three hundred yards west of the shuttle. Poda Nem showed them how to use a shovel and stood back to watch while Sato mastered the art of digging and spraying dirt on anyone within ten feet. All of the missing components were there, but were caked with moist soil. Jarred reported to Dane that half a day would be required to disassemble and clean them all. She assigned the three of them to work through the hours of darkness.

"We can't leave the shuttle here as planned," she said to Jenny, "now that we know there are hostile Patrol in the area. But Regent believes we'll be fired on if we take it much closer to the city. I'm going to have Mendel take it out over the ocean and wait until we call him."

"After we find Buto."

"Yes. We'll go up as soon as there's light."

Shimas was glad to see the night coming on. Darkness meant that he had to stop and rest, as his body demanded but his mind would not allow. He'd walked for uncounted hours though the deep woods, grateful for the cover provided by the treetops. But he suspected, after he'd passed what appeared to be the same small clearing twice, that he was traveling in circles. The wind had long since stopped. Several times he'd climbed to the top of trees, dizzy beyond anything he'd ever known, hoping to see the shuttle. That it wasn't to be seen increased his sense of dread; if Jenny could, she would be searching for him.

He was unprepared for the sudden cold and the noises that seemed to come from everywhere as darkness approached—and then, it seemed within seconds, became total. He could no longer see any part of his body.

He felt an odd sense of embarrassment about his situation. Where, in such a place, does one sit or lie down for the night? He decided that it was best to move up against a tree. That might protect him from the wind, if it began again. Stretching his hands out before him, he walked carefully ahead until he found a tree. It was a small one, barely as thick around as he was. But it seemed as good a place as any to stop for the night. He sat down and leaned back against it, wishing he knew more about the local stars. A few of them were visible through the canopy above. But they gave him no sense of place or direction.

Or of time.

He didn't know how long he'd been asleep when he jerked awake and leapt to his feet. There was a sharp cry and the sound of running feet just a few feet ahead of him. Moving away. He began perspiring heavily as he recalled what had seemed to be a dream—the feel of hot breath on his cheek, and the reek of spoiled garbage. The running stopped. Whatever had been there was not alone. From the darkness came fast clicking sounds and a rumbling *jee-ummm . . . jee-ummm*. The sounds came from every direction. Careful and slow this time, circling.

Whatever the creature had been, Shimas had frightened it away by sudden movement. More of the same was indicated. He kicked at the undergrowth and shouted, feeling more than a little foolish when he realized that he was flailing his arms wildly, adding nothing to the noise he was otherwise making. Still, it seemed the right thing to do.

A low-throated *jee-ummm* to his right caused him to turn. As he did, he was hit on that side and pushed to his left. Searing pain erupted from the point of impact. He brought his arm down and caught the wriggling creature's neck in his hand, pulling it away as his uniform and flesh were torn by sharp teeth. The animal was hairless where he gripped it, with thick cords of muscle around a neck nearly as thick as his upper arm. He squeezed his hand shut and felt bones snap. He was hit again, low in the right leg. Again he caught the creature, but this time broke its neck before pulling it from him. The teeth had locked shut; the tearing and the hot pain were just the same as the first time.

He heard more of them around him, clicks and guttural snarls circling in the darkness. The thought came to him as if someone had spoken: Here, *you* are meat.

The world seemed to explode with intense light, no sound.

"Fall down," he heard. "We'll take care of them."

Shimas was nearly blind from the sudden glare, but still he could see that some areas were darker than others. The darkest ones were moving, still circling.

"Fall down! They won't go away if there's something moving and bleeding." It was a woman's voice, he thought, but the cacophony of animal sounds was so loud he couldn't be sure. He dropped to his knees and lay down, tucking his head to his chest and drawing up into a fetal position. His hands went to his wounds and found lacerations the length of his palm. He pressed down to stanch the bleeding. "That's good. Now don't move." A strong light was placed near his head, its glow visible even through closed eyes. "You two," the voice said. "Let's make a circle around him and keep the lights pointed at the jummers. Nobody move."

Several minutes passed. His side and leg ached and burned, pounding with every heartbeat. Blood seeped between his fingers. Finally there came a tap on his shoulder.

"You can sit up now," the voice said.

Shimas brought himself up slowly, keeping his hands in place. He opened his eyes and saw the outlines of three people. They seemed to be green and far away. The color was the result of his damaged night vision, he knew. And the oddity of distance resolved itself when he realized that they were small children. His eyes began to adjust.

One of the children, a girl, came close to him and held out a hand. "They got you," she said. "Open your mouth." Shimas complied and received a small, flat piece of soft material, which he guessed to be vegetation. "Go ahead," the girl said. "Chew on it. Swallow as much of the juice as you can, but don't swallow the whole thing yet.''

''Ren, that's all we brought with us,'' another, a boy, said.

The third was also a boy. He said, ''Heth, do you plan to get bit?''

''No, I'm not stupid,'' said the boy.

''Neither are we. So we don't need it. But he does.''

Shimas chewed, and found the taste bitter but not unpleasant. Because he'd had nothing to drink for a full day, he had difficulty producing saliva.

''You need water?'' Ren asked.

Shimas nodded to her. He estimated her age at about seven, with Heth and the other boy a year older. The boys were both dark and looked enough alike to be twins. Ren was light-skinned, with hair the same color as the orange-yellow glow from the lights. All three were dirty, wearing clothes that were torn. Only Ren had shoes. She left for a few seconds and returned with a bag. From it she removed a green ball the size of Shimas's fist. He remembered seeing others like this, growing from ropelike tendrils wrapped around the bottoms of several trees he'd passed. ''Bite into it and drink,'' she said, handing it to him. ''But remember not to swallow the ligax leaf.''

The thin liquid was warm and extremely sweet. Shimas felt his body absorbing energy as it poured down his throat. When the ball was empty, he gave it back to Ren. She looked at him quizzically and tossed it away. ''Now chew some more. That's so you don't die.''

''Thank you. My name is Buto Shimas.''

''I'm Kiber Ren,'' the girl said. ''These are my brothers Heth and Seth. I never heard of the Buto family. Are you from the city?''

''No,'' Shimas said. ''Will those things come back again tonight?''

''The jummers? They won't,'' Seth said. ''You killed two of them. The other four dragged them away and will eat them, so they won't be hungry until tomorrow night.

Anyway, we have the lights. Why are you out here?"

"I was separated from the people I was with," Shimas said.

"That's what Seth thought," Ren said. "You passed by us twice today. Seth thought we'd better follow you, because it didn't look like you knew where you were going."

"Then we decided you were a hunter," Heth said. "From the way you were making so much noise after it got dark. My father does that to bring the jummers out. But he has a suit they can't bite through, and you don't. Why were you acting so stupid?"

"I've never been in a place like this before," Shimas said. "I didn't know what to do."

"Well," Ren said, "next time remember that jummers never attack anything that's alive and bigger than they are unless it's dying, or they're afraid. And you're a lot bigger than they are. If you weren't moving, they would have smelled that you weren't dying and gone away."

"And never drink the boles until they're dark green," Seth added. "And always keep ligax with you, because jummers aren't the only things that can kill you with small bites. Sometimes you have to follow a stream for a few days before you find some, but you'll find it if you look for the yellow berries with black spots. But don't eat the berries."

"That's right," Heth said. "And don't eat any animals that have three toes or a split tongue. And don't eat any plants that have white and purple together on them."

"Not until after it snows," Ren said.

Heth nodded solemnly. "Not until after it snows a few times, to be safe. So you should never gather food when it's dark because even with these lights everything looks different than it does in the day."

Shimas understood that they were reciting, proudly sharing their knowledge with him. "When it's light again, would you take me to where you live? Maybe your parents will help me find the people I was separated from."

"We live here," Seth said, gesturing all around him.

Heth said, "Seth and I have the same mother and father. But Ren's father is married to our mother now, so we're all second-family. Our parents are away in the city. First he went, and then she went to look for him."

"But you're children. Did she leave you alone?"

"Rol stayed with us. He was Ren's brother. He was a grown man."

"He died," Ren said. "When our parents come back, we have to tell them."

"How long have they been gone?" Shimas asked, suspecting that he already knew the answer.

"A long time," Heth said. "They'll be proud when they see how well we did while they were gone. Seth is the one who knows everything, but Ren and I helped him."

"Do you know where the River Complex is?" Shimas asked.

The children looked at one another, held their noses, and giggled. Ren said, "We bring herbs to the cooks there and they give us cakes and milk."

"How far is it from here?"

"Less than eight miles," Seth said. "Do you want us to take you there?"

"I would be grateful," Shimas said, shocked that he'd walked so far but traveled so small a distance. "I have a son who is a little bigger than you three are. We can alter some of his clothes to fit you."

"The cooks don't *have* to give us anything," Ren said, looking down. "We'd still take the herbs to them, because they don't know how to find them for themselves. That's the right way."

"Besides," Heth added, "your son's clothes belong to him. You shouldn't promise to give them away without asking him first."

"You're right," Shimas said. "I'll ask first. Will you take me?"

"If you can walk that far," Seth said. "Jummer bites hurt the next day, even with the ligax."

"I'll be able to walk," Shimas promised.

Seth asked, "What about the others?"

"I don't know what you mean."

"There are two groups of Patrol between here and the complex. I think they're looking for someone. Is that you?"

"Possibly," Shimas said. "It would be best if they don't see me."

"I don't want them to see us, either," Seth hold him. "It used to be that Patrol were everyone's friends. That's what my mother always said. But there's a bunch of them that come by here sometimes. They're not friendly at all. They take food and tools from the complex."

"Rol worked there," Ren said. "The Patrol killed Rol because he chased after them. Would you rather die or be cold, Buto Shimas?"

"What?"

"You're still bleeding. With jummer bites, it doesn't stop by itself. If you give me part of your clothes, I can make bandages and wrap mud in them. Otherwise you'll die like Rol did. But he was dead before we found him."

"The fabric is stuck to me," Shimas said. "If you have a knife, I can cut it away."

Seth took a light and searched carefully over the ground where Shimas had been attacked. He returned with several small objects in his hand. "These are jummer teeth," he told Shimas, and gave one each to Heth and Ren. "Don't cut yourselves. We don't have any more ligax."

"Wait," Shimas said. "The medals I'm wearing are held in place by pins. Can you use them?"

"Were we supposed to think of that?" Ren asked, looking down again.

"No," Shimas said. "I've got to learn to think like a . . . to be as smart as you three are."

Ren smiled at him. "Don't worry, we'll teach you." Minutes later the upper half of Shimas's uniform had become layers of bandage separated by cool mud, circling his waist and right calf. The children selected a nearby tree to serve as temporary quarters. Shimas found a wide notch twenty feet above the ground and, to his surprise, was falling asleep within minutes.

Day 54

"Buto Shimas! Buto Shimas!"

Shimas awoke to Seth's urgent whisper and found the small boy crouched near his head, pushing and pulling on his shoulder. The green canopy above sparkled with morning sunlight glistening off beads of moisture. For the first time since his arrival on Canopal, the air smelled pure and fresh. He inhaled deeply, finding that the forest smells no longer seemed alien.

"What is it?"

Seth's hand covered his mouth. "Shhh! They're down there. It's my fault, Buto Shimas. I should have brought the empty bole up here with us. They found it."

Shimas gently removed Seth's hand and tried to sit up. He pushed himself slowly erect while his side and leg protested the movement with excruciating reminders of the jummer attack. Thirty feet out from the base of the tree, two men in green uniforms were walking, bent at the waist and pushing the undergrowth aside with the shoulder-ends of long portable weapons.

"Here," one of them said. "Another imprint. Bega, go stand where you found that last blood." The other man moved out of Shimas's sight. "Good," the first one said. "He's still moving in the same line." The man turned around and brought the weapon to his shoulder, using it to give him a straight line of sight. The rifle pointed directly at the tree.

For the first time, he looked up. It was impossible for Shimas to hide.

"Good morning, General," the man said. "I am Lieutenant Hanse Till of the Provisional Patrol. We have met, but you were unconscious at the time. Please come down."

He lifted a hand over his brow and scanned the tree. "And your companions as well, sir."

"I'll come down," Shimas answered. "There is no reason for you to bother with the children."

The lieutenant had come close enough for Shimas to see his scowl. "My people are engaged in preventing the destruction of this world, General," he said. "We're not interested in three children. Follow my orders, and they can go."

"No!" Ren climbed down from her branch and made her way beside Seth, who was standing protectively in front of Shimas. "You're the people who killed Rol," she called out. "We won't let you hurt Buto Shimas."

"It's all right," Shimas said. "They won't—"

Ren pitched forward and screamed. Before Shimas could reach out she was gone, tumbling through the air. He heard her small body thud against the ground twenty feet below.

"Tilam Bega!" Hanse Till shouted. "You had no authority to fire!"

Bega's voice came from the opposite side of the tree. "I've been up all night looking for this spacer, Lieutenant. I'm tired and I'm hungry. Now tell him to get down from there before I shoot the other two."

"Like you killed those three Patrol at the complex?"

"That's right, sir. Now let's get moving."

Heth climbed down to Shimas and wrapped his arms around Seth. The two began to cry. As if from a great distance, Shimas heard Hanse Till. "I regret what happened, General. You have my assurance that you will not be harmed. We need you to bring an end to all of this."

"And the children?"

"They can stay where they are."

"Agreed," Shimas said. "But you'll have to be patient. I'm wounded." He whispered to Seth, "You two sit down. Don't watch, and don't move."

"But they—"

"Stay here! Don't move!"

Shimas edged out of the tree notch and began the climb

to the ground. He kept his right leg bent, using the left and his arms to support his weight as he carefully lowered himself from branch to branch. Grimacing as though the pain were worse than it truly was, he squeezed both wounds, causing them to bleed down onto the ground below.

"I didn't know you were hurt that badly," Hanse Till called up. "I'll send Bega for the others. We can lower you down with a rope."

"I'll make it," Shimas said.

"Go slowly, General. We need you alive."

Shimas was nine feet from the ground when his left foot slipped from its purchase. He cried out and reached for an adjacent limb before dropping like dead weight to the ground. He landed on his back.

"General!"

"I'm all right," Shimas grunted. He attempted to sit and collapsed. "No, I'm not. I can't feel my legs. I don't know if I can walk."

"We'll get help," Hanse Till said.

"First you'd better roll me over," Shimas said. "I landed on something that's cutting into me."

"Bega," Hanse Till called, "come here and keep your rifle trained on him."

The other Patrol arrived and took a position ten feet from Shimas. "Go ahead, Lieutenant."

Hanse Till went to his left side, keeping Shimas between him and Bega's rifle. "The other way," Shimas said. "My right side has to be elevated."

"Agreed." After Bega shifted to a position behind Shimas's head, Hanse Till crossed around Shimas and attempted to push him over, toward the tree. "You're a large man, General. It took four of us to carry you from your ship. You'll have to help me."

"Here," Shimas said. He raised his right arm and put it around Till's shoulder. "I'll count to four," he said, "and we'll push together. One . . . two . . . three . . . four!" At the last count Shimas gripped Till's head from the top, his wide fingers digging into the recess below the lieutenant's eyebrows. A backward pull snapped Hanse Till's upper spine cleanly apart.

Shimas was on his feet in a fraction of a second, charging Bega with Till's corpse thrust ahead of him as a shield. The Patrol fired once, threw the rifle at Shimas's legs, and turned to run. Shimas overtook him within ten paces and leapt onto Bega's back. The smaller man screamed, and was dead before his legs folded and collapsed beneath him.

Shimas returned to the tree and bent over the tiny, face-down body of Ren. She was breathing in shallow gasps, her right arm curled beneath her. The rifle's beam had burned a narrow hole through her left shoulder. Her clothing was torn over numerous abrasions along her right side.

"She's alive," Shimas called up to the boys. "We're going to find my people. Hurry, before more Patrol arrives."

To his astonishment, Seth jumped from his perch. Shimas caught the boy and set him down just as Heth launched himself. When they were both safely on the ground, Shimas examined Ren more carefully, probing gently for broken bones and then moving her onto her back. He lifted her eyelids to check for pupil dilation. Satisfied, he took her in his arms and stood up slowly.

"You're bleeding again," Heth said.

"Then we'd better get started," Shimas replied.

"I'll run ahead and look for more Patrol," Seth called out, turning to lead the way. "Heth, stay with Buto Shimas and protect him and Ren." Three seconds later he was gone from sight, disappearing silently into the foliage.

Heth came to stand close to Shimas and looked up. "Buto Shimas, is Ren going to die too?"

"No," Shimas said. "I promise you she won't."

The small boy smiled and touched Shimas's leg. "You're not as tall as my father, but I think you're stronger. I'll find us things to eat on the way."

Four hours later Shimas walked into the clearing that had held the shuttle. In each of his hands was the neck of a

Patrol, both men struggling to maintain their balance as they were half pushed and half carried backward. "Where is Boothe LawNis Regent?" he demanded. "I want to talk with her."

Startled, the large woman spun around to face him. Behind her were Ten and Mill. "You're General Shimas?" Regent asked.

"Yes. Where is my family?"

"Most of them are looking for you," Regent said. "Let those two go before you hurt them."

"What do you mean, 'most'? Who's still here, and where are they?" He heard an answering voice from far to his right.

"Dad! Are you all right?"

Shimas looked, but could not see Jarred until he emerged from the treeline. Martin was just behind him. The two ran across the clearing. "Mom and Dane and Sato are out in the shuttle," Jarred said. "Regent and her Patrol are helping us, Dad."

"I don't trust Patrol," Shimas said.

"Nor do we trust you," Regent said. "But for now we have little choice but to pretend. Now, please let them go."

Jarred nodded. Shimas released the two. Each man was unsteady on his feet, but not hurt. "There are three small children with me," he said. "One of them has been wounded. Do you have a doctor here?"

"Yes," Regent said. "I'm a physician. Where is this child?"

"I'll get her."

Shimas walked back into the woods and carried Ren into the clearing. Seth and Heth walked at his side. Regent met them and took Ren from Shimas's arms. "What happened to her?"

"Your Patrol," Shimas said through clenched teeth. "One of them shot this little girl through the back. She was twenty feet up in a tree, Regent. She fell."

"It must have been an accident."

"No, it wasn't," Seth said. "They killed our brother Rol and they tried to kill her too."

"Are you good Patrol, or bad Patrol?" Heth asked.

Regent looked at the three of them, and then at Ren. "Spacers lie," she said to Shimas.

"Then believe these children," Shimas said.

"I'll take care of her," Regent responded, eyebrows arched. "With luck she'll be recovered by the time you decide to kill her. Along with these boys, and everyone else on Canopal."

"That's not true!" Heth screamed. "Buto Shimas wouldn't hurt Ren! He said she wasn't going to die! He promised!"

"Did you?" Regent challenged, matching Shimas's furious glare. "Did you say that?"

Shimas spun on his heels and stamped away. "Jarred!" he called over his shoulder. "Do we have a radio unit here?"

"Yes, sir."

"Call your mother and tell her where I am."

"Yes, sir. But Dane is in command now."

"I don't care *who's* in command. Call her!"

Before Shimas said a word about his shredded uniform or the new bandages he wore, before he explained who the children were, Dane knew. For eight years, tracking him often, manipulating and influencing him to the extent of her Stem training, pleading with him as a daughter, she had tried to reach his mind and soul. She knew, the moment she saw him enter the shuttle followed by two wide-eyed little boys, that he'd been reached. She embraced him and then broke away, running down the shuttle steps and into the woods, where she sat down and wept.

When she returned, Buto was in a new uniform. Jenny sat beside him in the passenger compartment. The two were laughing while Sato tried to instruct the boys in proper etiquette as they ate, filling their mouths as fast as their small hands could move. "Your water doesn't taste like anything,'' Seth said, swallowing. ''But everything else is good.'' They were freshly bathed, each wearing a uniform of Sato's that had been cut short at the arms and legs. Even with the alterations, their small bodies looked as if they were wearing cloth bags.

Shimas looked up at Dane and smiled. His smile faded as she turned and ran back down the steps. ''What's wrong with her?'' he asked.

Jenny shrugged, drawing her arm tighter around her husband's shoulders.

''Then you would classify the Grounders as hostile?'' Trikal asked.

''No, Generals,'' Shimas replied. He was in the pilot's seat. Next to him, Dane listened. ''I believe 'distrustful' is more accurate. The only difficulty we've encountered is transportation.''

''Please explain.''

Shimas had never lied to a superior officer. He found it surprisingly easy. What disturbed him was that the comm patch was through *Alee*, leaving Kay-Raike free to monitor the conversation. ''We had trouble with the shuttle,'' he said. ''It's repaired now, but our liaison here has advised that flying near their central city is forbidden. It's just turning night here, Generals, and because of wild beasts in the area, the local terrain cannot be safely traversed without sunlight. We plan to take groundcars tomorrow.''

''How much more time do you require?'' Depluss asked.

''I request five days,'' Shimas said, ''in addition to the three originally authorized.''

''Wait.''

Two minutes later, the reply came. ''Very well,'' Trikal said. ''I will allow it. Six days from now you are to be aboard *Alee*, preparing your final report. But, Shimas, don't ask again for more time to complete a simple assignment. Your presence is required on the council.''

''I understand, Generals. Thank you.''

The patch was ended, followed by Karnas Kay-Raike's

voice. "General Shimas, may I ask if your discussion with the Generals will affect our mission here?"

"Weren't you listening, Kay-Raike?"

"Sir, that is an unnecessary insult."

"Very well, I apologize. I'll confine myself to the necessary ones. The answer to your question is yes. We will remain down here for an additional five days, if necessary."

"I see."

"Have you had recent contact with that unidentified ship?"

"No, sir. I've had twenty of my ships conducting a patterned search of the system. The intruder has either gone or shut down on one of the planets. Would it be possible to speak with Mendel?"

"Not at this time, Kay-Raike. He's outside on sentry."

"*Outside?* Is my brother being punished, sir?"

"No. We will all stand outside duty. Mendel is merely first."

"Why do you need sentries, if the Grounders aren't . . ." Shimas laughed. Another "mistake." "Why do you need sentries, sir?"

"Wild beasts, Kay-Raike. It's always best to be prepared for them."

"I understand. Would you relay a message to my brother?"

"Go ahead."

"Please tell Mendel that Dorothy is not feeling well. There appears to be nothing to worry about, but she asked me to tell him that she misses him and looks forward to his return. We both regret that he cannot send a direct response to this message."

"I'll tell him."

"Thank you, sir."

Shimas broke the connection. "Satisfactory, Commander?"

"Yes, Buto," Dane said.

"You were saying that you planned to leave the shuttle with Mendel while we're in the city. I'd advise instead that we bring him with us. Jarred can stay aboard.''

"Why, sir?''

"I want Mendel and Martin to see that city,'' Shimas said. "Maybe they're less Kay-Raike than Karnas is.'' He looked at her, and scowled. "Dane, what is *wrong* with you today?''

"It's nothing, sir. The air here causes my eyes to water.''

"Do you agree with my recommendations?''

"Yes, I do.''

"Good. I'm going to sleep now.'' He stood and walked toward the passenger compartment. "Good night, Dane.''

"Good night, Dad.''

⇛19⇚

Day 55

"That was the entire message? Are you sure, Martin?"

"Yes, sir. 'Please tell Mendel that Dorothy is not feeling well. There appears to be nothing to worry about, but she asked me to tell him that she misses him and looks forward to his return. We both regret that he cannot send a direct response to this message.' That was all. I hope everything is all right, sir."

"What? Oh, I'm sure it is."

"I didn't know that you had married, sir."

"You've lived apart from us for eight years, Martin. Help me up." Mendel extended a hand and allowed the younger man to pull him to his feet. "This uniform will never be clean again," he said disgustedly, brushing away loose soil. Four hours before dawn the sky was clear, presenting a wreath of stars in unfamiliar formations directly overhead and above the circular treeline that defined the clearing. "There have been those clicking sounds there, and there," Mendel said, pointing to two sections of the forest. "I assume they were made by the 'jummers' General Shimas spoke about."

"Yes, sir. Apparently the clicking is an organic radar. They can run at full speed through complete darkness, but their eyes are always ready to react to light. Isn't that fascinating?"

"Yes, yes," Mendel said impatiently. "Our area of responsibility extends from there," he said, pointing again, "to there." His hands bracketed the northeastern quadrant. "Regent's people are watching over the rest."

"I'm ready to relieve you, sir."

"I stand relieved."

Mendel had gone two paces when Martin said, "Sir, may I ask you something?"

"Yes."

"I've been watching Jarred with Generals Marsham and Shimas. And then those three Grounder children, who probably don't have parents now. I've come to a decision."

"Be quick, Martin. I'm tired."

"When we get back to *Alee*, would you speak for me? I want to transfer back aboard."

"*What?* Are you *insane*?"

"He's my father, sir. As much as we disagree, I'd like to be with him again."

Mendel's surge of resentment was so powerful he nearly struck the young man. Eight years ago Martin had been given freedom from Karnas Kay-Raike; that was the one gift Mendel himself coveted above all others. To gain it, he was prepared to assassinate a council member and his family. The risks were daunting: To fail his brother was death. To succeed was also death, if the Fleet had the barest suspicion that he was involved in the assassinations. But taken in perspective those were minor considerations, compared to what complete victory would bring: a life with Dorothy, who was everything to him, and their child. And freedom from the malignant beast that fate had cast as his brother. What kind of fool would throw away such a precious gift? But he could not refuse Martin's request. If Karnas were to learn that he had . . . yes, he thought bitterly, death; everything about Karnas Kay-Raike meant death. "What do you want me to say?"

"Tell him that I'm loyal, and that I never believed the rumors that he killed my mother. Tell him that I haven't said a word about our first attack here."

"Think about that, Martin. Do you really want me to remind Karnas Kay-Raike that you're a potential threat to him? He knows he can control every man, woman, and child on his ships. But he may not be as confident about you."

"He'd never harm me, sir, but I understand your point. That's why I'm asking you to intercede. You know him better than I do. You'll know what to say."

"Martin, you haven't seen . . . You don't know . . ."

"I know some of it, sir. But he wants to change. He told me he's loyal to the Generals, and only wants the opportunity to prove it."

"You *believe* him?"

"Yes, I do. And I know that he's going to face trouble if Council Member Shimas finds what he's looking for."

"Do you believe he will?"

"If he does, my father will need me beside him. I'm determined to join him, sir, with or without your help."

"I see." Mendel clasped his hands behind his back and stared at the younger man, hoping to create or find a trace of indecision that he could exploit. Finding none, he abruptly turned toward the woods. The darkness there was suddenly, oddly, compelling. It was a savage and alien place, where a real person could not survive for long. But at that moment it seemed the only possible escape from the new trap this foolish boy had inadvertently built around him. Now that they had been attacked by Grounders, Mendel was free to carry out Karnas's instructions. He was having difficulty formulating a plan because those instructions included the death of Martin—but he wanted the boy to live. Martin was not his brother's biological son, but his own.

The death of Martin's mother during the Battle had had nothing to do with Enemy action. In a moment of anger she had, correctly, accused Karnas of sending fifteen clan ships into a skirmish and then, in fear, failing to support them. Fortunately for Mendel, his brother's rage had been so overwhelming that he'd killed her quickly. She'd neither been tortured nor given the opportunity to speak—and therefore had not confessed, or taunted her murderer with the truth about Martin. Vivian Kay-Raike had been a courageous woman whom Mendel remembered with more respect than affection. Their one coupling had not been the result of mutual desire; it was a spontaneous act, an attempt by both of them to strike back at the man who even then dominated their lives.

Mendel had hoped to kill the others in a way that would leave Martin believing that Grounders had done it. Karnas might then agree to let him live, as a witness who could undergo interrogation and say what needed to be said. But now . . . The boy was asking for the fate that Karnas meted out to those closest to him; first kill the spirit, and then the mind, and eventually the body. Saving him from that, even if it meant taking his life, could only be seen as an act of mercy. But there was another possibility: Keep Martin alive as he had hoped, and tell him the truth. Mendel rejected the idea. Inevitably, Karnas would learn everything.

His options were limited; a quick death for Martin, or torture and death for both of them. As Mendel pondered his dilemma, he realized that the dark woods were indeed the solution to this trap. But not in the impulsive way he had thought just moments before.

"All right," he said, facing the boy again. "After we get back, I'll speak for you." And he would, but probably not soon. Mendel believed in ultimate justice; someday, perhaps years from now, Karnas Kay-Raike would find the hand of destiny tearing at his throat. At that moment Mendel would whisper in his ear that the "son" he'd murdered, the only one he would ever have, had loved him. Had begged for the opportunity to be reunited with him.

"Thank you, sir."

"There's no need for that," Mendel said. Along with the regret that he would never come to know this young man came a sense of relief. Martin had condemned himself. There was nothing he could do to change that; and so he was now free to act. The first message about Dorothy—and their child, if that part was true—was a reminder to Mendel that they were hostages to his performance. This last one told him that Karnas was becoming impatient. *"We both regret that he cannot send a direct response to this message."* How clear could it be? Very well, then. There *was* a response he could send that would reassure his brother.

Now, before his resolve failed.

Mendel returned to the shuttle and assured himself that everyone was asleep. Entering one of the lavatories, he locked the door behind him and went to work. From a compartment within his new prosthetic he withdrew a small hand weapon and a tool kit.

Seventeen minutes later, he approached Martin and offered him the weapon. "I forgot to leave this with you," he said.

Martin took a step backward. "Sir, those are against regulations, except when conducting supply runs. Even then, they have to be specifically authorized."

Waving away the objection, Mendel said, "Your posting here is to protect the shuttle and the people in it. We know that if the hostile Patrol attacks, they won't hesitate to kill you. It is your duty to live long enough to warn the rest of us. A ridiculous regulation is not an excuse for failure, Martin. Not to a Kay-Raike."

"I understand, sir."

"Good. Have you practiced with one of these before?"

"Not since I was a boy, sir. But I remember how to use it."

"This," Mendel pointed out, "is the safety switch. When you go into the woods, slide it forward. If you hear jummers, fire toward them. I did that myself, and they didn't come anywhere near me. Also, don't use the lantern in the woods, or you'll make yourself a target for any hostile Patrol. If you think you hear them, don't shoot and don't go looking for them. Come back and alert us immediately.''

"That's the second time you've mentioned the forest, sir. Dane's instructions were to remain within the clearing at all times.''

"That,'' Mendel replied, "is because she has no experience with security. Regent's people are patrolling *their* areas, aren't they?''

"I wasn't aware of that.''

"Of course they are. Even Grounders know better than to sit passively and wait to be attacked. As a Kay-Raike, you should understand that instinctively.''

"You're right, sir. I'm sorry. But shouldn't we have Dane's authorization? I'm sure she'd understand the need.''

Mendel shook his head, sighing. "If that were so, she'd have ordered it already. I went in once an hour because it was *my* watch, and *my* responsibility to protect the rest of you. I don't need a Grounder's permission to do what any fool can see is necessary. But you're not under my orders, Martin, and I'm tired of your arguments. Do as you see fit.''

Martin accepted the pistol and then snapped to attention, eyes narrowed and jaw set with determination. "I'm my father's son, sir. I'll go in *twice* an hour.''

"It's up to you,'' Mendel said. He turned and walked away, absolved.

Dawn was still an hour away when Mendel returned to find the sentry post deserted. From the north, faintly, he heard the characteristic clicking and the throaty rumble of jummers. He was startled by the sound of footsteps behind him. He turned, part of him relieved, expecting to see Martin.

"Good morning, sir,'' Jarred said.

"Jarred . . . Where is my nephew, Lieutenant?" he demanded. "He was ordered to remain here."

"I don't know, sir. I left the shuttle just now, to relieve him early."

"Then he can't be aboard," Mendel said. "But where else could he be? You're faster than I am, Jarred. Take a run around the ship and see if he's in sight."

"Yes, sir."

Three minutes later Jarred returned to report, "I didn't find him, sir."

"Very well. We'll have to assume he's been taken by hostile Patrol. I'll begin the search there," he said, pointing northward. "You go back aboard and alert the others. Tell them which direction I've taken, to avoid overlapping our efforts."

"Yes, sir."

With a portable light to illuminate the way, Mendel followed the sound of jummers thirty yards into the woods. He found Martin face down beside a fallen tree. Unseen animals paced the undergrowth and cried menacingly, warning him away from their feast. He took care to move slowly and to keep his eyes from what remained of the boy. Finally he located the pistol whose insulation he'd removed, causing it to deliver a paralyzing shock upon activation. He slid the switch to the safe position and began a slow walk away from the beasts. Ten yards from the clearing he stopped to bury the weapon, and at that moment heard voices. In the chaos of trees and undergrowth, he could not determine their direction or distance. He bent and quickly replaced it inside his prosthetic leg. And then, running unsteadily toward the shuttle, he called out, "Here! Here, I've found him! We need a doctor, fast!. Someone get Regent!"

Twelve minutes later, Regent said, "There's no need to approach him any closer. You can all see as well as I can." She turned the light away from Martin. "I'm sorry, Mendel. Your nephew is dead."

"Then so am I," Mendel replied, looking at the ground

and turning back toward the shuttle. "It was my job to protect him." He said over his shoulder, "I'll get blankets and wrap . . . a father shouldn't see his son like this."

"Buto Shimas, Buto Shimas."

"Shhh," Shimas whispered, bending down to remove Seth's hand from his trouser leg. "We're not supposed to talk. We have to show respect."

"Yes, sir. But I want to go down now. I don't like this place."

"We'll be back on land soon," Sato said quietly. "There's nothing to be afraid of."

Holding the recovering Ren, Dane watched Karnas Kay-Raike glaring at her and the four children from the other side of a gray metal box. His face was twisted in grief—or a good mask, she thought. Beside him at attention stood Mendel, who was making no effort to wipe away the tears coursing down his cheeks and disappearing into his beard.

Jarred spoke briefly for Martin before the Marshams and the three children of Canopal left the Kay-Raikes alone in *Alee*'s airlock. Jenny had asked for a moment alone with Karnas after the ceremony. She despised the man, but she understood his grief.

"There is nothing to discuss," he'd said. "Except that I question your leaving him alone outside, knowing that he was vulnerable to hostile Grounders and deadly beasts."

"I don't know why he wandered off," Jenny replied. "He was safe near the shuttle. Mendel assured me that he stressed to Martin how important it was to remain there."

"That," Karnas said, "is the only reason Mendel is alive at this moment. Part of the fault is yours, and part is mine. I should have kept the boy with me all these years, and trained him properly. You should not have given him an assignment he was not qualified to undertake. But the real blame lies with that world. It killed two of my crews, and now it has killed my precious son."

"I am sorry. I liked Martin, very much. He was a fine young man."

"He was that and more, General Marsham. He was the future of our clan. But he's gone now, isn't he? After my son has been committed to space, I'd like all of you to return to your shuttle and wait there for Mendel. I'm asking as a father who wants and deserves justice. Please return to Canopal and complete your assignment."

After the seven of them were gone, the box carrying the remains of Martin Kay-Raike was propelled into space while Karnas and Mendel watched from outside the airlock.

"His sacrifice was for the future of all of us," Karnas said. "My son will be remembered as a hero of the clan."

"Yes, sir, he will." Uncertain about Karnas's reaction now that the boy was dead, Mendel said again, "I had nothing to do with what happened, sir. It was a genuine accident."

"Why are you repeating yourself? And what difference does that make?"

"None, I suppose. May I see Dorothy before I go?"

"She's resting," Karnas said. "Her health is still not what it should be."

"Just for a moment?"

"No. When your work is complete, you'll have the rest of your lives together, aboard your own ship. And you will be free of me. Isn't that what you've always wanted, Brother? Isn't that enough? Or have you decided to demand more?"

"Of course not, sir."

"Good. Martin died at a good time. Now we have a few minutes alone."

"Sir?"

"You don't have a comprehensive plan yet, do you?"

"I'm considering a number of possibilities, sir."

"As I thought. Tell me how the Grounders are reacting to Shimas and the rest of his party. Do they trust them? Are they divided in their reactions?"

When Mendel was finished, Karnas smiled. "It couldn't be better. Now listen very carefully."

●   ●   ●

As Shimas piloted the vessel back to the clearing north of the River Complex, he keyed the intercom and asked Dane to come forward. When she was strapped in beside him, he asked, "I'm still unclear as to why you insisted that the children accompany us aboard *Alee*. Would you explain?"

"There were a number of reasons," Dane answered. "First, they asked. I thought it was reasonable that since Kay-Raike invaded their world, they might invade his."

"At the funeral service of his only son?"

"That was another factor. They lost their parents and their brother but have never had a ceremony that would allow them to say good-bye. I believe that their imaginations will link what they've just seen with what they've lost. It will help them reach a closure."

"I see. I'm still curious, though. You must have known how their presence would upset Kay-Raike. Was that part of your motivation, to add to his pain?"

Dane's inclination was to say, *What* pain? She understood the two Kay-Raikes sufficiently to interpret their movements, expressions, and tonality under extreme stress. She was certain that Karnas felt nothing but the need to project anguish. That was not unexpected. But Mendel had surprised her. His every nuance pointed toward a genuine sense of loss far deeper than seemed appropriate for a young man he'd rarely seen, and who was the son of a brother he feared and hated. There was something else in Mendel that puzzled Dane: remorse, as if he had been somehow responsible for Martin disobeying orders. Karnas Kay-Raike may have made such an accusation. But to accept it as valid was out of place in a man she judged to be sane. "No," she said. "It wasn't."

"I asked because I've never known anyone more deserving of hatred than Karnas Kay-Raike. But at the same time, I've never known anyone more incapable of that emotion than you. It was an interesting juxtaposition. If I offended you, I apologize."

"No, Dad," Dane replied, wishing within part of herself that he and Jenny understood her better. "You didn't offend me."

⇒ 20 ⇐

Day 56

Momed Pwanda lay at ease beneath an ersatz sky seven feet above him. Recreated with remarkable accuracy from descriptions he'd given Marana Beviney, it perfectly captured a warm and listless late afternoon on the equatorial plains of his native Pan'Omo. Sun One hung heavy and fertile, golden above the broad reach of the distant, violet-hazed Koomer Mountains. Just now rising twenty-three degrees to the south was her tiny and coquettish consort of poem and song, Sun Two. On this night he would begin his approach to her, only to shy away five days later and hide until the winter solstice. Then he would return, to begin once more the eternal cycle of life. This was the vista his parents had presented to him at the end of his eighth day of life, when he had received a name. He had no conscious memory of the event. But a painting of it adorned his bedroom wall during all of his childhood and years at the university.

"We'll go back to Pan'Omo for the original painting," Marana Beviney said, nestling his head on her lap. Her fingers massaged his temples in a slow rhythm as she watched his eyes move from one feature to another.

"That would be nice," Momed said, covering her hands with his. "When?"

"When we can present it to our first child." She still could not bring herself to look at the disturbing simulation for very long. Nor could she believe that as of nine hours ago, the handsome face she watched so happily was that of her husband. This was the first formal union between one of her people and a Dirt . . . NO! He was above that now . . . in the history of the Gold Fleet. By the Nomarch's agreement, the precedent could not be repeated without her direct authorization, which she did not intend to grant. But who knew? If there were other men and women out there as skilled in life and love as Momed Pwanda, why not use them as rewards for her own officers?

"Yes," Momed said in a half-whisper. He had spent a lifetime studying emotion—its signs, effects, and manipulation. But no amount of study and field experience had prepared him for the now-total union with Marana. Never had he felt so content, invincible, and fulfilled. "Yes," he repeated. "That will be nice."

"Sleep well, husband."

He sat up and spun his body around to face her, laughing. "Sleep? Already? You must be joking."

"Oh, I was," Marana replied, also laughing. She leaned forward and placed her hands on his hips. "I was, I was."

I don't know if I can control her, Momed thought as he returned the embrace and lifted Marana onto his lap. *But is that important? Her love for me is as total as mine for her. We are one person now. And so she'll keep her promises about Dane and The Stem.*

The three groundcars were packed tightly with Regent's people and those from the Silver Fleet. As they wound single file along a narrow dirt road toward the City of Dreams,

Jarred piloted the shuttle over them once in a low salute and then shot his craft skyward. He banked sharply and set in a course toward the ocean, where he would wait alone to be called.

In the middle car, Ren and Heth sat on Shimas's legs while Seth pushed back comfortably against Jenny and promptly fell asleep. In the seat ahead of them, Dane sat against the door while the ample Regent drove. Sato was squeezed between them. On the roof were Ten and Mill. Neither cared for cramped quarters, and both considered themselves superior lookouts.

Atop each of the vehicles, two Patrol with shoulder weapons lay at the ready. The third car in line carried the supplies for both groups crammed into the rear seat. In the front, Mendel rode with Poda Nem. He was relieved to be away from the others, especially Dane, for a while. Although she'd been subtle about it, he was certain that she had been watching him closely since their return from *Alee*. But she'd listened and agreed when he explained to her that he needed to be as alone with his grief as the travel arrangements allowed. He considered it a good piece of luck that he was assigned with Poda Nem, who seemed less hostile than the other Patrol.

Mendel watched the closely spaced trees pass by the window as he shifted continually to find a comfortable position in the jolting vehicle. He attributed every movement in the woods to jummers, each a reminder of Martin's last moments. Had the boy suffered? Did the shock kill him immediately? Or was he conscious when the beasts began tearing at his flesh? Mendel forced himself to forget about Martin and concentrate on the plan Karnas had given him. It was dangerous, but he admitted that it was more likely to succeed than anything he'd thought of. He decided to start with the small man seated to his left.

As Mendel opened his mouth to speak, Nem's voice startled him. "Want some of this?"

"What did you say?"

"I asked if you want some." Mendel turned to see the

man holding a black cube in his hand. "It's chew," Nem explained. "It keeps you from getting hungry, thirsty, or tired. And it tightens you up down below so you won't need to go into the woods for a while. Go ahead, it's a long trip."

"How long?"

"Anywhere from five to twelve hours. It depends. There's a settlement three quarters of the way to the city, and it's possible that renegade Patrol will be waiting for us there. I suppose Regent will have us detour around it. That would mean leaving the road, so it's hard to guess. You want some, or not?"

"Thank you, but no," Mendel said. He knew what a road was supposed to be, and was dismayed to hear the word applied to the rough ground they were traveling over. He couldn't imagine, and didn't want to, what "leaving the road" would bring. It occurred to him that the modified pistol could be jarred into activation, or the hidden radio could be damaged. But there was nothing he could do about that now without arousing the curiosity of Poda Nem.

After a few minutes he said, "Nem, what do you think of all this?"

"It's beautiful," Nem replied. "When we retire, my wife and I are going to build a cabin in a place like this. The children will be grown by then, but we hope they'll come out with us. I never did care for crowded settlements and all the noise that—"

"I meant us," Mendel interrupted. "What do you think about us being here?"

Nem shrugged, chewing thoughtfully. "I don't think about it very much," he said. "That ruins thinking about retirement and the cabin. And the children, and then someday their children. I guess what I'd like is for this to be over, and for you spacers to go away. As friends, I mean."

"That won't happen," Mendel said.

Nem glanced at him, then away as the groundcar wheeled into a rut. Fighting it back out, he asked, "What do you mean? Regent says your Generals told her that if they can prove we were attacked first, we'll be safe.''

"Yes," Mendel said. "I know she said that." He turned away, giving Nem time to ponder what he'd said. A beast he couldn't identify broke from the foliage and ran parallel to the car. It was long and graceful, brown with white stripes, with what appeared to be two bones protruding from its forehead. As Mendel was wondering what threat it might pose, the beast's side exploded in red. It stumbled and pitched forward, tumbling end over end until it came to a halt. Poda Nem gave two blasts on the vehicle's horn and applied the brakes. The vehicles ahead stopped also. Mendel watched as two Patrol leapt from the groundcar's roof. Between them they put the dead beast in a large bag and carried it back up to the roof. Nem honked again, and the convoy resumed its slow pace.

"Was it dangerous?" Mendel asked.

"No," Nem said. "It's dinner. What did you mean before? About you spacers not leaving as friends."

"We will certainly leave," Mendel said. "But we'll never be friends. Nem, I'm going to tell you something that even Regent doesn't know. My brother Karnas commands the ships surrounding Canopal. It is he who will decide whether those ships leave you intact, or destroy this world. He is not interested in anything Generals Shimas and Marsham may find. All that concerns him is your ability to fight back."

"I don't think I understand you."

Mendel thought for a moment and said, "Suppose that beast just now *had* been dangerous, and strong enough to overcome these vehicles if attacked."

"You mean, like a tark?"

"If you say so. What would you have done?"

"We'd have left it alone and hoped for the best."

"But because it was an easy kill, it is now dinner. My brother feels the same way about Canopal. It was he who ordered the original attack here. Do you understand now?"

"Then you spacers have been lying all along," Nem said

angrily, the fear in his eyes unmistakable. "The Provisional Patrol was right."

"No. Your renegades wanted to use us as hostages to bargain for their safety. That is a sure course to suicide. Secondly, Generals Shimas and Marsham believe what they've told you. But my brother is also a renegade, against the Fleet. Whatever proof they bring back won't matter. The very fact that you allow them to return will prove to him that you're weak, and afraid of us."

"And then he'll attack again?"

"Yes. And this time he won't stop."

"But your Fleet would punish him, wouldn't they?"

Mendel shook his head sadly. "You don't understand us at all, Nem, and I'm truly sorry that you don't. Once the others in my party demonstrate to Karnas that you're defenseless, he'll kill them all and destroy whatever they've found. The second thing he'll do is begin the attack on Canopal. The Fleet leadership won't punish him because it knows he would never surrender to authority. My brother has many allies. Going after him would bring about an internal war that neither side wants."

"That doesn't make sense. How can your leadership maintain discipline if—"

"I'm sorry to say it, Nem, but judged against keeping order in my Fleet, your world is a trivial matter. No one will go to war to protect it or to avenge its destruction. Think of it in your own terms. Regent hasn't ordered you to hunt down your renegade Patrol and execute them, has she?"

"No, of course not. She believes they'll return to us when this crisis is over."

"It's the same with our council. We're alike in many ways, Nem, even if you don't understand us."

"I surely don't. Why would your brother . . . do that to us?"

"Because you humiliated him. Because you killed two of his ships and damaged eight others. Because his only son died here. Because he'll lose the respect of his own officers if he doesn't at least test your strength and resolve. But mostly because the spacers with me are going to prove that he *can*."

Poda Nem was quiet for several minutes. His hands shook at the controls, sending the groundcar from side to side on the road, slamming into ruts the vehicles ahead easily avoided. "Why are you telling me this?" he asked at last.

"Because I've decided to die."

"*What?*"

"Generals Shimas and Marsham and their children are going to be killed. Whether you do it, or my brother does, won't matter to them. The only way *I* can remain alive is to return with them to my ship. And that would mean the death of you, your wife, your children, and every human being on Canopal. My life isn't worth that, Nem. No one's life is worth that much. You have to kill us. It's the only way my brother will believe that you're not afraid of him. If he's uncertain about you, he won't risk his ships again. He'll take them away. As I said before, it won't be as friends. But he'll respect you and he'll be gone. And you'll be alive."

"Until more of your Fleet comes for revenge."

"No. Coming here was Council Member Shimas's idea. His status gave him that right, but our leadership made it clear that the risks are his alone."

"How could we kill him, if he came here to protect us?"

"Nem, you're foolish to trust a spacer. Shimas is not what you think he is."

"What do you mean?"

"Among other things, he personally led a raid on a world called Walden. He ordered the killing of thousands of people there. As you know, Dane is not his true daughter. He took her as a slave on that world. When my brother petitioned the council for permission to come back here, Shimas had no objection because he doesn't care about you, or any world. But then he saw the opportunity to embarrass my brother, and make himself more important in the Fleet. That is why he came to Canopal.''

Nem gripped the wheel and looked straight ahead. "I don't think I like any of you very much," he said at last. "But I still can't believe that your Fleet won't retaliate if we kill a council member."

"One of the things we've learned over centuries of war against the Gold Fleet is to accept casualties when necessary. Particularly when they're caused by a foolish commander acting for purely personal motives, as Shimas is. No more ships will be put at risk here. And that is for the most basic of reasons. You have nothing worth the life of a single ship."

Nem thought about that, and nodded. "But whatever his motive, General Shimas *is* trying to protect us. And so is his family."

"Yes. But there's only one way they *can* protect you. I think you understand that now, don't you?"

"Suppose we just report all of you dead? And confine you until your brother leaves?"

Mendel was ready for the question. "It wouldn't work. As a safety precaution, all spacers assigned to work on planets are implanted with devices that respond to a broadcast signal with the wearer's vital signs. My brother would know we're still alive. But yes, you have to report us dead when it's true. And challenge him to retaliate. He'll be satisfied that he can go no further, and his officers will know that he did all he could without endangering them. That is how things are done in the Fleet. When we see strength, we measure potential loss against gain. When we see weakness, we attack. It's really as simple as that. A demonstration of confidence and defiance is the only way you can defend yourselves."

Nem was perspiring, his breath coming fast and shallow. "I don't know whether to believe you or not," he said. "But if you're willing to die—"

"You don't have to believe me," Mendel said. "Tell Regent, and let her decide."

"Yes! Yes, that's what I'll do."

"Thank you. May I make a suggestion?"

"What?"

"Tell all of your Patrol what I've said. Not just Regent. It's their lives, and their families' lives as well. But I hope you'll agree not to let the other spacers know. When all of you decide as you must, let it be fast and unexpected for them. As you said, maybe it doesn't matter why Shimas came here. But it's certain that the rest of them are sincere. There's no reason to make them suffer."

"You're right. I'm sorry they have to die, but it was your Fleet that started this."

"And tell Regent that I'll answer any questions she has."

Without conscious intent, Poda Nem had accepted Mendel as his superior. "Yes, sir. What about Ten and Mill?"

"What about them? They're your friends. Just keep them out of this, and when they see my brother's ships leaving, they'll thank you. But for my sake, Nem, do it quickly. I'm not a brave man. The sooner this is done, the better for all of us."

"I think you're the bravest person I've ever known," Nem said. He sounded the horn twice, bringing the three vehicles to a halt.

"What are you doing?"

"I'm going to tell Regent that I'm tired of sitting with you, and ask to be reassigned to the first car. That will give me the chance to discuss this with them. Later, we'll find a way to talk with Regent and the other two Patrol riding with her."

"Very well, go ahead." As if an idea had just occurred to him, Mendel added, "Regent is only one person."

"Sir?"

"The fate of every human being on Canopal depends on what you do next. This is too important for one person to decide alone."

It was as Mendel had hoped—as Karnas had predicted. Once the idea of assassination was accepted, a small mutiny wasn't a problem. "You're right again. If we're unanimous, Regent will have to follow *our* orders."

"I know it isn't easy, Nem. But it's the only thing you can do." Mendel smiled reassuringly and looked away. More of the odd, graceful beasts could be seen just inside the woods. They ran parallel to the convoy with no apparent recognition that one of their number had just been sacrificed. Dinner, to keep their hunters strong for the next kill. Typical Grounders. "When you build that cabin," he said, "remember me."

"I will, sir. All of us will."

"Who is the most aggressive among your Patrol?"

Nem grinned. "That's easy. My youngest sister, Poda Sela."

"How does she feel about spacers?"

"She hates you. A lot of the Patrol does."

"And for good reason. Your sister is the one I should talk to next. She's in the lead vehicle?"

"Yes."

"Good. Tell her I'm being a nuisance."

"Yes, sir."

"Could I have some of that chew now? My stomach is—"

"I understand, sir."

There was one flaw in his plan, Mendel thought as Nem left the vehicle. Buto Shimas was not an officer to be taken easily, as two competing factions of armed Patrol had already seen. Leaning over the seat, he quickly found what he wanted and went to work. Now, he told himself, Shimas's prowess will be irrelevant.

Six minutes later, a tall young woman approached the third groundcar. As she slammed the door shut and began driving, she said, "Nem says your snoring was driving him insane, spacer. I'm not like him, and I don't care how tired you are. So stay awake if you don't want to be tied down on the roof."

"I'll use this," Mendel said, opening his hand and showing her the black cube. "Would you like some?"

• • •

Momed Pwanda awoke from a dream of home and was startled to see the familiar vista above him. He was startled again to realize that the sky he saw was a representation, and that he was on the Gold Fleet flagship *Noldron*. Part of his dream had been about his older brothers, Ahken and Murak, whom he had never seen. They were legends in his village, bold and restless young men who'd taken to the skies, never to return, months before Momed was born. The stories about them told of their daring, their defiance of both Fleets as they commanded smuggling operations involving weapons and supplies, and most dangerous of all, ideas, to the local worlds victimized by centuries of war. Momed knew from his parents that the stories were greatly exaggerated; Ahken signed onto the pirate vessel *Sword* as a cook, while Murak, gifted in mathematics, was to study navigation while assisting Ahken in the galley. But the truth did not diminish their courage in Momed's eyes, and he never agreed with his parents' privately held belief that they'd thrown away their lives. When his own opportunity to fight against the war came, he took it without a moment's hesitation. And while he may have accomplished more than his brothers, he knew that they had risked as much as he had. The irony, which struck him as he came fully awake, was that they were heroes at home. He, by contrast, would be remembered by his village as a precocious young man and then a professor of engineering who had unaccountably—unforgivably—severed contact with the people who'd given him everything.

Marana had spoken of visiting Pan'Omo when their first child was born. The idea had delighted him. But in the cold clarity that now overcame him, he faced the question, How could he ever return? He was the son, the cousin, the friend, who had disappeared for a reason he could never tell them. Worse in their eyes, he was now married to the highest-ranking officer in the hated Gold Fleet. First a deserter. Now a traitor.

He looked to his left on the bed, where Marana had slept.

The warmth of her returned, along with the blissful languor of physical and emotional fulfillment that had eased him into sleep. She would be going about her duties now; enthusiastic, efficient, occasionally brilliant. Always ruthless when it came to Fleet operations. But his total empathy with her had unlocked something his years of observation had never identified: a well of kindness, tenderness, compassion. Love. He'd found it in her mind, her touch, her total surrender to the sweet passion that had engulfed them both—giving, wanting so desperately to please.

Momed's professional self knew that he had achieved a prize beyond measure in the centuries-old struggle to contain the Fleets. From the beginning, The Stem had acknowledged that they could not be defeated militarily; change had to be forced from within. Marana could never again become the same cold and dispassionate killer she had been; he would see to that. In the same way, the Fleet she controlled would inevitably change. He would see to that, also. And in the bargain he himself was happier than he had ever been.

Why, then, did he feel such a burden of loss? The only clear answer that came to him was that the home he'd had, the esteem of the village he had so prized, were irrevocably gone. But those were consequences of his work he should have anticipated and then accepted, years ago. Still, there was something else. Momed decided that if it was important, it would come to him. For now he would allow the question to percolate on its own, and reveal itself when the time came to deal with it.

He leapt out of bed and attacked his routine of stretching and calisthenics with a vigor he hadn't felt in years. In the lavatory of the quarters he now shared with Marana he showered and shaved, then returned to the sleeping area to put on a fresh uniform from the still unpacked boxes Marana had ordered brought from his old quarters.

"Oh!" A young supervisor, one of Marana's personal staff, brought her hand to her mouth, then snapped to at-

tention as he entered. "I apologize, No'ln Pwanda! There
was no answer at the door, so I thought—"

Pwanda suppressed a laugh as she blushed and turned to
face away from him. With a towel around his waist and
another over his shoulders, he was informally dressed but
presentable by the standards of most worlds he'd visited.
"That's quite all right, Supervisor. What is it you came
for?"

"I was going to write out a message for you, No'ln
Pwanda. No'ln Beviney is in the Battle Control Center, and
asks you to join her there before the morning meal."

"Please tell her I'll be there in ten minutes."

"Yes, sir."

Minutes later, Pwanda was in the corridor. Everyone he
passed, supervisor, coordinator, or crew, deferred to him
and greeted him politely, by title. As he entered the red-
tinged relative darkness of the Battle Control Center he met
No'ln Bishop, Beviney's second in command, coming out.
For the first time in eight years, the stiff old man smiled at
him. "You're still dressed like a Dirt, Pwanda," he said.
"I'd think you'd have a proper uniform by now."

"You're right, Bishop," Pwanda said, matching his tone.
"See to it personally, would you?"

Before Bishop could reply, Marana saw him and called
out, "Momed!" Obviously on cue, every person in the
compartment came to attention, held the position for three
seconds, and then applauded. Pwanda grinned and gave
them an elaborate bow. He knew that the affection they'd
been ordered to display was genuine in many cases. He'd
worked directly with many of the people here over the
years. And six of the supervisors whose faces he could see
in the dim red lighting had been in this room with him
during the Battle, during which he'd personally directed a
number of successful sorties against the Silver Fleet. Many
believed—and they were correct—that his advice to Beviney had averted a Fleetwide catastrophe. What they did not
know was that he and Dane Steppart had engineered the
catastrophe specifically to prevent it from happening, in a

way that guaranteed balanced and large-scale casualties on both sides. And elevated themselves to positions of prominence within their respective Fleets.

"I wanted to show you something," Marana said, crossing the compartment and taking his hand. She led him to a broad table beneath whose transparent cover was displayed a planetary system. Momed's first impression was that this was his home, Pan'Omo, and that she was about to announce a visit there. But while thinking of a carefully worded argument, he looked more closely. There were eight planets there, the fifth and seventh gas giants, as was true of the bodies revolving around Sun One. But this was not a binary system. The depicted planetary paths were much too regular to allow for the subtle influence of Sun Two.

"You and I are leaving *Noldron* for a while," Marana said. "We're going to relax and enjoy ourselves, and do nothing but have fun. How does that sound, husband?"

Pwanda answered guardedly. He'd never heard her use the word "fun" except to describe combat. But then, she would never leave *Noldron* if an armed conflict were impending. "Uncharacteristic," he said.

"You're right," Marana laughed. "But this is by direct order of the Nomarch. When I spoke to him this morning, he asked me why I looked happy, and what was wrong with me. I told him that *you* made me happy. He said, and I'm quoting, 'Then go away and play with him, and come back when you're normal again.' "

Pwanda had a question, but it could not be asked within the hearing of others. He said, "I think it's wonderful, Marana. Can we discuss it while we eat? I'm famished."

Across a private dining table half an hour later, he said, "Marana, you've never taken time away from your duties. Will this jeopardize your position in the Fleet?"

"Dear, dear husband," Marana said affectionately. "I know my staff, and my fellow No'ln Supervisors. Most are loyal to me to the point of death. Others are questionable, and are here only because they enjoy the favor of the No-

march, or provide exceptional service. The first group is by
far the larger. They'll guard against any challenge to my—
our—authority. I'll brief them in detail before we leave. So
don't worry.'' She put her hand to her lips, and then held
it out to him. ''But your concern is touching. Thank you.''

She was absolutely confident about that, Pwanda saw.
He relaxed and took her hand. ''So tell me, Marana. What's
special about that planetary system you had displayed?''

''That,'' she said, ''is what I meant about having fun.
It's only a day away if we make maximum use of hyperspace. We're taking fifty ships with us, and in accordance
with the Nomarch's orders, we're going to play. Do you
remember asking me about Karnas Kay-Raike?''

Pwanda's expression froze. ''Yes,'' he said.

=≥21≤=

Day 56

I don't know what she has in mind, Dane. Beviney detests Kay-Raike. But she still won't tell me if she's reached some sort of agreement with him. So we're either going to harass him, which could be what she meant by fun, or we're coming to aid in the destruction of Canopal.

Momed, I have to ask a personal question. How close have you gotten to her?

Close, Dane. But there are still things I don't know. If I had your skill in tracking, I could be of more help to you. I'm sorry.

Does she care for you?

Yes, she does.

As you said last time, I'm beginning to pick up the nuances of conversation in this mode. You're being defensive, Momed. I won't ask you why that is, because I know you'll tell me if it's important. My point is that if she cares for you, she'll know how you'd feel about seeing a world torn apart.

Not necessarily. As far as I can determine, she believes that my loyalty is to her personally, and her alone. But she may have doubts.

I see. Then witnessing the destruction of Canopal could be a test of your commitment?

Yes. Also, I'm convinced that she knows you're down there. But of course there's no way I can tell her that *I* know. If she plans to assist Kay-Raike, your death would mean to her that my past is completely severed.

She's jealous that you and I were married?

Yes. Even though she knows that our marriage was a working relationship, and never consummated.

How much have you told her, Momed?

Enough to get the information I needed. Yes, I know, I'm being defensive again. I apologize for that, but for now it's all I'm prepared to say on the subject. But any information you need, I'll give you as soon as I get it. I promise you that.

I trust you, Momed. And I know that I've been asking you for help while giving you none in return. I'll be waiting to hear more. For now, there's a situation developing here that requires my full attention.

Good-bye, then, Dane. We'll reach your system tomorrow. I don't know what to say, except to wish you good luck.

Good-bye. And thank you.

She'd first noticed it hours before, as the convoy crept toward the City of Dreams. Regent had shown no sign that anything was out of the ordinary. But every half hour or so, the vehicles would come to a stop and whoever was driving with Mendel Kay-Raike would be replaced. Even the two lookouts on the roof with Ten and Mill had been rotated. That might be standard procedure, but those emerging from the third groundcar glanced toward Dane or the others in her party with expressions that varied from worry to fear, to unconcealed hatred.

She knew, by exchanging looks with Jenny and Buto,

that her adoptive parents had also noted the pattern. The situation became clear when the two Patrol atop the first car turned themselves to face Regent and her passengers.

Shimas said conversationally, "Regent, how well do you know this area?"

"Other than this road, not at all," Regent replied. "Why do you ask?"

"Have you ever commanded a Patrol unit before?"

"No, not directly. General, is there a point to your questions?"

"She doesn't know about it," Dane said to Shimas.

"About what?" Regent asked.

"Regent," Jenny said. "You're about to face a mutiny. We need to know right now, before the groundcars stop again. Whose side will you take?"

"What are you all talking about?"

"In a few minutes," Dane said, "sound your horn and stop. Tell the others that Ren's injury has opened again and that she can't go on for a while. Order them to continue ahead, and make sure the way is clear."

"But why—"

"They'll argue," Dane continued, "but they'll leave us if you're firm with them. After a while they'll stop and decide among themselves what to do. By the time they come back for us, we'll be a good distance from here."

Seth bounced on Jenny's knee and asked excitedly, "Are we going to hide again?"

"Yes," Shimas answered.

"But . . ." Regent began. "Are you certain this is necessary?"

"I've commanded troops all of my adult life," Jenny said. "I should have recognized them sooner, but the signs are unmistakable. Now stop the groundcars and give the orders. Otherwise our mission here will be over before it really begins. And you know what that will mean."

Regent sounded the horn twice, and the vehicles ground to a halt. "We'll have to leave the car here," she said. "It won't make it a hundred feet into those woods."

"Never mind," Shimas said. "Once we've found a safe place, we'll call for Jarred and the shuttle."

"But we can't approach the city by air! They'll—"

"We'll find a way," Dane said. "Please, get out of the car and give the orders. Don't allow them the opportunity to speak first, or time to think about what's happening. They don't want to hurt you, Regent. That's our only advantage right now."

Regent looked at the faces around her, and made her decision. She left the car and strode purposefully to the first vehicle in line, gesturing for the occupants to remain inside.

Dane and her party watched as the large woman bent to speak directly into the car's open window, punctuating her commands with animated arm movements.

"Good," Dane said. And then, to her amazement, Regent reached into the vehicle and pulled a man out through the window. She held him a foot off the ground by his uniform blouse, bellowing loudly into his face.

"I don't understand a word of that," Shimas said, chuckling. "Except that his name is Taro Peth. It must be colorful invective, though. I've never seen a face turn that shade of red."

"No, Dad," Sato said with a laugh. "I think that's purple."

Regent tossed Taro Peth onto the vehicle's roof and pointed to one of the Patrol who'd ridden there as guard. Immediately the man jumped to the ground and gave her his rifle, then opened the car door and got in. The other Patrol on the roof passed Regent her weapon, as well. With a final shout, Regent pointed to the road ahead. The vehicle jolted to a start and resumed its customary pace.

"Here," Regent said as she approached Dane's car. She thrust the weapons through the window.

"We'll need the radios," Dane said. "They're in a small red bag in the third car."

Regent nodded and continued on.

"Mendel must have started this, Dane," Sato said. "Shouldn't we kill him?"

Dane winced. "No. They've obviously accepted him as their leader. So they won't leave him behind, and he can't travel fast. He'll slow them down."

"I suppose you're right," Sato replied.

"She's exactly right," Jenny said. "Sato, killing your enemy is not always the best way to win. Think before you speak, and think twice before you act."

The third vehicle edged past them on the narrow road. At a shouted order from Regent, the two Patrol atop Dane's car jumped onto the other as it followed after the first. Mendel Kay-Raike was slouched down, only the top of his head visible. "Hiding," Shimas observed. "As if we'd forget about him." When Regent joined them again, he said, "Nicely done. You'd have made a fine Fleet officer."

"And you'll suffer for that remark," Regent said. "But yes, I did do well, didn't I?"

Ten jumped down from the roof. "Would someone tell me what we're doing?" he asked.

As the two vehicles ahead disappeared around a bend in the road, Dane stepped out of the car. "We're going to hide until Jarred can pick us up," she told him. "You and Mill should stay here. The Patrol is coming back for us soon, but they don't have any reason to harm you. Regent, I think you'd be safe here, also."

"That sounds reasonable," Ten said. "We're not forest people. But what about Seth, and Ren, and Heth?"

"They'd better come with us," Regent said. "It hurts me even to think about it, but they could be taken hostage because of the spacers' affection for them."

"You're going?" Ten asked. "Why?"

"Because these people are my responsibility," Regent answered. "And they'll need me when we reach the city."

"They'll need us as well," Mill said, jumping down to stand beside her husband. "That's why we came along, remember? We're going too."

Seth, Ren, and Heth spilled out of the car, followed by Sato. "We'll go that way," Seth said, pointing westward.

"Seth," Regent said, "that way is all uphill. My legs aren't as young as yours."

"Uphill means we might find some caves to hide in. Heth," he said, turning to his brother, "you go in the lead. Ren, Buto Shimas will have to carry you. Don't let these people make a mess. I'll stay behind and make a false trail for the Patrol to follow. Sato, I think you're strong enough to help. Do you want to come with me?"

"Yes!"

"I don't think that's a good idea," Jenny said worriedly.

Shimas disagreed. "These children know the woods better than you know engines. He'll be fine."

"Is what I said all right with you, Dane?" Seth asked.

"Yes," she replied. "You three are the experts here. I'm glad you're with us."

Regent gave Dane the red bag and took the rifles out of the car. She kept one, and gave the other to Ten. "There's nothing else here that's useful to us," she said to Dane. "Are we all ready?"

Dane nodded, and Heth ran into the brush alongside the road. "Let's go!" he called back.

"Slowly, child," Regent said quietly. "Please."

⇻22⇺

Day 57

Flagship Sovereign

"You've heard my thoughts," Tabba Depluss said. "What are yours?"

"Yvonne Tillic and Merrill Rhodes are gone and not yet replaced," Mosh Trikal said. Attached to him by their common arm, Depluss nodded. Surrounding the Generals was a curtain of silver light, opaque and soundproof. "With Buto Shimas away," Trikal continued, "the council numbers six. But despite the even number, I find it inexcusable that they can't render a majority recommendation. And worse, they've added nothing what you and I have already discussed."

Depluss nodded again, disturbed that Trikal found it necessary to state the obvious. She'd known him for more than thirty years, far longer than they'd been joined. Decisiveness had been one of his foremost qualities. But twice in

227

the past months when they'd been divided on a question, he'd refrained from overruling her, as the "attack" half of the Generals was permitted—required—to do. Now he seemed unable even to form an opinion. And the way he'd set this meeting could only be described as bizarre. "Mosh," she said quietly, hoping her condescending tone might anger him to full alertness, "perhaps you need me to review the situation again."

"Yes," he said. "That would be helpful."

Depluss sighed. "Very well. First, regarding the performance of the council. You told them that we're conducting an exercise to test their ability to reach a decision in diminished numbers. They consider the test an indignity, and therefore are not focusing on the question as they normally would. And I agree that we're insulting them by presenting this as a simulation."

"You're repeating yourself," Trikal said. "Very well, so will I. They are not to know about that scout ship we sent to keep an eye on Kay-Raike. What is it called again?"

"*Ansel.*"

"Yes, that's right. The ability to penetrate and spy so effectively on our own ships has been a closely held secret ever since Major General Marsham devised it. The council has no need to know about it."

"I concede the point, Mosh."

"Good. And it is we who should be offended. They've been told to assume that one of Kay-Raike's officers defied him and passed information on to us. That alone should be enough to engage their minds, but not one of them has seized on it to argue that Kay-Raike is vulnerable. But let us concentrate on reality. Go on."

"*Ansel* reports that fifty Gold Fleet ships are approaching Kay-Raike's position above that world."

"Canopal."

"Yes. The Enemy ships are well within his detection range. But he has not notified us of their presence."

"Why?"

"That is what this 'emergency meeting' is about," Depluss said.

"The question was rhetorical," Trikal snapped. "We know the man is arrogant. He would not consider fifty Gold Fleet ships a threat."

"Yes. But Kay-Raike understands regulations as well as our more loyal officers. He is required to report any unanticipated Enemy movement."

Trikal nodded. "Which suggests that the Gold Fleet ships may have been expected. Why?" Holding up his free hand, he said, "Again, Tabba, rhetorical." After a moment, he said, "No, the question is genuine. I cannot imagine what he plans to do."

"The council is evenly divided," Depluss reminded him. "Half would want to bring him back here for court-martial. The rest would want to leave him alone, and wait for his explanation. The latter position is that with Shimas there, even Kay-Raike wouldn't disobey a regulation without good cause. I agree with the former."

"And you want to send in a squadron of one hundred ships."

"Yes."

"That would take four days?"

"It can be done in three. As I said before, Canopal has come to represent too much. Kay-Raike's failure to report those Gold Fleet ships is all the justification we need to abandon the mission entirely."

"My instinct tells me we should order him back to *Sovereign* for immediate retirement, and never mind a divisive court-martial. That squadron you want can retrieve Shimas and his family. But," he said, scratching his forehead, "to all appearances Kay-Raike has submitted to the council. If we summarily retire him, his sympathizers throughout the Fleet would cause more trouble than the death of one renegade officer is worth. And so you're partially right. All of this has taken on a meaning far beyond itself. But I can't agree to end the mission prematurely. Kay-Raike is a threat. This is our best opportunity to retire him. But when we do, he has to have been given every opportunity to defend himself. We're trapped into cooperating with him.''

"And allowing him to flaunt regulations?''

"Yes.'' Lowering his eyes, Trikal said, "I hate compromises, Tabba. The need for them is the one thing that surprised and disappointed me after accepting this rank. Our predecessors made it look too easy.''

"I was joined to Tobok Ishmahan for nearly a year,'' Depluss said. "He and Menta Carole were no different than we are. Except that they were better at concealing the compromises they were forced into. And the deceptions,'' she added in an ironic tone.

Trikal nodded. "I don't like this either. But I've suspected for a long while that one of the council members is in collusion with Kay-Raike. Unless it was Rhodes or Tillic, that individual is still with us.''

"I don't share that opinion,'' Depluss said.

"I'm aware of that. And I hope you're right.'' Clearing his throat, Trikal continued. "Very well, then. For now, we will assume that Kay-Raike may have a legitimate reason for his actions. But, as a safeguard, we'll send the hundred ships. They will remain outside the system and will avoid detection at all costs. We'll communicate with the squadron leader using the same 'noise' code we've established with *Ansel*.'' He smiled, the relief at having made a decision clear in his eyes. "Colonel Saddhurst and Captain Jeffers. They're really quite clever, aren't they?''

"It's a brilliant advance in communication,'' Depluss said. "Apparently the idea was hers, and he was able to put it into operation.''

"I foresee a good career for both of them. Are we agreed, then, on what we will do?''

"Yes, Mosh. I defer to you.''

The opaque curtain dissolved.

"I have conferred,'' Trikal said to the six council members. "I am disappointed that this council was unable to reach a majority recommendation. The meeting is concluded. I expect better results during our next simulation.''

The council members stood sullenly, and filed out of the chamber.

That evening in their quarters, the Generals sat before a large communications console. Added to the array of equipment was a green fist-sized cube, attached to the console by cables from five of its six surfaces.

First, Trikal recorded his message.

"Colonel Saddhurst, one of your 'noise' units has been shuttled to the flagship of Squadron V-223, which under my private order will approach but not enter the Sentaura System, seventy-three hours from now. Squadron Leader Keitel will contact you with her unit's parameters and the details of her orders when the installation is complete. Have you anything additional to report?"

Grinning at Depluss like a child with a new toy, Trikal routed the recording through the cube and depressed a toggle switch. The process created a hyperspace pulse analogous to standard communication, but only milliseconds in duration. Undeciphered, it was indistinguishable from the random noise generated by a universe that seemed forever to be talking to itself in codes no human would ever comprehend.

The reply was only moments in arriving.

Saddhurst sounded as if he were approaching panic. "Generals! I tried to reach you an hour ago. I hope that squadron arrives in time."

Exchanging a look with Trikal, Depluss sent, "Take a deep breath, and tell me what's happened."

"Pardon me, Generals. First, let me remind you that *Ansel* is attached to a rogue asteroid which has now passed its closest approach to Canopal."

"I am aware of the technique," Trikal said. "And your communications device has exponentially increased its value. I am also aware of your position."

"My point is that what you're about to hear was monitored sixty-seven minutes ago. We've got only one side of the conversation because the reply was evidently sent back to Canopal in a line-of-sight mode. Also, what I have is weak. I've clarified it as thoroughly as possible.''

"Understood, Colonel. Proceed.''

Only parts of the broadcast could be understood.

"... *news to report, sir*" ... seconds of static ... *"abandoned the groundcar and went into the trees with Regent."*—clean break—*"She's the foremost Grounder leader, sir."*—clean break—*"Yes, sir. The area is no doubt full of the beasts"* ... static ... *"Martin."*—clean break— *"I understand how important General Shimas and his family are, sir. We'll find them all. I have several Patrol"* ... static ... *"now, and we've been searching since"* ... seconds of static ... *"three Grounder children with them who know how to"* ... static, long break—*"Sir, I won't disappoint you. I ... Karnas, the Patrol is coming. I'll have to put the radio back"* ... static.

"That was all, Generals,'' Saddhurst sent. "Shall I repeat it?''

"No,'' Depluss said. "It's recorded here. Are you certain there's nothing else, Colonel? I'd like to know why Shimas and his party abandoned their planned route.''

"I'm sorry, Generals. That was all.''

Trikal asked, "Have any of Kay-Raike's ships gone down to the surface?''

"I don't know. They've been maintaining a stationary orbit. Minutes after the transmission you heard, they passed to the far side of Canopal. I won't see them again for ... wait, let me calculate the path of this asteroid ... ten hours thirty-one minutes.''

"And the Gold Fleet?''

"They're holding a more distant position. They haven't approached Canopal closely, and I've detected no communication between them and Kay-Raike. Of course, that doesn't mean that they're *not* communicating.''

"Very well, Colonel. If Shimas hasn't been located by the time Keitel's squadron arrives, I'll instruct her to assist in the rescue.''

"Generals, may I ask a question?''

"Yes.''

"Has Kay-Raike informed you of this?"

"No," Depluss said. "He has not."

"This is my first position of command, Generals, but shouldn't that have been his initial response?"

Trikal answered slowly and calmly, in response to Saddhurst's frantic tone. "Let me tell you something every officer learns eventually, Colonel. There are circumstances under which the safest way to acknowledge a major problem is to report it solved. The Fleet can be of no immediate assistance to Kay-Raike. In this instance, I would expect a reasonable delay in contacting me."

"I understand, Generals. But if I may make an observation, I've listened to that recording dozens of times now. There is nothing blatant in it to suggest anything other than an ongoing rescue attempt. But neither is there anything to rule out the possibility that the officer speaking may be *chasing* Council Member Shimas and his family."

"Thank you for the analysis," Trikal said tersely. "But what you suggest is unthinkable. Do you have anything else to report?"

"Yes. In forty-seven hours, *Ansel* will be too distant from Canopal to be of use to you. That will be a full day before the squadron arrives."

"Understood. Continue on station until Keitel arrives." Trikal switched off the cube.

"He could be right," Depluss said.

" 'Unthinkable' does not mean 'impossible,' " Trikal responded. "Of course he could be right. But if so, there is nothing he can do to help Shimas."

"He could let Kay-Raike know that he's being watched."

"That is precisely why I ordered him to remain on station. Think about it, Tabba. Assuming that Saddhurst is right, revealing *Ansel* would be the worst possible thing he could do. Kay-Raike would immediately send another line-of-sight message and warn his officer to make no further broadcasts. We'd be left with nothing except that one recording, which would be useless in a court-martial." Ab-

sently scratching his cheek, he continued. "Shimas and his
party may be sacrificed. We cannot physically prevent that
from happening, if it is Kay-Raike's intent. But I will not
have their deaths count for nothing."

Depluss considered what he'd said, and smiled. "You've
returned, old friend."

"What?"

"I was worried about you. But your performance just
now was vintage Mosh Trikal."

Trikal touched their joined shoulder with his free hand.
"I've been worried also, Tabba. But there's nothing like
having a traitor in one's sights to stimulate the mind."

Canopal

Already bored with the routine, Jarred piloted the shuttle in
its three-hour cycle to a position above Canopal that would
allow direct radio communication from Dane. After ten
minutes of silence, the vessel returned to its station above
a choppy ocean, safe once again from any misguided attack
from panicked Grounders.

The darkness in the cave was total, the silence broken
only by the cacophony of eight exhausted people breathing
in individual rhythms. Dane lay awake, the sleeping Ren
cradled in the crook of one shoulder. She told herself again
that Jenny had been right; no one could have foreseen that
sometime during the previous days, Mendel Kay-Raike
would manage to—or want to—disable both of their radios.
Jenny took responsibility for storing them together in one
bag. And Shimas assured her that when light came again,
he would try to repair at least one of them, with wiring or
components taken from one of the rifles. But there was no
comfort to be found in any of this. Their safety was an
obligation she'd accepted. She had misinterpreted Mendel's
behavior since the death of Martin. Or perhaps her error
had begun the moment he'd joined them. Now only he

could contact Jarred and their shuttle; and Jarred had no way to know what awaited him when he responded. That could only be described as negligence on her part. Further, she'd hesitated to act when she first saw signs of the mutiny, relying instead on Regent's experience with the Patrol to recognize impending trouble. It was Buto, not she, who'd asked the crucial question: "Have you ever commanded a Patrol unit before?"

The conclusion was stark and unavoidable: The talents she'd developed all of her life were not complementary to the skills of command; the one distracted her from the other. In the morning, she would ask to be relieved of the duties Jenny and Buto had offered her. And hope that the damage she'd done could be rectified.

Dane's reverie was broken by Ren, who stirred and whispered, "Seth is coming in."

Dane heard nothing, and was not aware of Seth's approach until she felt his small hand on her shoulder.

"Dane," he said quietly. "Are you awake?"

"Yes."

"There are two Patrol coming this way. I don't think they've found our trail, because they're pointing their lights everywhere and not moving in a straight line."

"How far away are they?"

"Remember the last creek Heth led you through? That's where."

"Seth, you were able to follow us through that."

"Don't worry," Ren whispered. "No one is as good as Seth is."

"But we'd better make sure," Seth said. "I need two of you big people to help me dig out some spoor from the back of the cave."

"Some what?" Dane asked.

"This used to be a tark's home," Ren explained. "That's what that strong smell is. If we dig through the mounds, we'll find some that's still wet from groundwater. But the dry part on top will be hard, almost like a rock."

"Ten and I will help," Mill whispered from a distance

away. "It can't be any worse than cleaning out *Suram*'s bilges when we first bought it."

"That was a hundred tons of stink," Ten agreed. "My nose hasn't worked right since."

"Follow me, then," Seth whispered. "And stay bent over." Minutes later came the sounds of muted grunting and scraping, soon followed by a stench that filled the cave and brought tears to the eyes. The others pressed against opposite walls as Seth could be heard emerging from the rear of the cave, leading Mill and Ten. "I was wrong," Ten whispered. "But this time my nose is ruined for sure."

"What are they going to do with it?" Sato asked as the three left the cave.

"Probably," Heth said, "Seth will have them make small piles a little way out from the entrance and mash them in the ground. Then he'll go on ahead and try to find some jummers. If he does, he'll use the spoor to drive them to where the Patrol is. Jummers are scared of tarks. Our brother Rol used to do that when the bad Patrol came close to our house."

"That was before they killed him," Ren said, whimpering. "And now they're *all* bad Patrol."

Dane pulled the little girl close to her. "No," she said. "They're just afraid of us, and confused about what to do. But, Ren, I don't want you to be afraid. If they catch us, they won't hurt you or your brothers."

"I'm not afraid," Ren said. "My brothers take care of me, and sometimes I take care of them. Besides, you're smart. And Jenny Marsham is brave, and Buto Shimas is strong. And Mill and Ten are good helpers, and Regent is a doctor."

"What about me?" Sato asked in the darkness.

Ren pulled Dane's head down and whispered in her ear, "He's handsome. But he doesn't know much."

"Do you hear it?" Heth asked suddenly, excitement in his voice. "He found some."

"I hear it," Ren said.

As the others strained to hear, the sound grew until it

was audible to their untrained senses. Faint clicking, low-throated rumbling, and a high-pitched whine that quickly became dominant as the jummer sounds receded into the night.

"They're running away," Ren said, laughing. "Our father can hiss just like a mother tark with babies to protect. Seth can't do that, but they're afraid of him because of the spoor. That will chase the Patrol away."

Ren was mistaken.

"No," Mendel said, shaking his head adamantly in the weak starlight. "Shimas reported that they won't attack a large animal unless it frightens them. And they won't come near these lights."

"Sir," Poda Sela said, "do you hear them crying? And smell the breeze. They're running from a tark. In a frenzy like that, they'll attack anything."

"Can a human run faster than jummers?"

"No. But they're not intelligent animals, and at night they guide themselves by radar, not sight. If we're all moving in the same direction, they may take us for two of their own."

"Assuming they don't stop to investigate."

"They won't, not in the panic they're in."

"Very well," Mendel said. "But I can't run. We'll walk." As they began their slow pace away from the oncoming pack, a thought occurred to him. "Sela, what does a tark eat?"

"Anything," she replied. "Including you and me, if it overtakes us. Can't you walk any faster?"

Mendel suppressed a surge of horror. The thought of being consumed was terrifying; but he was less afraid of an unknown beast than he was of the familiar one circling his ships high above Canopal. "Suppose," he said, "the tark chased the jummers away from a meal. Is that possible?"

Poda Sela made an error that Seth hadn't anticipated; he

knew that tarks were not scavengers, while she did not. "Yes," she replied. "It's possible."

"Then that meal could be one or more of my companions. Send up the signal."

"Sir, I only said it's possible. That could be a female guarding its young. Or it could be—"

"Send the signal."

"That is not a good idea," she said firmly. "You'll endanger the rest of the Patrol."

"Send it!"

The trail of blue luminescence shot to the sky and opened at the top like a giant spring flower, making a sharp popping noise. Seth knew what it was. "Stupid Patrol!" he muttered, turning to run back toward the cave. "A real tark would find you and kill you now. Don't you know anything?"

Inside again, he burst into tears. "I fooled the jummers, but now *all* the Patrol are coming. I thought if they believed I was a tark, they wouldn't look for us here."

Shimas followed the sound of his sobbing and lifted the small boy. "Dane," he said, "with your permission we're going out."

"I was going to tell you later, Dad. I don't want command anymore."

"Very well; there's no time to discuss that now. Jenny, please keep the rest here, and don't allow any noise. We should be back before light."

"Good luck, Buto," Jenny said.

Once they were outside, Shimas put Seth down. "You've done everything well," he said. "We're all proud of you, Seth. Your parents and Rol would be proud of you also. Now I need you do two more things. All right?"

"All right, Buto Shimas."

"Good. I want you to help me find some of the Patrol who are looking for us. And on the way, I want you to tell me how a tark kills."

•   •   •

Morning light was just beginning to cast dim shadows when Poda Nem found the cave entrance. The stench was almost unbearable, the first sign that the cavern was in active use. The next sign was pieces of torn carcasses strewn on the apron of solid rock leading to the cave. A good hunt, he thought gratefully, relieved that the animal inside would likely be asleep. And then he looked closer to the entrance: Broken shards of bone protruded from scraps of uniform and a boot, all lying in fresh pools of blood. Nem fell to his knees and vomited. When he had control once more, he pushed himself erect and walked unsteadily back the way he'd come. Within a few minutes he reached his companions and motioned for them to follow him. He said nothing until he had gone another hundred yards and stood before Mendel Kay-Raike. "They're not here," he said in a shaking voice. "But I found Taro Peth. Wend was right; a tark took him. The only thing left was his boots and scraps of uniform."

"He's dead?" Mendel asked. Peth had been reported missing when his partner, Renath Wend, joined the rest and begged for help in finding him. She and one other Patrol were still out searching.

"He's in the stomach of a tark, spacer. Yes, he's dead! Sela told you not to launch that signal. And now Peth is dead!" Nem brought his hands up and rubbed his face, then ran them through his hair. "I apologize, sir. With what you're doing for all of us, I have no right to shout at you. You made the best decision you could. But Peth was my wife's brother. It was me who talked him into joining the Patrol."

"I'm sorry for your loss," Mendel said. "But is it possible that he wasn't the only victim?"

"No," Nem said. "Peth's are the only human remains there. Tarks don't take food into their dens. They eat outside, and leave what's left to mark their territory. When the pieces rot, scavengers will come and drag them away. There hasn't been time for that to happen with the other spacers."

Mendel let out a long breath. As if someone had brushed cold fingers against his neck, he could feel the presence of Karnas Kay-Raike accusing him of yet another failure. "Very well," he said. "We'll find a safe place and rest for a few hours. Then we'll break apart again and continue the search. Is there some kind of ceremony you want to hold for your friend?" These Grounders, he had come to learn, held death services in many ways similar to those of the Fleet. One of the Patrol had assured him that when he died, it would be painless. And accompanied by a ceremony that would be repeated throughout Canopal for centuries to come.

"Not here," Nem said. "Unless we want to be food ourselves. When this is over, we'll meet with my wife and Peth's other family members."

Mendel had made the offer as a gesture of solicitude, knowing that he should have listened to Poda Sela. Another mistake could cost him the loyalty of these people. Or his life; they didn't need him to find and kill the others. In truth he was an impediment, as he'd just demonstrated. His best hope of survival was to remind them constantly of the sacrifice he was making for their survival. "When this is over," he repeated, looking down. "I hope that's soon. I told you, I'm not a brave man."

Nem put a hand on Mendel's shoulder. "When it's over," he said gently, "we'll try to find a convincing way for you to escape back to your brother."

"I can't ask you do that," Mendel said. "I might say something that would make him suspect the truth. It's too much to risk."

"You won't betray us, sir, or yourself. We've all talked about this. I won't promise anything, but we've got to try."

The others nodded, or spoke their agreement.

Mendel smiled. He knew exactly how it was going to be done.

Twenty minutes later Seth released the branch he'd clung to and made his way down the tree, keeping its trunk between himself and the direction the Patrol had taken.

"They're gone," he announced as he entered the cave. "All of them are gone."

Shimas removed his hand from Taro Peth's mouth. "Behave," he said, "and we might feed you."

⇒23⇐

Noldron

"Frankly, I'm disappointed," No'ln Beviney said. "I expected to hear from you by now that you'd fulfilled your agreement with me, and that a large faction of your Fleet is rallying behind you. I expected to come here and view the remains of a world that had dared to offend the great Karnas Kay-Raike. Instead I see this pathetic rock intact, you're *still* here, and you report that Shimas and his family have escaped along with six Dirts. You know where their shuttle is, but you haven't captured it. And I see your ships idle, with nothing accomplished. After how long? Five days?"

"No'ln Beviney, I've—"

"So tell me, Kay-Raike. Are you afraid, or merely incompetent? Or do you have no intention of honoring our agreement? Have you decided you don't need my help to take command of your Fleet?" Alone in the quarters she now shared with Momed, Beviney was pleased that she'd established an audio-only communication. If Kay-Raike could see her face, he would know she wasn't angry; she was having *fun*.

The man she was tormenting, however, was nearing apoplexy. "No'ln Beviney, I've told you that I can't speak freely now."

"Because you don't want to be overheard? That is nonsense. This communication is focused, from my ship to yours. None of your captains can monitor. I want an explanation, Kay-Raike. Now. Or we have no agreement."

"Very well, No'ln Beviney. First, I remind you that my brother has disabled their radios. They can't contact their shuttle, and we know they're approximately forty miles from that city. They'll be found soon."

"I want to know what *you're* doing. I want to believe I can have confidence in you."

"Everything is arranged, No'ln Beviney. The Grounders will kill Shimas and the rest, and then issue a challenge for me to respond. Until that occurs, I cannot proceed. But when it does, I will relay their message to every ship in my Fleet. Hundreds of them will react. With or without permission, they'll take revenge on any world they happen to be near. At that moment the Generals and the council will lose some of the unchallenged authority they've had for centuries, and significant portions of the Fleet will see that I've been right all along. They'll also understand that they're acting under *my* leadership. After that, it will be just a matter of consolidating power."

"If it's all so easy," Beviney said, taunting him, "why do you need me?"

"Because as I've said before, you're respected within my Fleet. I need *thousands* of ships to react, not merely hundreds. Your participation in massive strikes against the worlds will inspire them and make them ashamed that for eight years they've ignored Fleet tradition. They will no longer be willing to follow the current leadership, whose inaction has allowed the worlds to believe they can assassinate a council member without fearing the consequences.

They'll know that only *I* had the courage to act. And they'll follow me.''

"I see," Beviney said. Kay-Raike hadn't responded with an answer; he'd given a speech. Which meant that he'd waiting for her to ask that question. Further spoiling her fun, he sounded much too sure of himself. She decided to take the offensive again. "Perhaps I'll begin my 'participation' here and now.''

"No! Don't you understand? It must be *me* who acts here, in response to the assassination of a council member. I forbid you to interfere—''

"Forbid?" Beviney sat up straight, her amusement gone. "Kay-Raike," she continued angrily, *"never* presume to give me orders. I want those people dead. If you're incapable of so simple an assignment, I will see to it myself." She knew as she spoke that she was pushing him too far. But she would never accept an implied threat, or *orders*, from the Silver Fleet.

When Kay-Raike's voice came back seconds later, he spoke slowly, with a calm that was clearly forced. "I apologize, No'ln Beviney. Please understand that everything depends on what happens here, and on the *way* it's done. With all humility and respect, I beg you to take no action at this time.''

Astounded by Kay-Raike's capitulation, Beviney said, "I'll stand by for now. Good-bye." For minutes she sat at the console, considering what had just taken place and feeling a sickness wash over her. *Beg?* Her earliest memories centered around hatred of the Silver Fleet, beginning with stories she heard from her parents, brilliant hunters and killers who correctly saw her as the most gifted of her family in generations. Until her marriage to Momed Pwanda, her greatest pleasure in life had been the pursuit and destruction of the Enemy. Their ship commanders were inept, often paralyzed by fear, and without the loyalty she inspired within her own Fleet. But even after she'd crippled them, as she closed in for the kill, none of them had ever *begged*. She'd imagined it happening; and had assumed that it would be a pleasant reminder of her own superiority, an invigorating renewal of the contempt in which she held the Silver Fleet. The reality was far from that. "*I apologize . . . Please understand . . . With all humility . . . I beg you . . .*" The Fleets were enemies, but they shared a common heritage that elevated them above groveling Dirts or the animals that crawled on their horrid rocks. Kay-Raike's shameless display left her feeling degraded. Ashamed.

Beviney removed the recording of their conversation from the console. She passed it from hand to hand, thinking, growing angrier with every second. How could she have misjudged Kay-Raike so badly? He had no courage, no pride. An officer without those qualities had no chance to succeed in a plan as bold and dangerous—as exciting—as the one he'd proposed. Kay-Raike could never gather the power he'd promised, the power she'd intended to take from him and bestow as a gift to her husband. She'd been cheated. Worse, Momed had been cheated.

Her eyes focused on the flat blue rectangle in her hand. Acquiring it was the primary reason she'd made the journey. This recording was to have been a source of control over Kay-Raike when he took command. But now . . . Yes! she thought. He'd spoken of broadcasting the Dirts' message to every ship in his Fleet. Wouldn't they be more entertained by hearing him confess treason? But first, she decided, he would watch as she took his prize from him. The thought brought an ironic smile to her lips: Kay-Raike would be forced to plead—beg—in defense of a world and people whose destruction he desired above all else. She hoped, in the end, he would have the decency to offer a good fight.

Replacing the recording, she prepared the console to transmit in her personal code. "No'ln Bishop," she said when the connection was established, "I want two hundred ships here tomorrow."

"They'll be there," came the reply. "May I ask—"

"No, you may not."

• • •

Beviney could not sleep that evening. She was restless, her mind unable to find the contentment that being with Momed had brought her the day before. She listened to him breathing rhythmically beside her, and pictured the delight that would have been in his warm dark eyes as she presented him with a shattered Silver Fleet to use or destroy at his whim. For the first time since early childhood, she felt tears spilling down her cheeks. She kissed her husband's forehead and climbed out of bed, careful not to disturb him.

Pwanda was awakened by the sound of Marana's sharp expletive.

"Is something wrong?" he asked.

"I scraped my shin. I'm sorry I woke you."

"What are you doing?"

"Getting dressed. I'm restless."

"Switch on a light before you hurt yourself."

"No, you go back to sleep." She laughed in the darkness. "I want you rested when I return."

"I live to serve," he said, smiling and rolling over.

Minutes later he was awakened again by a soft droning signal, accompanied by a steady yellow glow from the communications console. The illumination was sufficient for him to make his way to the seat without additional light. Approaching the unfamiliar unit, he heard No'ln Bishop's voice. "She isn't here," he responded to the greeting.

"You have her code, Pwanda?" Bishop asked.

"No. If that's what we're using, she must have left it set in."

"Oh? That is most . . . Please tell No'ln Beviney that her orders have been carried out. They will be complete in sixteen hours."

"Bishop, I'll call her here if you like. You can speak directly. And privately."

"That won't be necessary. This is merely a courtesy report. Please tell her what I've said." The transmission ended, and the yellow glow died away. Pwanda crossed the compartment to switch on the lighting, and began to dress.

Earlier, when Marana had asked him to leave their quarters for an hour, she'd been secretive about the reason, saying only that she was arranging a surprise for him. Everything in her manner suggested that whatever the secret was, it was a matter of playfulness between wife and husband. But something was clearly disturbing her now, and it was out of character for her to leave the communications console set to her personal code. Even Bishop had reacted to that. Why had she contacted *Noldron*, and what orders had she given? Something was happening, and Pwanda was sure he needed to know what it was.

Before going to look for Marana, he returned to the console to memorize the switches and dials as they were now arranged. It was then he noticed a holostat of himself and Marana on the console desk. It was an old one that he had never seen, capturing the two of them locked in eye-to-eye determination over a game of Disks. At the base Marana had inscribed, "My dear Husband, We have both won the best Game of all." He lifted the holostat and kissed her image. Setting it back down, he saw the open slot and the recording inside. This, he thought, might answer his question about Marana's call to Bishop.

Beviney returned to their quarters three hours later. Her plans were complete, her mind finally at rest. "Momed?" she called softly in the darkness. Receiving no reply, she walked carefully to the bed and reached down to rouse him from sleep. He was gone. When she'd illuminated the compartment, she saw the note where he'd left it, on her side of the bed.

Dearest Marana,

I have been unable to sleep, consumed with curiosity about the surprise you promised. And it occurred to me that I must do something for you, in return. I am certain that the planet below will have the minerals I need to create the most astounding—

"No!" She threw the note aside and ran to the intercom mounted near the compartment's entrance. Within a minute, she had confirmed her fear. Momed had taken a shuttle and gone. She screamed at the supervisor, who reminded her politely that he could not question the order of a No'ln Supervisor; No'ln Pwanda was adamant that no one be informed of his departure. Yes, he answered her next question, No'ln Pwanda had gone alone. Nearly three hours ago. Furious and nearly frantic with worry for her husband, Beviney broke the connection and snatched up the nearest heavy object, a hull fragment from the first Silver Fleet vessel she'd defeated in combat. She hurled it across the compartment, where it impacted dully against a wall and dropped—shattering the holostat she'd left as a surprise for Momed. She crossed the compartment, lifted the pieces, and wept. *Everything I want to give him breaks! First my arrangement with that begging coward, and now* . . . In a rage she lifted the fragment and brought it down time after time against the console until it was a mangled mass of wires and metal. The recording of Kay-Raike's voice was ruined. She didn't care; at this moment he meant nothing to her. But Momed . . . Lifting the shattered holo again, she slowed her breathing. *Never mind*, she thought. *It's only a holostat. It can be replaced. Momed cannot.*

She glanced at a chronometer and calculated: By now he was on that detestable rock, searching for whatever it was he needed to make her gift. Her mind eased somewhat when she told herself that Momed was too cautious to approach an area where Dirts lived. And it *was* a big rock; the chance of his discovering that his former wife and the others were down there also was close to zero.

Minutes later she was in the Battle Control Center. The voice of Karnas Kay-Raike reassured her further. The first thing he said was, "I assume you have a good reason for dispatching a reconnaissance shuttle, No'ln Beviney. But for safety reasons you should have notified me first. Of course, I've issued orders to leave it unmolested."

"Of course." She had no intention of revealing how important the craft's occupant was to her. Kay-Raike could easily take him prisoner, giving him an advantage. "The shuttle is searching for a type of mineral I need, Kay-Raike, and it isn't the reason I called you. I want to know . . . wait." She was silent for a minute, and then resumed. "I'll speak with you tomorrow. There's something important that needs my attention now."

"Very well. Good-bye, No'ln Beviney."

Turning to a junior supervisor, she said, "Try again to contact the shuttle."

⇛24⇚

Day 58

Canopal

Pwanda could not control the shaking in his hands. *Isolate,* he thought. Isolate the pain. Gather it all into one place, make it small, move away from it. An elementary technique, basic to Stem training. But this time it would not work; the pain was everywhere, and he could find no inner core of being to separate it from. He did not blame Marana. Her love for him was genuine, and profound. But it was not the transforming dynamic he had allowed himself to believe it would be. Marana was Marana. Their connection added to all that she was, but did not change the essential person. Why had he believed otherwise? *I'm an expert. I can create a level of empathy so deep that she will be lost in the joy of bonding with me. But I am in control. I will not change.* That was his mistake: supreme arrogance, believing that a lifetime of specialized training had equipped him to succeed where a hundred thousand generations of lovers had failed.

He'd been warned at the beginning of his Stem training that people who lead secret lives are alone. A sense of purpose, perfect confidence that he was acting in a noble cause, had always been enough to sustain him. Never, until now, had he felt *lonely*. And never would he have imagined the depth of anguish that feeling carried with it. And self-loathing. Because if nothing more than the lives of Dane and the others were at stake, he knew he'd have found a way to accept their deaths—so long as it kept him close to Marana, secure in the belief that he was pursuing a greater good. Paradoxically, it was fortunate for Dane and their work that hundreds of worlds, billions of lives, were at risk. No amount of arrogance or self-delusion could rationalize a loss on that scale.

The radio squawked once, and once again he ignored it.

Dane, he sent.

Momed!

Where are you? I mean, specifically?

I don't understand.

You and the others are hiding with six Canopalese. You don't have a functioning radio or access to your shuttle. I've got to find you.

How do you know the details? And where are *you*?

I'm . . . I've left the Gold Fleet. Right now I'm alone in a shuttle on the night side of Canopal. I've been here for hours . . . I have to find you, Dane. After I'm with you, Shimas can contact Marana . . . No'ln Beviney . . . and tell her you've taken me hostage. She will force Kay-Raike to withdraw. Or she'll die trying.

Momed, you're not well. Why would she do that?

I'll explain while I'm on the way. Apparently you're about forty miles from a city.

Yes, directly south.

Can you describe it?

Momed, you can't fly over the city. You'll be fired on.

I've spent the last seven hours recording infrared im-

ages of major cities, but none of my approaches has been close. One of them is emitting heat in a distinctive pattern, as if Fleet weaponry had been at work there not long ago. That's got to be the one you came to visit.

Kay-Raike didn't try to stop you?

He wouldn't dare. He's terrified of No'ln Beviney.

But you can't come here. He'll be watching you.

I'm sure he will. I plan to approach you indirectly, and touch down several times on the way at random locations. When I reach you, I'll take you all aboard and continue as before. Even if he guesses what I've done, though, I don't think he'll interfere. If I'm right, he'll assume that No'ln Beviney is impatient and wants to kill you herself. That would actually simplify things for him, so long as she gives him your bodies. No, don't ask. I'll explain that too.

Oh, no.

What?

Seth—he's one of the children with us—is telling Buto that two of the Patrol are coming in our direction again.

Quickly, then, I need to verify that I'm right about the city. Tell me what you saw in that holo Kay-Raike made before he attacked. Also, describe any mountains, bodies of water, or prominent landmarks near you.

Wait. I'll have to ask one of the children about the landmarks.

Forty seconds later she gave him the information he needed.

Thanks, Dane. I'll be there as soon as I can.

"Go ahead."

"Yes, No'ln Beviney."

Marana paced through the Battle Control Center, listening as the junior supervisor sent out another single pulse. Why wasn't he responding? He would have to leave the shuttle to find what he was after. But for eight hours? She thought of him lying injured, or worse . . . the victim of animals, Dirts, an accident . . . "Try again in one hour," she ordered as she left the compartment.

Arriving in her quarters, she found three repair personnel installing the new communications console.

"We'll be finished in two minutes," the senior among them reported.

"One minute," Beviney ordered. When they were gone, she sat and thought. The additional two hundred ships should be entering the system within six hours. If necessary, she could deploy them in a comprehensive search, and threaten Kay-Raike with annihilation if he interfered. But six hours was too long to wait. Somewhere down below was the only person who had ever truly known her, loved her. So much so that he was risking his life to bring her a gift. She couldn't bear the thought of him down there, alone. There was one thing she could do immediately, to ease her panic. Kay-Raike had had no objection to one shuttle. He couldn't object to a second.

Ansel

"There it is again," Naomi Jeffers said. "A seventh pulse, all exactly an hour apart."

"I've run it through everything we have," Saddhurst said. "It's a clean, single tone. There's nothing coded in it. It has to be a preset signal."

"But from the Gold Fleet? Who would it be meant for?"

Saddhurst smiled and rubbed his eyes. "I thought it was my turn to ask our favorite stupid question."

"I'm ready to relieve you, William. Try to sleep this time."

"I'm fine, Naomi."

"No, you're not. Listen, Keitel's squadron will be here in two days." Naomi put a hand on his arm. "Dane is a strong person, William. She'll be all right."

"Is it that obvious?"

"There. Now you've come up with a new stupid question."

Canopal

"Your eyes are sharper than mine, Wend, but I see it this time. Can you identify the type?"

The woman peered into the distance and said, "It isn't one of our flyers. It must be from your ships."

"Very well. It will be trying to detect weapons emplacements. Hide yourself and don't move. I'll be back."

"Where are you going, sir?"

Turning away, he said, "Some things are private, Wend. And urgent."

"Yes, sir. Please be careful."

Mendel wondered what the problem was this time. Obviously Karnas wanted to be contacted, and right away. As he walked to a distance he judged to be beyond hearing range, the vessel came into view again. This time it was closer, passing in full profile. *Gold Fleet.*

His breath coming fast, Mendel hid beneath a cluster of undergrowth and snatched the radio from the compartment in his prosthetic.

"Yes," came the reply minutes later. "I assume you're ready to report success. Finally."

"Sir, there's a Gold Fleet shuttle here! I've seen it twice now."

After a pause, Kay-Raike's response came as a shout. "Is that why you've disturbed my sleep? Brother, are you so half-witted as to believe that I would not be aware of an Enemy presence on Canopal? That . . . *Quiet!*" Mendel heard the sound of flesh striking flesh, and a grunt of pain. "Go, get out. You can dress in the corridor. *Go!*" There was silence for a few seconds. "Mendel," Kay-Raike resumed, "the shuttle is irrelevant to me. But if it's searching for Shimas, it means everything to you. You do not want to be beaten to your objective. Do you understand?"

Shaken, Mendel hesitated before answering. "Yes, sir. I understand. Completely."

He rejoined Renath Wend, and was surprised to see another Patrol with her. "Nem," he said, sitting down to stop the trembling in his legs. "What are you doing here? You're supposed to be with your sister."

"We went back to the tark cave, sir. Poda Sela is still there."

"Why?"

"Ever since yesterday morning when I found what was left of Taro Peth, I've been thinking about it. Something didn't seem right."

Mendel looked up at the man with keen interest. "Yes?"

"When the remains of a carcass rot, scavengers—"

"You've explained that," Mendel interrupted, climbing to his feet. "The point is, you went back. And you found something wrong."

Flushed with pride, Poda Nem was not to be denied his moment of glory. "The point, sir, is that there should have been pieces of old kills, not spoiled enough yet for the scavengers to risk taking. I didn't remember seeing or smelling any. Early this morning, I figured out that that's what was bothering me."

"So you went back," Mendel said excitedly, "and you were right."

"No, sir. I was wrong."

"Nem!"

The small man laughed. "Now, there are carcasses there in all stages of decay." He added significantly, "They made a mistake. They didn't think the same people would look twice."

Grinning, Mendel put his hands on the smaller man's shoulders. "Nem, you're a . . . Wait. Why didn't you signal the rest of us?"

"The ship from your Fleet," Wend answered for him. "He saw it before we did."

"Good. Nem, were you seen from the cave?"

"I doubt it, sir. But that doesn't matter. Poda Sela is armed, and waiting in a tree. She's very good. If any spacers come out, they'll be as dead as *real* tark food."

"Hurry, then," Mendel said, motioning for Renath Wend to join Nem. "Don't wait for me; go and help Sela."

"Yes, sir," Wend said. "We can build a fire and use the smoke to drive them out."

"Not yet. Don't do anything until we're sure that shuttle is gone. Then we'll call in the rest of the Patrol. Go now. Hurry."

When they were gone, Mendel checked his chronometer and smiled. Jarred would be aloft now, monitoring. Everything was working for him, at last. He extracted the radio again and set it to a different, secure frequency. "Jarred," he called. "You're to pick us up in four hours. Approximately forty miles south of the city, come to low altitude and circle above the highest landmass you see. I'll guide you down."

"Yes, sir. I'll need to speak to Dane."

"She's with Regent and the others," Mendel said. "They're saying good-bye. I don't care for such nonsense, so she asked me to contact you."

"I understand. Four hours."

Mendel whistled, a song that was one of Dorothy's favorites. He took his time walking, mentally saying good-bye to dirt and rotting carcasses and Grounders. There was no hurry. Soon enough he'd have everything he wanted.

From within the cave, the outside world was reduced to an irregularly shaped splotch of light.

"You've been away from the sea too long, Regent," Ten said. "You've lost your eye. That's not a man, it's a woman."

"All right, then," Regent said testily. "Don't kill *her*. You'd better be as accurate with that thing as you say you are."

"He is," Mill said. "But he can't control how she falls. You should have shot them both when they were closer, and we could guarantee that they'd only be wounded."

"I expected them to leave and tell the others to look elsewhere. We all agreed, Mill."

"Quiet, now," Ten said. "I need to concentrate. Everybody turn away and cover." He took a deep breath and began letting it out slowly. There was no sound, but the darkness was relieved for a fraction of a second by a dim burst of green. "Now my eyes are worse than yours," he said. "Next time we do this, remember to bring goggles. What happened?"

"You hit her," Regent answered.

"In the leg," Mill said. "She dropped the rifle but didn't fall. She's collapsed onto a branch."

Before anyone could stop him, Seth ran out of the cave to get a closer look at Poda Sela. "She's not awake," he said when he returned. "But she's breathing all right, and she's not bleeding as bad as Ren did."

"I'll see to her when you're gone," Taro Peth said.

"Good," Shimas said. "Then let's go."

"We could wait here," Dane suggested, recalling that Momed was on his way. "They'll think we ran."

"No," Jenny said. "We fooled them once. This time they'll check."

Momed, where are you?

Close, Dane.

We're leaving the cave. I'll let you know which way we travel.

A little patience, please? I've come a long way.

What is that? Are you laughing?

Step outside and look up. But tell the others not to shoot.

I'm no longer in command, Momed.

Wonderful. All right, give me a minute before you come out. Let's just hope they recognize my handsome face. Act surprised.

"Wait," Dane said. "Is there someone moving out there?"

"Where?" Seth asked.

"There. Next to that boulder, a little to the left."

"I don't see anything," Ten said. "But my eyes aren't right yet, thanks to Regent."

"I don't see anything either," Ren said. "But I hear something. It's whispering, like that little ship we rode in up to the big one."

"Shuttles don't make noise," Sato said.

"Move back, as far as you can go," Shimas ordered quietly. "Ten, give the weapon to Regent. Mill, you're ready with the other one?"

"I'm ready, General."

A large shadow was the first thing they saw, twenty feet out from the rocky apron leading from the cave. It grew steadily smaller until the bottom of the craft was in view.

"Gold Fleet!" Shimas whispered, stunned. "What is . . ."

And then the vessel touched down, its open door framing a smiling Momed Pwanda. "Does anyone need help?" he called out.

"Taro Peth," Dane said urgently, "go to the back of the cave and hide. We're going to take that shuttle, but you don't need to be involved anymore."

"I agree about Peth," Shimas said, "but that's Momed—"

"Yes, our enemy," Dane said, interrupting. "Peth, go!"

An hour later, Mendel Kay-Raike approached the cave, exhausted but enthusiastic. His happiness dissolved when he saw what awaited him. Renath Wend sat near the entrance, bent forward with her head down. Next to her sat Poda Nem, holding the hand of his sister as she lay prone on a makeshift stretcher, cushioned by leaves. Sela's legs were tied to straight pieces of wood.

Failure. The word echoed through his mind and brought with it images of torture, and death, and Dorothy.

"What happened?" he called out.

Wend looked at him, and then down again. "They were gone when we got here," she said, barely audible. "Poda Sela is unconscious. She's been hurt."

The next word that came to Mendel was *Jarred*. If the boy flew too close, he might well see Shimas and the others fleeing, and take them aboard. His Patrol would never catch them. Pretending physical urgency, he again moved a distance away. "Jarred," he radioed, "where are you?"

"Just over five hundred miles from the position you gave me, sir."

"Go back to your station and wait for us."

"But why? Is everything all right?"

"Jarred, if there was a problem we'd tell you. Dane has decided to prolong the good-bye. There are more officials from the city meeting us here. I assume she has some diplomatic purpose in mind, but I'm not a part of the discussions."

"Then everything went well?"

"For you, yes. But not for my brother."

"Why can't I come in now?"

Mendel was perspiring, straining to keep his voice calm. "Who understands Grounders? The ship would probably frighten them."

"All right, I'll be waiting. Same schedule as before."

"Very well," he said, releasing a breath.

Mendel rejoined the others to find Nem gathering more leaves. "How is she?" he asked.

Nem turned to face him, eyes filled with tears. "They shot her through the leg," he said. "It looks like she held onto the tree, and then grew so weak she fell. Both of her legs are broken." He added bitterly, "At least Regent had the decency to dress her wounds before they ran. Or maybe it was Taro Peth. He left a note on her in case any of us came back before he found more Patrol."

"He left her unprotected?"

"The tark smell," Nem said. "Nothing would bother her here. But he'll be back, with or without other Patrol."

"Nem," Renath Wend called. "She's waking up."

The younger man ran to his sister, while Mendel followed behind. Sela's eyes were open wide, and she was smiling. "Well, Nem," she said. "It's been an interesting day, hasn't it?"

"I gave you onynote for the pain," Nem said. "How are you feeling?"

"Just wonderful," Sela replied. "But I'm going to be

very sad when those ships start killing us. Maybe we should all take some onynote.''

"We'll catch them," Mendel assured her.

"Oh, hello, sir! No, I'm sorry, but you won't. Your shuttle already took them away."

Mendel flushed, feeling his stomach convulse. "My shuttle?"

"Yes sir, the one Nem and I saw." Looking toward her brother, she asked, "Didn't you tell him about that?"

"I told him, Sela. That's why I walked, instead of sending up the signal. Remember?"

Laughter crinkled her pale face. "I know that. You're the one who was fooled yesterday, not me. I . . . I think I can fly after them! Do you want me to try, sir?"

"Not yet," Mendel said. "I need you to stay with us now. Can you tell me exactly what happened?"

There were two points of her story that fascinated him. The first was the direction taken by the shuttle; instead of returning to orbit as might be expected, it had taken an overland route, flying barely above the treetops. The second point provided a possible answer for the first, and renewed his hope that he might live, after all. When she'd finished and asked for permission to sleep, Mendel nodded. He asked Nem, "How strong is that drug? Could it affect what she remembers?"

"I don't think so," Nem said. "It might change the way she feels about things, but not the facts."

"Will she be all right?"

"She'll live for as long as any of us do."

Mendel stood and paced, his mind racing. Karnas hadn't seemed concerned that a Gold Fleet vessel had joined the hunt. In fact, he'd used it as a taunt. But nothing could explain what Sela reported. Or thought she saw. Something was going on that his brother didn't know about; something that might be valuable enough to persuade Karnas to forgive him.

"You've done everything you could for us," Nem said. "If we send up the signal now, your ship may see it and come back for you. The three of us will stay in the cave until the rest of the Patrol reaches us."

"The shuttle has reached its destination by now," Mendel said. "Do you two need help carrying her inside for the night?"

Nem shook his head no.

"Go ahead, then. I'll call in the Patrol and bring the weapons."

Poda Nem and Renath Wend lifted the stretcher and had gone but a few steps when the blast caught Wend in the back, severing her spine and piercing her heart. She died instantly. Nem gave a startled cry as Wend collapsed and Sela tumbled to the ground. He dropped prone and looked around at the woods, calling for Mendel to get down.

"I told you once," Mendel said, taking aim, "that you couldn't trust us. You should have believed me." He fired, killing Nem with a shot through the head.

"You *liar!*"

Startled, Mendel turned to see Taro Peth charging at him from the woods fifteen feet away. He brought the weapon around and fired repeatedly, unable to hold himself steady enough for a clean shot. Peth had closed the distance to six feet before a thin bolt of energy shot through his stomach and, as Mendel held down the trigger, sliced upward. Momentum carried him into the larger man. Mendel fell backward and impacted hard, his head slamming against the apron of rock. The last thing he felt before losing consciousness was two hands, astonishingly strong, tearing at his face.

⇉25⇇

Day 59

"I did it to avert a war," Pwanda said. His passengers had bathed and slept, and were now gathered in the single compartment behind the pilot's station to share a meal. The shuttle was nestled among a large group of boulders twenty miles west of the city, situated so that only a craft directly overhead might detect it. "But this time against the worlds, not between the Fleets."

"You wouldn't mind if we all killed one another," Shimas said. "I don't mean to sound ungrateful, but isn't that the truth?"

Pwanda shrugged.

"And you haven't explained how you found us."

"The only thing that matters to you, Buto," he said. "is that if we survive, which is not likely, you owe me a debt. A personal debt."

"The last time you helped me, you wanted Dane as your wife. That was not a satisfactory arrangement for my

262

daughter. I hope you have something else in mind this time.''

He loves you very much, doesn't he?

Yes, he does. Momed, I know how much it must hurt you to think you've lost—

Not now, Dane. Maybe not ever.

"When we reach *Sovereign*, I may want to be released back to the Gold Fleet,'' Pwanda said. "For now I'll accept a solemn pledge from all of you that you will never reveal to anyone, your Generals, council, friends, neighbors, or *anyone*, that I came to you voluntarily.'' **Even if she doesn't know, she may decide never to forgive me.**

I think she will, Momed.

I'm getting careless. I didn't mean to send that.

"Done,'' Jenny said. "I can speak for Buto and our two children here. Jarred doesn't need to know.''

Seth nodded. "We won't tell.''

Regent agreed. "Three citizens of Canopal know. There will never be any others.''

With a laugh, Pwanda said, "Oh, you can arrange for my heroism to become known here in a few hundred years, Regent. I wouldn't mind being a legend somewhere.''

Like your brothers?

Yes, Dane. Like Ahken and Murak.

I've offended you again.

No, it's my fault. I—

You connected with her, didn't you? Totally?

All right, yes. Dane, you can't imagine what this feels like.

To an extent I can. I bonded emotionally and mentally, but not physically. She died.

Then you understand, to a point. I'm very sorry you do.

"I think,'' Pwanda said aloud, "it's time to contact No'ln Beviney. Are you ready, Buto?''

"I'm ready, Momed.''

The call traveled in a focused beam from the shuttle to a relay they'd positioned on a distant mountain. From the relay it left the surface of Canopal in a direct line toward the cluster of Beviney's ships, where it was received and fine-tuned to her temporary flagship. From there it was sent back down to a shuttle 6,800 miles from its point of origin. Once the contact was made, the time lapse was infinitesimal.

"Momed! Are you all right? Where are you?"

"No'ln Beviney, it's good to hear your voice. You may not want any of your personnel to overhear what I have to say. Do you remember the game I taught you, Disks?"

"Yes."

"Enter the sequence for your innovation on the Prince's Relay to represent zero. For the digit one, use a recent significant date in your life. I'm sure we'll choose the same one."

The process took less than ten seconds. "Now tell me, please, are you all right?"

"No, he isn't," Shimas said. "In fact, he's under the same threat the rest of us are facing."

"Who is this?"

"Council Member Buto Shimas. We've met."

"What have you done to my officer?"

"I believe you mean your *husband*, Marana?"

"I'm sorry," Pwanda said. "I saw three Canopalese with children, waving at me in apparent distress. When I landed and stepped outside, General Shimas came out of hiding. Marana, they were going to kill me and take the shuttle. Telling them about our marriage was the only way I could stay alive."

"You did the right thing, Momed," Beviney sent.

"Marana, why—" Pwanda's voice broke.

You have to say it, Momed.

And drive her insane with guilt?

Yes, if there is as much at stake as you say.

I'd always believed that between the two of us, I was the one most capable of cruelty. No, you don't deserve that. I know you're right.

"Marana," Pwanda continued, "General Marsham insists that if you've spoken with Kay-Raike, you must have known that she and her family were down here. Is that true?''

"Why do you want to know that?" The edge in Beviney's voice told the two Stem agents that jealousy was indeed a factor, as Momed had suspected. It was a factor that needed to be dealt with immediately.

Wincing as he drove the blade in deeper, Pwanda asked, "Why didn't you tell me? All I wanted was to give you something special. I would never have put your plans at risk, whatever they are." In the same way, he implied, she had put him at risk.

The reply was a long time in coming. "I didn't know what your reaction would be, husband. I am so sorry."

"No, I acted impulsively. This is my fault." In a rushed voice he continued, "Marana, don't let these people force you to do anything because of me. I don't trust—"

On cue, Shimas pushed Pwanda away from the radio. The sound of his fall carried throughout the shuttle compartment and to the distant No'ln Beviney. "Stop! Shimas, if you hurt him, I swear I will bring you more pain than you can possibly imagine. Tell me what you want, and release him."

"You'll have your husband again when we're safely returned to *Sovereign*. In the meantime, tell Kay-Raike to withdraw. Make sure every one of his ships leaves the system."

"I was planning that already. I have reinforcements arriving soon."

"Try to avoid a battle if you can. I want him to face a court-martial."

"You still plan to gather evidence against him?"

"That's why we came here, Beviney. I don't want any of his followers in the Fleet to doubt his guilt."

"Council Member Shimas, none of this is necessary. Bring me my husband and you'll have what you want, including safe passage. I give you my word."

"No," Jenny said. "I've had recent experience with the value of your word."

"And I'm expected to trust *you?*"

"Yes," Shimas said.

After a pause Beviney said angrily, "All right, Shimas. I agree."

"Good. For now, I need to arrange passage for us. Give me a comm patch to *Sovereign.*"

"Release Momed and you'll have it."

"I don't intend to bargain with you, No'ln Beviney."

"You already have, and we've reached an agreement. If you expect something further, I expect to be compensated for it. You have only one thing I want."

"Safe passage is a part of our agreement."

"Yes, it is. And I can provide it. But if you let him go, you can make whatever arrangements you like."

"The answer is no."

"Then so is mine. You won't hurt him, Shimas. Even the Silver Fleet isn't that stupid."

"Very well; we've reached an impasse. A warning: Don't try to find us. Our agreement ends if you're successful."

She's good, Momed.

She's everything, Dane. Even I can't guess what it costs her to take orders from the Silver Fleet.

You should sleep. We'll start walking as soon as it's dark.

"Dad," she said aloud. "Jarred should be coming into position now."

"Thank you." Tuning to another frequency, Shimas reached his son a minute later.

"Are you ready, Dad?"

"Jarred, don't respond again. We're all right. But you'll need to set down somewhere and remain undetected until we contact you again. Don't broadcast under any circumstances until we do. Be careful, Son."

● ● ●

Half of the ninety-minute transit to her ships had passed when Beviney changed her mind and reversed course. Remaining on the rock below would allow her to feel closer to her husband, more protective. She was furious with herself for the childish and unthinking tantrum she'd thrown. If she still had Kay-Raike's confession of treason, she could deliver it to Shimas and save the time needed for him to gather additional evidence. She called her temporary flagship to confirm that the two hundred ships had arrived in the system, and ordered a communications patch to Kay-Raike. Her plan was to entice and, if necessary, threaten. She would try to leave him hope for a future association. But if he proved difficult, she now had an overwhelming advantage in firepower.

"Kay-Raike," she said when the connection was established, "our situation has changed."

"Yes," came the angry reply. "By a factor of two hundred ships. What have you done, Beviney?"

Mendel woke to a universe of pain, the sharp points of light in his eyes finally resolving themselves into stars. He raised his head and winced as a surge of memory brought back the moments before he'd lost consciousness. His uniform was soaked with blood. Next to him lay the body of Taro Peth, hands outstretched, face frozen in a grimace of agony and hatred.

Moving slowly, Mendel rolled away from the corpse. His own injuries seemed to be minor. One eye was swollen nearly shut, the vision blurred. His jaw ached when he moved it, but there was no bleeding in his mouth. As clarity returned, he remembered Sela: his one remaining chance to live.

She was still where she'd fallen, but fresh blood indicated that the wound in her leg had opened again. He pressed an ear against her chest and heard a weak but stable heartbeat.

"Karnas," Mendel said when he had the radio out.

"You can rot where you are, Brother. We're leaving orbit. It's over."

"No it isn't, *Brother*. I have someone here you'll want to speak with. But she needs a doctor. Fast."

"General Shimas?"

"Yes, No'ln Beviney."

"Kay-Raike has begun to withdraw as we discussed, but *Alee* will be remaining for a short while."

"Please explain."

"I'm allowing him to send a shuttle for his brother. Depending on where you are, you may see it. I'm informing you now to avoid any misunderstanding."

"Why did you agree?"

"He believes we'll be working together again. To refuse his request would tell him otherwise and could start that fight you want me to avoid. If the shuttle deviates from the route he's given me, it won't survive. I have two hundred fifty ships here now."

"Very well," Shimas said. "I'm curious, No'ln Beviney. How did you persuade Kay-Raike to accept your instructions?"

"He expects to explain to your council that I took you prisoner and threatened to kill you if he informed them of it before I announced the terms for your release. I'm to make that broadcast in two days, as he's transiting back to *Sovereign*."

"And you gave him your word that none of us would be returned alive?"

"Yes. May I speak with my husband now?"

"Of course."

⇒26⇐

Day 60

"I've synthesized more of the drug from her blood samples," the physician reported, entering *Alee*'s dispensary. He set the vial on a table and smiled ingratiatingly at Karnas Kay-Raike. "That was an inspired suggestion, sir. I've mixed it with a mild stimulant and can now proceed without risk of harmful interactions. She'll feel pleasure from the Grounder drug, but she'll be perfectly coherent. With your permission, I'll begin restoring her to consciousness."

"Yes," Kay-Raike said. "Now we'll see if she can substantiate what my brother says."

"Sir, I promise—"

"Quiet! Mendel, any fool would have brought along the medication she needs. But you don't *have* the intelligence of a fool, do you?"

"No, sir."

"And so six hours have been wasted while this Grounder slept."

"Yes, sir."

"Sir, she's coming awake."

"Thank you, Doctor. Darken the lights, and you and I will leave now. Mendel, you won't mistake the recorders for child toys and shut them off, will you?"

"No, sir." The blatant reference to his future daughter brought a flash of rage, but years of practice kept it from his expression.

Minutes later, Poda Sela opened her eyes for the first time since Mendel had given her permission to sleep. Now he stood above her, holding her hand as Nem had. She looked around, moving only her eyes, and then focused on Mendel's face. "I can't see very much. Where are we, sir?"

"We're not far from your home, Sela. How do you feel?"

"Good. Very good."

"Nem has been worried about you. He'll be here soon."

"I'm glad. What happened?"

"We're all safe now. As I promised, my brother's ships are gone."

Sela's face brightened. "You caught them? How?"

"It wasn't us. Their shuttle flew too close to the city, and was shot down. Do you remember the shuttle?"

"Yes."

"As it happens, we're lucky they were able to overpower the crew."

"Sir?"

"You told me that when it landed near the cave, the spacers rushed out and attacked the crew."

"I'm sorry, sir, but I didn't say that. There was no fight. The man on the shuttle and the others, they were all friends."

Success! "Perhaps I misunderstood you. Are you sure they were friends?"

"Oh, yes, sir. The very best. Dane especially. Smiles and hugs, it was a beautiful thing to see. Beautiful. Can I have something to eat?"

"Of course. But first tell me everything again, from the beginning." He smiled at her. "We're writing your world's history, Sela. It's important to have all the details right."

Well beyond the range at which ship movement around Canopal could be detected, *Ansel* clung to its asteroid and waited for permission to break for hyperspace and join Opina Keitel's squadron, now thirty-seven hours away.

William Saddhurst was in a state of exhausted sleep when "BATTLE CONTACT! BATTLE CONTACT!" sounded over the alarm circuit. He was still waking up as he made his way through two narrow corridors to the tiny ship's Control Center.

"Too far away to see them individually, sir," Naomi reported as he entered. She pointed to the display hovering above a wide table, where a single silver mote moved relative to the asteroid's path. The characteristic emanations designated the oncoming ships as belonging to the Silver Fleet. More specifically, Saddhurst noted, to Karnas Kay-Raike.

"Their course is tangential to ours," Naomi said. "And so it's likely that they haven't seen us. I recommend shutting down main power before they do."

Saddhurst crossed to a console and made the necessary adjustments. There was a flicker of darkness before emergency lights engaged, bathing the compartment in a faint yellow radiance. The display above the War Table had changed to a simulation based on the most recent data. "Naomi," he said, "go and prepare a message for the Generals . . ." His breath caught in his throat as he turned to face her. *Dane?* He nearly said it aloud before the illusion, caused by his fatigue and the softer lighting, passed. "I'm sorry."

"It's all right. Are you awake now?"

"Yes. Assuming no change, how close will they come to us?"

"In another twenty-three minutes," Naomi said, "they'll pass just inside weapons range."

"Apparently they aren't in any hurry."

"It's another indication that they haven't detected us,"
Naomi said. "But I wonder why he's moving so slowly. If
he's leaving the system, he should have entered hyperspace
by now. And if he isn't, what *is* he doing?"

"For now, it doesn't appear to involve us."

"I don't want to give you the impression that we're entirely safe here. If Karnas is happy, he may celebrate by
shooting at anything that moves, and we're attached to the
only thing moving out here. If he's upset, he's likely to do
the same, but more aggressively. Fortunately, our rotation
will put the asteroid between him and us as he passes. That
should provide adequate protection."

"But maybe it won't, and we can't take that chance."
Saddhurst had paled at the words "If Karnas is happy."
Maybe he'd already killed Dane and the others, as Saddhurst was certain he intended. Or they might be aboard
with him, in which case there was nothing he could do to
help them. *But if Kay-Raike hasn't been able to find them
. . . or if he's still in the system because he intends to report
Dane and the others dead and wait for permission to begin
the destruction of Canopal . . . or if I've been wrong and
the Grounders have taken them . . .* Keitel was still more
than a day away. "Naomi, you have more direct experience
than I do. How long would it take us to run for hyperspace?"

"William, I know what you're thinking. The second we
leave normal space we're undetectable. But even it we
make it to hyperspace, come out, reset, reenter, and then
make it to Canopal, it could all be for nothing. The Gold
Fleet may still be there."

"How long to enter?"

"We can begin the procedure here. But they'll know
where we are as soon as we start. And the Generals have
ordered us—"

"Never mind the Generals. I'm not going to risk dying
here when we may be needed. I want an answer, Captain
Jeffers. How long will it take?"

Naomi studied the simulation with an expert eye. "Assuming running at one hundred percent capacity . . . Once we lift off, we'll need six minutes eighteen seconds. But *Ansel* is a scout ship, with a small power plant. We can't overcome their relative speed advantage. If he goes to maximum acceleration right away, he'll close to weapons range about thirty seconds before we're gone. Our chance of survival is minimal."

"But acceptable," Saddhurst said firmly. "We're a small target. And that thirty seconds grows with every second we wait. Begin the procedure, at one hundred ten percent capacity. That should reduce our vulnerability to twenty seconds."

The display switched to real time again as Saddhurst restored main power and Naomi busied herself with the details of preparing for hyperspace. As she'd predicted, the silver motes—distinctly thirty of them now—changed course and accelerated, directly toward *Ansel.*

Saddhurst stood aside and watched, knowing that any attempt to assist her would be more of a nuisance than genuine help. He ignored the radioed demands to identify his ship, and decided against contacting the Generals; Mosh Trikal himself had said that the safest way to acknowledge a problem was to report it solved.

Ansel was forty seconds from reaching hyperspace when Naomi reported, "They're firing, sir. At this distance it's nothing but intimidation. I estimate another nineteen seconds before they're in effective range."

"Very well." To his surprise, Saddhurst was enjoying himself. A look at Naomi told him that she shared the emotion. *Research be damned,* he thought. *This is what I was meant for.* "I'll fire back," he said. "Just for the thrill of it."

"I wouldn't recommend that," Naomi said. "We need all power for acceleration."

"Oh, very well." He looked at a chronometer. "Eight seconds to weapons range, twenty-nine to hyperspace."

Joy turned to fear moments later when *Ansel* jolted

sharply and main power flickered twice before holding. "Damage?" he heard himself shouting.

"We weren't hit, William. The primary power coupling couldn't take the overload."

"Meaning?"

"That this is an old ship, poorly maintained."

"Naomi!"

"Sorry. The secondary is engaged. We can still enter hyperspace, but I'm not sure we can do it more than once."

"Maybe we should—"

"Stop and surrender?"

"No! I was going to ask about evasive maneuvers."

"Again, I recommend against anything that would slow us down."

"You're right. Why did the Generals make *me* the captain?"

"Because I was a Kay-Raike. Some stains are not easily removed."

Saddhurst did not hear her. He was staring at the War Table display. "Two, one . . . Brace yourself. They're close enough now to fire effectively."

As he turned, Naomi dropped her hands to her sides and took a step back from her station. She swept the instruments with her eyes, then sat down.

"What's wrong?" he asked.

"Nothing," she said, laughing. "We made it."

He looked back at the display, which had switched back to simulation mode. "We're in . . . ? But—"

"I lied about the time."

"But . . . why?"

"It was a good opportunity to enhance your development, Colonel Saddhurst. Now you know something about yourself you weren't sure of." She stood and returned to the instrument array. "We'll need to return to normal space for a course correction. If the secondary holds, we should reenter the Sentaura System in less than four hours."

●   ●   ●

"BATTLE CONTACT! BATTLE CONTACT!"

As the dispensary lights grew stronger and acceleration increased, the doctor entered again and smiled reassuringly at Poda Sela. "Everything is fine; don't worry. I want to be sure you don't fall from the table."

"Who are you?"

"It's all right, Sela," Mendel said. "We'll talk a little more, and then you can eat."

She tried to sit up against Mendel's hands on her shoulders as the doctor began securing her to the table.

"Don't struggle!" Mendel shouted.

"I want Nem here. *Where am I?*"

"She's going to reinjure herself," the doctor said. "I'd better put her to sleep again."

"Make it light. I need more information, and soon." Seeing the contempt in the man's eyes, he said. "My *brother* needs the information."

"Of course."

When Poda Sela was unconscious Mendel made his way to *Alee*'s War Room and remained there only long enough to see that Karnas was directing the pursuit of a small scout ship. He left and passed through empty corridors, encountering no one. When he arrived at his destination, he opened a power panel and verified that the monitors inside were off.

"Open the door," he said. Without waiting for a response, he forced it open. As he'd expected, he found his wife there. She was strapped to Karnas's bed. "Does he leave you like this, or did you strap in for the battle contact?"

Twelve years his junior, Dorothy Kay-Raike was small and olive-skinned, with a childlike face framed by space-dark hair. At the sight of him, she began to tremble. "Mendel. I didn't know you were back. You shouldn't be here. I . . ." Sobbing, she said, "I'm sorry. He—"

"I know," Mendel said quietly, shutting the door behind him. He crossed the compartment and bent to kiss her, his tears falling to mingle with hers. "I know, Dorothy."

"You shouldn't be here," she repeated.

"I've been ordered not to go to our quarters, as if I thought you were there. He didn't say anything about coming here."

"You knew it was me."

"When he hit you. Yes, I heard. Dorothy, are you pregnant? A girl?"

"He told you?"

"Yes."

"She's yours, Mendel. He . . . tried, twice. He's impotent."

"Oh?" He straightened and said, "I have to go now."

"He said he'd kill you if I refused to stay with him, or told you about it. And then when the baby is born—"

"I understand."

"What are you going to do?"

"Does he hurt you?"

"No. He even apologized for hitting me. He thinks I'm happy with him."

"Then I'm not going to do anything that would jeopardize our future."

"That's wise."

"Can you bear it?"

"For you and our daughter, yes." With a look of relief she asked, "Do you know why he wants to believe I'd rather be with him than with you? It's because he knows you're a better man than he is."

I was, he thought, and smiled. "You've said so often enough."

"And it's true. Go back to your work, Mendel. Please."

"I will." He nodded to her and left the compartment.

He returned to the War Room to find Karnas in audio contact with the Generals. Trikal was speaking.

"Today is the day Council Member Shimas's party was due to be back aboard *Alee*, Kay-Raike. Why did you wait for me to call for him before you informed me of their disappearance?"

"There was nothing you could do, Generals," Karnas

replied. "I had hoped to find them by now. We're continuing the search, of course."

"Very well. I expect to hear from you very soon that they've been recovered, and are safe."

"I understand, Generals." Trikal broke the connection.

Turning to see Mendel standing behind him, Kay-Raike said, "What do you want? And why are you staring at me?"

"The Grounder is asleep again, sir. The doctor will notify me when she wakes. In the meantime, I'd like to go to my quarters and see Dorothy."

"I've told you, Brother, that you'll see her when your information is corroborated. Has that happened yet?"

"Not completely, sir."

"Then get out of my sight."

"Yes, sir."

Trikal attempted to contact Saddhurst. When there was no response, he keyed the noise unit for Opina Keitel.

"Yes, Generals?"

"Squadron Leader, have you communicated recently with *Ansel*?"

"Not since I last reported to you."

"When we're finished here, begin making the attempt. Let me know if you get through."

"I will, Generals."

"Kay-Raike acknowledged just now that Shimas and his party are missing, but he made no mention of the Gold Fleet presence there. Unless you hear from *Ansel* during the remainder of your transit, I will consider the ship lost. You are then to enter the system and proceed directly to Canopal. You will locate and take aboard the council member's party while regarding Kay-Raike's force as an enemy, along with the fifty Gold Fleet ships. But do not initiate hostilities."

"I understand."

⇒27⇐

Day 61

They'd been walking for six hours when Ren, atop Shimas's shoulders, said, "Look!"

"What is it?" he asked.

"Behind you, Buto Shimas. In the sky."

He turned and saw the craft, a darkened spot against a pale moon. It was traveling from north to south. "It won't see us," he said, "unless it changes course. Keep looking, Ren. And good work."

"Thank you, Buto Shimas."

"Buto," Jenny said. "The next time we may not see it in time."

"I plan to do something about that, Jenny."

Half an hour later they came to an elevated clearing that offered a view to the distant mountain where they'd placed the relay. When the signal was locked on, he keyed the radio. "I believe I warned you about looking for us," he said. "Order your shuttles to return."

"If you see me, I must be close."

"You?"

"Yes, I'm down here. There is only one shuttle, and I'm alone aboard it."

Pwanda called out, "Marana, there are renegades here. They control weapons capable of destroying a ship. Please don't endanger yourself."

"Kay-Raike told me about them," Beviney replied. "I don't care."

Pwanda put his face in his hands. **I can't do this, Dane. I'm killing her.**

She just wants to be sure you're all right.

She knows I'm all right. What she wants is to be near me. Even if it means exposing herself to fire from the city. And don't remind me of who I am, or how much damage she's done. I don't think I'm rational anymore.

If you weren't, you couldn't form that thought.

Small comfort. Look, I'm warning you, while I still can. Watch me. Treat me as if I *am* your enemy.

"General Shimas," Beviney said, "you must have guessed that Kay-Raike was receiving reports from his brother."

"Your point?"

"I know who's with you, and where you're going. If my intentions were hostile, I'd simply wait for you there."

"No you wouldn't. First, it's a big city and you don't know precisely where we'll be entering. Second, you can't approach it safely." He did not want to tell her that they were no longer aboard Pwanda's shuttle. "We have clearance, but they'd never agree to two flights."

"General Shimas . . ." There was a long pause before she said, *"Please."*

"What do you want?"

"I want to be with my husband. You'll have two hostages."

Marana, I love you.

Dane did not respond, other than to glance at Pwanda. He was looking at the western sky, his tears flowing freely.

"That isn't possible, No'ln Beviney."

"I'll give you that comm patch to *Sovereign*. You can have it right now, through my ship. Set your frequency controls and tell me when you're ready."

Good, he thought; he'd convinced her that they were still aboard. "I expect to have this business concluded within twenty-four hours," he said. "My Fleet is four days away. Do you want to wait that long?"

"What do you mean?"

"When we're finished, we'll be arriving at your ship in the shuttle that brought us here. Momed will remain inside with us until we reach *Sovereign*. But you can come aboard, during the transit. If all goes well, you'll be together tomorrow. Is that satisfactory?"

"Yes! General Shimas, isn't there a way I can help?"

"You can return to your ship, and don't be seen. You'll make the people in the city nervous."

"I will. Thank you."

"You handled that well," Pwanda said when the radio was secured. "Letting her aboard is a good idea. I'm grateful also."

"I'm sorry," Shimas said. "But now that I've thought about it, I can't take the chance."

"You lied?"

"I spoke too hastily. We'll have to keep the shuttle pressurized and sealed at all times. If we open the door even for a second, we're vulnerable."

"You *are* a liar, Buto," Pwanda said angrily. "Do you know how difficult it was for a woman like Marana to say *please*? She's been completely truthful in everything she's said to you, and she's done all that you asked. In return you forced her to humiliate herself, and you lied to her."

"As I told you," Shimas said, his color rising, "I spoke hastily."

"Then call her now and tell her the truth."

"You do it." He tossed the radio to Pwanda. "And when she's killed trying to find you—"

Pwanda threw back the radio, forcefully. Shimas caught

it two inches from his face and advanced on the taller man, who clenched his fists and strode toward Shimas.

Dane and Jenny stepped between them. "Please," Dane said. "Don't."

Shimas stopped and took several deep breaths. He put his hands over Jenny's, which were pressing against his chest. "I apologize, Momed. And when this is over, I'll apologize to Marana."

"No'ln Supervisor Beviney, to you." Pwanda glared at him, then turned and began walking in long strides toward the city. **Tell them to keep up with me, Dane. I want this finished.**

Regent can't match that pace, Momed.

Then she can stay here.

Momed, she has to be with us when we get there.

Shimas can carry her. Let's go. But just before he left the clearing, he stopped and waited for the others.

Alee

"I had you brought aboard because you were dying," Mendel said. "Nem begged me to help you. I didn't tell you where you were because I didn't want to frighten you. We're on the way back now, to take you home."

The onynote had taken effect, and Sela was calm and talkative. "Your brother is going to let me live? Why?"

"I told him about all the weapons emplacements I'd seen," Mendel said, winking. "He was grateful for the warning."

"I'm glad we don't have to kill all of you," she said, understanding the joke. "Seriously, I'm grateful too. You saved my life."

"You can do something for me, if you want to," Mendel said. "I have to know about that shuttle again."

"Why?"

With a frown, Mendel said, "I'm a little worried about a head injury I received."

"I didn't know you were hurt, sir."

"I fell while I was helping to carry you into the cave. You were unconscious at the time."

"Are you all right?"

"I thought so. But now I'm not so sure. I was certain you told me there was a fight when the shuttle landed."

"Do you want me to go over it all again?"

"Yes, please. And when you're finished, I want to hear what Nem was going to say when he reported the spacers killed."

"Oh, it was good," she said, smiling broadly. "I wrote it myself."

"Excellent." He winked again. "Frighten me with it."

"Are you satisfied, sir?" Mendel asked an hour later.

"So it's true," Kay-Raike said, smiling with satisfaction. "The same story, twice, no contradictions." The two officers were alone in *Alee*'s dimly lit War Room, the holo of Poda Sela frozen above the table between them. "Pwanda betrayed his wife for that . . . *her*." He laughed, switching off the display. "It's all mine again, Mendel. I'll give Beviney the proof, including the Grounder for interrogation. Once she's convinced, she'll be eager to reestablish our partnership. She'll deal with her husband and, in gratitude, give the rest to me."

"How would you like it done, sir? Shimas, I mean."

"This time there will be no mistakes, Mendel. I'll take personal charge. First we'll 'discover' the bodies, covered with dirt and vegetation."

"And their son, Jarred?"

"If we can find him soon enough, we'll invite him to participate in the search. His testimony could be valuable. Otherwise we must reluctantly consider him lost, and report as such to the Generals." Kay-Raike closed his eyes for a moment, envisioning their "discovery." "It will look as though the Grounders tortured *her* . . . horribly, Mendel . . . and then executed all of them. As further proof we'll transmit Poda Sela's voice announcing their deaths and issuing

Canopal's challenge to the entire Fleet. And then we begin.'' He tapped his fingers excitedly against the table. ''You did well, Brother. Finally.''

''Thank you, sir. May I see Dorothy now?''

''Yes. I'll go with you.''

''Why?''

''I want to present you both with the orders for your new command.'' For the first time since they were children, he clapped Mendel's shoulder in a gesture of affection. ''I'll make it a proper good-bye.''

At the last corridor intersection before reaching his quarters, Mendel turned left, but was restrained by Karnas's hand. ''The orders,'' he said, pointing to the right, ''are in my stateroom. We'll stop there first.''

Telling Mendel to wait outside, Karnas entered the compartment and shut the door behind him. As the long minutes passed, Mendel heard laughter from inside. By the time the door opened again, his eyes were dry, and he was ready.

''Oh!'' Dorothy, her hair and uniform disheveled, one arm around Kay-Raike's waist, put a hand to her mouth and took a step backward.

''Come in, Brother,'' Kay-Raike said, in the same genial tone he'd used when ordering that crew to shatter his legs.

Mendel's face was without expression. Taking three steps forward, he said, ''Martin loved you, Karnas.''

Kay-Raike stared, not comprehending. ''What does that—'' As the larger man continued approaching, he backed away.

Mendel stopped walking. ''He loved you, Karnas. Before I killed him, he begged me to intercede with you.''

Looking into his brother's eyes, Kay-Raike realized that this time, his brother understood what he had in mind for him: first humiliation, and then execution. ''Dorothy is here as a joke, Brother,'' he said. ''A joke, to send the two . . . three of you on your way.'' He moved bit by bit to his left, circling, hoping to position himself between his brother and the door.

"He was proud of you. He wanted to be with you, as your son. To help you against the council."

As the smaller man took another half-step, Mendel raised his left arm and pointed the pistol at his chest. Kay-Raike's eyes went wide. "You were *ordered* to return that to the quartermaster!"

"I forgot, Brother."

Kay-Raike judged the distance to the door; too far. He stopped.

"That's why I killed him. Because he loved you."

"You said it was accidental."

Mendel smiled, tight-lipped. "A Kay-Raike, lying? Imagine that."

"Why are you telling me this?"

"I promised myself I would, before you died."

Dorothy said from behind Kay-Raike, "Mendel. Don't do this."

"We're going to be free," he said, his eyes never leaving Kay-Raike.

"Free? We'll be killed."

"He flaunts you, Dorothy! There is no ship for us as he promised. What other freedom is possible now?" He raised the weapon minutely, concentrating his aim.

"Mendel, please!" Kay-Raike said. "I told you, this was meant to be a joke. You're to leave today for your new command. I swear it!"

"What ship, Brother? What is the name of my new command?" When Kay-Raike hesitated, he laughed. "There's a Grounder saying, Karnas. Even a fool is wise twice in his lifetime."

"Think about your family," Kay-Raike said, using his hands as ineffective shields. "You know what will happen to your wife. And your *child*."

Mendel hesitated, slowly lowering the pistol. But then he raised it again, and held it for several seconds before lowering, then raising, it again. His hand shook. "I can't . . ." he said, and was silent, until the hardness entered his eyes again. "All I ever wanted from you was my freedom," he said. "Now I'm going to have it." But still, he hesitated.

"Give me the weapon, Brother," Kay-Raike said, holding out his hand. "I say again, it was meant as a harmless joke. You misunderstood. But I'm at fault here, not you."

"Mendel," Dorothy said. "While we're alive, we have a chance. Please don't take it away."

"You misunderstood," Kay-Raike repeated.

Judging the time to be right, Mendel nodded. "Here," he said. "Take it."

Weapon in hand, Kay-Raike backed three paces. "Grounder sayings," he said, smiling, taking aim. "Is that what you've come to, fool? Dorothy, come here." As she stood beside him, he put his arm around her waist. "Choose between us," he said confidently. "If you choose him, I'll let you both go. On the honor of my mother, I will."

"On the honor of . . ." Mendel said, shock and then relief in his eyes. "Dorothy, he means it! We can go." He stepped toward her, arms outstretched.

"No! I'm sorry," she said. "Mendel, I did care for you, once. But you're weak. You've never had a future."

Mendel slumped, his eyes downcast. He had believed her. Despite the lie about Karnas's impotence, which he thought was meant to comfort him, he'd believed her. "So it's him you want, and now . . . You didn't tell him I was here before?"

"No."

"Why?"

"To protect you."

"And as usual," he said, "I was wrong about everything." Looking at her again, he said, "Take care of our child, Dorothy."

"I will, Mendel. I promise you that."

Kay-Raike sneered. "You think he deserves your kindness after trying to assassinate me? Tell him the truth."

"Karnas, I . . ."

"Tell him!"

"There is no child," Dorothy said. "I thought believing there was might inspire you. But you nearly failed again."

Angrily, she continued. "Why are you so stupid? You and I could have had a good life together, a prominent place in the Fleet. Karnas has given you every opportunity to advance, to become valuable to him. This time you succeeded only because a Grounder happened to see something after one of your customary mistakes."

"You knew everything?"

"The plan you were to carry out was hers," Kay-Raike said, pulling her closer to him. "She's been very helpful, Brother. For a very long time. The only error she made was in convincing me to tolerate you for as long as I have. Today that error nearly cost me my life." He took her hand, and placed the weapon in it. "Go ahead, Dorothy."

"Karnas, I don't want to do this."

A knife appeared in his hand. "If you don't, I'll keep him alive for days. He's your one mistake. Kill him."

She leveled the weapon. Mendel began to speak, but remained silent.

"I'm sorry, Mendel."

"So am I, Dorothy. Good-bye."

She squeezed the trigger and opened her mouth as if to scream. Spasms wracked her body as she shook her arm, unable to release the object that was causing her such agony. She collapsed and writhed, doubled at the waist, her head snapping grotesquely against the metal floor.

Mendel charged around her at Kay-Raike. But the smaller man, younger and quicker of reflex, was ready. The knife entered below Mendel's sternum and was snatched away as Kay-Raike took a step backward. Again Mendel lunged, this time closing his hands around Kay-Raike's throat. He squeezed as the knife pressed against his own throat, cutting him, the pain soon forcing him to move back and release his grip. Kay-Raike pulled away, and as Mendel stumbled toward him he bent and attacked. This time the blade found soft flesh in Mendel's right thigh and twisted. But still he tried to fight, bellowing and swinging his fists through the air as Kay-Raike easily evaded the blows.

"Stop!" Kay-Raike backed away. "I'll bring a doctor here."

"So you can make it last for days?" Mendel grated out.

"Yes!" Kay-Raike moved toward the door.

Weakening fast as the blood poured from his wounds, Mendel pointed at the barely twitching figure of Dorothy. "That's how Martin died," he said in a barely audible voice. "The boy who loved you, Brother. Our mother would have been proud of him. But you killed her, too."

Kay-Raike froze. "*Me?* I had nothing to do . . . *She* made the choice!"

"Yes. But you've never forgiven yourself for her death."

"That's absurd."

"No," Mendel said weakly, swaying on his feet. The pain was becoming unbearable as the combat-induced adrenaline ebbed away. "It's not absurd." He knew he would bleed to death—if given time. "It's insane. And it's the truth. The doctors know it. All of your crews know it. They laugh at you, Karnas."

"Liar!"

I am well trained for lies, he thought, and pressed on for a quick death. "You kept me alive all these years because only *I* can forgive you. But I never will. You killed your son, who loved you." Mendel's legs folded beneath him. He landed on his knees and pitched forward, catching himself with his hands, grimacing, knowing that he was close to death—and victory. "And our mother . . ."

Kay-Raike raised the knife and ran at the fallen man. He stabbed repeatedly as the room swirled around him, closing in, suffocating him. "Liar," he said, panting, as Mendel collapsed. "No one knows! No one laughs at . . ." And then, in the phenomenon Dane had seen while tracking him, he was suddenly calm. "You won't die so easily," he said quietly, withdrawing the knife and tossing it aside. He lifted Mendel's head. "Do you understand me?" And then he opened his hand and screamed in rage. Mendel had cheated him, beaten him. He was dead.

That Dorothy was also added little to his misery. After examining her, he tried to stand and could not force his legs to be steady. He rolled onto the floor and shook, hearing again above her last consoling message, the terrifying accusations of his mother. And a voice he had never really heard before. Martin's.

₹28₹

Day 62

Pacing her stateroom, Beviney waited impatiently for Shimas to reply to her message, broadcast an hour before and now repeated every ten minutes. They must be within the city now, she reasoned, and outside the shuttle. *Answer!* she commanded silently.

Her first response to the report that a Silver Fleet squadron was approaching the system had been visceral: anger, and the anticipation of battle. But then she realized that their presence could be of help to her—if Shimas would agree to accept one hundred ships as the safe passage he wanted. She would have been content to be with Momed aboard the shuttle during the transit to *Sovereign*. But how much better it will be, she thought, to have him safe in their stateroom, Shimas and his party aboard their own ships, and the Fleets parting company.

Her conversation with Squadron Leader Opina Keitel had been cordial but understandably guarded. Keitel would not reveal her orders. And so Beviney had said little, other than that she knew Shimas's approximate location and had no objection to the squadron approaching Canopal—provided that no ship entered the atmosphere. That, she explained, could incite the Dirts and endanger "one of my officers" who was traveling with the council member.

Ansel

"Can we reenter hyperspace?" Saddhurst asked.

Naomi emerged from beneath a thick black cylinder, the vessel's secondary power coupling, and jumped lightly to her feet. There were new cuts on her hands, and her face and uniform were stained with white lubricant. "It may hold," she said. "But not more than once. The parts I could salvage from the primary were not in good condition. What about propulsion?"

"The diagnostics are under way," Saddhurst said. "So far everything looks good."

"How much longer until you know?"

"A few hours. I'm going to sleep."

"So am I," Naomi said. "I only wish there were enough water for a bath."

"Isn't there?"

"No. I've had to dedicate the recycle system to provide cooling."

"No need to worry," Saddhurst said. "Where we're going, there are oceans."

When he reached the summit of a hill and had his first view of the City of Dreams, Shimas stood silently for a minute before turning and motioning for Jenny to call a halt. He took her aside as all but the children sat on a carpet of grass.

"Is something wrong, Buto Shimas?" Ren asked after Pwanda had set her down. "We're not tired."

"Wait, please," Shimas replied. He led Jenny back toward the place where he'd been standing. "This far out," he said to her as they walked, "they didn't recover the bodies."

Jenny reached the summit and gasped. "I don't want Ren and her brothers to see this."

"And Sato?"

She put her hand on his shoulder and said, "I can't decide that. Not alone."

"Then ask me," Sato said from behind them.

"Sato," Jenny said. "You were told to wait."

"But I was ordered to be a part of this. Remember, I'm quickly becoming a man."

"Very well," Shimas said. "Come here."

The scene below was a boneyard. Between the hill and a cluster of small buildings ahead lay scores of human skeletons, few of them intact, scattered over a broad field among piles of ashes. Here and there were blackened but still-standing stone ovens. There were the sun-bleached remains of animals, most of them jummers. "When the first meal was over," Shimas observed, "they were next."

"Buto," Jenny said. "Those people . . . nearly all of them so small . . . They were children."

Shimas nodded in agreement. "This was probably what Dane calls a play area."

Sato was quiet, his face expressionless.

"Do you want to go on?" Shimas asked. "There may be much worse ahead."

"I'm quickly becoming a man," Sato said in a quiet voice. "But there's nothing wrong with being a child a little longer. I've seen enough." Turning from them, he walked away.

Jenny returned to the base of the hill with the four children while Buto led the others into the city. Regent spoke with the few people they encountered, explaining to them what she was looking for. The residents answered tersely that they didn't know of any recordings of the attack. But they were all willing to relate what they'd seen. When they learned that their testimony would not be of help, many of them told their stories anyway, following the group or acting as guides.

Dane was gratified that Shimas did not order them to leave, or to be quiet. He listened, and asked questions.

It soon became apparent that contrary to Fleet tradition, Kay-Raike had not concentrated his fire on buildings and city infrastructure. His interest had been the killing of as many people as possible. And he'd been efficient. The guides led them past a gravesite bearing hundreds of markers. "There are dozens of these," a young woman said. "They were shelters. From over there," she said, indicating a small copse of trees, "I watched a ship hover and shoot down into the one you just saw."

"How did the spacers know they were shelters?" Mill asked.

"People were still running into them."

This area, she told Shimas, had been assailed during the first attack—before two Kay-Raike ships had been destroyed. "You don't want to see where the second attack came."

"Yes," Regent told her. "He does." She took the lead, and an hour later they crested a two-story pile of debris. The heat at the top was intense, nearly unbearable. Below them stretched a half-mile or more of smoldering pits bordered by plateaus of devastation. No structure remained.

"This was the core of the city," Regent said, turning to face away from the carnage. "There were hospitals, schools, government centers, trade markets. My staff estimates that on the day of the attacks there were more than eighty thousand people in that one area. But this isn't the worst. Nearly all of our housing was there." She pointed north, and then swept her arm eastward. "We'll never know the actual number of dead," she said. "Many escaped into the countryside, and more of them return every day to help rebuild. But we're guessing that you spacers murdered at least two hundred thousand people. That's seven of every ten citizens in the city."

"I never thought," Ten said, staring at the vista before

them, "that even spacers were this bad." Turning to Dane, he said, "It's good I didn't know about this when you came aboard *Suram*. You'd've all been shredded like the eels we ate that day."

Unable to take her eyes from the destruction, Dane did not hear him.

"She isn't one of them," Pwanda said. "And we've got to find enough recordings to prevent this from happening again."

"Follow me," Regent said. "The university observatory and three weather stations survived. They'll have what we need."

Shimas wheeled around to face her. "You knew where we needed to go, Regent. Why did you allow us to waste time?"

"Smell the air," Regent said. "It's clean right now. But once or twice a day there's another collapse below ground. Sometimes blood is forced up by the pressure, and you can see it spurting and bubbling in pools before it boils away. Do you know how many crushed bodies that implies? For a day or more you can smell them burning down there. That's a pleasure your Fleet has added to our lives, General Shimas. I would have been rude if I hadn't at least tried to share it with you."

He isn't going to tell her what happens when a ship explodes, is he?

That's exactly what he did when my mother pleaded with him to stop the destruction on Walden.

You told me. That's why I asked.

No, I don't think he'll do that now.

Dane was correct. Shimas began making his way back down the pile of debris, saying nothing.

Karnas Kay-Raike lay in bed, shivering as two doctors wiped perspiration from his face. "No more medication," he said through clenched teeth as one of them raised a vial to his mouth.

"But, sir, you need to sleep."

"Get out."

"Let us change your uniform first, sir. We have a warm and dry one here."

Kay-Raike struck the woman's face with his fist. "Get out!"

When he was alone, he sat up dizzily, wrapping himself with his arms. "I am a Kay-Raike," he muttered, finding strength in the words. "I am *the* Kay-Raike." He stood slowly and, taking his time, removed his soaked clothing and put on the fresh uniform. He felt better.

At the radio console he made the connection and began speaking with No'ln Beviney.

Moving at maximum normal-space speed, *Alee* and Beviney's temporary flagship closed to within fifty miles of one another. The shuttle carrying Poda Sela covered the distance in minutes and returned to *Alee*.

It was her greatest fear, and therefore the one she had clung to most tenaciously. Poda Sela was unconscious now, her screams forgotten. Beviney sat slumped in a chair. The unadorned wall ahead of her filled with images of her husband's face, the movements he made while sleeping, the things he did when he wasn't aware that she was watching. And then the wall showed her Momed and Dane Steppart, embracing, laughing together. With that special smile, the one that was—she had believed—meant for her only. Not a hostage. He was as Kay-Raike had said: a traitor.

"No'ln Beviney." She heard the voice as if it had been filtered through layers of thick cloth. "We've rejoined our ships."

Opina Keitel was forced by circumstance to keep her squadron relatively close to the Gold Fleet formation. She had been monitoring Beviney's attempts to contact Shimas, and wanted to be in position to intercede if necessary when he was located. A small, frail-looking woman of fifty, she was deceptively strong physically and too experienced a commander to be lulled by the open cooperation she had received so far. Her ships were on high alert status, the individual captains ready to respond to Enemy provocation.

Still, she was shocked by the speed of the maneuver displayed above her War Table. One second the golden mites were sedately keeping station, one of them having just rejoined the rest. And then as quickly as her eye could follow, they formed into a three-dimensional wedge aimed directly at her flagship. And accelerated.

Their coordination is astonishing, she thought as her hand reached for the alarm.

"BATTLE CONTACT! BATTLE CONTACT!"

"X-7-12," she said calmly into the squadronwide battle circuit. "Execute, but do not fire without my authorization." Weapons range was less than a minute away, if the Gold Fleet maintained its acceleration.

The silver-hued ships turned in unit formation to face the charge and held position.

"Squadron Leader," she heard from behind her. "No'ln Beviney is calling for you."

"Patch it to here," Keitel said. The signal was audio only. "What are you doing?" Keitel asked.

"Games, Squadron Leader," Beviney replied. "We thought you might be as bored as we are."

"You're creating a dangerous situation," Keitel said.

"It is exciting, isn't it? Your General Marsham did well the last time we met like this. I wonder if you have her nerve."

"Forty seconds to weapons range," Keitel said. "I request that you change course." Jenny Marsham was an old friend of Keitel's. Privately, she had told her of the Grounder game pebble-hand, which had guided the encounter Beviney alluded to. She had to consider the possibility that Beviney was attempting to entice her to fire, thus losing the game—if it was a game.

"You're well within our range already," Beviney said. "If you were involved in our conflict of eight years ago, you know that. What are you going to do?"

Keitel had commanded a ship during the Battle. She knew that an undetermined number of the Gold Fleet vessels had sacrificed shield strength and maneuverability for enhanced range. But none of the golden mites had lagged behind the others when the Gold Fleet took its present formation. And so thirty-three seconds remained before either side could fire effectively. "You'll know what I'm going to do very soon, No'ln Beviney. Unless you change course, as I once again request."

"If you're frightened, why don't you try to run?"

"I have an assignment here."

"Not anymore," came Beviney's cold reply. The communication ended.

Keitel rested her hand next to the switch that would send her voice to all Silver Fleet ships. She watched the display as the seconds passed. The Gold Fleet formation passed into weapons range, but did not fire. Nor did it alter course or speed.

Twelve more seconds had elapsed when Beviney's voice came back. "Nicely done, Squadron Leader. I'll reverse course now. General Marsham will be proud of your—"

At that instant, the slaughter began. Two hundred fifty Gold Fleet ships fired as one, concentrating on fifty of the Silver Fleet vessels. Within a second, forty-three of them were fatally damaged. At Keitel's order the survivors broke formation and returned fire, turning to run for hyperspace.

Beviney's force split into fragments and pursued.

Knowing that she was lost, Keitel initiated an emergency transmission to *Sovereign* that had just begun when the ship seemed to lift beneath her, suddenly spinning out of control. The next series of impacts ended with the disintegration of the innermost hull. As all air vanished into the vacuum of space, her lungs expanded until they burst.

Fifty-one Gold Fleet ships perished in the fight. None of Keitel's squadron reached the safety of hyperspace.

⇒29⇐

Day 63

Pebbles, Dane thought. Four red bulbs. Smaller than grapes, harder than stones, virtually weightless. Inside her uniform pocket she closed her hand around them protectively. The information they contained meant the difference between life and death for countless worlds. If they could be delivered to *Sovereign*.

Ahead of her walked Buto Shimas, his enormous shoulders nearly bowed under the weight of two cloth bags. Each contained two of the primitive, by Fleet standards, recorders that had produced the bulbs. Those too would be examined by the council to establish that there had been no deceit.

Dane was excited, her fatigue disappearing as they neared the shuttle. Seth had estimated that they would arrive just before dawn—already the sky was a light gray, with ghostly shadows falling away from trees and boulders. She thought of Regent, who was probably now rousing from slumber to resume her role in the rebuilding of the

City of Dreams. Of the many incredible things Dane had seen in her life, one of the most surprising had been the sight of Regent and Buto Shimas embracing warmly as they said good-bye and wished one another good luck. Like many strong people, Shimas could accept change within himself only if it grew from his own experience and honestly held convictions. But never in her memory had he accepted . . . *scolding* was the most appropriate word she could think of . . . from anyone but Jenny Marsham.

"There it is!" Sato called out. "See that big tree with the broken branch? Twenty yards beyond that are those boulders with the one that looks like a jummer's head. And then we'll be at the shuttle."

"You're really smart," Ren said. She was stronger now, and had walked for the past three hours.

Sato looked at her, blank-faced. "I've been trying to tell you that," he said with great dignity.

Heth burst into laughter. Unable to stare him into silence, Sato joined in.

"Wait," Shimas said as the children began to run ahead. "Stay with us. We'll be there soon."

"Buto Shimas, can I be the one to call Jarred?" Seth asked.

"Yes," he said. "You've earned it."

"They'll like it aboard *Suram*," Ten said to Jenny. "They'll cry some more about their parents, but in no time at all they'll be as happy at sea as they were in these smelly woods."

"I thought they'd want to stay with Regent," Jenny replied.

"They're not city children," Mill said. "They'd feel crated in there. Now they'll have a whole ocean to explore."

Pwanda walked silently behind the others, wondering where home would be for the rest of his life. He was the last to come in sight of the shuttle. But he was first to see the figure walking out from behind it.

"Good morning, husband," Marana Beviney said.

• • •

Karnas Kay-Raike sat on the floor in his darkened state-room, hands on his knees, head lowered. Between his feet was the holostat of his mother. Perspiration dried on his face as he breathed deeply, smiling. The vigil was over. Through the night he had searched her face for evidence of the obscenity Mendel had spoken, the one he had believed for so long, never giving it words. Her eyes looked back at him. There was no condemnation, no forgiveness. There was nothing. She was dead.

He lay back and laughed, pounding the floor with clenched fists. How could he have been so stupid? What was the point of all his years of suffering? She was *dead*.

She knows, Dane. It was all for nothing.

Beviney gave a sharp pull on the length of cord she held. Following her out came Jarred, stumbling, face bloodied, blindfolded. His arms were tied behind his back.

"Beviney." Shimas began walking toward them.

"Come ahead," Beviney said, releasing the cord. Jenny rushed to Jarred and led him back. "I wanted to see what you would do first, Shimas. Come for your son, or secure your *hostage?* I believe that particular game is over now." When no one answered, she raised a radio to her mouth and said, "Now."

From below the northern horizon two streaks of gold appeared, gleaming in the morning sun. With a thunderous clap the warships covered the distance in seconds, hovered for a moment a mile away, and as the explosion of sound came again retreated beyond sight.

"Other than those two," Beviney said to Shimas, "I'm alone. What are you going to do?"

Look at her face, Dane. She wants to be killed. May God forgive me for what I've done to her.

"What do you want?" Shimas asked.

"The joy of destroying a squadron of your ships that came to help you," Beviney said. "But I have already had that pleasure. Did you find what you wanted against Kay-Raike?"

"No," Shimas said.

"Yes, Marana," Pwanda said. "We found it."

"Give it to me."

Shimas indicated the two bags he'd set down. "There," he said.

Beviney advanced boldly and hefted the bags. "There seems to be a great deal," she said, her eyes challenging Shimas to strike at her. "Is this all of it?"

"No," Pwanda said. "Dane has four capsules in her pocket. They're what's really important."

For the first time Beviney looked directly at him. She held his eyes until he lowered his face. Turning to Dane, she said, "Give them to me."

"It's all right, Dane," Jenny said. "We have no choice now."

Dane looked at Beviney, and saw the unutterable pain in her eyes. "He loves you, No'ln Beviney. It was never about me. It was about preventing Kay-Raike from—"

"Give them to me."

Dane reached in her pocket and hesitated.

"Now," Beviney said, extending her hand.

Dane looked at Shimas, who nodded. Her closed right hand emerged from her pocket and touched Beviney's.

The blow, a solid left fist to Beviney's temple, surprised Dane as much as it did the others.

Pwanda ran forward and caught his collapsing wife. Beviney had discarded the radio and was reaching for his face when she lost consciousness. Pwanda glared at Dane as he lowered Marana gently to the ground.

Shocked by her action, the first time she had ever struck another human being, Dane sent, **Bond with her when she wakes, Momed.**

No more deception, Dane.

Deception? **Momed, tell her the truth.** *Heal* **her!**

Why should she believe me? Yes, I'll try, for her sake. And if any of you comes near her again, I'll kill you.

At that moment the two Gold Fleet ships appeared with the same booming thunder as before, stopping directly overhead. The ground around them began to burn, trees and undergrowth erupting in flame. The inferno was so sudden and all-encompassing that within seconds they were gasping for oxygen.

"To the shuttle!" Marsham cried out. Pwanda lifted Marana into his arms as Dane, Shimas, and Marsham each picked up one of the children.

"How do you open this thing?" Mill, the first to arrive at the vessel, called. Immediately behind her, Jarred grasped an inset lever just aft of the door and twisted it to the side.

"It's locked," he said.

"Let me try." Shimas took hold and grunted with effort, pulling at the unyielding lever until it tore from its socket. "Gold Fleet garbage," he said in disgust, hurling it at the door.

From above came the sound of shrieking, tearing metal. Through gathering clouds of smoke, one of the Gold Fleet ships could be seen to rock unsteadily before darting away, disintegrating as it fled. As the smoke obscured everything beyond it, a series of explosions ripped through the pall.

She did want to die. But how could her ships react so quickly?

On signal, Dane. She must have keyed the radio before she passed out.

The city was firing on them, Shimas realized. He looked in every direction and saw only solid walls of flame. All of them were on the ground now, faces close to the dirt, drawing in the last of the air. His reserves depleted by the struggle with the door, he barely had the breath to say goodbye to Jenny and the children.

Beyond the inferno, ten Patrol sent by Regent as an unseen escort ran around the flames, desperately seeking a gap in the burning wall. Three approached too closely and were nearly overcome by the intense heat before retreating helplessly. The Patrol's calls of encouragement were lost in the roaring, snapping chaos.

The circle of fire raged closer. Dane and Jenny lay atop the four children, trying to shield them with their bodies.

Choking, Ten gasped, "Maybe that fire isn't so thick. I'll call if I get through." He had taken only three steps when he fell. Mill crawled toward him.

This is my fault, Momed. I'm sorry.

What does it matter? I'm glad it's over, Dane. No one will ever hurt her again. It *is* their fault, Pwanda told himself bitterly. They should've killed Kay-Raike years ago. *She* would have. And it isn't my fault they don't carry breather-pellets as *we of the Gold Fleet* do. The sooner they're gone from the galaxies, the better. Cradling Marana in his arms, watching as her chest rose and fell, he was unafraid of the burning death only minutes away now.

"Water," he heard. Turning, he saw Seth crawling toward him. "Water," the boy said again. "Please, Momed Pwanda, help me." He struggled to lift one of the rifles, pointed it at Pwanda. "Help me."

"I can't," Pwanda said, his heart breaking for these children who were condemned by their elders' stupidity. But why should here be any different from the rest of the universe? "Lie down, Seth. It will be easier that way."

⇒30⇐

Day 65

No'ln Bishop received the report in his quarters, thankful that the junior supervisor, his niece, had had the foresight to use his private code. "And the Silver Fleet ships?" he asked.

"We destroyed that squadron, sir. As for—"

" 'As for' is what I'm asking about, Verna. I know about the squadron. What about Kay-Raike?"

"His thirty ships are still here, No'ln Bishop."

"Do you believe he knows what's happened?"

"I don't see how he could, sir. None of his ships has entered the atmosphere. The fire was very small, and impenetrable. Exactly as you ordered."

"And neither of our ships survived?"

"No, sir. The Dirts got one of them as it was recording Shimas and the rest of them burning."

Bishop held the transmitted holo in his hand, nodding. "And the second ship?"

"They got the other one when it returned later to confirm that the shuttle had been consumed. There was nothing left but a burned-out hull."

"Unfortunate," he said, smiling. "Stand by."

Bishop severed the connection and began making another one. He sincerely regretted the death of Marana Beviney. She had been an able administrator, and the finest battle commander the Fleet had produced in centuries. But unlike himself, she was a person of limited vision. Kay-Raike had offered her the chance to take total power over the Silver Fleet. She had accepted, but only to please her husband. How could she have been so naive as to believe that he, No'ln Ferstead Bishop, did not know her every plan? He could have forgiven her for that lapse and guided her to take the correct action. But to bring a Dirt into the highest and most honorable echelon of the Gold Fleet—into the ancient community of Noldron Supervisors, to which his family had belonged for eight centuries—effrontery! No, that could never be tolerated.

The connection had been established for several seconds, Kay-Raike repeating his name, before Bishop broke his reverie and responded. "No'ln Beviney is dead," he said. "So are Shimas and the others. No evidence exists against you."

"How did it happen, No'ln Bishop?"

"I'll explain in a minute. You and I are to be partners, equally. Beviney never offered you that, did she?"

"No, sir."

"My name is Ferstead. With all respect, Karnas, I recommend that you return to *Sovereign* immediately and show your Generals what I'm about to transmit to you. In the meantime I'm calling my ships back to *Noldron*, where the captains will testify before the Nomarch."

"Testify to what?"

"That the worlds are a grave danger to all of us. Everything, exactly as you've said. Now please be patient, and listen."

•　　•　　•

Kay-Raike smiled as he listened, pacing his quarters with renewed energy. Gingerly he stepped around an open box containing the wrapped body of Dorothy, on whose stomach rested the holostat of his mother. "Good, Ferstead," he said at last, lowering the box's lid until he was alone again. "I'll leave immediately."

⇉31⇇

Day 75

Sovereign

Some members desperately trying to conceal their outrage, others basking in the glory of victory, the council, as one, smiled benignly while Karnas Kay-Raike entered the austere compartment and took his place among them. The Generals had not yet arrived, and so the talk was informal. Those whose beliefs had been vanquished joined in the easy banter, pretending an affection they did not feel for the usurper, and the future—a return to the past, with a vengeance—he represented. Kay-Raike was magnanimous to all. He answered their polite questions about the murder of Council Member Shimas and his family, their anguished faces plainly seen in the holo, so cruelly burned to death as Grounders encircled the blaze and jeered. The holo had been graciously provided by the Gold Fleet's new Senior No'ln Supervisor in the belief that they must now cooperate against a newly powerful and audacious common enemy. And then there was that Grounder's boasting of their deaths, challenging the Fleet to respond. All of them flushed as Kay-Raike recited the words yet again.

When the Generals arrived, all came to attention. Mosh Trikal welcomed Kay-Raike and invited them to be seated. "One detail," he said. "I have decided to attempt the retrieval of any remains of our colleague and his family before Canopal receives Fleet justice."

The council nodded its approval; Shimas and General Marsham deserved no less.

"Karnas," Depluss said, "are you certain of the coordinates involved? I don't wish to risk one of our ships unnecessarily."

Kay-Raike was mildly surprised at the Generals' sudden announcement, wondering if they still distrusted him. No matter, he thought. Any foray to Canopal would only confirm what he had told them. And hasten their fall from power. "Of course, Generals. I'm certain."

"Good," Trikal said. "Please excuse me while I make arrangements for the attempt."

In their quarters, the Generals sat down at the communication console. Trikal engaged the noise unit. "Colonel Saddhurst," he said. "Proceed with the information I gave you."

"Thank you, Generals," came the reply. "Again I apologize for not contacting you sooner. But we were stranded out here for quite some time."

"You've explained that, Colonel. The personnel responsible for the maintenance of *Ansel* will face appropriate charges. Whatever remains you may find, leave the atmosphere as soon as they're aboard. An escort squadron will arrive in four days."

"Understood, Generals. Thank you."

"The idea to bring them back should have been mine," Depluss said. "I am sorry for your loss, Colonel." Not waiting for the surprised reply to be completed, she ended the transmission.

• • •

Mill's burns were the worst, but she would survive. They waited now while she healed, with little else to do.

Twelve days before, the fire had threatened to consume them all. But again Seth preserved their lives.

The rifle's beam had sliced neatly through the ground as Pwanda focused its energy over the spot beneath which Seth had heard the rush of flowing water. He had cut in a circular pattern, and at last the beam penetrated. Shimas crawled to the spot and threw his bulk against it, disappearing as the ground gave way. There was a splash from the cavern below before Shimas called out, "The hole's too deep for me to climb out, but there's air here." Pwanda could feel it rushing out, pure, sweet, and cool. "Get the others down, Momed. Please."

Marana was first, followed by the children. Dane, Jarred, and Jenny were able to crawl to the spot and drop through. Mill and Ten needed to be dragged. As the flames closed in around him, Momed jumped through the hole into darkness.

The cold water shocked Marana into consciousness. They had no choice but to flow with the stream, which was too rapid to fight against. She, Jenny, Shimas, Jarred, and Sato could not swim. But this was not a problem for most of their hour-long journey through total darkness, the water only occasionally exceeding knee level. Ten had revived and pushed ahead of them, floating on his stomach and pulling against the mud with his hands. The rest followed, the spacers walking bent over at the waist.

"Good thing there's low tides here, too," Ten called back to them. A spot of light ahead grew larger as they approached. Ten could be seen profiled in it, waving them onward. When they reached him, he pointed downward. "About fifteen feet of sheer rock," he said, "then a pool below. Who wants to test the waters?"

"Wait until our eyes adjust," Shimas said. "Then—"

"You're not in command here," Pwanda snapped. "No'ln Beviney, with your permission?"

She stared at him for a long while before nodding. "Be careful," she said.

Pwanda turned from her, his face contorted, wet from sudden tears of hope. He leapt feet first into space, knifing sharply into the pool. For long seconds Ten and Marana watched the roiling water. At last his head broke the surface and he waved, grinning. "Deep," he called up to her. "No rocks."

Without hesitation, Marana jumped.

Shimas was last, dismissing his fear and emulating the courage of Jenny, Jarred, and Sato.

Seth led them in building a shelter against a heavy rain that began to fall. By dusk it was completed and they were sitting around a warming fire, facing away from one another, drying themselves and their hung clothing as harmless smoke fluted up the shelter's conical shape and disappeared. Two of their number were not there. Marana and Pwanda walked outside together, heedless of the drenching torrent.

Day 83

Sovereign

Following the unprecedented jovial mood of the Generals, laughing with the other council members, Karnas Kay-Raike turned with all of them as the chamber door opened.

The five entered by rank. First No'ln Beviney and her husband. And then Buto Shimas and Jenny Marsham, followed by Dane.

"I assume you're prepared," Beviney said. "My husband and I intend to testify only once."

"A moment, please, No'ln Beviney," Trikal said. "Dane?"

Ignoring Kay-Raike, who was babbling and white with shock, Dane walked to the Generals and extended her right hand. Mosh Trikal reached out. They opened their hands together, and Dane showed him four pebbles.

"An interesting game," he said cheerfully. "We all win."

Day 100

The three ships formed a triangle: *Suram* lay serenely at anchor in a placid sea, surrounded by a honor guard of five smaller vessels from the port of Metia. Beyond the cloudless blue sky were *Sovereign* and *Noldron*, both with outriders. At the agreed-upon time, each of the Fleet ships launched a shuttle. *Suram* dispatched a freshly painted dinghy.

The rendezvous was over in minutes. At the prow of *Suram* Mill, Ten, and Regent watched as two streaks, one silver, one gold, vanished into the invisible blackness beyond Canopal. Next to Regent stood Poda Sela. Permanently blinded, she whispered, "Please, never come back."

Dinner was formal that evening, with *Sovereign* and *Noldron* linked by real-time holography. Marana Beviney and Momed Pwanda sat alone at an ornate table. But seeming to share that table were the images of Buto, Jenny, and Dane.

"I don't believe the question is proper," Shimas was saying. "But under the circumstances, I'll answer it. Naomi Jeffers and William Saddhurst have received promotions. She will command a warship, while he will lead an elite unit conducting research into an area I will not discuss."

"I see," Beviney said. "I asked because, unlike the rest of your Fleet, those two are worthy of respect. He will be relatively safe aboard *Sovereign*, but I will probably have to order Naomi Jeffers killed the next time we meet. For once, I will regret having to give such an order."

No one replied. Dane noted that while the remark was clearly a threat, it contained a seed of hope: regret at the death of an enemy. She smiled, realizing that Beviney's statement represented perfectly the delicate balance sought by The Stem. Unity of the Fleets was unthinkable at this time. But if the present generation of leaders bore that seed, it could be carefully nurtured until the time was right for an end to hostilities. When would that be? Probably not in her lifetime, she reflected. For now it was enough that Bishop and Kay-Raike had failed to plunge the galaxies into a final darkness; once again, the worlds had the precious gift of time.

I'm resigning from The Stem.

Dane was disappointed, but not surprised. She could not imagine leaving her life's work. But the power of the link Momed had established with Marana Beviney was a mystery, even to The Stem. Who could say what she might do under the same circumstances? That thought led naturally to another as her mind wandered for a moment. "Worthy of respect." William Saddhurst was certainly that. And perhaps much more. Dane raised a fork to her mouth and lowered it, deciding to save her appetite for the late dinner she'd agreed to with William.

Dane?

I assumed you'd resign, Momed. I had a speech prepared to change your mind, but I know it wouldn't make any difference.

You're right. I've given this a lot of thought. No matter what the stakes, I am not capable of causing further harm to Marana. That makes me more of a liability than an asset. Thanks for understanding.

What about your implant?

There's no reason not to say hello now and again, is there?

Dane smiled openly at him, not caring how odd that would appear to everyone else present. **No reason at all, my friend. Thank you for everything.**

Marana and I wish you well, Dane. But at a safe distance.

EPILOGUE

The City of Dreams would be years in the rebuilding. Tireless workers labored from sunrise to sunset, always with an eye surveying the heavens, an ear tuned to sudden attack. But as the great statue for which the city had been named once represented hope, a new, living monument now reminded them daily that justice was not impossible. Even from the Fleets.

The twin cages were suspended from cables directly over the worst of the devastation. Ferstead Bishop could bear the heat. He could bear the meager food and water, and the hostile or horrified eyes that sometimes glanced up at him, and as quickly looked away. After all, they were only Dirts. His personal hell was that he could not reach into the cage next to him and put an end to the shrieking, pleading madman there. He knew the unbearable noise would never, never stop.